BEYOND THIS HOME

Book IV
Beyond Those Hills Series

Beyond This Home

Vernal Lind

© 2012 by Vernal Lind. All rights reserved.

Published by Redemption Press, PO Box 427, Enumclaw, WA 98022.

No part of this publication may be reproduced, stored in a retrieval system, or transmitted in any way by any means—electronic, mechanical, photocopy, recording, or otherwise—without the prior permission of the copyright holder, except as provided by USA copyright law.

Unless otherwise noted, all Scriptures are taken from the *Holy Bible, New International Version*®, *NIV*®. Copyright © 1973, 1978, 1984, 2011 by Biblica, Inc.™ Used by permission of Zondervan. All rights reserved worldwide. www.zondervan.com

Unless otherwise noted, all Scriptures are taken from the *King James Version* of the Bible and are quoted by the characters as in the story.

Scripture references marked NASB are taken from the *New American Standard Bible*, © 1960, 1963, 1968, 1971, 1972, 1973, 1975, 1977 by The Lockman Foundation. Used by permission.

ISBN 13: 978-1-63232-211-1 (Print)
978-1-63232-212-8 (ePub)
978-1-63232-213-5 (Mobi)

Library of Congress Catalog Card Number: 2011933423

An Introduction From The Author

As I introduce this fourth book in the *Beyond Those Hills* series, I wish to dedicate this book to my family: first in memory of my parents, Alfred and Marie Lind, who exemplified so many Christian values; then to my sisters, Juneal and Marlys, and their families; and finally to my extended family.

In a broader sense, family is the fabric that knits a society together. The strength of our country and its culture depends on the stability of the family. In this novel and in the earlier ones, I have endeavored to present a family with its strengths as well as its problems. This fictional family is a reminder of the importance and influence of home and family.

Families grow and spread out. Keeping track of family members in a story or real life becomes more of a challenge. Who is related to whom? How are they related? These relationships become more complicated and puzzling. Perhaps this list will explain relationships, review some characters from earlier books, and update characters of the younger generation.

The last book, *Beyond the Darkness*, ended in 1947. This novel continues the story in 1962. Several in-laws as well as a number of children have joined the family.

MATTHEW'S PARENTS:
JOHN ANDERSON (PA). 1862–1940. Strong immigrant, farmer, man of faith. Patriarch of the family. Community leader. Married Elizabeth in 1887.
ELIZABETH OLSON ANDERSON (MA) 1868– . Mother, grandmother, and more. Survivor. Became stronger in determination to live independently, but now declining in physical and mental health.

MATTHEW AND HIS FAMILY
MATTHEW ANDERSON 1900– . Farmer. Loves the land and loves his family. Quiet leader, sensitive. Man of faith. Married Ellen in 1923.
ELLEN JOHNSON ANDERSON. 1899– . Retired country school teacher. Loving wife and mother. Strong personality.

JAMES ANDERSON. 1924– . Oldest son. College professor. Would-be writer. Married Ruth in 1950.
RUTH ROBERTS ANDERSON. 1925– . Teacher and wife. James and Ruth have three children: RICHARD. 1951– . ; COLEEN. 1953– : MELISSA. 1955– .

JOHNIE (JOHN) ANDERSON 1925– . Matthew's favorite. Loved the farm and farming, but became a minister. Married Laura in 1952.
LAURA (MALMSTROM) ANDERSON 1925– Originally a nurse. Now a pastor's wife and mother. She is struggling with cancer. They have three children: JANELLE. 1954– ; JACK (JOHNIE). 1956– . LEAH. 1958– .

MARGARET ANDERSON NELSON 1927– . The ideal daughter who first became a country school teacher and then a farmer's wife and mother. Married Joe Nelson in 1947.
JOE NELSON. 1921– . Formerly hired man to the Andersons, now farms on the home place, where Matthew grew up. They have six children: MATT (MATTHEW). 1948– . DAVID. 1950– DEBORAH. 1952– . JOEL. 1953. JUDITH. 1953– . MARLENE. 1957– .

CAROL ANDERSON STEVENS 1928– . Rebel daughter who got into trouble. Married JEFFREY GRANT in 1945, but was widowed in her teens. Married LEE MCKENZIE in 1951, but divorced him in 1959. Recently married HANK STEVENS in 1962. CAROL has three children: JEFFREY GRANT. 1946– . NICHOLAS MCKENZIE. 1952– .NICOLE MCKENIZIE. 1954– .

MICHAEL ANDERSON 1939– . Youngest son of Matthew and Ellen. Loves the farm and is very much like JOHNIE. He has returned from the Army, a troubled young man.

MATTHEW'S SIBLINGS AND THEIR FAMILIES

MARTHA ANDERSON CARLSON 1888– . Matthew's oldest sister; has been a widow for many years. Was like a second mother to Matthew in his early life. She has three daughters.

RACHEL. 1907– . Matthew's niece. Has a family, and is not in the story.

JANE. 1908– . Matthew's niece. Has a family, and is not in the story.

CORRINE CARLSON WESTBERG. 1911– . Matthew's favorite niece. Married to WARREN WESTBERG. They lived in the area and were friends to Matthew and Ellen. They have three daughters. They now live in California.

VICTORIA ANDERSON 1892– . Retired high school teacher and principal. Strong, independent and forceful. Has a special interest in Matthew's children.

P.J. ANDERSON (PAUL JOHN) 1893–1940. Took the farm that rightfully belonged to Matthew. Had criminal connections. Source of problems in the earlier novels.

RITA. 1895– . Impressed with wealth and position. Lives "out east." "Southern Bell." There are two children:

NOREEN. 1914– . The family doesn't know her whereabouts. She has been married, has two girls.

LARRY ANDERSON 1915– . Changed from a troubled youth to a responsible husband and father. Good looking and talented. Works well with youth. Matthew's special nephew. Married JOAN in 1940.

JOAN ANDERSON 1921– . Joan and Larry have three children: LOWELL. 1941– . LISA. 1946– . LORRAINE. 1948– .

MARY ANDERSON HANSON 1901– . Sister of Matthew and close friend of Matthew and Ellen. Suffered with TB a few years back. Has health problems. Now lives in California. Married ED HANSON in 1923.

ED HANSON 1891– . Brother-in-law to Matthew and friend for years. Now in California. A strict disciplinarian with a temper. Had been hard on his children, especially his son.

BETH. 1925– . Had been tomboy and cousin and friend to James and Johnie. A single teacher, now in California.

JACOB (JAKE) 1926– . Father and son never got along. Married LORETTA in 1951. Has two sons, and lives and farms in southern Minnesota. NICK. 1952– . JACOB. 1954– .

IRENE. 1928– . Cousin and good friend to Margaret and Carol. Married WILL BARTLETT in 1950. Live in the Twin Cities. They have three children: Margaret. 1952– . Bill. 1952– . JEAN. 1954– .

MATTHEW'S COUSIN:

PETER ANDERSON 1892– . A childhood and adult friend. Lives on the Iron Range. Visits infrequently. Married to ALICE 1894– .

MATTHEW'S LONG-TIME FRIEND:

GLENN ROBERTSON 1900– . Farms nearby. Matthew's closest friend. Married to MABEL 1902– . They have several children. Glenn's son TIM was a suitor of Margaret a few years back, but now farms and is a "wheeler-dealer." Married with a family.

As you continue the story of the Anderson family,
I pray that the Lord will richly bless you.
Vernal Lind

Contents

Prologue

May 1962

Matthew Anderson listened intently as his wife read the words their daughter Margaret had written. Ellen's voice and face showed a depth of feeling she did not ordinarily show.

"My dear Father and Mother." Ellen read the words slowly and precisely.

"It is Mother's Day, May 13, 1962. Somehow, I want to honor both of you and express my love. You built a home for me and four other children. Your love and faith provided a foundation for all of us. It is the home that you established that has made me what I am today.

"Home. What a beautiful word! That word brings to mind all the people who mean the most to me. All those special times. While home reminds me of joy, I am also reminded of sorrows. The loss of special people—Grandpa. And Grandma, growing old, leaving for the nursing home.

"I am almost overwhelmed with my role as mother and wife, as well as my part in the extended family. But it is the Lord who provides this added strength.

"This house is on the spot where Grandpa and Grandma lived so many years. John and Elizabeth Anderson made a big impact on the whole community. But they started a family and leave a legacy of faith and love. Not everyone has followed their ways. But their example serves as a guiding beacon. Even now Grandma at 93 serves as a silent reminder of this way of life.

"I am finding it hard to believe that I am now thirty-five years old. Except for Michael, your children are all in their thirties. At this time, I feel a need to reflect on all our lives and the direction we're going.

"James. You must be especially proud of him. With a doctor's degree, he now will be the head of the English department at Riverton State College. I'm told that is quite remarkable for a man only thirty-eight years old. And Ruth, the ideal wife and teacher, fits right in with the Andersons. I wish we saw more of them and their three children.

"I wonder if James will ever fulfill his dream of writing that great American novel."

Matthew had wondered the same thing. People could become so preoccupied with earning a living and getting ahead that they forgot their dreams and what might be more important in life.

"John—or we all know him as Johnie. We always thought he would be the farmer, but he's become a fine pastor. What sadness we feel now that Laura is struggling with cancer. Yesterday, I heard that she's doing better. And Johnie and Laura have blest you with three grandchildren.

"And I, Margaret, function as mother and teacher. I wonder sometimes how I can get everything done. I couldn't have asked for a better husband. I don't know what I ever did to deserve such a devoted and hard-working husband. I think I fell in love with Joe at the tender age of twelve or thirteen. And now we have six children!"

Matthew interrupted. "I remember so well when Joe came into our lives. He was always around when we needed him. It's great that we have Joe and Margaret just a few miles away."

Ellen nodded agreement and continued reading. "Carol. Oh, how I miss my sister. I don't understand her leaving Dr. Nick McKenzie for Hank. Apparently, Hank Stevens is a millionaire businessman. Divorce hurts. Those three children have been badly hurt. I'm afraid my sister has lost sight of some of our important family values.

"That leaves little Michael. Only he isn't little. I think he's the same height as Johnie. His time in the service seemed to lead him into habits that aren't good. I hope and pray he will get his act together. If he's taking over the farm, he needs to get serious. He's twenty-three and it's time for him to settle down.

Prologue

"Look at our family size. Fifteen grandchildren. The five of us with our spouses add up to nine. And with the two of you, we are twenty-six. That's the change from six—or seven after Michael was born.

"I think there's always that desire to come home. I feel an urge or a nudge that something is calling all of us home. Maybe there is an instinct within that wants to return to the safety of home—that creates in me a desire to see my brothers and sisters and my aunts and uncles and cousins as well.

"I wrote to James. He is serious about taking a break this summer. I think I need to remind him of his dream about writing that great American novel. And, Johnie is sure that he can take a Sunday away from the church. However, I haven't heard from Carol. Of course, Michael should be around. I think Aunt Mary and Uncle Ed and many of the cousins will be coming. That should mean we can have a big family reunion.

"I may have become sidetracked from my original purpose. I want to thank you for being the parents you have been. How can I ever pay a proper tribute to you and the wonderful home you have provided? Our hearts and minds come back to that home, but your children and grandchildren are going far beyond this home.

"May the Lord guide and bless us all. And may we all come together in our Eternal Home."

Ellen wiped her eyes. Matthew looked away, not trusting himself to speak. They sat in silence for several minutes.

Ellen broke the silence. "I don't think we realize life as we live it. The decisions we make and the lives we live impact many, both in the present and in the distant future."

The wall clock chimed the hour.

Matthew stood up. "It's time for chores. The milking won't wait."

Chapter 1

June 1962

Matthew stood by the garden gate, looking at his handsome 1910 farm home. The new coat of paint gave the house a touch of class. In a few weeks the front porch would welcome a host of people for a midsummer family reunion.

He glanced at the garden nearby, and several healthy red strawberries caught his attention. His mouth watered at the thought of a bowl of luscious strawberries with rich cream and sugar. The garden, as well as the hay and grain fields, displayed the lush green of June. Spring brought with it the hope for a good life.

Matthew wore well his sixty-two years. Dr. Baker had said his heart seemed strong, and his brush with death and those past stomach problems were far behind him. This lean farmer appeared to have some good years ahead of him.

Matthew reached down for his pocket watch. The time on his watch and the appearance of cattle in the barnyard reminded him of milking time.

"Michael's not back yet." Ellen's voice startled his reverie. "You shouldn't do the milking all by yourself. I'll help."

"I wonder what's keeping Michael. It's a quieter time at the elevator. And he's supposed to be off the job by four."

Ellen cleared her throat. "Matthew, dear, you know very well what's keeping him."

"I hate to admit it. Liquor destroys lives. It helped destroy my brother P.J., and it could destroy Michael."

Matthew herded the cows into the barn. With the new bulk tank and the new machines, milking was simpler in some ways. He didn't have to lift those heavy milk cans. Yet, there was all that cleaning and rinsing and disinfecting that had to be done. He and Ellen had learned to work as a team when Michael was in the service. But now Michael was supposed to help. After all, he would be taking over the farm.

There were times when Matthew wished he were back on the home farm—the farm with those pleasant memories of childhood. But that special place also had the memory of P.J., who had essentially stolen the farm from him. He was thankful that the home farm was back in the hands of the family, namely his daughter Margaret and son-in-law Joe.

He surveyed the hills and fields nearby. This was truly his place, his home—not a place that other family members could lay claim to. He dreamed that this home would be the place where his children and grandchildren would return.

Matthew and Ellen said little as they did their work. By a quarter after six they finished the milking. Matthew let the cows out of the barn, and Ellen returned to the house to finish getting supper ready. Still there was no Michael.

As Matthew entered the kitchen, Ellen made an announcement. "Things can't go on this way. Michael has to settle down, or we sell the cattle. We need less farm work, not more work."

Matthew knew Ellen was right—as usual. "I had hoped Michael would get over this habit of stopping for a few beers."

"We've been patient long enough."

Matthew had an uneasy feeling about Michael's actions and where they would lead.

An hour later, Ellen put away the last dishes. Matthew was outside, probably tinkering with the new motorized lawn mower. She looked and saw Margaret get out of the car.

Chapter 1

"Mother," greeted Margaret. "I thought we should do some planning for the family reunion."

"I guess we should, Ellen answered.

"I hope this reunion isn't going to be too much for you. It's a lot of work to have all those people here. It's enough with just us sisters and brothers and our kids."

"I may be sixty-three, but I'm feeling just fine. I don't do as much as I used to, but it will be fun to be all together."

Ellen didn't look her age. She was still petite, though not as slim as she once was. Her blue gingham dress accented the brilliant blue of her eyes. Her hair was now completely gray—almost white. Her face, with only a few wrinkles, still remained youthful.

Margaret, a younger version of her mother, seemed always to be in motion—working or planning something. It was easy to see why this girl was Matthew's favorite daughter.

In moments, with writing pads in hand, mother and daughter were busy planning menus and other important details that go into a family reunion. Both mother and daughter loved the idea of bringing the whole family together.

"Isn't it about time for coffee?" asked Matthew as he and Joe entered the kitchen.

"We've been busy," replied Ellen, realizing they had lost track of time.

"I'll get the coffee going." Margaret got up and filled the coffeepot with water and put the grounds in. "By the way, where's Michael? I thought he was with you fellows."

Ellen hesitated and gave Matthew that knowing look. "I'm afraid he hasn't come home from work."

Joe, always the quiet one, spoke up. "I think I know what's been going on. And you don't want to talk about it."

Margaret looked bewildered. "Am I missing something?"

"He stops off for a few beers after work," said Matthew. "He's supposed be finished at the elevator before four. I'm afraid it's not just beer. It's whiskey and some of the stronger stuff."

Ellen could see that her daughter was not one to hold back where Michael was concerned. She had been like a second mother to her younger brother, and she was not afraid to scold.

"So this has been going on for a while?" Margaret questioned. "And I didn't know about it!"

Ellen looked to Matthew for reassurance. "It's happened several times. He doesn't seem to have purpose in life."

"He's twenty-three. He's an adult!" exclaimed Margaret. "We've babied him long enough. He needs to act like an adult and take responsibility."

"Don't be too hard on the boy," said her father.

Ellen began to think aloud. "I'm afraid he was the baby, and we spoiled him."

"As big sister, I'm afraid I spoiled him, too. He was so cute, and I bought him those extra gifts when I started teaching."

Joe smiled at his wife. "Michael has some of that male Anderson charm. And even his sisters can't resist that."

Margaret gave her husband an annoyed look. "That charm will not work. When I see him, I shall have something to say."

Ellen knew her daughter could be sharp with her words. "Please be careful. I'm afraid Michael is hurting for some reason. We may have little idea what that hurt is all about."

By this time, the coffee was ready.

"Let's have the coffee and relax," said Matthew.

Ellen went over to the refrigerator and brought out sandwich meat. "This meat is good. We can make ourselves sandwiches. And I baked some chocolate chip cookies this morning."

For a short while their attention was taken away from Michael and his habits. Ellen thought of the Scripture used in a prayer—a prayer about "leading a quiet and peaceable life here on earth." Most of the time Matthew's and her lives had been "quiet and peaceable." And that's the way life was supposed to be. That's the way she wanted it.

As they finished coffee and their visiting tapered off, Joe pushed back his chair. "It's time to go. Five o'clock morning chores time comes awfully fast."

Just then came the sounds of a car followed by squealing tires and a sudden stop. The look on Matthew's face told Ellen he was both relieved and concerned about the return of his son.

The car door slammed.

"I wonder what's coming," said Ellen.

The four waited tensely. The Andersons were not used to this kind of behavior.

Ellen silently prayed for patience and wisdom. Michael's walk up the back steps and onto the porch told her that her son had been drinking.

Chapter 1

Michael entered the kitchen. Awkward silence greeted him, save for a few awkward hellos.

"I guess I'm a little late," he mumbled.

Ellen managed to say, "We were worried. Why so late?"

Michael stood unsteadily by the door. "I needed to relax a little. I lost track of time."

"The cows didn't lose track of time," said Margaret.

"I'm sorry, Dad."

Margaret stood up and walked toward her brother. "Michael, do you realize what's happening? Look at Mom and Dad. They're not so young anymore. They keep the farm and milk business so you can take over. Then, you don't show up to do chores. Dad works twice as hard to build up the herd, and you have Mother out there doing chores with him. That's not right."

Michael looked down, avoiding his sister's gaze.

Margaret backed away and clenched her fist. "What do you have to say for yourself? That smell of liquor is filling this room. You're disgracing the family."

Michael's words were barely audible, "I'm sorry." He backed away.

Joe went over to his wife, placing a protective hand on her shoulder. "Margaret's right. I know what it's like to get out of the service and back to civilian life. It's hard. Remember, I was in heavy fighting in the South Pacific. And Johnie fought in Germany. There are terrible memories to erase. But you didn't go through any of that terrible bloodshed. You were in the Army during peace time."

Ellen looked at Matthew and saw tears in his eyes. Tears filled her eyes; yet she felt anger at her son and at herself.

Margaret's voice rose sharply. "Mother and Dad are too kind and nice to speak up. You need to face up to what you're doing to yourself and to them!"

Michael's apologetic mood changed suddenly to one of belligerence. "Oh, you're always so perfect, Margaret. You do everything right. I can't do anything right."

"We're not talking about me. We're talking about you and the way you're not living up to your agreement with Mother and Dad."

"I need my friends. And I go where they go."

Ellen stood and walked toward her son. "Yes, son, you choose your friends. But those friends determine who you are. You become like your friends. And look what your friends are doing to you."

Michael looked down and backed away, avoiding his sister's gaze.

Margaret grabbed her brother's arm. "You know better than to do what you're doing. Liquor is not a part of Anderson life. You're wasting your life. You're destroying yourself!"

He moved away, freeing his arm. "So what, it's my life. I can do with it what I want."

Ellen felt the eyes of everyone on her. She knew they were waiting for her to speak. Her eyes showed the gentle love of a mother but the stern discipline of a teacher.

"My dear Michael, my youngest, you know something else very well. Your life is not your own. You are accountable to God. You will face Him at His judgment seat. Please, don't go on the way you are."

Michael let out an angry laugh. "And if God cares so much, why does He let some people starve? And why are some people under the yoke of communism?"

Ellen knew her words were falling on deaf ears, but she had to speak. "Michael, God gives people choices. I'm afraid if they choose evil, He lets them do that. But they and others reap the consequences of those choices."

For a moment Ellen thought her son was about to break down and cry. The smell of liquor seemed to permeate the whole kitchen. It was almost as if an evil spirit took over.

"I'm not so sure I even believe anymore. I've had it with all this church and religion. I want no part of it!"

For the first time Matthew spoke. "Are you giving up on God? Are you saying you want no part of us or of the farm? Are you giving up this life?"

"I don't know! I don't know!" Michael yelled. "I can't take anymore of this badgering."

Margaret grasped both of her brother's arms. "You just stop what you're saying. You owe something to your family. Mom and Dad loved you and took care of you. You've done these stupid things, and they've put up with you. You've caused more pain than the rest of us put together. You can at least have the decency to come home and help with chores."

Michael backed toward the door, pushing his sister away from him.

"You know where you can go."

Ellen saw the anger in Joe's eyes as his whole body stiffened. Though several inches shorter but husky in frame, he moved forward and took hold of Michael.

Chapter 1

"Don't you dare speak to my wife that way—or the rest of this family. Mom and Dad mean as much to me as any real mother and father. If you treat them this way, it's best you get out."

Michael's fist aimed unsteadily at Joe. But Joe caught his fist and pushed him onto the porch.

Michael stumbled and then lunged toward Joe. Despite Michael's larger size and strength, Joe pushed him away. Michael was too intoxicated to fight.

Ellen heard the loudest scream she had ever heard. Not until Margaret held her back did she realize the scream was hers.

Michael stood up slowly and backed away. He looked down, avoiding his family's gaze. Then, he opened the door and went out, slamming it. He ran but half-stumbled toward his car. He got in the car, started it and gunned the motor. He turned the car around, leaving a cloud of dust behind.

Ellen rushed outside, followed by the others. "What will happen to that boy? I'm afraid he'll kill himself."

That night Matthew and Ellen found sleep would not come. They tossed and turned for several hours, hoping Michael would return. But he did not return.

"There's nothing we can do," said Ellen. "As Joe said, if we'd follow him, Michael would only become angrier."

"It's almost like my brother all over again. Once P.J. began drinking it seemed he couldn't stop. He had to have those drinks no matter what."

"Let's pray that something stops Michael before he gets to that point."

They lay in silence for what seemed like hours.

Finally, sleep came to Matthew, but it was not a restful sleep. Nightmares blended the past and the present.

P.J. appeared in those nightmares. P.J., dark and handsome and charming, seemed to take the form of the very devil himself. Matthew became that little boy while P.J. locked him in the attic. P.J. stood below, taunting and ridiculing him.

Then P.J. stood before him and Michael. Matthew became an adult and stood on the sidelides, watching as P.J. signaled for Michael to follow him. P.J. kept on offering Michael beer and other drinks. Michael followed.

Suddenly, P.J. changed into Michael. Michael was shouting out in fear as he kept on falling—falling into an abyss.

Matthew called out. "Michael, come back." He reached out to his son. "Son, I'll help you. Please don't go that way."

Matthew sat up, fully awake. He kept seeing Michael stumbling toward his car and driving away.

Deep within he knew something terrible was about to happen.

CHAPTER 2

Matthew dreaded what this day would bring. However, life went on and chores had to be done. Ellen called to him as he walked toward the barn.

"Michael's probably sleeping it off in the car some place."

"I hope that's the case, but I'm afraid this could be more serious."

When they finished chores and sat at the breakfast table, Matthew knew it was time to talk. They had to make some drastic changes.

Ellen broke the silence. "Matthew, we're not going to keep on doing this work. I think we should sell the cattle. We can live comfortably on the other income. And we could even put the land into the Soil Bank program."

"I know this work is too much for us at our age. If Michael were taking over, I'd be happy to help him get started."

Ellen's next words startled him. "Perhaps we need to sell the farm and move to town. As we get older, it's not good for us to be alone out here in the country if something should happen to one of us."

Matthew had thought of this dreadful possibility. "I know I'd never want to be alone out here in the country. I think I'd go crazy."

"And I could never be alone. I'm too old to learn to drive, so I'd be stuck out here."

"I've been a country man all my life. But a lot of farmers have moved to town. They seem happy there."

"You'd do just fine. We could still have a big garden. Maybe we could keep some land down by the lake and have a cottage built."

"We've talked of having a cottage there. Maybe that can be more than a dream."

Ellen poured another cup of coffee.

Matthew's thoughts went back to an earlier time. "Michael has always loved the land and the animals. He seemed like another Johnie when he was growing up. I used to make the mistake of calling him Johnie. He was proud of being so much like his brother."

"When did he start to go wrong?" wondered Ellen. "He led such a good life all through high school—and even those two years after graduation when he was farming with you. He was active in church, and we thought he might follow Johnie's footsteps and become a minister."

Matthew thought back over the last months. "He came back from the two years in the army, and he was different. Silent, much of the time. It was as if he were living in a different world."

Ellen began to clear the table. "You're right. He didn't seem to be our son when he came back. I wonder what happened to change him."

"We may need to do some listening—if he'll talk."

"Or—" Ellen paused. "We may need to make drastic changes if he goes on this way."

"Right now, it's time for me to check if the alfalfa is ready. Glenn and Tim have agreed to do the baling, and our grandsons will help."

Matthew experienced a peace as he walked beside the alfalfa field. He looked once more at the hills and spoke the words of Scripture. "I will lift mine eyes unto the hills from whence cometh my help. My help cometh from the Lord, who made heaven and earth."

He said a prayer for Michael and then got on the tractor to go home. "God is good. I give this problem to Him."

An hour later when Matthew walked toward the house, he knew something bad had happened. A deep fear, almost a panic, filled his being.

Ellen hurried out to meet him. "I have bad news. Michael's been in an accident. He's in the hospital. He's unconscious."

"What accident? Car?"

Chapter 2

"He smashed up his car. It happened west of River Falls. A winding country road."

Matthew's mind raced ahead. "Was he alone?"

"He was driving fast and missed a curve. He went into a ditch filled with water. He was cut badly—hit on the head. He hasn't regained consciousness."

"This is serious, isn't it?"

"Yes. Matthew, we have to get to the hospital. I laid out your clean trousers."

Matthew moved without thinking. Within minutes he and Ellen were on their way to River Falls.

Ellen watched her husband intently as he drove the thirty miles to River Falls. His pale face frightened her. At times like this she wished she drove. As they got out of the car, she noticed his hands trembled.

"Matthew, are you okay?"

"I'm all right. Don't worry about me."

Ellen knew he wasn't all right. They hurried into the hospital and were directed to Michael's room. Ellen's mind returned to a stormy winter day twenty-three years ago when Michael entered the world. She had barely made it in time for her baby to be born. And now there was a possibility she could lose him.

Ellen stood beside the bed. The bandages covered part of his face. The cuts and bleeding were still evident. Otherwise, Michael's blond hair and other handsome features were visible even though he was unconscious.

"Michael." She wanted to tell her son how much she loved him.

A sudden thump startled her. She looked down, and there lay Matthew on the floor. "Help!" she called out. "Something's happened to Matthew."

A nurse entered and bent down. "Sir, can you hear me? Do you have pain anywhere?"

Matthew started to get up. "I don't know what happened. I feel light-headed."

The nurse smiled. "I think you fainted." She took his arm and helped him up. "Come over here and sit down." Matthew sat. "Now, put your head down."

For those moments, Ellen wondered if both her husband and son were in serious condition.

The nurse began to take Matthew's pulse. "Your husband's all right. I think seeing your son was a little too much for him. Dr. Baker should be in soon, and he'll check you."

"I'm all right. It was stupid of me to let that happen."

"Perfectly normal reaction," reassured the nurse.

"Has Michael been conscious at all?" questioned Ellen.

"No, I don't believe so. Otherwise, considering the seriousness of the accident, he seems pretty good. Possibly cracked or broken ribs. It could have been much worse."

The next two hours seemed like days. Dr. Baker checked Michael, but there was no news and no change.

Matthew paced back and forth in the room and then in the halls. He talked with nurses and visitors. Ellen sat with folded hands next to Michael. She silently and desperately prayed for her son.

As the afternoon wore on, Matthew said to Ellen, "I guess there's nothing I can do. There are chores to do. Someone needs to do them."

"You go ahead home. Someone should be here when he wakes up. I'll stay."

In that moment Ellen realized another terrible possibility. It could happen that he would not wake up. The loss of a child was too terrible for a mother to bear.

"I hate to leave. I can't think of anything else but Michael. I keep thinking of the kind of boy he used to be. This angry young man isn't really our Michael."

The two sat in silence. Ellen felt stronger because Matthew was beside her. They had weathered the storms of life together for thirty-nine years.

Ellen reached over to grasp Michael's hand. "I thought Margaret and Joe would come. When I called her, she said she'd see us at the hospital."

"Did I hear my name?" Margaret entered the room, and then stopped abruptly as she observed her brother. "Oh no, he looks so pale."

"We're glad you're here," said Ellen.

Chapter 2

Margaret found herself in her father's arms. "Oh, Dad, this is hard. Why did Michael have to leave the way he did?" After a long hug, she came over and gave Ellen a kiss.

"There's been no change since we came," said Ellen.

Margaret stood close to her brother. "I can't believe this has happened. Everything seems so unreal."

Ellen moved to the other side of the bed. "I'm afraid this has been coming on for a long time. Michael's been angry and hurt. We can't understand why."

"Something must have happened when he was in the army."

Matthew reached down and brought out his pocket watch. "I guess I need to think about chores. You should stay here."

"Dad, that's taken care of. I would have been here sooner, but Joe and I arranged for Matt to be in charge of our chores. Joe and the twins will go over and take care of your chores. That's the advantage of having six children."

"Thanks, dear."

Ellen watched her husband fidget. "Matthew, why don't you go outside and take a walk. Margaret and I will wait here."

Matthew seemed happy with their suggestion. Ellen knew her husband all too well. He didn't like being cooped up inside. He liked the hills and open spaces.

Ellen and Margaret talked for a while and then sat in silence. Michael showed no change.

Once Matthew was outside, he inhaled deeply the fresh June air. This month, in many ways, was the most perfect time of the year. The poet echoed his thoughts in saying, "Oh, what is so rare as a day in June."

But he remembered other times when he had been in this place. He looked up at the modern, recently-built new hospital and then across the street to the old hospital. That old building contained more memories. That was the place where he came close to death almost twenty-five years ago.

Then, he thought of his brother P.J., lying in that hospital bed. It was P.J., who had stolen the family farm and had done other immoral and illegal deeds. Those deeds had caught up with him during his last hours.

His final moments of life had been spent in torment. Matthew would never forget those last words: "I want to make things right, if I can."

But P.J. never had that chance. It was only after many problems that the family farm did come back to a family member who wanted to farm.

Matthew walked the streets for an hour, thinking of the past but always coming back to Michael. After Johnie had gone to the seminary, Matthew's hopes transferred to Michael as the son who would take over the family farm. And now it seemed those hopes were dashed.

"What if Michael doesn't regain consciousness?" Matthew thought and spoke the words aloud. In that moment it seemed his dreams of leaving the farm for the family were completely destroyed.

Something within him urged Matthew to return to the hospital room. He hoped and prayed that Michael would regain consciousness.

The minute he entered the room, Matthew knew there was no change. Michael remained in an almost a death-like stillness.

Ellen spoke the obvious. "No change. Matthew, you and Margaret go and have some supper. I'll wait here. Someone should be with him when he wakes up."

Margaret objected. "Mother, you really need a break."

"No, I'm okay."

Matthew realized Ellen would not leave the side of her son. "I don't feel like eating, but I probably need to."

Margaret persuaded her father to go to the hospital cafeteria. Every time a stressful situation came into his life, Matthew felt those pains in his stomach. It was almost as if his ulcers were returning.

Waiting that afternoon and evening seemed endless. The nurses came in frequently to check vital signs. Dr. Baker tried to be encouraging, but what he didn't say left Matthew and the others wondering.

Matthew found himself pacing back and forth in the hall or on the streets. He thought back to this morning and last night. Michael's angry words kept repeating themselves in his mind. Then, he heard Ellen's words, "There's been an accident."

Why couldn't life be the way it was when Michael enjoyed the hard work on the farm? Why was he angry? Was this a repeat of the last generation, when P.J. had left the family to pursue what was immoral and wrong? Could there be such a thing as a curse that found itself in the next generation?

"Lord," he prayed aloud, "bring Michael back to us—in body, mind and spirit. Please help me to be the father I should be. Even though my boys are men, they still need a father. And more than anything, Lord, they need You. Bring Michael back; You are that loving father who welcomes back the son who has gone astray."

Something prompted Matthew to return to the hospital room. Perhaps there was a change.

"Dad," was the word coming from a familiar voice.

Matthew stood for a moment, speechless. "Johnie, I'm surprised to see you."

"Laura's better. The moment I heard about Michael, I wanted to come. A pastor deserves a day off now and then. And I wanted to see my little brother."

Matthew choked with emotion as Johnie spoke. Johnie extended his arms and moved toward his father. Soon Matthew found himself in his son's arms, his tears flowing freely.

Time seemed to stand still. Matthew felt a sense of relief and release as Johnie comforted him.

He stepped away. "Well, son, you do the job of a pastor well."

"Dad," said Margaret, "I've never seen you cry before. I've seen tears in your eyes, but this is the first time."

Ellen smiled."Your father has a tender heart. He has more love for you children than you'll ever realize."

Johnie moved over to the bed where his brother lay. "We kids have been fortunate to have a wonderful home. We owe you more than we could ever repay."

For several moments no one spoke.

"I think," began Johnie, "we should stand close to Michael and pray for him. I have felt the Lord's healing touch, and I'm confident Michael will come back."

Ellen sat beside the bed and grasped Michael's hand. Johnie stood on the other side and placed his hand on his brother's forehead. Matthew and Margaret stood close by.

Johnie began slowly. "Our loving and merciful heavenly Father. We come before You with heavy hearts. We know that You heal the brokenhearted. But we come to You, knowing that You are a God who heals and transforms lives. Thank You for coming into our lives. Thank You for changing me from a depressed and suicidal veteran to a man who wants to tell of You and Your love.

"We pray for Your healing touch upon Michael. We want him to know Your love and compassion and mercy. Please, Lord, we need this young man—as son—as brother. Lord, we claim Your healing touch on Michael. And now, we thank You in the name of Jesus Christ, Your Son, our Lord.

"And now let us pray the prayer You taught us. Our Father—"

As they finished the prayer, the hospital room was filled with a quiet reverence that Matthew rarely experienced even in a church building. An unusual warmth moved through him. The worry lines in his face disappeared. God was indeed present and at work.

"I think I felt his hand move," said Ellen.

Matthew and the others looked down. Matthew saw without a doubt that Michael was grasping Ellen's hand.

Johnie touched his brother's forehead. "Lord, please bring Michael back to us."

Chapter 3

Johnie slept restlessly during the night, but at least he slept. Part of the time, he thought of Laura. After months of treatment that didn't seem to affect the cancer, suddenly Laura was doing better. He prayed that she would somehow recover. He didn't know how he could live without her.

His mother had insisted that he sleep in the extra hospital bed. She should have slept in the bed. After all, at sixty-three she wasn't so young anymore. But, typically, Ellen Anderson insisted on being close to her son and sacrificing for her children. He and his mother convinced his father to go home and get a good night's sleep.

Johnie had been confident Michael would awaken. As he sat up now and looked at his brother, he somehow wasn't as certain. Michael looked so pale and lay still as if he were dead. He remembered when one of his parishioners had a similar accident and never recovered. The death of one so young did not seem fair.

Johnie got up quietly and moved over to the window. He looked out at the deep green of the oak and elm trees. There was no more beautiful day than a day in June. Today, the early morning sun shone on the lush green that was a part of late spring or early summer. This type of day encouraged him to worship and praise his Creator.

He turned back to Michael. He whispered aloud, "I wish I could take you in my arms, brother, and hold you the way I did when you were a child. You were so much like me. I just wanted to spare you the hurts I went through."

Johnie recalled the dark nights of the soul. The wounds and memories of those battles in Germany could never be erased. The death and killing on the battlefield were too terrible to describe. In a sense they were fading into the distant past; yet there were times he remembered the bloody battles as if they took place yesterday.

He tiptoed quietly toward the door, trying not to waken his mother.

"I must have dozed off." His mother sat up straight. "I had such crazy dreams. I thought for a while I was pregnant with Michael. It was all so real."

"Good morning, Mother."

"Good morning," she replied. She looked at Michael and reached out to touch him. "Still no change."

"Mother, I'll get some breakfast from the cafeteria, unless you want to come with me. There's nothing we can do here."

"No, son, I'd rather stay. But I think I'm hungry."

"I'll get you some scrambled eggs and toast. I'll be back." He hurried down to the cafeteria and ordered two breakfasts.

It took longer than he expected to order and receive the breakfasts. When he returned to the room, he handed his mother the tray. He sat down, and said a quick table grace. Soon mother and son were enjoying the hospital breakfast.

As always, food seems to stimulate conversation. Johnie began to tell his mother about each of the three children as well as some of those experiences that ministers have from day to day.

He recalled for his mother one of those embarrassing but funny situations. "We had our friend Mary over for dinner last Sunday. Mary loves to talk, but she lives alone. And she makes up for it when she's with people. Well, Mary got going on a story just as Laura brought out our meal. We were ready for the table grace, but Mary kept on talking. Finally, little four-year-old Leah spoke up. 'Why don't you stop talking so we can eat?'" Johnie couldn't help laughing as he finished the story.

Ellen laughed. "I met Mary when we visited you. That's one of those stories you won't forget."

A weak voice interrupted their laughter. "What's so funny?"

They both looked at Michael. "You're awake!" exclaimed Johnie.

"Thank God," added Ellen.

"I ache all over, but something smells terribly good."

Chapter 3

"Thank God!" repeated Ellen. "You're back with us. Thank God!"

"We'll see that you get your breakfast."

Michael straightened himself. "How did I get here?"

"You were in an accident," said Johnie.

Michael sat up slowly. "What are you doing here anyway? Shouldn't you be off preaching or visiting your church members in hospitals?"

Johnie smiled. "You gave us all a real scare. That's why I'm here."

At that point the nurse entered. "Michael, welcome back. The doctor is going to want to see you." She hurried out.

Soon a doctor entered and began to examine Michael.

Johnie and Ellen stepped out of the room, anxiously waiting for the doctor to give his opinion.

To Johnie the minutes that followed seemed like hours. Michael had regained consciousness, but were there other problems? He had heard dreadful stories of accident victims who never came back to a normal life after such trauma. Somehow, he couldn't imagine young Michael in any way except as active and lively.

His mother took his hand. "I'm thankful he's back, but I'm scared."

Johnie spoke, but may not have been as confident as he sounded. "The Lord is faithful. He will see us through, and He does heal."

"O ye of little faith. That describes me."

"Mom, you're a woman of great faith. You're part of the reason I am what I am. But I give God the real credit."

His mother leaned toward him. "Son, I'm proud of you."

Johnie thought he saw tears in his mother's eyes. "Thanks, Mom."

The door opened. The doctor spoke in his businesslike way, not the personal way of Dr. Baker. "I think we can be optimistic. We'll do some tests this afternoon, but Michael has sustained amazingly little damage after such a terrible accident. It looks like cracked ribs and some nasty cuts and bruises, but that's all. He's a lucky man. Lucky to be alive."

The doctor left.

"I'm starved!" exclaimed Michael. "I need food."

Johnie felt a sense of relief. "You're my little brother, and I'm glad I have you back."

"I'm not so little. I'm bigger than you."

The night before, Matthew had decided to go home to the farm. He lay awake for hours that night. The house seemed to be haunted by ghosts of the past—Ellen and the five children. In his mind the childhood voices echoed throughout the house. Then, emptiness pervaded the place. He would never want to live here alone.

His namesake slept in the boys' room. In many ways fourteen-year-old Matt was like Johnie and Michael. He loved the outdoors. He loved his 4-H calf and cared for the heifer so that it would be Grand Champion material at the county fair.

He got up and dressed quietly. "I'll let the boy sleep. Matt's a growing boy, and he worked hard yesterday."

The sun was just rising. The cattle began to move about in the barnyard. He put out the feed, let them into the barn, and then went about the task of cleaning the udders. Yes, he had this more sophisticated milking machine, but it required extra preparation to keep the cattle clean. That was the price of selling Grade A milk for a higher price.

Matthew went through the motions of doing the work. As he walked around each corner, he felt Michael would appear. Two days ago, he and Michael had worked together, doing the chores. He had hoped that this would continue. An ache and emptiness filled his whole being.

"Grandpa, you were supposed to wake me." Young Matt appeared and began to check for the work he could do. "I'm here to help you."

Matthew reached over and gave the boy a gentle nudge. "You're young. I thought you needed your sleep. Growing boys need sleep."

Grandfather and grandson went about finishing the milking, cleaning the equipment and letting out the cattle. The morning chores were done.

As they walked toward the house, Matthew saw that Margaret had driven over and was already busy in the kitchen. He should have known she would come over to help. He entered and smelled the delicious aroma of bacon and eggs. Even a person who had a small appetite would become hungry after smelling her cooking.

"Good morning, Dad. I knew Matt would be hungry, and I knew you needed a good breakfast to start the day. We don't know what this day will bring."

Margaret gave her father a hug and a quick kiss.

"I couldn't ask for a more thoughtful daughter. You're just like your mother. I don't know what I'd do without your mother taking care of me."

And so, the day began.

Chapter 3

Several hours later, Matthew and Margaret entered Michael's hospital room. Matthew's heart beat quickly when he saw the empty bed.

"What's happened? Where is Michael?"

Margaret's face showed concern, though she tried to hide it. "Oh, they've probably moved him to another room."

At that moment Ellen and Johnie walked toward them. One look at their faces told Matthew that the news was good.

"He's regained consciousness!" Ellen called out. "He's going to be all right!"

Such a sense of relief came over Matthew that no words came. In a moment this reserved Swedish gentleman held his wife in his arms. He thought of the scripture, "Tears last for the night, but joy comes in the morning."

"They've been giving him tests," said Johnie. "He should be back in his room any time now."

At that moment a nurse came, pushing Michael in a wheelchair. "Here's your patient. He's a little too frisky for his own good."

Michael's voice showed annoyance and irritation. "I'm tired of being treated like an invalid. I want to get up and walk."

The nurse announced, "We have good news. Aside from a serious bump on the head, some cracked ribs and some scratches, Michael is doing well."

"I'm ready to go home."

The nurse quickly replied. "No, you're not. The doctor will talk to you, but we're keeping you here for observation. You've had a terrible jolt. When you're hit on the head that badly, you have to be careful."

"Little brother, you need to listen to your doctor and nurse."

"But," objected Michael, "I need to get home and help Dad."

"Well, brother, you haven't been around to help that much. Dad's been doing most of the work by himself."

Matthew was surprised at Johnie's directness.

Michael blushed in embarrassment. "I guess you're right. That's going to change."

They returned to Michael's room. Matthew felt a sense of relief sweep over him. Michael would recover. But then he felt a gnawing fear that his son would return to his old ways.

Johnie decided to stay around a few more days. Two days later, he told his parents that he would go to the hospital to pick up Michael. He knew it was time for them to talk. A "big brother lecture" is what Michael would call the conversation.

Johnie had learned that prayer changes things. He prayed about Michael, but he still wanted to wring his brother's neck for his actions during the past weeks. How could he lovingly reprove him and point out the error of his ways?

When he arrived at the nurses' station, Johnie found Michael sitting contentedly in a wheelchair. "Michael, it looks as if you're ready to go home."

Michael looked up. "I'd like to have you meet my special nurse. This is Erma. My brother, Pastor John Anderson."

The young woman extended her hand. "Nice to meet you, pastor."

"Glad to meet you. I'm surprised you can keep my brother in the wheelchair."

"It's my job to deliver the patient to the hospital entrance."

Michael looked up at Erma. "I couldn't ask for a better nurse."

Erma laughed. "You say that to all the nurses."

Johnie felt like a third wheel as Michael and Erma talked back and forth. He hadn't had such an experience in a long time.

When Michael got out of the wheelchair, he stooped down and gave Erma a kiss—not a light one, but a passionate one on the lips. The nurse held back at first, but then returned the kiss.

As Erma left, Michael called out. "I'll see you soon."

Johnie looked askance at his brother. "I didn't think nurses were supposed to fraternize with their patients that way."

Michael smiled smugly. "I'm not just any patient."

Michael's joking and good humor persisted during the time they were driving home. Michael made light small talk, but Johnie wanted to talk more seriously.

Finally, Johnie stopped Michael in mid-sentence. "Michael, you've got to get serious. There are some things we need to talk about."

"Let's talk about Erma. I have a date with her Saturday night."

"Get serious," Johnie repeated. "At this point you don't have a car. You seem to forget you smashed your car. That's beyond repair."

"There's Dad's. He'll let me use his. And I'll be getting a new car."

"Can you afford one?"

This time Michael was at a loss for words.

Chapter 3

Johnie pulled off to the side of the road. "Michael, we've got to talk. You can't go on the way you've been going. You had a brush with death. If you go on drinking and partying this way, you're in serious trouble. And what's more, Mom and Dad aren't so young. Dad shouldn't be spending time doing your work."

"I'll come home in time for milking."

Johnie had just started; he was not about to quit. "You should be ashamed of yourself. Mom and Dad have been worried sick about you. If you don't change, they're going to have to give up farming. Or, maybe they'll even sell the farm."

Michael's mood changed. "I can't imagine Dad not being on the farm. I don't think he could survive in town. That would kill him."

"Then you better change the way you're living. You can't go on the way you are. You have to change."

Michael looked away. "When I was in the army, I saw the other side of life. I know I didn't get into the middle of fighting the way you did, but I saw the other side of life. It's like two worlds out there."

"What do you mean?"

"When I was stationed out East, I went with a buddy to his home in Appalachia. I saw the poverty. That was dreadful. Then, our unit was stationed a week in North Africa. I saw squalor and poverty and crime there. It was unbelievable."

"But, Michael, you didn't have to witness your friends blown to bits or limbs blown off or injured in other ways."

Michael thought a moment. "No, but I'm restless now. I want to get out and see the world and maybe do something. I'm not sure I can stay home on the farm the rest of my life."

Johnie found anger rising within himself. "That's good enough for you. But think of Dad. He's working hard so that you can take over the farm. And then you worry them half to death when you get drunk and almost get killed."

"I'm sorry about that."

"Yes, being sorry is fine. You need to be sorry enough so that you change your ways. And you need to be fair with Mom and Dad. If you're not interested in the farm, you need to let them know."

Johnie saw his brother's face redden in anger.

"That's all right for you to say. These times are different than when you grew up. Farming's changed. Look at the people who have left their farms. A farmer can't make a living off the land. He has to make a big investment, and then the prices can be rock bottom."

Johnie lowered his voice, hoping to communicate a gentle spirit. "But Michael, you have an advantage. The farm will be yours without question. You won't have the expenses that many young farmers have."

Michael avoided the gaze of his brother. "I want to go out in the world and meet people. I want to date girls like Erma and just have fun. Then, someday I'll settle down."

"You're twenty-three. It's time to settle down."

Michael tightened his fist and pounded it on the dashboard. "It's my life, and I'll do what I please."

Johnie wanted to say more, but there seemed to be little use. He paused, "I guess it's time to get back home."

Matthew loved family gatherings of any kind. It was Friday night, and James and Ruth and their children had arrived only an hour ago. They were busy inside the house, getting settled. James had a week off from teaching at the college, meaning the family could spend a few days at the farm.

Johnie had left that morning. After all, a minister had his big task on Sunday morning, and Laura needed him even though the cancer seemed to be in remission. Matthew loved all of his children, but he loved Johnie as a man after his own heart.

Matthew reviewed what had happened these past days. He had to be thankful that Michael had survived the accident so well. Even now, though, Michael needed time for healing. Perhaps that was healing both of body and mind. Matthew always enjoyed these moments alone as he thought about life and enjoyed the beauty of an early June evening.

"Dad." James' voice broke his reverie. "How are things really going? How are you?"

"Oh, fine." Matthew shrugged off the question.

"Dad, I know something's bothering you. And it's more than Michael's accident. Come now, you need to talk about it."

Matthew wasn't sure how much he should say. "You know all about Michael's drinking. There's not much to say that hasn't already been said. Johnie gave him a good talking to."

"There's more, Dad."

Chapter 3

Matthew thought a moment. "It's the farm. I can't see working so hard with cattle and the field work. I'm ready to give it up. Maybe we should move off the farm."

"Are you ready for that?"

"My good friend Glenn Robertson is thinking about it, and several other farmers have moved into town."

"Dad, it's up to you."

Matthew felt a need to share his burden. "I've come to love this farm and this way of life. I had dreams of a life that would continue here. The world is changing so fast. And farming has changed as well. I guess I wanted to have this farm be a place where children and grandchildren and other family members could come back to."

"Ruth and I love this place. We consider it home."

"But, James, we can't go on this way with Michael. He has to decide one way or another. And I don't know how long I can take this added work."

James placed his hand on his father's shoulder. "These things will work out. We kids are here to help."

At that moment two cars came up the driveway. First came Matthew's sister, Victoria. Even at seventy-two, neither her driving nor her life had slowed down. A safe distance behind came Joe. More like a son than a son-in-law, he brought precious daughter Margaret along with the six children.

Soon James and Ruth's three children joined Joe and Margaret's six, and there was delightful merriment, soon to become a lively game of softball. This was life as it should be.

The women hurried inside. There was planning to do. The men, Matthew and Joe and James, remained outside, watching the children. Michael was nowhere around; he was supposed to be resting.

Matthew listened as the women chattered and the children shouted while they played. There was a pause in the men's conversations. He looked once more to the hills. He whispered the words, "I will lift my eyes unto the hills. My help comes from the Lord, who made heaven and earth."

He felt a peace beyond all understanding.

Chapter 4

Matthew felt like a child anticipating Christmas. Only this was June 22, the Friday before midsummer, the weekend of the Anderson family reunion. This weekend, his organized and predictable life would be filled with the unpredictable. He eagerly awaited the arrival of each member of the family.

But, he wondered if Carol would come. She had not visited the family for over two years. It was then that she had divorced Dr. Nick McKenzie and soon married big-time businessman, Hank Stevens. She had never brought Hank to meet the family. Letters and telephone calls had been infrequent.

The rest of the family should arrive at any minute. In the meantime, Matthew picked up twigs that had fallen from the trees during the last thunderstorm. He found this work relaxing. And now with Michael doing more of the farm work, Matthew could enjoy more of the simple pleasures of life. He hoped Michael had learned his lesson and would settle down.

A car drove up, and noise and activity followed. It was James and Ruth. They had driven from Riverton, where James taught at the state college and Ruth taught second grade at one of the schools. The three children, each two years apart, quickly greeted their grandfather with hugs and kisses. Richard, eleven, followed by sisters Coleen and Melissa, headed for the barn to visit their old friends, several cats, and whatever other pets might greet them.

Ruth joined her mother-in-law in the kitchen. Once the luggage was taken into the house, James joined his father on the front porch.

James didn't waste words. "How's everything working with Michael? He surely gave us a scare."

Matthew wanted to believe the best. "He's been coming home in time for milking in the evening. I'm afraid he still goes out for a few drinks."

"I hope he's just going through a phase. He needs to settle down. It's time for him to take life seriously."

"I'm trying to be patient."

"Dad, you're the most patient man in the world. You're too patient."

Before they could go on with the conversation, a car and a pickup came up the driveway. The back of the pickup was filled with noisy kids. The six children belonging to Margaret and Joe had been joined by Johnie and Laura's three. They had enjoyed a breezy ride from the old home place, now occupied by Margaret and Joe.

The nine children jumped down and ran over to their grandfather. Matthew stood straight and tall, proud of these grandchildren. Each gave a quick hug and hurried on.

At the same time, Johnie and Laura got out of their car. That meant most of the family had arrived.

Matt, now fourteen and the oldest of the children, shouted to the others. "Get your swimming suits. We're off to the lake."

"Some adults need to go down with you," said Johnie. "I remember a time long ago when three little girls disappeared."

"Oh, you would have to remind me of that," said Margaret, as she gave her brother a little nudge. "Johnie, why don't you go with the kids? And maybe Michael can also. Joe can drive all of you down to the lake in the pickup."

The other three children came out of the barn. That only added to the noise of all the cousins being together for the first time in several months.

It took only a few minutes for the children to run and get their swimming suits. Some disappeared quickly and got into their suits. Young Matt shouted out, "Hurry! We can change when we get down to the lake. Plenty of trees to change behind."

Joe started the pickup and soon all the noise of the children faded into the distance.

Chapter 4

"Where do they get all that energy?" James asked his father.

"I wish I had a small part of it."

Father and son walked up to the porch and seated themselves on the swing. The women went to the kitchen, no doubt to prepare some evening lunch as well as plan for the bigger celebration tomorrow. That event would feature many more of the Andersons, the homecoming event of the decade.

The two men sat in silence for several minutes.

James spoke first. "Dad, do you ever regret leaving the home place when P.J. got the ownership? Somehow, both these places seem like home."

Matthew thought for a moment. "Your mother has been happier here, that's for sure. She always thought that some other family members felt they owned the other place. Also, I realize that I have a better and bigger house and barn on this farm. In reality, I'm better off here."

"We kids were so excited about moving. I remember all the new adventures we had here. There was the attic as well as that old house to explore. But I guess I'm partial to the home place. I'm glad that Margaret and Joe live there."

"Your mother always says, 'Home is where your loved ones are.' I guess that's true. We've talked about moving into town. But now it looks as if Michael will stay around. We'd want to stay until he gets married and settles down."

"I wonder about him. Michael doesn't seem ready to settle down."

A door opened. "Did I hear my name taken in vain?"

James quickly replied, "Nothing bad. I just said I didn't know if you were ready to settle down."

"I thought you were down at the lake with the swimmers," said Matthew.

"Dad, you forget I have to be careful. My ribs are healing."

"Johnie and Joe are there looking after the kids so they don't get into any trouble."

Matthew heard the telephone ring. No longer were there three long rings. Instead, only one ring, though one other person was on the party line.

"Michael, it's for you," called Ellen. "It's long distance."

"Thanks, Mom." Michael wasted no time going inside to answer.

The long distance announcement piqued Matthew's curiosity. "I wonder if that's another one of Michael's girlfriends."

"Does he have a special girl?"

"No, I don't think so. All the girls his age are either married or have left the area. Most young people go to the city for work."

"But Michael always loved the farm. I thought he would be the one to stay."

Matthew couldn't help thinking how convenient that would be. Michael would remain on this farm and take over in a few years. He might continue working in the elevator a few hours in order to supplement his income. That way he could have a comfortable life.

"You can never tell what life brings." Matthew kept thinking of how transitory life is. "Tomorrow when the family gathers, many will be together. In all probability the same group will never again be together."

The two sat silently, trying to hear the voices from inside the house. The voices of the women drowned out Michael's words. Then, Michael returned.

"I suppose that was another one of your lady friends," teased James. "You've got girls all over the place, I bet."

"Don't I wish. All the good looking girls leave for the cities or get married."

"Have a seat," invited James. "The swing's big enough for three—or even more."

"No thanks."

Matthew sensed that his son was hiding something. He wanted to ask, but something held him back.

"What have you been up to lately?" asked James. "Are you feeling okay after that accident? You seem to be healing fast."

"I'm getting better, but I have to be careful. I can still feel those ribs."

James went on to ask the question that Matthew wanted to ask. "Well, isn't it time to settle down? Aren't you planning to take over the farm so Dad can retire? Remember, Dad's not so young anymore."

Michael looked away, saying nothing.

James repeated the question. "Are you planning to take over the farm?"

Michael began, "Well, I don't know about that." He hesitated. "I didn't want to say anything yet. I'm not ready to take over the farm. In fact, I don't know what I want to do."

Matthew knew what Michael was thinking before he spoke the words. He desperately wanted Michael to say something different.

Chapter 4

"But," said James, "my brother, now is your chance. If you don't take this opportunity, there may not be a farm for you to take over."

Michael looked alarmed. "Dad, you'll be here for many more years. I can't see you living anywhere but here."

Matthew hesitated once more. "It's about time for me to retire. Sell the cattle. Rent out the fields or put them in Soil Bank. I'm ready. And maybe it's time to move to town."

"But Dad," Michael objected, "your whole life is tied up in working on the farm. You love this place."

Matthew said nothing.

James spoke quietly, almost whispering. "What happens is up to you."

Michael avoided the gazes of his father and brother. Then, he spoke. "I've made a decision. That phone call was a job opportunity at Minneapolis Moline in the cities. I have to try this. Maybe I'll be back on the farm. But I don't fit in around here. I have to see what that world is like. I had a taste of it in the army. And I know there's more to life than the town of Lake View and farming."

Matthew's heart seemed to skip a beat as the reality became clear. Underneath, though, he had known this was likely to happen. Young men were no longer satisfied to stay home on the farm. They wanted something more.

"Are you certain you know what you're doing?" asked James.

"Yes, I'm very sure."

Matthew sighed. "You have to make the right decision for you. I guess we won't be passing the farm on to the next generation."

Ellen sighed. The first family gathering was winding down. She had hoped Carol would come, but she had not. If Carol had come with her husband and children, the Matthew Anderson gathering would have been complete. Carol, probably the wealthiest one in the family, had been her biggest disappointment. This child had rejected the values that the family held in high regard.

Lunch had been served. Immediately afterward, the twelve children of the younger generation hurried outside to play their own games. The adults visited quietly on the front porch. No one seemed in a hurry to go home or to retire for the night. The shadows of evening stole across the landscape, but the mosquitoes had not yet made their presence known.

Ellen couldn't help noticing how pale Laura looked. This daughter-in-law needed her rest. The terrible cancer was making itself known.

Johnie must have sensed it was time. "I think we better get back to the old home place and the little house. Laura needs her rest."

"The beds are all made and ready for you," said Margaret. "You can sleep as late in the morning as you wish."

How handy it was to have Grandma's little house as an extra place for guests, especially since Margaret and Joe's big house was full with their six children.

At that moment a car came up the driveway.

"It's late, but could it be Carol?" questioned Ellen.

"It's Aunt Carol!" shouted one of the kids.

The yard light revealed a stunningly beautiful woman. Blonde hair. A fashionable dress in the style of the best-dressed women who appeared on television. Two children stood close to her.

Ellen hurried forward to meet her daughter. "O my dear child, how wonderful it is that you are here. I was afraid something had happened so you couldn't come."

"Mother, I'm glad I'm here."

Carol opened her arms, and mother and daughter embraced.

The next moments were pandemonium. Five children, three spouses and a total of fourteen grandchildren meant much noise and confusion. These were the sounds of a joyful family reunion. For the first time in two years the family was complete—almost complete.

Margaret spoke above the many voices. "Didn't you bring your new husband? We were eager to meet him. And what about Jeffrey?"

"Hank was so involved in business deals he couldn't make it. He might be able to come on Sunday."

Margaret repeated her last question. "What about Jeffrey? We haven't seen him in a long time."

"Jeff is with his grandmother. Mrs. Grant insisted he spend time with them."

Ellen sensed there could be trouble brewing. Mrs. Grant had interfered in Carol's marriage to her son and then tried to take her grandson away from Carol.

Johnie and Laura and their children said their goodnights, and Margaret and Joe said theirs as well.

Chapter 4

"We'll move into the living room and porch," said James. "Then you can have our bedroom."

"Thank you, James, but we made arrangements to stay in the motel in Lake View. We knew it would be more than a little crowded out here. We've already checked in."

"I'm sorry," Ellen managed to say. "But come out for breakfast. We'll have our Saturday farmers' breakfast along with cinnamon rolls."

"Mother hasn't lost her touch."

Carol moved back toward the car. "We'll see how early we get up."

Ellen felt a kind of rejection from Carol. It seemed Carol was not only rejecting the family values but also her mother.

Ellen tried hard to smile. "We'll see you tomorrow."

Later that night, sleep would not come to either Matthew or Ellen. There had been too much excitement for them to settle down. They lay in bed, not ready to go to sleep. Matthew sensed something was bothering his wife.

"What's wrong, dear? Something's bothering you. Is it Carol?"

"Yes and no. I'm concerned about Carol. We haven't been together for a long time. It's almost as if she doesn't want to be part of this family."

"I couldn't help thinking about Aunt Rita. Carol seems to be going Rita's way of a high society lady."

Ellen turned toward her husband. "There's something else that I wasn't going to tell you tonight, but it's best I do."

Matthew knew what Ellen was about to say.

"It's about Laura. Johnie told me that her cancer is back worse than ever. The doctor says she may not have much time."

Matthew cleared his throat. "Somehow, I knew Laura wasn't doing well. She looked so pale."

"There's nothing we can do—except pray. I don't feel optimistic. And Johnie's been through so much. And those three lovely children."

"God never gives us more than we can handle. He gives us the strength to get through those tough times."

"I know it's true, but I'm having a hard time really believing it."

"So am I. And I found out something, too. It looks as if Michael will move away—at least for now. He has a job opportunity."

"I heard snatches of the conversation," said Ellen. "I was sure that move was coming."

"It looks as if we need to make some changes." He thought a moment. "Life never stays the same, does it? Living life means changing every day."

"We need to move forward, but I'm not sure I'm ready."

Chapter 5

James stood back from the activity that was taking place. Today was the day all the cousins and relatives of the Anderson clan would gather. He walked over to the old oak tree that had been there all the days of his life. Dad had come to the same spot. This was one of those perfect June days, and he wanted to savor the moment.

James spoke the words, for he knew these lines were Dad's favorite as well: "'And what is so rare as a day in June? Then, if ever, come perfect days; Then heaven tries earth if it be in tune, And over it softly her warm ear lays; Whether we look or whether we listen, We hear life murmur, or see it glisten.'"

"Thanks, Son, I used to know that whole stanza. This is such a day."

"I see that sadness in your eyes, Dad. Is something wrong?"

"I'm thinking of other family gatherings at this same spot, but so much has changed. Some of those people are no longer with us." Matthew stopped a moment. "Our family is here today. We will never all be together at the same time. I think of Ma and her time on earth."

"We're fortunate to have Grandma with us. Not too many people live to be almost ninety-four years. She's had a rich life."

"But I keep thinking how we will never all be together as we are today. We must make the most of every moment."

It was strange, thought James, how his father, who had less than an eighth grade education, made such profound observations. "Dad, I have come to appreciate your wisdom more than ever. You are a wise man."

"I've lived a few years, and I try to learn. The Lord teaches us many lessons."

Father and son savored the next moments. There were times when words only interfered with fellowship and communication.

"Ma made an interesting request. She wants to see and talk with each family member in order. She wants to see each of her children first—in order. Then, each of her grandchildren by family."

James remembered a scene from the past. During the last hours of his life his grandfather, John Anderson, lay on his bed in the little house down the hill from the big family home, and he had heard Grandpa speak to those of his family who were present. During his last moments of life, Grandpa had blessed each child and then each grandchild.

"Grandma wants to bless each one of us—just the way Grandpa did. Those are moments I will never forget."

In his gentle way his father suggested, "Son, you should write about what happens here today. What is said and done may influence people for years to come."

"Yes, Dad. I've thought of writing about this day. I'd like to write that great American novel, but now I feel I can't even do justice to writing about this family."

"Son, you can do justice to it, and you will."

That evening, James wrote in his journal his account of and insights about the events of the day. Somehow he would like to get inside each person and tell their story. But after trying, he realized that was impossible.

In some ways Grandma seemed unchanged. Her hair had always been white, combed back in a bun—called a pug in those earlier days. The lines in her face had become deeper, but otherwise her face showed more of a gentle quality. Her blue eyes that had been so bright and observant had now dimmed. She needed to hear the voice before she knew who the person was.

Chapter 5

Grandma, along with his parents, had been the constant presence in the whole of his life. These family members helped give him the strength and security so important in a chaotic and unpredictable world.

James tried to put himself into the mind of Elizabeth Anderson. What would she be thinking and feeling now? How would she look at people and life? He listened and tried hard to remember all that was important.

He found a quiet corner and began to write and the words flowed easily. "I, Elizabeth Anderson, have lived a full and rich life. When John died and I was only in my seventies, I felt that three score and ten was the complete life God intended for me. But then I looked to my family and friends and to Holy Scripture. I still had purpose in life. The Lord permitted me to live for a reason.

"I'm feeling the ravages of age. I see little. I have to feel my way around. People have to lead me. At first I resented the help that people wanted to give. Now, I feel an intense love for the person. I pray for and bless each person who helps me.

"Sometimes, I think John is present. I tell him about our children and grandchildren and great-grandchildren. He would have been so proud.

"I miss Lucille. That's one tragedy I couldn't understand. I intend to ask God some questions about that. Why did He permit Lucille to suffer and die at such a young age? She would have been the perfect mother. It was Lucille who helped bring me closer to You, Lord, and then I lost her. Why? Why?

"And Paul John, or P.J. I brought him up the same way as the other children. Why did he turn out to be a liar and cheater? I spent more time praying for him than for any of the others. Did You ignore my prayers? Why?

"I keep remembering my early life. My mother and father. The hard times. My brothers and sisters. Those early school days. The hard work on the farm. The church. Changing from Swedish to English. That was hard for the older people. John and I were ready, and we knew this was the only way.

"I'm getting terribly forgetful. Sometimes I'm dizzy, and everything around me seems unreal. I fell the other day. I didn't know what had happened, and all of a sudden a nurse was helping me up. Thank God I didn't break a hip or anything else.

"If there's anything I'm afraid of, it's falling and breaking a leg or hip. I've seen this happen to many people.

"Sometimes, I feel so alone in this world. All of my brothers and sisters are gone. Almost all of my friends have died. Lord, isn't it time for me to go Home?

"I used to think death would be so awful—especially those moments when you knew you would die. Now, I feel I'd like to leave these aches and pains. And Heaven means reunions with Mother and Father and sisters and brothers and friends. It also means I will meet my Lord.

"But I am alive now. I must bless and encourage each person in my family. I rejoice in the way God has worked in my life and in the lives of my family."

Most of the words that James wrote were thoughts that he imagined Elizabeth Anderson would have while some were words she had spoken. Throughout the day he had stayed close to this frail and precious lady.

James had decided he wanted to be an observer. He greeted many people and talked with them, but he wanted only to listen. Listening was a part of gaining both information and wisdom—a part that most people neglected.

Aunt Martha was the first to come to Grandma. In a sense, she had been second mother to Matthew Anderson. There was a special bond between them. Though she spent much of her life away from the rest of the family, her return always brought an excitement to everyone else. One could never say that Martha Anderson Carlson was fat, but she was that jolly woman who obviously enjoyed the fruits of her own cooking. And that was part of her warm and loving personality.

"You are my firstborn," began Elizabeth Anderson. "You have been the one who nurtures your own and other children. Your life has not been an easy one. You lost your husband before you were forty-five. You have been a source of strength for your three daughters and for the grandchildren and great-grandchildren as well. Somehow I know that there is Anderson blood in distant California. The Lord is with these loved ones even to the end of the world."

Martha grasped her mother's hand. "It was you, Mother, who showed me the way. I've looked to you as my example. Even though I was far away, I always thought of you and wished that I were close by."

"I was never far away," replied Elizabeth. "You were held close in my heart and in my prayers. Never a day went by that I did not pray for you."

This is my heritage, thought James. Grandma and Grandpa built their home on a foundation of faith. Then, Dad came out of that home, and he and Mother built a home that carried forward that heritage. And now I see what I must do.

At that moment a little girl ran up to Aunt Martha and Grandma. Grandma reached down and took the young child's hand. "What is your name, my dear one?"

The young eyes looked up into Elizabeth Anderson's. "My name is the same as yours. I'm Elizabeth."

Grandma reached down and with her failing strength brought the child up onto her lap. "I'm so glad you came. I love you."

"This is Corrine's granddaughter. It's Susie's little girl. But now we call her Susan rather than Susie. And Elizabeth is your great-great granddaughter."

This small encounter was one of many that James witnessed. He tried to remember each one. Later he wrote feverishly, hoping not to forget any part. The influence of one home had gone far beyond the home and beyond these beautiful hills of Minnesota.

"It's Victoria, Mother." Victoria sat down beside her mother and placed her hand in the old woman's frail hand.

The woman that James had known as principal and teacher did not look quite so tall and commanding. Her dark hair had many strands of gray. Victoria, now more than seventy years old, was beginning to show her age.

"I'm so thankful you're back home. I've missed you."

Victoria began to tell of her latest trip. "I've always dreamed of seeing London Bridge and Westminster Abbey. Now I've done what I always wanted to do."

"I'm glad you're home. But you have your purpose here, and it's not just me. There's more for you right here in Lake View."

"Yes, Mother, I think I know."

"When you visit me and talk with the other residents in the nursing home, it is special. And when you read the stories and poems, you give a whole new meaning to our lives. And your tutoring of the children who have reading problems, that is important."

Elizabeth Anderson seemed to grope for words. "I don't think as fast as I used to. But I want to say something. When your father died and I was alone, I thought my life was over. Now that you're no longer a teacher, you have a new purpose in life. Take advantage of these new opportunities."

Victoria smiled. "I'm finding there are times when I have to reevaluate my life. I guess that happens when a person is over seventy."

"The Lord guides each step of the way. My life is changing, too, as I become weaker and weaker. And I keep hoping the Lord will take me Home."

"But, Mother, we don't want you to leave us."

James looked around at the older relatives. Grandma had become frail. She was now the only member of that generation. Uncle Ed looked ever so much older. These loved ones would leave this earth—and Mom and Dad weren't so young anymore. Life seemed to move forward like a fast-flowing river.

Matthew took his turn with his mother. James listened intently and tried to remember all he heard.

Elizabeth spoke slowly and deliberately. "You have been a wonderful son. You have been there when I needed you most. And Ellen seems more like a daughter than a daughter-in-law."

"Ma, I don't think you realize how much you gave to each of your children—and your grandchildren as well."

"You have done more to carry on the Anderson heritage of faith than anyone else. Even though your part seems less important now, what you are and do makes a great difference."

His father said something, but James couldn't quite hear. Then he spoke louder and James heard the words.

"I'd like this farm and the home farm to be places to come back to. At least Margaret and Joe will be on the home place. Ellen and I hope to live here for a few more years. But right now, it looks as if Michael won't be staying."

"Time will tell." Grandma reached out for her son's hand. "Somehow, I believe Michael will decide to return. He's a farm boy and can't get away from the land. It's hard for some young men to grow up and take on responsibility."

His father spoke quietly. James sensed the sadness in the words he couldn't quite hear.

Grandma tightened her grip on her son's hand. "My son, my son, I love you more than I can say. I can't thank you enough for all you've done for me. May the Lord bless you beyond all measure."

Moments of reverent silence followed.

When Aunt Mary approached Grandma, James noticed how much older she looked. The dark hair was no longer dark, but gray and almost white in places. The last years in California had not been easy years.

"Mary, I've missed you ever so much. I wish you weren't so far away."

Chapter 5

Mary quickly defended herself. "These cold winters are getting too much for me, and it's even harder on Ed. Beth isn't that far from us. And Irene and her family think about moving to California."

"But Jake and his family are in the southern part of the state."

"We're happy in California, but we miss you."

Grandma's voice quivered. "I didn't mean to sound critical. I'm sorry."

"Mother, I understand."

Grandma began again. "I have to say that I'm sorry. I'm afraid that when you were born, I had not been feeling well. I often feel that I failed you—that I wasn't the kind of mother to you that I should have been. I was ill so much of the time. I'm sorry."

Mary smiled. "Mother, you were a great mother. And look at me: I turned out all right."

In the next moments, James moved away, for it seemed these were private moments for mother and daughter alone. In her own way, Grandma blessed her youngest daughter.

As Mary left, cousin Peter stooped down and kissed his aunt on the cheek. Grandma went about the business of visiting with Peter and giving him her blessing. In many ways, Peter had been like an uncle to James. James had to admire the way Peter had won his struggle with alcoholism.

His mind traveled back in time. James saw his brothers and sisters when they were young. Somehow, the years had slipped by. Except for Michael, they were now middle-aged parents who were busy with their children and jobs and church and community. A new generation was replacing the generation of his parents.

"James." His grandmother's voice broke into his awareness. "James, could you help me into the house? I'm tired. I'm afraid I need to rest a little while."

James stooped down and helped her stand up.

"My dear boy, there are so many things I'd like to say to you. I don't know where to begin."

"I'll be around awhile this summer. There will be other days."

Grandma's voice seemed to weaken. "I'm afraid if I don't take my chances now, I won't have another opportunity."

James sighed, hating to think of losing his grandmother.

"My boy, I think you spent more time with me than any of the other grandchildren."

James remembered. "Yes, I practically lived down in your little house. I remember many of the stories you used to tell. Many of those family members and their stories I will never forget."

"Write them down. Tell them. Tell them to your children that they may know their roots. Tell them that they may appreciate their heritage."

"Yes, Grandma."

James took his grandmother's arm, and they began to walk toward the house. She leaned on him.

"Never forget, my dear, the Lord in your life. Next to that, your family is more important than money or jobs or anything in the world. But you must also follow your dream."

"I know, Grandma. I won't forget."

As James completed his journal about the day, he spoke his thoughts aloud. "Am I losing track of what is most important? Am I forgetting my dream?"

CHAPTER 6

"We're moving forward like a fast-flowing river." Matthew thought of the truth of the words James had spoken earlier. These days would quickly end.

Yesterday, Ma had visited some of the grandchildren but then became too tired to go on. Matthew hoped that today all of them would have an opportunity to be with their grandmother. Getting old was not easy.

Today, the Anderson family filled the Oak Ridge Church. The balcony was full, and chairs had to be brought in. For that hour on Sunday morning, they were all together in a quiet worship service. Even Michael, still without his own car, was present.

Matthew loved the old hymns. He wanted to experience each of those words:

> Children of the heavenly Father
> Safely in His bosom gather;
> Nestling bird nor star in heaven,
> Such a refuge ne'er was given.

The words swelled even more on the next verse.

God His own doth tend and nourish
In His Holy courts they flourish.
From all evil things He spares them;
In His mighty arms He bears them.

As they finished the final verse, James and Johnie moved to the front of the sanctuary. Johnie's voice boomed out: "Now, I invite those of you who know the Swedish to join my brother and me in singing those words."

Matthew felt a catch in his throat. He looked over at Ma and thought he saw tears in her tired eyes.

Trggare kan ingen vara
An Guds lilla barna skara;
Stjarnan ej pa himla fastet
Fageln ej i kanda nastet.

In that moment Matthew experienced the greater truth that he had realized so many years ago. Many changes take place on this earth, but "Jesus Christ is the same yesterday, today, and forever." He whispered under his breath, "Lord, thank You for never changing. You are with me now and forever."

Some of that peace and security seemed to fade during the afternoon. Back at the home place, Margaret had everything organized. Ellen and Victoria had also brought baked chicken. The women all seemed to know what to do in bringing food, and the men managed to get chairs and tables in place. This was Midsummer's Day, and a picnic in the Swedish tradition was the only way to hold a family reunion.

As the meal ended, Matthew and his brother-in-law Ed walked toward the barn. Warren, niece Corrine's husband, joined them. This is what they would have done twenty years ago. At these times the men shared what was on their minds.

Ed, who had always been strong and outspoken, was the first to speak. "I miss Minnesota in spite of these weather extremes. Mary and I think about coming back."

"Then, it would be like old times."

"Mary's holding back because of Beth. Beth has a good teaching job about fifty miles away. She's alone. You know her fiancée was killed a few years ago. She has a lady friend living with her. But otherwise, she's alone."

"But," added Matthew, "Jake and his family are in southern Minnesota, and Irene and her family are in the cities."

"We think of that. We'll probably move back in another year." Ed paused a moment. "I'm afraid I won't see much of Jake. He still resents me. I know I was too hard on him when he was growing up."

Matthew thought it best to say nothing. He was all too aware of Ed's violent temper and the way he had punished his son.

"It's easier to raise girls," said Warren. "I guess I left most of the responsibility to Corrine. She's a wonderful wife and mother."

Matthew felt himself becoming nostalgic. "Remember the days when the three of us talked just this way. That seems like such a long time ago."

Warren went on. "I'd like to come back, too, but all three of our girls are settled in California. Corrine would never want to leave. Corrine's sisters don't even care to come back here to visit. Only Corrine and Susan feel a real connection."

"Families seem to come apart," said Ed. "We're not close the way we used to be."

Matthew realized the truth of what they were saying. "It's sad, but families do grow apart. I'm afraid we're losing something along the way. The next generation doesn't feel the connection we did. There was also a connection to the land."

Ed grunted. "Yes, that connection to the land meant working from sunrise to sunset and barely earning a living!"

"But," interrupted Matthew, "on the farm a man's his own boss. He doesn't have someone telling him what to do. And when I plow the fields, I feel a sense of nearness to my Creator. The Lord is very near."

Ed started to say something, but stopped.

"I like raising oranges and other good things in my backyard." Warren added details about his gardening.

Ed's fist tightened. "Mary's been such a good person. She does all kinds of things for the church. And God doesn't seem to favor her. She's had all kinds of health problems."

Matthew thought of his only explanation. "Ed, I'm afraid we live in a fallen world. We've all had our health problems—and other problems."

Warren began to say what Matthew had been thinking. "There's Heaven. Grandma's been talking much more about Heaven. She keeps telling us that she wants to go Home."

"Now that I'm getting older," said Matthew, "I begin to think more about the end of my life—and about what Heaven will be like."

Ed avoided his brother-in-law's gaze. "I wish I could believe. God seems far away and not too interested in what's happening down here."

Matthew wanted to disagree, but an interruption stopped him.

It was Victoria, announcing the agenda. "You're supposed to come. Everyone's getting together and the photographer is taking pictures. And we're having a little program."

Matthew walked slowly back to the gathering. He walked even more slowly, for weariness had taken over. With Ed and Warren walking ahead, he couldn't help wondering if there would be another chance for the three to talk in this way. Family gatherings are wonderful, he thought, but they remind us how mortal we humans are. And these gatherings seemed to bring out both the best and the worst in people.

Victoria, using her leadership capabilities as principal and teacher, called the family together. Though retired, this sister had not lost her ability to stay in control and order people around.

"I want to welcome all of you to our midsummer Anderson reunion. It has been a real blessing that we could all be together, or at least as many as could travel and get away at this time. And now that we have a minister in the family, I want to call on my nephew, Johnie Anderson. Or we should call him Pastor John Anderson?"

Matthew always felt pride about all his children, but especially about Johnie. He had to admit that Johnie had always been his favorite. Johnie, the boy who loved the land and the outdoors and tractors. The boy who spent more time with him than any of the others.

"I can't begin to tell you how much I appreciate being here with all of you. Family is important. My own family of Laura and our three children mean more than life itself. And all of you are a part of this larger family. Let us now pray and give thanks."

Matthew bowed his head. He couldn't help thinking of other gatherings at this very place. Ma and Pa's golden wedding. Corrine and Warren's welcoming gatherings. Other family and community gatherings. Margaret and Joe's family gatherings. All of these memories flowed through his mind.

"Almighty God, our loving heavenly Father, we come to You with hearts full of gratitude. We thank You for family. We thank You for the home we all came from. We thank You for the homes that we are now a part of. It is in these homes that we come to faith and learn to walk in Your ways.

Chapter 6

"Lord, this is a time of change and uncertainty. Our world is changing fast, and we do not understand some of what is happening. Help us to rely on Your wisdom and Your strength. Your strength is made perfect in our weakness. We thank You that You are the same yesterday, today, and forever.

"We ask Your blessing on each family member present here today. May each one know You in a personal way. May each individual seek Your guidance.

"We thank You for many material blessings. You have given us wealth beyond all measure. We live as well as royalty lived in the past. In our time of wealth and prosperity, we pray that our nation will not forget You—but will remember and acknowledge You as the source of our blessings.

"Guide and bless our fellowship here today. May we build up one another in our most holy faith. May we live and honor You in all that we say and do. We pray all this in the name of the Father, Jesus the Son, and the Holy Spirit. Amen."

A hush had fallen over the congregation of family members.

Victoria broke the silence. "The Andersons have always loved to sing. So we'll start by singing a favorite. And then afterwards we'll hear from each family—starting with the oldest." She looked at Martha, who smiled. "No, we'll leave the oldest until last. We'll ask Mother to give us her blessing. First, we'll sing a favorite."

Ellen played the introductory notes, and soon the Anderson family lustily sang.

> What a friend we have in Jesus,
> All our sins and griefs to bear!
> What a privilege to carry
> Everything to God in prayer!
> O what peace we often forfeit,
> O what needless pain we bear,
> All because we do not carry
> Everything to God in prayer.

The family sang a number of other hymns, all of them family favorites. Then, Johnie shared some thoughts about what Scripture says about family. This is more powerful than any Sunday morning sermon, Matthew thought.

Family sharing time followed. Martha told about the two older daughters and their families in California. Those families seemed distant—not just in a physical way. Then, Corrine stood and introduced Susie and little Elizabeth. The family had expanded into a new generation, a fifth generation.

Victoria joked about her place as second. "I'm second best. And I've already talked too much. Some of you who were my students got to know me better than you wanted to."

Some light remarks interrupted her words.

James spoke out. "We may not have appreciated you at the time, but we did afterward. You made us learn history. We're all grateful for what you did. And we learned the difference between right and wrong."

Victoria brushed off the compliment. "But now we go on to the family of P.J."

Larry Anderson moved to the area that served as the platform. Matthew remembered all too well the Larry of twenty years ago, the Larry who stretched the law and stole from others. Larry's transformation had been more dramatic than any other. He had changed from a wild kid who broke the law to a dedicated and responsible Christian husband and father.

Larry spoke softly. "Most of you know my story. I was a really rotten sinner. I went to jail for my dishonesty. But while I was in jail, Christ came into my life. I became a different person. My dear wife Joan can attest to that. I wasn't even around when my son was born. It was Uncle Matthew and Aunt Ellen who took her to the hospital and stayed with her. But the Lord turned me around.

"I have three children. I want them to stand up." The three stood. "Lowell is twenty-one and will be a senior in college. Lisa is sixteen and will be a junior in high school this fall. And Lorraine will be a freshman. That's my family—and, of course, Joan, the woman who helped me all these years."

"Tell us about Rita, your mother," requested Victoria.

Larry looked aside as if he wanted to avoid the request. "I haven't heard from Mother for a while. She has a busy social life. She hasn't been back for some time. She's been in the hospital several times. She has breathing problems—because of all that smoking. My sister Noreen is out East. She has two children. I've tried, but we don't have much contact."

"It's too bad they couldn't be here."

Chapter 6

Matthew could see some of the children were trying hard to sit still.

"Let's move along. I think the kids want to get out and have their game of softball." Victoria looked to Matthew and Ellen.

Matthew let Ellen do the honors of introducing. Ellen quickly moved through the children in order. James and Ruth and their three. Johnie and Laura and their three. Margaret and Joe and their six. And Carol, whom she barely recognized, with her new husband and three children. And, finally, Michael.

That left Mary. Matthew had missed the close fellowship of Mary and Ed. It had now been seventeen years since they had moved to California. Matthew's four older children and Mary's three children had been inseparable in their growing-up years.

Mary nervously grasped a handkerchief as she stood to introduce the two children who were present. As Beth stood, Matthew couldn't help seeing her as a younger and shorter version of Victoria. She seemed to have that same presence and authority that her aunt had—probably part of being a teacher. Irene, a young version of Mary, stood and introduced her husband and pointed out her three children. Her children and others were becoming restless.

Jake had chosen not to come. Matthew knew that this son harbored much resentment against his father. Ed had always treated him in such a rough way.

Victoria raised her voice. "Now, last of all, but most important, we want to hear from our mother and grandmother and great grandmother, Elizabeth Anderson."

Young Susie called out. "Remember, we have a great-great granddaughter here as well."

"I stand corrected."

Family members moved closer as Elizabeth Anderson began to speak.

"I am overwhelmed as I see so many of my family together. I'm at a loss for words. It can be hard to grow old. At times, my mind is not so clear, and I forget things. That's part of growing old. But I know the Lord is with me even in the valley of the shadow of death. I fear no evil, for the Lord is with me."

Matthew observed that his mother was "old and full of years," as the Bible said. Yet, he remembered her as a much younger woman. The woman who taught him many of the great truths. She had taught him how to pray. He listened closely to the words that followed.

"I want to tell you about a very simple truth—yet a very deep truth. I believe it is love that has brought you here. It is love that has brought me to this very place. Love is so completely associated with home. And that little house over there was home to me for many years. The big house replaces another house that was home to the Andersons.

"But all of this love comes from a greater love—my heavenly Father's love. I feel your love flowing freely. My heavenly Father's love has touched mine and yours.

"I'm an old woman, and I don't think so fast, but I want to bless you all. I've talked with my children and many of my grandchildren. I want to bless each of you. When God blesses us, He is involved in our lives. And He changes us and does what is best for us.

"What I want to say above all is this: Seek first the Kingdom of God and His righteousness. Then, other things will be added. Seek His love, and then love one another as He has loved us."

With trembling hands, she motioned to Johnie. "Let's pray the benediction together. You get us started."

Matthew stood in amazement at the quiet that had settled over the group. From the very youngest to the oldest, everyone was listening.

Johnie said a few words and then led the family in the prayer: "The Lord bless us and keep us. The Lord lift His countenance upon us and give us peace. In the name of the Father, the Son, and the Holy Spirit. Amen."

For a few moments everyone remained quiet. Matthew hated to see this time of worship come to an end.

Victoria broke the silence. "Now, it's time to visit. And how about that game of softball down in the west pasture? And later there's afternoon lunch, of course. I guess we Andersons always need to have another lunch."

The silence changed to laughter and talk and noisy family fellowship. The younger generation and some older members walked and ran to the west pasture. Little time elapsed before the game was in full swing.

Matthew walked toward the pasture more slowly. Larry had stayed back with him.

"Something's bothering you, Uncle Matthew, isn't it?"

Matthew hesitated. For a number of years, uncle and nephew had confided their concerns to each other. "Yes, and you probably know what it is."

"It's Michael, isn't it?"

Chapter 6

"He's settled down a bit, but he still goes back to the bars. He seems to lack direction. Just last night, he told us that he's planning to leave the farm."

"I'm sorry. And you were counting on him to take over."

Matthew stooped down and picked up a blade of grass. "Yes, the blade withers. The grass dies. And another generation takes over. We fixed up the barn and got the new equipment for Grade A milk. I was sure Michael would take over. Right now, this is too much for me, especially the larger number of cattle."

"I wish I could do something."

"Ellen and I have been talking about selling the cattle and renting out the land. We might even sell and move to town."

"It's hard to imagine you and Aunt Ellen in any other place than on the farm."

The two men reached the fence and stood, talking and thinking.

"I have a hard time imagining myself anywhere else. I'm a farm boy at heart. Give me a field and horses or a tractor, and I'm happy."

Larry placed his arm on Matthew's shoulder. "Let's think about it and pray. Something will work out. Remember how I changed. Michael will change also."

With those words the men joined the others and watched the softball game.

Ellen breathed a sigh of relief when almost everyone took off for the west pasture and the softball game. Even Victoria and Martha had walked over to watch the game. Her mother-in-law was in the bedroom, lying down. The people and activities had been a little much for her.

"Mother," asked Margaret, "what's bothering you? Has anything happened that I don't know about?"

"I suppose it's nothing new. I always feel concerned about your father. Michael's been so irresponsible. Your father can't go on this way. We'll have to do something if Michael doesn't come around."

"Perhaps Matt should come over and help for the summer."

"That still wouldn't take care of the problem. I think we're going to have to act. But Matthew loves the farm. He doesn't want to leave."

"What do you think, Mother?"

"I'll do whatever is best for Matthew. I think we should stay on the farm for a while. We have no guarantees about life. Most people do not live to be the age of Elizabeth Anderson."

Mother and daughter began to work with sandwich meat and buns. In a short time hungry children and adults would descend on them, looking for food. The mother-daughter kitchen work spoke of the continuity of life. Women preparing lunch for their families was an activity that went back for generations.

As they finished making a large platter of sandwiches, Carol entered the kitchen.

"We haven't had much chance to talk," said Carol. "I should have stayed to help with all the work."

"Everything is under control," assured Margaret. "We haven't had much of a chance to visit with your new husband."

"Hank hasn't exactly felt welcomed to the Anderson family. He's an important man. Most of the leading people of Chicago know the name Hank Stevens."

Ellen saw the same waywardness that caused trouble for Carol and the family years ago. It almost seemed that some people never changed.

Margaret spoke Ellen's thoughts. "Remember, we loved your Dr. McKenzie. He treated Jeffrey as his own, and he was a wonderful father to Nicholas and Nicole. We don't understand why you left him."

"I didn't think you would," came Carol's sharp reply. "I felt stifled by that marriage. I was merely his wife. I wasn't a person in my own right."

Ellen couldn't help herself. She had to object. "But you promised to love and honor him so long as you both shall live."

"I'm afraid I couldn't take it anymore. There is more to being a woman than just being a wife and mother. I want to do something more with my life."

"I've been a teacher," began Margaret, "but I find nothing more satisfying than being a wife and mother. I couldn't ask for a better husband than Joe. And I have six wonderful children. I feel completely fulfilled."

Carol's voice became tinged with sarcasm. "I guess I knew we had to have this talk. And, Margaret, the favored one, does things right. You always did what the family expected, and I could never do things right."

"That's not true," interrupted Ellen. "We never expected the same of you, Carol. You are two entirely different people."

"I should have known." Carol began to walk toward the door.

Chapter 6

Ellen found tears coming to her eyes. "Are you suggesting that my life didn't really have meaning? I tried to do the best to be a good mother. I wanted to do the best with all my children."

Carol turned back. "I'm sorry, Mother. You were a wonderful mother."

By this time Margaret had something to say. "Now, you feel fulfilled with high society and Hank Stevens. I expect that in another year you might grow tired of your husband and want to move on to something more fulfilling or exciting. Isn't that what you're saying?"

"No!" exclaimed Carol. "I love Hank with all my heart. Dr. Nick McKenzie might have been a great father. He spent all the rest of his time being a doctor and friend to hundreds—no thousands—of people. But he forgot about being a husband."

Margaret responded as only a sister could. "Did you remember to be a wife? Or did you forget your role?"

"That's not fair."

Ellen and her two daughters continued to talk. The sharp disagreements remained and there was no resolution.

All at once, the boisterous talk and noise of other family members interrupted them. Ellen felt relieved as the conversation ended, but she wanted to talk more with her wayward daughter. However, she was certain that the conversation would not take place.

Victoria, Martha, and Mary returned to do their part in arranging the lunch. It was hard to get people's attention so that they could sing the table prayer. Finally, Victoria, using her schoolteacher authority, and Johnie, using his ministerial voice, managed to get everyone's attention. They sang the table prayer. In moments the family ate lunch and visited and had their fellowship.

After the rest of the family had gone through the lunch line, Margaret and Ellen sat down. All the delightful confusion of family filled the house and yard. Many clipped, short conversations took place.

Matthew hovered around his mother. Elizabeth Anderson once more came alive following her afternoon nap. In many ways everything seemed right with the world except for the directions of Michael and Carol. But, somehow, Ellen had faith that these problems would work out in their own time.

During one of those few quiet moments, Carol tapped Ellen on her shoulder. "Mother, we need to be going. Hank wants to get us back home."

"I wish you didn't have to leave so soon. Can't you stay another day so we can see more of the kids?"

"I'm sorry, but Hank and I both have obligations." Carol paused and then stooped down and gave Ellen a kiss. "I'm sorry for the hurt I've caused you. I'm afraid I'm a slow learner. Sometimes, I do stupid things, and I know I've made mistakes."

"I love you, my daughter. I love you."

"Mother, I love you. And I wish that I could be the kind of mother you have been. I wish I could provide the kind of home you have given us."

"Thank you."

Carol held back tears. "I may be the rebellious daughter, but it is you and your home that helped make me strong. I love you more than I can say."

From a distance away, Johnie's loud, clear voice came through. "Some of you will be leaving. Let's have a word of prayer to bless us on our way.

Ellen felt an inexpressible pride as her son prayed. Some of the words remained in her mind and heart.

"Lord, we thank You for the home established by John and Elizabeth Anderson. It is their home that pointed us all in the right direction. And this home and this faith have been brought into the next generations. I thank You for my home established by Matthew and Ellen. They have provided the light that guided me.

"Lord, guide us all as we go our separate ways. These home fires have reflected Your love and goodness. Help us never to forget who we are. And may we always honor and glorify You. And now let us join together in praying the prayer You taught us."

As the family reverently prayed the Lord's Prayer, Ellen felt a love and strength and presence she rarely experienced. Truly, God was present.

The prayer ended, and spontaneously the family joined in singing:

God be with you till we meet again,
By His counsels guide, uphold you,
With His sheep securely fold you:
God be with you till we meet again.
Till we meet, till we meet,
Till we meet at Jesus' feet—

CHAPTER 7

Matthew always experienced a let-down after big family events. The day after the midsummer family reunion was such a day. James had stayed and was helping him with milking. It seemed almost like old times except that the big machines and the bulk tank made the whole milking process feel less personal.

James let the cattle out of the barn, and Matthew took care of washing the machines. There were times he would have preferred to go back to the old ways. Those ways were simpler.

The two men stopped outside the barn and talked of yesterday's events.

James interrupted their talk. "Dad, have you ever thought that a young couple might like to come and live here and run the farm? You could stay on and take life a bit easier."

"I keep thinking Michael will decide to come back and take over. If I hang on long enough, that might happen."

"We can't be sure he will."

"Farming's so much in my blood that I can't see myself anywhere else. I can't imagine myself sitting around and retired. At least not until I'm much older."

"You should take advantage of Margaret's offer to have Matt come over here for the summer. That would be good for both him and you."

Matthew looked away toward the hills. "It's not fair to take him away from his family. I don't want to take advantage of anyone."

"But, Dad, that might be the answer for now."

"We'll see."

Ellen called to them from the back porch. "The first pancakes are ready—along with some crisp fried bacon—just the way you like it."

Matthew smelled the delicious aroma. His mouth watered.

In minutes they were seated at the kitchen table. Ruth had come down and was helping Ellen. The kids were still playing.

"Where's Michael?" asked Matthew. "Isn't he up yet?"

Ellen placed a plate of pancakes on the table. "He got up about a half hour ago. A buddy of his stopped by. Michael said he was getting a car of his own."

Matthew said nothing. He knew Michael plus a car could mean trouble.

"I need to have another talk with my brother."

Ellen didn't hesitate. "James, you know that won't do a bit of good. He might listen to Johnie, but I wonder if he would even listen to him."

For the next moments as they talked, Matthew felt he had the burdens of the world on his shoulders. Problems seemed everywhere. Carol's waywardness, her divorce and re-marriage. Michael's stubborn rebellion. And Johnie's Laura had looked so pale and tired. Could she survive the cancer?

It seemed the lives of Margaret and James were in good order.

An hour later, with breakfast finished and children outside playing, Matthew still sat at the kitchen table. The coffee tasted especially good today. And it was pleasant to talk quietly with Ellen and James and Ruth.

Ellen brought up a question that had moved to the far corners of Matthew's mind. "Son, you've been successful at the college. You've been promoted to head of the English department. What about your dream of a career in writing?"

Ruth quickly responded. "Yes, James, I think your mother has asked a good question."

Matthew observed a faraway look in his son's eyes.

"I'm afraid my writing career is on hold. I want to write some of these family stories. These are stories I must remember, and others should remember them, too."

"That is good," said Ellen, "but you've always dreamed of being a writer. Shouldn't you find time to follow your dream?"

Chapter 7

Ruth didn't hesitate. "James, I could do full-time teaching. You could cut back and teach part-time. Then you could write."

James stood up and walked over to the window and looked out. "I can't turn down this promotion. I love my teaching and my students as well. But I haven't given up on writing."

Usually the one to hold back, Matthew stood up and went over to his son. "James, you have a dream. You need to follow that dream. You won't be happy unless you do."

"Yes, son, your father has spoken wisely. You must do what you feel called to do."

James turned to Matthew and the others. "Thanks, all of you. You're right. I have this dream of telling stories of this family and community. I want to show how families can live together in love. I want to show the mistakes and wrongs done, but I want to tell stories of lives that are changed. As Grandma said yesterday, I want to show how God's love can flow through family and community."

"Why don't you?" asked Ellen.

Slowly James answered: "I guess I'm afraid. Afraid my writing may not be quite good enough so that a publisher will want it. Or good enough so that people will want to read my books."

Matthew couldn't help thinking of his own fears of not measuring up. He remembered how he had felt inferior. He had compared himself to his sisters and brother who had far more education.

Almost in chorus, wife and mother said, "We know you can do it!"

Matthew found words coming to him easily. "Son, I've always felt I didn't measure up. Years ago, I failed that Geography State Board exam in seventh grade. I felt discouraged. Then, it was too easy to stay home and do farm work. I never finished eighth grade. But I have learned something. I have studied Scripture and read magazines and books. The Lord gives wisdom and knowledge to all who ask. I have asked, and He has given me much. I have seen how the Lord has helped me go far beyond my weakness and mistakes."

James, Ruth, and Ellen were silent.

"And, son, you must listen to what the Lord is telling you. If He says that you should write, then you must."

James threw open his arms. Father and son embraced.

"I'm proud of you, Matthew," said his wife.

"Dad." Ruth always called him Dad. "You have more wisdom than most college graduates. James, you have a great role model."

"And now," said James, "it's time for us to be on our way."

"Don't forget what we've said." Ellen gave her son a hug.

"I won't forget. I will pursue my dream. Though it may not happen at once."

Ellen poured a cup of coffee for Matthew. When Matthew wasn't out in the field, he always came in for his three o'clock coffee. It was at times like these she learned what was on his mind.

"Matthew, what's bothering you?

Matthew took a sip of coffee. "I guess we'll always be parents who worry about our children. I think James is doing fine—except he needs to follow the dream. And when I think of Johnie, I think of Laura."

"Laura looked so pale. She looks years older though she hasn't lost her hair."

"It doesn't seem fair that God should let this happen to a wonderful woman like Laura. And Johnie's already been through so much. He's a fine pastor."

Ellen knew she didn't have an answer. "We definitely live in a world where disease and problems are everywhere. That's part of it. But Margaret and Joe are doing well."

Matthew had sensed something else. "Yes, they are. But look at all the responsibility Margaret has. Joe. The six children. Then, she does so much in the community and church. And she's always ready to take care of a family gathering."

Ellen had to admit her husband was right. Matthew was probably the most sensitive man she had ever known. "And then we have Carol and Michael. I worry more about Carol. It seems somehow I failed her."

"No," Matthew objected. "You never failed her. She failed you."

"Thanks." She paused. "Then, we have Michael. He's so young and impressionable. I hope somehow he'll come back to us."

"I'm praying for that."

The screen door slammed, and Johnie entered. "I promised we'd stop before leaving for Maple Valley."

Ellen got up and brought over the pot of coffee and a cup. "Where's Laura? And the kids?"

Chapter 7

Johnie chuckled. "Well, the kids headed straight to the barn to play with little kittens. And Laura's tired all the time. She's taking a nap back at the little house."

"I'm worried about Laura."

Johnie's handsome face showed lines of concern. "She was doing so well for awhile. The cancer was in remission. But now, I'm afraid something's happening."

Ellen wanted to reach out and shelter her son from the hurt.

It was Matthew who replied. "All we can do is pray."

Johnie folded his hands as if to pray. "Now, I'm facing the very thing my church members are facing or have faced. I have to live what I preach."

"It's not easy, is it?" answered Ellen.

During the next minutes, Johnie poured out those concerns to his parents.

Ellen couldn't help remembering those precious times when she stood at the bedsides of her children, hearing their prayers at night. Then, they were all safe within her care. But now they faced a world that was sometimes vicious and cruel.

A door slammed.

Michael walked unsteadily into the kitchen. "It's soon chores time. I'm here to help."

Johnie stood up abruptly. "You don't look as if you're in a condition to do much of anything except to sleep it off."

"Oh, come now, brother, don't get so high and mighty. Just because you're a minister doesn't give you that right."

Ellen quickly brought out a cup of coffee. "I think you need some of this." She handed him a cup.

"Maybe I do." He accepted the cup and sat down at the kitchen table.

An uncomfortable awkward silence followed.

Ellen knew something had to happen. Michael could not go on this way. Matthew couldn't go on with all the responsibility of the farm. Michael's actions would destroy himself and others as well.

Johnie looked steadily at his brother. "Michael, look at me. I have something to say, and you need to listen."

"You don't have the right to tell everyone what to do. Well, I'm not listening. I've got a good job. I'm getting out of this blasted place."

Ellen noticed the hurt in Matthew's eyes.

"Michael, you sit there and listen. You've had too much to drink. If you drive that car, you'll be in another accident, worse than the one before. You'll kill yourself."

"I can handle a few drinks."

Ellen moved over and placed her hands on Michael's shoulders. "Son, you are killing yourself. You're hurting both your father and me."

Ellen silently prayed for Michael. A terrible tension filled the kitchen, normally a place of peace and contentment.

Without warning, Michael burst into tears.

A day later, Matthew wondered what would happen next. After Johnie had confronted him, Michael seemed sorry for his drinking and other actions. It looked as if he would change his ways.

Once more, Matthew sat at the kitchen table. Ellen, Michael, and he had finished dinner. Michael had just picked at his food.

"Michael," said Ellen, "you need to eat. Is something wrong? Is there something you want to tell us?"

"Mom. Dad. There is something I have to say."

Matthew searched for the right words. "Son, we're not going to hold anything against you. You made some mistakes. We forgive you."

"Dad, I know I've been a first-rate jerk. You shouldn't have to put up with that."

Matthew waited for Michael to go on.

"I've made some decisions. First, no more drinking for me. I can't handle booze. But, I know I have to do something on my own. At least for now. I'm going to take that job in the city. I'll work with tractors in that manufacturing plant. I have to see more of the world."

"I understand," said Matthew. "I think a man needs to get away from home to find out who he really is."

"Yes," said Ellen. "I left home when I traveled away from Prairie Center and taught thirty children in a rural school. That's when I found out who I really was."

"I'm glad you understand. I plan to leave tomorrow morning."

All at once, Matthew saw what he needed to do. "Your mother and I will stay, but I'll scale down my farming. Sell some cattle. Rent out some of the land. We'll be just fine."

Chapter 7

Matthew saw the look of relief in Ellen's face.

"Then, maybe in a few years, I'll come back and take over."

Ellen smiled. "You haven't eaten. Let me warm up the potatoes and meat and gravy. I think we're hungry now."

"Right on, Mother."

Matthew felt that the warmth of family love had once more returned to the Anderson kitchen.

CHAPTER 8

July 1962

Johnie, known by his parishioners as Pastor John or Pastor Anderson, looked on with pride as eight-year-old Janelle washed dishes. They had had a late supper that Sunday, and Laura needed to take it easy. He had just finished a phone conversation with his mother.

"Good news," he announced to Laura and the kids. "Michael's straightened around, but he has left for the cities. He has a place to stay, and he starts his new job tomorrow."

"Why doesn't Uncle Michael stay with Grandpa and Grandma on the farm?" asked six-year-old Jack. "That's where he belongs. You said so yourself."

Johnie knew this was explanation time. "Well, son, we're not all called to be on the farm even though we'd like to see your uncle stay on the farm. I'm a minister. Your Uncle James is a professor at the university. And your Uncle Michael wants to work with machines."

"But," interrupted Janelle, "Uncle Michael was acting awfully funny. He didn't seem like an uncle at all."

Laura smiled at her husband. Johnie knew there must be more explanation.

"Sometimes people have problems and make mistakes. Your Uncle Michael was in that accident, and he was still recovering. That's what was happening."

"He smelled funny," added four-year-old Leah.

Laura winked. "I think you better explain that one."

Johnie knew there was no way out. "Let's finish washing these dishes and then we'll go in the living room. I'll explain."

"Is this complicated?" asked Janelle.

"Yes." Johnie put away the last of the dishes.

"What is complic—?" questioned little Leah.

"Sometimes you ask too many questions." Johnie thought again. "But I hope you never stop asking questions. Questions are good. Complicated means that you don't understand something."

A few minutes later, Johnie and Laura and the three children sat on the old hand-me-down davenport. The children seemed to be in the mood for non-stop questions. Most of the time, Laura sat quietly, not her usual talkative self.

Johnie figured this time might be one of those teachable moments.

"Remember the time we drove through the city later at night," began Johnie.

Each of the three seemed to remember something different.

"Well," Johnie continued, "think of the time that man ran out in front of our car. I stopped the car just in time, or we could have killed him."

"I was sleeping. But I woke up when I hit my head."

"That's what happens when someone drinks too much. People start out, maybe, drinking just a little bit. But then they drink more and more. And then they can get into accidents. They can even get killed."

"Why do they do such stupid things?" questioned Janelle.

"That's really dumb," echoed Jack.

"Big people make these mistakes because the drink tastes good. And it seems to make them feel good at first."

"Like when Uncle Michael acted funny?" Janelle's statement came as a question.

"Yes, Uncle Michael started to go with some friends who did these bad things, like drinking. That's why you should watch who your friends are. If your friends do bad things, you can start doing bad things, too."

"Will Uncle Michael be all right?" asked Joel.

"We hope and pray that he will." Johnie looked over at Laura and realized how tired she looked. "It's just about time for bed."

Chapter 8

Leah nestled close to Laura. "Mamma, won't you tell us a story. You haven't told us a story for a long time."

"And you tell good stories," added Jack.

"I'm afraid your mother's a little tired."

Laura straightened herself. "You kids go up and get ready for bed. Then, I'll come and tell a story. How's that?"

The children bounded up the stairs.

Johnie looked tenderly at his wife. "Be sure you don't over-do."

Johnie followed Laura upstairs to the girls' room. Janelle and Leah cuddled together in their bed, Jack sat in the rocker, and Laura sat on the edge of the bed. Johnie kneeled on the floor and looked up at Laura and the children.

Once Laura began her story, the children were spellbound. It wasn't so much the story itself, it was the compelling way she spoke.

"My story begins on a cold winter night. It was January. Snow had come down all day. I was working a double shift at the hospital in North Wood. My relief nurse came in at eleven. I had just checked on all the patients.

"I had had a hard day. Several patients had come from accidents—not life-threatening ones. But they needed to stay for observation. I was anxious to get home. Your grandmother was there with your grandfather. Your grandfather was not well. He needed constant care."

"Is he the Grandpa we have in Heaven?" asked little Leah.

"Yes, Grandpa is in Heaven. The nurse who was taking my place told me that I shouldn't try to drive the five miles out in the country. I wasn't about to give up. I figured I was a good driver, and my dad needed me.

"The wind blew and the snow came down. I had no trouble seeing the road when I was in town. At first the road didn't seem bad at all. Then, a mile down the road I needed to turn onto a township road. Everything looked white. I became dizzy with the snowflakes coming at me. But I knew the road well. I kept on driving.

"It seemed to take forever. Suddenly, I was sliding. I hit the brake gradually. I stepped out of the car. I was halfway into the ditch. I began praying. Lord, I said, help me out of this. Please get me home.

"I got back into the car, shifted into reverse, and backed up onto the road. I continued on my way. The road went straight for another mile. I had no trouble, but I was all over the road. Then, I came to the wooded area, where there would be many hills and curves.

"I made it down one hill and around a curve and up another hill. All of a sudden, a gust of wind practically blew me off the road. I was determined. I kept on driving. I had to slow down. The wind and snow came in such a way that I didn't know where I was. I stopped and started again. Suddenly, I jerked forward and realized I was in the ditch.

"I could barely open the car door. I realized the temperatures were dropping. I was at least a mile from home. I prayed harder than ever. Oh, Lord, save me. I could freeze to death. What should I do? I realized I might be safer if I stayed in the car. There was a blanket in the back seat. And I carried a flashlight and matches and a candle.

"I tried starting the car, but it wouldn't start. Something was wrong. I knew it wasn't safe to walk. And who would come along this late at night?

"I stepped outside once more. I could hardly see where the road was. I returned to the car, got in and closed the door. I felt a terrible panic. I had to do something. If I stayed in the car, I could freeze to death.

"Once more I got out. I began to walk. The temperature was colder than I had realized. There were no farms nearby. I had heard terrible stories of people freezing to death just a short way from home. I stumbled along. Soon I felt a warmth coming over me. I needed to sit down and rest a minute. It was almost as if I didn't care what happened.

"As I was about to give up, bright lights startled me. There, coming out of this pickup, was a blond, handsome young man. He called out to me. 'What are you doing out here on a night like this? You should be home in bed.'

"He picked me up and carried me. I was almost asleep. He opened the pickup door. 'I'm getting you home.'

"I was awake enough to feel all tingly in other ways. This man was everything I felt a man should be. In a moment, I loved him." Laura paused a moment. " And can you guess who this is?"

"Daddy!" came the chorus from all three children.

"And that handsome man took me safely home."

Johnie got up and sat next to Laura, enfolding her in his arms.

"That was a beautiful story," said Janelle.

The younger children echoed the same response.

Johnie felt a tenderness that words could not express. The love he felt for Laura and for the children had to be a love that only God could give.

"It's time for your prayers," said Laura.

The children prayed.

Laura stooped down and kissed each child. "I love you," she said.

Chapter 8

Johnie wanted these moments to last. Love filled his whole being and seemed to light up the room.

"God is good." Johnie spoke the words quietly. "God is love."

That night Johnie held Laura in his arms as they prayed for each of the children. The roughness of his youth had passed, and tenderness filled his spirit.

During the night hours that followed, Johnie experienced a deep sleep that shut out everything in the world around him. A sleep such as this sometimes is characterized as the sleep of the dead—that is, a sleep of preparation. And, in a sense, that sleep prepared Johnie for what lay ahead.

He awakened with a start, knowing something was wrong. He reached over to touch Laura. Her cold body instantly told him that she was no longer in the land of the living.

"Lord," he whispered, "help me! Somehow I knew this could happen, but I didn't expect it right now. I need Your strength."

Johnie moved quietly out of the room and downstairs to the phone. Strangely, he went through the motions with little feeling. He called the ambulance as well as Dr. Hughes. The doctor came immediately because he lived nearby.

Dr. Hughes, a dignified gentleman who was probably Johnie's father's age, spoke words of comfort to Johnie. "Laura passed away in the best way possible. No doubt the cancer was just too much for her weak heart. Her heart just gave out. That's what happened."

"But Laura was so good last night. A little tired maybe. I knew her time might be short, but I didn't think the end would come this fast. She told the children a beautiful story. Then, she lay in my arms as we prayed. In minutes she was sound asleep, and I had one of the deepest sleeps I've had in months."

The doctor placed his hand on Johnie's shoulder in a fatherly way. "I'm going to say something that is out of the field of medicine. For some reason, unknown to us mortals, it was Laura's time. The Lord took her from you in the kindest way possible."

"She didn't suffer, did she?"

"I would say her pain was minimal."

Johnie held back his tears. "I have calls to make. And I must tell the children."

The ambulance, which also served as a hearse in this small town, arrived. Dr. Hughes cautioned the men to proceed quietly. They worked, making little noise. It was only as they took Laura's body out the door that Johnie broke into tears.

"Oh, Lord," he cried in anguish, "what do I do now?"

"You carry on. I'll have my wife come over and help with the children." Dr. Hughes turned as he went out. "Your friends and the church will help."

Johnie didn't have to wait for the children to come. First, he heard Leah coming down the steps. Then Jack and Janelle followed.

Leah ran into Johnie's arms. "Where's Mommy?"

Johnie could not find words to tell them.

"Is she in Heaven with Jesus?" asked little Leah.

Johnie looked away. "Yes, she's in Heaven with Jesus."

"That's not fair," said Janelle, "We need her here."

Johnie stooped down and then fell on his knees. He gathered his three children into his arms. "God will take care of us."

Chapter 9

The minute Matthew saw Ellen on the porch steps, he knew something was wrong. The strange feeling in his stomach reminded him of his close call with death.

Ellen walked toward him. Her face told him this was grave.

"Matthew, it's Laura. Johnie called. She died during the night."

Somehow Matthew had had a premonition that Laura would not survive the cancer, but at the same time he had thought there would be more time. In the next moment he knew he wanted to be with Johnie. They had that special bond.

"We have to go and be with Johnie," he said.

"What about the chores?"

Matthew thought a minute. "I think we can get someone to take care of the chores. Maybe we should wait a day anyway."

During the day that followed many things worked out. Matthew learned that there would be a funeral service at Maple Valley Church on Friday. The following day another funeral and the burial would take place at the Oak Ridge Church. Laura would be buried with Andersons—that meant the beginning of a new plot in the cemetery.

When death and tragedy occur, people have a way of coming together. Friends seek their own family and friends. That was the case with Matthew. He found time to drive over to see Glenn. Then he stopped to see Larry. And, of course, he went to Joe, who was much more than a son-in-law.

"I'll see that your chores are taken care of," said Glenn.

Then, Larry said almost the same words and added, "Lowell is going to be around for a while this summer. He's looking for work."

Matthew observed to Ellen that next evening, "It seems that someone has to die before we appreciate them. And then all at once we begin to appreciate each other."

"I think of that play we saw last fall, *Our Town*. When Emily looked back on life beyond the grave, she realized something. We don't really see each other. And she said something to the effect that life is too wonderful for us to realize or appreciate it."

"There's a lesson isn't there? We need to appreciate life and each other when we live each day."

Two days after Laura's death, Matthew and Ellen arrived in Maple Valley. The parsonage was a beehive of activity. Laura's mother, Mrs. Malmstrom, had assumed the role of coordinator of all that went on. Women of the church had brought food for the family and any other visitors. There seemed to be no lack of people who had come to express sympathy by being there or bringing something or helping in some other way.

When Matthew saw Johnie, he sensed his son's tiredness and sadness, but he saw a man of strength. Johnie first embraced his mother and held her for a long time. Then, Matthew felt himself enfolded in his son's arms.

Johnie spoke through his tears. "I miss her so much. I feel so empty without her."

Matthew could not imagine the emptiness that he would feel without Ellen. The three children ran into their grandfather's arms.

Words were not necessary to express the sadness or the love.

Life seemed to move in slow motion. Matthew and Ellen had tried to help for those two days before the funeral. The Fourth of July celebration was quiet. The children didn't even seem interested in the candy or the parade. But life kept moving on.

In some ways this funeral was different from any other Matthew had attended. This was a close family member of the next generation. Even so, he heard the familiar Scripture and sang some of the familiar hymns. "I am the resurrection and the life. Whoever believes in Me should not perish but have eternal life."

Chapter 9

Eternal life. How distant it seemed at this moment. Even so, Matthew thought of those who had gone before. Pa would welcome his grandson's wife. Pa would have loved this loving nurse and granddaughter-in-law. Thank God for this future in eternity!

Friday evening, Matthew and Ellen returned home to Oak Ridge. Johnie and his mother-in-law and the children came home as well. The end of life summoned people to the place called home.

That night, Matthew experienced the comfort of being home in his own bed. Johnie was down the hall in his old room. The children were in the girls' old room. Michael would be coming home tomorrow. They hadn't been able to reach Carol. She was on one of those trips.

The strains of "Going Home" drifted through his mind. When all of these struggles of life were over, man returned Home—his body returned to the dust. The Christian returned to his Creator.

"One of these days," Matthew said to Ellen. "I'll be going Home."

Ever since that night when Laura died, Johnie had felt a sense of unreality. A mysterious strength propelled him through the days that followed. He comforted the children. When people tried to comfort him, he went through the motions of comforting them. He didn't feel like a pillar of strength, but that's what people said he was.

Through this sense of unreality, Johnie felt a keen awareness of people's actions and words. Some words and actions he would remember to his dying day.

As he looked at Mom and Dad, he realized they were no longer young. They were in their sixties and beginning to show those signs of growing older. They tried so hard to say the right things and to be strong. He wanted to tell them, "Let me be strong for you." In one way he would always look to them for stability and strength. But in another way, he wanted to shield them from harshness and illness.

Now, it was early Saturday morning. He must face another long day. Today would be the second funeral for beloved Laura. Once more, he must be strong for the sake of the children.

He got out of bed quietly. Even now, he wanted to reach over for Laura's hand, but that would be no more. He left his room and went down the hall to the children's room. He looked at Janelle and Leah in the big bed his sisters had shared. Their closed eyes told him that they had been crying. His namesake, who they called Jack, had doubled up fists as if he were ready to fight.

Downstairs, he heard his parents getting up. It was time to milk the cows. Perhaps Lowell would come over once more to help with this task. Without a second thought Johnie hurriedly dressed. He wanted to be out in the barn with his father.

When he entered the barn, he announced, "I want to get back to the reality of life. Milking cows has a way of bringing a fellow down to earth."

Matthew didn't hesitate. "Johnie, you don't need to. I can handle this myself."

"I want to. I need to."

Father and son divided the tasks. It didn't take long before the milking was finished and the barn cleaning was done. The cattle were let out so that they could roam the pastures for the day. Johnie felt in touch with the mundane realities of life.

One reality hit him like one of those old oak trees coming down. The care of his children. How could he bring up three children and go about his ministry?

"Care to talk?" asked his father.

"I'm afraid I'm overwhelmed by responsibilities. I need to look ahead. Laura's mother wants to move in and take over. I can't see that. She is not at all like Laura."

"Laura was always so kind and gentle. Yet, she could discipline when she needed to."

Johnie looked aside to the garden nearby. "Mother Malmstrom wouldn't permit her grandchildren to be children. Children need some freedom to play and dream and be themselves. She wouldn't permit that."

"Son, you make the decision. You're the boss."

"But," Johnie conceded, "I need help. I need someone to help with the children."

"You will find a way," reassured Matthew. "God will show you the way."

"Thanks Dad." Johnie smiled. "Well, I managed to get her to stay over at the little house with Mary and Ed. I simply told her that two grandmothers in the same place were like too many cooks in the kitchen."

Matthew chuckled at Johnie's sense of humor.

Chapter 9

These moments would be the only truly quiet moments of the day. "Dear Lord," Johnie whispered, "I need Your strength. I can't face this alone."

I wonder why Protestant funerals have to be held in the afternoon, thought Johnie. I wish this funeral could be in the morning. Morning seems like a better time. Maybe this will change in the future.

The sense of unreality stayed with Johnie through most of the day. It was as if he were having a terrible nightmare that would end and life would return to normal. But in this case death was real. He went through all the motions of appearing to be a strong man of faith. The children crowded close to him as if they were afraid of losing him, too.

Later, he would remember little from the funeral. Pastor Young, who had been the pastor for almost fifteen years, delivered the sermon. It seemed to Johnie that this pastor had little to say. He knew much about psychology, but he provided little comfort to Johnie.

Reality returned suddenly and harshly at the cemetery.

The closed casket was placed above the hole that had been dug. Johnie held Leah in his arms while Janelle and Jack snuggled close. Mrs. Malmstrom tried to move into her grandchildren's space, but they avoided her and clung to their father. Ellen and Matthew stood by Johnie's side. Margaret and Joe, with their six children close by, and James and Ruth, with their children crowded near the casket. Michael stood by Grandma, who remained in her wheelchair.

For a moment he thought of Carol. They had tried hard to contact her, but she was nowhere to be found. Her absence left a void. The family was not complete.

Aunt Victoria and Aunt Martha remained close to their mother. Aunt Mary and Uncle Ed stood farther back. A number of cousins, other relatives, and many friends filled the area nearby.

"Ashes to ashes. Dust to dust. From dust thou came, to dust thou shalt return."

Johnie felt an emptiness, deep and frightening. He had not felt this way since he had come to a deep personal faith. God seemed distant.

A reverence and peace settled over the congregation as the committal service ended. The audience prayed the Lord's Prayer. Then Pastor Young prayed, "May the Lord bless you and keep you. May the Lord lift His countenance upon you and give you peace. In the name of the Father, the Son, and the Holy Spirit. Amen."

The family and friends remained quiet. Johnie found himself kneeling with the three children huddled close to him. "Goodbye, Laura. I realize now how much I've loved you. And I miss you."

"She's with Jesus," said little Leah.

"Oh, for the faith of a child. And a child shall lead them." Johnie paused. "Dear Lord Jesus, I thank You for my years with Laura. I commit my dear wife to You. We shall meet again in eternity."

He stood up and looked around. There were no dry eyes.

"We'll be here for you, Son," said Ellen. "God will give you the strength you need."

Michael wheeled Grandma close to Johnie. She reached out and touched him. "Johnie, I wish I had been the one. I'll be meeting her soon."

Johnie stooped down and kissed his grandmother. "Thank you, Grandma. It's so hard. I have faith, but I miss her so much."

"Even to this day," said Grandma, "I miss your grandfather. I think that's part of our knowing there's an eternal home. There's more to life than what we have here."

As people began to leave the cemetery, Johnie felt God's presence. God had spoken to him through these people. He experienced a peace and comfort that passed all understanding.

In many ways all funeral lunches were alike. The usual hot dish. Jell-O salad. Ham sandwiches. A variety of cakes. The church basement became noisy with family and friends visiting and catching up on the latest news.

Matthew watched his son. He wanted to shout out his pride in having such a strong son, a son who was also a minister of the Gospel.

As it neared chores time, most people left the church basement to return home. Matthew had been talking to a farmer by the name of Wickstrom. He was a leader in Johnie's church, and he seemed to have a fatherly interest in Johnie.

Johnie approached Matthew and Wickstrom. "Mr. Wickstrom, I want to thank you for taking all the trouble to come from Maple Valley to the Oak Ridge Church. You can never realize how much this means to me."

"I came because I wanted to. My wife and I love you—not just as a preacher of the Gospel—but we think of you as the son we never had. We know that this is a painful time for you."

"I need my friends and family and parishioners more than ever."

"I've been talking with the church board, and we've come to an agreement. I've talked with your father here, and I've seen how you love the farm and farming."

Johnie smiled. "I guess I never thought I'd be a preacher. I always figured I'd end up taking over the family farm."

Mr. Wickstrom continued. "We've seen how rough it's been for you for a long time. The board and I want you take some time off. We want to pay you as usual. We have a son of the congregation who is on vacation, and he will preach. We thought you should take time off and be with your kids and your family. Then, you can come back in the fall."

Johnie struggled for words. "I don't know what to say."

Matthew responded, "Wickstrom and I have been talking. And Margaret is in on this too. Your grandma's little house is now empty most of the time. You and the kids can stay there. Then, you can come over here whenever you feel like it."

Johnie repeated the words. "I don't know what to say."

Wickstrom spoke gently, "Think about it. Or you can decide right now. We want you back as our pastor. And there are people who will help with the kids. But we know you have suffered great loss. You need time to recover from that loss."

"I'm overwhelmed," said Johnie. "I can see I'm not much good for anything right now. I think I need to accept your offer."

Matthew hadn't expected Johnie to agree so quickly.

Johnie opened his arms and gave the reserved Swedish farmer a hug. Wickstrom graciously accepted the gesture. Then Johnie stepped back and opened his arms to his father. Matthew warmly embraced his son.

"Dad, you said it yourself. A man always needs a father. I need you more than ever."

Matthew gulped. "And I need a son more than ever."

CHAPTER 10

August 1962

In many ways the summer of 1962 was one of the most idyllic for the Matthew Anderson family. Matthew's family was complete—except for Carol and her family. Michael came home most weekends, and his life appeared to be under control. James and Johnie and Margaret were at home or nearby. Matthew loved the weekly family gatherings—most of them at the lake that was a part of his farm. This picnic spot brought back many memories.

Matthew experienced that warmth and sense of togetherness that often comes after tragedy. Johnie had agreed to take the time off that Wickstrom had offered him. The time off became a time of healing. Johnie and his three children accepted Margaret's invitation to stay at Ma's little house. They could stay there as a family and get used to being alone without a wife and mother. At the same time, Margaret and Joe and their children were nearby. And Matthew and Ellen were only six miles away and eager for the company of their son and grandchildren.

This was the summer for James to take time off from his duties as professor. It was his time to re-assess and consider his dreams of becoming a writer. James and Ruth and the three children stayed with Matthew and Ellen. Within a few days, Matthew felt the activity was like life when the kids were growing up. And his namesake, whom everyone called Matt, stayed in the boys' old room and helped with chores.

There was something of strength and security that came when families lived in close proximity. Matthew knew, though, that James and Johnie and their families had to go on with their lives. This was not a permanent arrangement.

Matthew remembered the good old days when life was simpler. Today, farming was highly mechanized; yet farmers seemed to be working all seven days of the week. Even though most neighbors did not follow his example, Matthew refused to do the unnecessary work on Sunday. He always did the chores, but other work could wait. Joe usually avoided the Sunday work, except during harvest when the work sometimes had to be done.

Today was one of those quiet Sundays in the middle of harvest season. But instead of tractors and binders and shocking, there were huge combines and big trucks. Harvesting was a whole different process. Joe had the latest machinery and combined the grain for Matthew as well as for a number of neighbors.

Matthew loved the noisy confusion of a picnic by his lake, known as Nelson Lake because of the previous owner, who was actually Joe's grandfather. A picnic table, which Matthew and his sons had built years ago, now stood on the spot permanently. This table held the traditional fried chicken along with hot dishes and Jell-O salad and breads and delicious desserts. Ellen and Margaret were in the center of the planning and organizing. At seventy-two, Matthew's sister Victoria seemed satisfied to remain on the sidelines.

Some of the children wandered down to the lake. Several tried to see how far they could get stones to skip.

Margaret gave one of those shrill whistles. This petite daughter always amazed Matthew. She could manage a family with six children and keep everything organized and on time. And this Sunday afternoon she saw that a meal for more than twenty people came off right on time.

"I'd like to have Johnie give the blessing," Margaret announced. "We have much to be thankful for."

The crowd quieted and Johnie began. "Let us bow our heads in prayer."

Matthew couldn't help thinking of Ma in the nursing home. He missed her presence at these family gatherings. No longer did she have the physical strength, and there were times when she became confused.

Chapter 10

"Our heavenly Father, we look at the clear beauty of this lake. We see Your presence in nature all around us. We thank You for this family and for all the love that is found around us. It is Your love and strength that gets us through. We thank You for the many memories of this place. It is a place we return to for renewal in our lives.

"Now we thank You for this delicious food that we are about to enjoy. Bless each of us and our fellowship together. Bless this food to our bodies. In the name of our Lord and Savior, Jesus Christ. Amen."

"Thank you, brother." Margaret raised her voice. "We'll let the kids go first this time. Then, in an hour, they can swim."

It didn't take long for the kids to load up their plates and find places on the ground to sit.

Soon the rest of the family filled plates with food and ate heartily. As Matthew finished his meal, he lay back and enjoyed the shade of the strong and sturdy basswood tree. August sun could be rather hot, and this tree afforded protection.

Matthew relaxed and Joe and his nephew, Larry, sat nearby. They talked of many things. When James and Johnie returned from watching the children swimming, the topics turned from farm concerns to national news.

"This Berlin Wall is a frightening separation," said James. "Then, only last week the Soviets began atomic testing."

"I'm not sure what all of this means." Johnie sat down near his father. "Some look at Russia as the superpower from the north. The Russian army will come down on Israel and play an important role in the End Times."

Matthew found these prophecies and speculations confusing. "Twenty years ago, we thought Hitler or Mussolini might be the anti-Christ. That didn't happen."

Johnie replied with the expected answer. "We do not know the day or the hour. Only God knows."

Matthew added, "The End could come today, or it could come in a thousand years."

It was James who changed the subject. "It seems to me we become so caught up in the frivolous. Just last week, Marilyn Monroe took her life. What a tragedy! But we can see how empty some lives are."

Matthew saw little sense in this whole entertainment business. People spent time going to movies or watching television instead of studying Scripture. Television seemed to be the guide for many people's lives.

For awhile the discussion became animated. Then, James and Johnie decided to walk back toward the farmyard. The women settled in their own area and talked quietly of other matters. That left Matthew and Joe and Larry to lie back and doze.

This was the day of rest that Matthew needed. Matthew strongly believed that God meant for man to rest on the seventh day. And modern-day followers chose Sunday because that was the day to celebrate the resurrection.

The leaves of the basswood rustled as a gentle breeze blew. The women's voices grew quieter, and the men were silent. The sounds of children talking and swimming had also come to an end. Their voices faded as well.

Matthew drifted into that in-between world of sleeping and waking, one with a perfect sense of peace.

A voice, filled with fear and concern, broke into Matthew's relaxed state. Johnie was calling out for Janelle and Leah. Then, James called for Marlene. He couldn't hear the words exactly, but he heard his sons scolding the older children.

Joe and Larry were up in seconds. Soon everyone, including Victoria, was down by the lake. Though he usually moved faster, Matthew was the last to arrive.

Margaret scolded her two older children. "Matt! David! You need to look after the younger ones."

"Mom, we did while we were swimming," protested Matt. "We got out of the water over half an hour ago. They just took off."

"Which way did they go?"

Johnie looked Matthew's way, and their eyes met. Johnie's expression told Matthew that he remembered another frantic search years ago.

At first no one seemed to know who had gone or which direction they had gone. What followed was a roll call of those present. Finally, it was determined that four of the girls were missing.

In the midst of the confusion, Matthew's mind went back almost twenty-five years. He remembered distinctly how his niece, Irene, and Margaret and Carol had disappeared. Then, after they found Carol, Margaret and Irene were not found until the following day. That had been one of the most dreadful days of his life.

"Lord," he whispered, "don't let anything happen to these dear little ones. Help us find them. Keep them safe."

Chapter 10

As he ended his silent prayer, Matthew raised his voice. "We need a search plan. We can't just run off in all directions. We'll waste time if we do that."

Johnie immediately spoke up. "Let's determine exactly where they were when we last saw them."

A number of answers indicated that the children had probably gone to the north and east. That was the direction the three young girls had taken years ago.

"We need to divide into groups!" shouted Johnie. "That's what Sheriff Walker had us do when Margaret and Carol were lost."

It was Margaret, who used her schoolteacher organization. "Mother and Victoria need to stay here—in case the girls come back by a different way. Someone should go back to the house and be there—possibly phone the neighbors."

"Let's not get the neighbors involved unless we have to," objected Ellen.

Johnie raised his voice. "Dad, you and I will go toward the swamp. We know that area better than anyone else."

Ellen's concern became evident as she moved toward her husband. "Johnie, remember your father is older. He can't go at your speed."

Johnie's voice trembled. "I'm sorry. But Dad knows the area better than anyone else." He looked down at his son. "Jack, you stay close to your grandmother. I don't want you getting lost."

Jack began to cry. "I'm scared. I don't want anything to happen to Leah and Janelle."

Ellen stooped down and picked up her grandson. "We'll be praying. Your sisters will be fine. We'll find them."

"Let's not waste time!" Larry shouted. "James and I'll lead away from the swamp. Joe will lead to the east. Quickly get in line with one of the three groups. Spread out, but follow your leader."

The confusion turned to organization and action. Matthew stayed close to Johnie. He saw in Johnie the same fear that he had experienced years ago.

"Lord," Matthew prayed in a whisper, "spare my son any more problems. He's had more than he can handle."

A sharp pain penetrated his stomach. For a moment, Johnie wondered if history was repeating itself in another way. Matthew had almost died of a perforated ulcer. Those stomach pains told Johnie that he might be having the same problem. After all, he and his father were alike in many ways.

"Slow down," said Matthew quietly. "We need to look in all directions." He turned his attention to Matt and David. "Why don't you boys run over to that clump of trees? See if there are any signs of the girls."

The boys obediently ran over to the grove.

"I'm sorry, Dad, I'm so afraid for those girls. Don't you have the Angus cattle in this pasture? And Black Angus are protective of their young calves."

"Yes, the Angus might be in this area." Matthew thought of Joe and the way he instructed his children. Marlene, though only five years old, would have been taught about the dangers of an angry mother Angus, and was probably cautioned sternly about the Angus bull. "If they listen to Marlene, they should be okay."

Matt and David came running, catching up with Matthew and Johnie. "The cows are over there."

"Did you see anything?" asked Johnie.

"Just the cows."

Johnie felt his heart beating faster, and the steady pain in his stomach became sharper.

The two boys stayed close to the men.

The brush became heavier, slowing them down. The boys were able to maneuver under the brush more easily. The prickly ash, which they called lemon brush, scratched Johnie's arms. One branch swatted him in the face, slowing him even more.

Johnie's mind seemed to jerk back and forth from past to present. He remembered when Dad and he had found Carol. Carol had crawled into a cave formed by a large tree having been blown down. He had crawled into that hole and rescued his little sister. He had never felt closer or more protective of Carol.

Johnie suddenly found his shoes sinking in the mud. The rains of the past years had filled the low-lying area with water. What had been dry was now filled with several feet of water.

"It's not likely the girls would be around here." Johnie stepped out of the mud.

Dad seemed to have the right idea of where to go. "If we walk on the edge of the swamp, we'll get to the road. A little more to the right is the corn field. There's lots of places to get lost in the corn field."

Chapter 10

"I guess I'm too upset to make good decisions."

Father and son and the two boys struggled through some more brush and up and down some more hills. The road was to their left and the corn field lay straight ahead. They were joined soon by a group of the children who had been searching elsewhere.

It was James's son, Richard, who said, "Dad and Cousin Larry went back for a car and the pickup. They said to wait here."

The excited talk of the children revealed nothing. There were no signs that the lost children had been anywhere they looked.

As he stood on the shoulder of the road, Johnie sensed the oppressiveness of the heat. This heat could lead into one of those late summer storms.

Johnie became oblivious to what was around him. He saw Laura, pale and unreal, in the coffin at the front of the church. This had to be some horrible nightmare that would soon go away. And then, the children, Janelle and Leah, stood before him, crying and helpless. How could these children be lost as well?

"Where's my faith?" he whispered aloud. "Lord, where are You now when I need You the most? Help!"

All at once, he saw himself in the Oak Ridge Church sanctuary in front of the stained glass window with Christ holding the lost sheep. He felt like that lost sheep. He longed to be in the arms of the Good Shepherd.

His thoughts traveled back a year to Maple Valley. The congregation had grown at a fantastic rate. He had become known as the most outstanding preacher in the whole county. If there was such a thing as success in the Christian church, he had achieved that success. With two congregations that had more than doubled in numbers, people seemed to worship him.

A new realization came to him like a lightning bolt. "Lord," he whispered, "have I lost sight of You in all this? Have I been so caught up in a successful ministry that I've lost my way? Save my girls. Save me from this terrible pride and hardness."

Though there was a time lapse of only a few minutes, it seemed to Johnie that he had spent hours in this struggle. At the end of that time, he experienced a peace beyond all understanding. Words not quite audible came to him. "Johnie, I am with you always. Even to the end of the world."

Johnie stood, half dazed, wanting that moment to last. In minutes several cars and a pickup came.

"We'll drive up the roads as well as the other trails," announced Larry.

"And," said James, "we need to go up and down the rows of corn."

Matthew walked over to James. "I know a place where we might look. I'd like to go there. I don't think it's likely they're there, but I'd like to check it out."

"Here, Dad, you take the car."

Johnie knew his father had a hunch. "I'll go with you."

Matthew got in the car and drove along the north edge of the road to another township road, where he turned. He kept looking around. Finally, he found an old driveway and turned in, stopping the car when it became overgrown with small trees.

Johnie knew where they were headed. "We're going to that same place where you found Margaret and Irene when they were lost."

"Just a hunch."

Johnie got out of the car and hurried ahead, leaving his father behind. This old driveway had not been used for years.

He wondered if the four girls had stayed together, or would they find some and not the others? There were dangers. such as rabid skunks.or an angry Angus, protecting her young one. Or there could be wolves that could attack a small child. Why did they have to wander off as they did?

All at once Johnie saw the old homestead. The boards on the front porch were broken and rotting. And the barn had no roof. They walked through the old house.

"Years ago, we found the girls in this house. They were huddled together—afraid and very tired."

Johnie sighed, disappointed. "They obviously aren't there now."

His father walked over toward the windmill. "There's something I wanted to check."

For a moment, Johnie felt panic that he experienced only rarely. "The old well. Those old wells could have deep holes."

He ran to the spot. The boards had rotted, and there was a hole. He looked into the hole. He examined the grass and weeds nearby. "Thank God. They're not here."

"I figured we had to eliminate this possibility."

For some moments Johnie felt a sense of relief. Then, the panic returned. He rushed ahead of his father. "We've got to keep on looking."

Chapter 10

Matthew watched Johnie rush ahead. He tried to follow as closely as possible, but Johnie was a young man. Instinctively, Matthew knew that panic never solved any problem. They needed to think back and imagine what the four girls might be thinking.

They reached the car.

"Hurry up, Dad!" shouted Johnie. "We can't waste time."

Matthew purposely stopped. "Son, you've got to calm down. Panic makes us run around in circles and accomplish nothing."

Matthew silently prayed for wisdom. "I have another hunch. But calm down. I know the children are safe."

Chapter 11

Johnie did not share his father's confidence that the children were safe. No one else seemed as concerned or upset as he. Maybe he was just overreacting because of all he had been through. There were times he felt so secure and certain of the Lord's guiding hand. Other times, everything seemed to be falling apart.

"I'll drive," his father had said. "You're upset. Calm down. We can't accomplish a thing when we panic."

Johnie knew his father was right. For a simple farmer with less than an eighth-grade education, Matthew Anderson was a smart man with more wisdom than many of Johnie's seminary friends.

The search parties had either gone into the fields and pastures and wooded areas north, or into the corn field. Children could find many places to play hide and seek.

His father kept driving toward home and turned in the driveway. "Where are you taking us?"

"I said they might be right under our noses."

Johnie wasn't sure whether he should be amused or annoyed. "You think they might be back at the house?"

"No, I don't think so." Matthew stopped the car when he saw Victoria on the front steps.

His sister called out, "You haven't found them, have you? Some of the neighbors came and are looking to the south and west."

Matthew got out of the car. "We haven't found them, but I have a hunch."

Johnie followed. "Where are you taking us?"

Matthew walked to the edge of the lawn, held down the barbed wire, and stepped over the fence. Johnie followed close behind. They kept on walking until they came to an opening in the woods. Before them stood the old house they called the Nelson house, a house that had been left unused for years. Johnie had forgotten about this place. Here's where James would go to be alone, and the girls would have tea parties.

Matthew walked ahead to the steps of the front porch. "Watch yourself. Some of these boards may be rotten."

Before either man could open the door, they heard the laughter of the girls.

Johnie paused, smiling with relief."They've been right under our noses all the time."

Matthew opened the door carefully, and Johnie followed. The girls were in the next room and didn't hear them. In their make-believe world, the four were having an animated discussion about their little children and problems when children were mean.

Matthew chuckled and nudged Johnie, "Listen to the way the girls are taking on the roles of concerned mothers."

Johnie stepped into the next room, the room that had been a kitchen years ago. "What are you doing here? We've been looking all over for you."

It was Janelle, the oldest, who replied. "You grownups were so busy; we thought we'd have some fun."

"It's time to get back to the family," said Johnie.

"We were having so much fun. Do we have to go?" pleaded Leah.

Their concerned grandfather began to explain. "When children disappear, their parents and grandparents get worried."

Johnie tried to collect his thoughts. "It so happens there are woods and swamps around here. And little girls can get lost."

"I'm sorry, Daddy," cried Leah.

In a moment, Leah was in his arms, and Janelle joined her.

Matthew picked up Marlene, and Melissa came to him and gave a hug. "Years ago, there were two girls who got lost and stayed out all night. They were very frightened. They were lost a whole day. They were scared and tired and hungry."

"We didn't want that to happen to you."

Chapter 11

By this time, the reunion was complete. It was time to get back and let everyone know that the lost had been found. The four girls were safe.

That night, Johnie heard the prayers of his children. They missed their mother, but they seemed to have more assurance than he did. "Mommy's in Heaven," said little Leah, "but we still miss her."

Many thoughts filled his mind as he went into the room that had been his grandparent's bedroom. His mind returned to that unforgettable day years ago. The family had stood around the bed; Grandpa had blessed each of his children and then had done the same with the grandchildren.

Grandpa had looked at him and James. "Never forget who you are. You bear the name Anderson. But more important—you bear the name of Christ. All of you, never forget that."

Johnie got into bed, but sleep evaded him. The events and concerns of the day kept running through his mind. His fears of losing his daughters kept haunting him. He didn't seem able to turn off those thoughts. But finally sleep came, and so did some strange dreams.

The dreams were neither comforting nor troubling. Johnie felt there were times when dreams were messages from God. People were so busy with the cares and troubles of the world that they didn't listen to what the Almighty wanted them to do. It was at such times that God chose to speak through the stillness of the night.

In this dream he saw Grandma in the nursing home, but suddenly she changed to the younger person he knew when he was growing up. As a little boy he sat at her table with a glass of milk and cookies. Oh, how he would love to return to those days of boyhood! Her eyes became clear once more—those clear blue eyes that were passed on to her children and grandchildren right on down to the fifth generation.

"John Anderson, my grandson," she said, "you have a special purpose in life. You must preach the Gospel to the next generation. Keep God's Word in your heart and life. You must go far beyond this family and home. That is your destiny. Never forget why God placed you here on earth."

Johnie heard himself speaking from the depths of his heart. "Grandma, I'm hurting. It's almost as if I've been hit in my stomach and can't get my breath. I can't seem to go on. I don't have the strength and the energy."

"You are weak, yes. But the Lord's strength is made perfect in weakness. You can't go on in your own strength. You must go on in God's strength."

Johnie felt like the little boy who had misbehaved, and Grandma or Mother was scolding him.

In the next moment, Grandma became terribly old. She looked even older than her ninety-four years. "My time is short. Be strong. You will preach my funeral sermon. Give a strong Gospel message. Give Jesus' message to come to Him. He will give rest to your souls."

Johnie, half awake, tossed about on the bed. Sleep once more quieted his spirit.

The dream resumed. Grandpa stood there at the foot of the bed. He said nothing. Johnie became a little boy once more. Grandpa lifted him high up the way he did so many years ago. Johnie shouted with that child-like exuberance. "I can almost touch the sky."

Without warning, Grandpa disappeared.

Then, Laura appeared. She was once more robust and healthy, dressed in her nurse's uniform. She smiled.

He felt a hand on his forehead. "My beloved husband, I know you feel great sorrow. Life is difficult. The children need you. The people of Maple Valley mourn with you. Do not mourn for me. Think of the Easter message. 'He is not here. He is risen.' I no longer live in this mortal body. I look forward to the final day and the resurrection."

He wanted to reach out and touch his beloved, but she was just beyond him. Then, a heaviness settled over him. It seemed the world was pressing down on him and he couldn't breathe. He wondered if this was the way a person would feel when he came to die. Was he now dying? Would he leave three orphan children?

Suddenly, he was awake. He got out of bed, though the night shadows had not disappeared. Morning would soon break.

In that moment, John Anderson knew exactly what he had to do.

Two days later, in early evening, Matthew surveyed the farmyard and the cattle contentedly grazing in the pasture nearby. "We've got to make some decisions," he said aloud. "Matt will be going home when school starts. It's time to sell the cattle and simplify life. This is too much work. And I don't think Michael's going to come back to take over the farm."

He felt a light touch on his shoulder.

"Matthew," Ellen said. "We're going to have to decide. That's what you're thinking about, isn't it?"

"You know, Ellen," Matthew began, "this has been one of the best summers. Except for Laura's death, of course. But we've had most of the family together. Michael's come many of the weekends, and he's behaved himself. We've had as many as we could ever expect to have around us."

"The grandchildren are growing up so fast. They'll be going their own ways. And, dear Matthew, we are growing older."

"Right now," said Matthew, "I feel very old." He paused a moment. "It's so quiet around the house now that James and Ruth and the kids have left. They need to go on with their own lives."

"School starts in another week. When school starts, I think it's in many ways like a new year."

Matthew nodded. "It's time for us to decide. I think it's time to sell the cattle."

At that moment a car came up the driveway. It was Johnie. They had not seen him for several days.

As he got out of the car, Johnie walked quickly and with a lighter step. Matthew immediately knew he had made some decisions.

He greeted his parents, giving Ellen a kiss and Matthew a healthy bear hug. Johnie was his old self.

"I'm going back to Maple Valley tomorrow," he announced. "I need to go on with my life. I'm ready."

"We figured this was the time," said Ellen. "School starts in another week."

"I've made some other arrangements. Mrs. Wickstrom is going to come in to do some cooking and help with the kids. Laura's mother needs to go on with her life. And I don't want her bringing up my children. I will do the best I can as a single father."

"You'll do great, son," said Ellen. "My dad did a wonderful job with seven children after Mother died. I'm sure it wasn't easy, but it can be done."

"The other day, I went back to Maple Valley to make the arrangements. I knew exactly what I had to do. Several nights ago, I had some strange dreams about Grandma and Grandpa and Laura. It was almost as if they were telling me what to do."

"A night's sleep can make some things very clear," said Matthew. "It's always good to sleep on an important decision."

Ellen added, "I believe God speaks to us at night in our dreams."

Johnie agreed.

Matthew realized he needed to tell Johnie about their decisions. "Your mother and I have made some important decisions also."

Ellen interrupted. "Your father's not so young anymore. When we made the improvements on the barn so that we could sell Grade A milk, we thought Michael would be taking over the farm. Well, that hasn't happened. It doesn't look as if it will happen."

Johnie's look showed his apprehension.

Matthew continued to explain. "We've decided to sell the cattle. I might keep some beef cattle, but I'll rent out most of the land. And in a few years we may sell the farm and move to town. That's what some of the other farmers are doing."

"But Dad," Johnie said, "you always wanted to have this place as a place for children and grandchildren to come back to. It was your dream. Do you think you'd be happy in town?"

"Your father will adjust. He'll make new friends in town," Ellen answered for him.

Johnie continued. "There are so many changes happening all at once. I'm finding it hard to believe this will happen, too."

Matthew tried to reassure his son. "This isn't all going to happen at once. It will take time."

"I was being selfish in wanting you on the farm. You have to think of yourselves."

"Your father and I hope to be around for you for a few more years."

Johnie smiled. "I hope so. I need you. And I love you. I should go now, We'll be leaving right away in the morning."

Ellen gave that knowing look. "We knew you were ready to go back."

"We'll come over and see you off."

"I'll bake some of my cinnamon rolls and bring them."

"Mom, you're the greatest. And you, too, Dad."

Johnie stretched out his arms and enfolded them around both his parents.

Chapter 11

Sometimes, everything happens at once. First, it was the four girls getting lost. Then, it was Johnie's decision to return to Maple Valley. And next, it was Matthew and Ellen's decision to sell the cattle and look ahead toward moving off the farm.

It was the last decision that was interrupted. Less than a half-hour after Johnie left, another car came up the driveway. This time it was Larry.

Matthew and Ellen were sitting on the front porch. Matthew had just observed, "Life will be much simpler when we sell the cattle. This is the most beautiful place on earth, and I can have time to enjoy it."

Larry approached his uncle. "I'm glad I found you home."

Matthew could tell immediately there must be a problem. "What can we do for you?"

"Joan and I have been struggling with a problem, and I'm beginning to think there might be a simple solution."

"Sit down," invited Ellen. "Tell us about it."

"It's a long story, but I'll try to give the shortened version."

In that moment, Matthew envisioned his nephew as a child. As a young uncle, he had been close to this boy. Though he had been in serious trouble later on, Larry had changed. Matthew felt pride in his nephew for turning his life around and for leading a life that helped many young people—especially young men who had been in trouble.

Larry looked down. "I'm embarrassed to tell you what's happened. We've always tried to bring up Lowell in the right way. He's been such a good kid most of the time. But, two years ago, he started to go on the wild side."

Matthew wanted to say something but didn't.

"Yes, Uncle Matthew, you remember how I was. I guess my son followed in my footsteps even when I encouraged him differently."

Larry stopped, groping for words. "We thought he was ready to go back for his senior year at college. But something's happened. It's not that uncommon." He paused, "Oh, he's not in trouble with the law as I was."

By this time Matthew had guessed.

"We arranged for Pastor Young to marry Lowell and Megan. That happened this last weekend. Lowell's wife is expecting. Their financial situation is tight."

"I don't understand what we can do?" questioned Ellen.

"I'm getting around to the possibility. Uncle Matthew, you told me something about quitting cattle and even selling this farm."

"I don't understand. Does Lowell want to buy the farm?" asked Matthew.

"I believe you really would like to keep the farm. Now, if Lowell works and rents for a year, that will give you some additional time to decide. Then, there's the possibility that Michael will come to his senses and decide to come back."

Matthew wasn't sure of what to think or say. "Is Lowell really interested in staying on the farm?"

"I don't think so. Last night, we talked quite seriously about his future. He wants to get the business administration degree, but with it he would like to study agricultural business. This is the wave of the future."

Matthew wasn't sure he liked this so-called wave of the future.

Ellen was quicker to respond. "Matthew, this might be a good idea. But I'm not sure it would be good for Lowell and his wife to live with us. They need to have their own home."

"I've already thought of that. I purchased a trailer house—a rather nice one. We could move the trailer down to your farm. They could live near here."

"Sounds almost too good to be true," said Matthew. "But I think we want to sleep on a decision. We do that for any of our big decisions."

"And I know you'll pray about it. Joan and I have sent up lots of prayers about our son and this whole situation."

"Let's plan to talk tomorrow."

Johnie always felt sad about leaving home. Grandma's little house had been a safe haven these past weeks. He experienced being a single father, but he had his loving sister Margaret, who advised and helped in so many ways. He didn't feature himself to be a cook, but there was much he could do. He realized he could cook and care for his three precious children.

This morning, Margaret had fried bacon crisp just the way he liked it. Debbie and Judy had scrambled the eggs, adding a little cheese and the right amount of seasoning. And Mother had brought over several pans of her famous cinnamon rolls.

Chapter 11

In the cool of this August morning, the family ate their special breakfast outside. The more than a dozen people sat around the two picnic tables. There was a certain amount of noisy excitement, but underlying the happy gathering was sadness about Johnie and his three children returning to Maple Valley.

As they were finishing breakfast, both children and adults became rather quiet. Departure time was near.

Margaret broke the momentary silence. "Life's going to be awfully quiet around here. We've had nine or twelve or more kids around most of the summer. I don't know how I'll take all the quietness."

Several of the six children yelled out, almost in unison. "We'll make plenty of noise!"

Joe, usually the quiet one, raised his voice. "Not that kind of noise."

"We'll miss our cousins," said Janelle.

Her cousins responded with serious comments as well as humorous jokes.

Johnie experienced something he had never before felt—not even when he left to go overseas as a soldier. It seemed he was leaving for another country or another life. These people were changing. Would they be here when he came back?

An overwhelming heaviness came over him. He wanted desperately to express what family and home had meant these past months.

Johnie stood. "I have something I'd like to say."

One of the kids piped up. "No sermon. It's not Sunday."

Johnie found himself laughing. "I want to say thank you, and I can't find the right words."

"You don't have to say anything," said Margaret. "We all know how you feel. It's been great having you here this summer."

"Life changes so quickly. I had hoped Laura would be with me the rest of my life. I miss her terribly, but my life must go on. There are family members we see very little of. There are those we may never see again in this life.

"But we're all here together now. We must enjoy and appreciate each other while we are together at this special time. We don't say these things very often. But I have to say how much I love each of you.

"Mom. Dad. You built a home for us. You have given us love. We have seen the love of God in all of this. We have experienced Christ and His love. Let us bask in the warmth of His love.

"I thank you all from the bottom of my heart. And my children—Janelle and Jack and Leah—thank you. We couldn't have made it through without your love and your help."

Johnie looked around. There were very few dry eyes.

Matthew stood up. "That's the best sermon I've heard. And your mother and I want to say that you will have our home to come back to as long as we live. Lowell and his new wife are moving into a trailer house on our property. They will live there during this coming year. Lowell will take over the cattle and most of the farming. I'll still have plenty to do."

"Thank God! I was afraid of losing this place to come home to."

"And you'll always have this place," said Joe.

Johnie hated to leave, but he knew this was the right time. "It's about time for us to say goodbye."

Ellen spoke up. "Let's sing a special song and then pray the Lord's Prayer."

The family joined hands, and rich voices blended together.

> Blest be the tie that binds
> Our hearts in Christian love.
> The fellowship of kindred minds
> Is like to that above.

Chapter 12

September 1962

"I shouldn't say this," said Ellen as she poured a cup of coffee for Matthew. "It feels good to be alone. James and Ruth and the kids were great. I enjoyed having them. And it was fun to have the rest of the family coming and going, but I'm tired out."

"We're not so young anymore."

"Our children and grandchildren need to live their lives at their own speed—not ours."

Matthew began to sip his coffee. "I think we need to go in and visit Ma. She's been going downhill since our big celebration this summer."

"That's a good idea. I need to do some shopping. We could stop and see Victoria."

Matthew and Ellen drank their coffee, quickly got ready, and drove into town.

Ellen kept noticing how Matthew held his hand over his heart. She didn't want to pester him because that didn't do any good. Should she insist that he go to the doctor? Matthew always avoided doctor visits.

Ellen led the way as they walked down the hall to her mother-in-law's room. She noticed several patients in wheelchairs and an old gentleman hobbling along.

"It's hard seeing Ma grow old and feeble," said Matthew. "I hope I never have to go to a nursing home."

Ellen couldn't help smiling. "My dear, I'm afraid you'd make a terrible patient."

Matthew agreed. "I like to take care of myself. I don't like someone telling me when to do it or where to go."

"I don't suppose any of us would like that."

As they entered the room, Elizabeth Anderson appeared to be waking up. She looked up, startled. "Is that you, John?"

"No, Ma, it's Matthew, your son. And Ellen."

Elizabeth's face looked perplexed. "I can't understand why John has been away so long. It's not like him to leave me this way."

"Ma," said Matthew, "Pa's been gone for years. He won't be coming back."

Ellen knew this objection would do no good.

"That man goes off and works and forgets all about me. He'll feel bad when I'm gone and he's all alone."

Matthew smiled, yet there were tears in his eyes. In reality, Ma had outlived Pa by more than twenty years. Objecting was futile.

Ellen saw that look in her husband's eyes, a look of sadness and discouragement. He flinched as if sudden pain shot through him.

"Matthew, are you all right?"

He turned. "I'll just take a walk and go outside for some air."

Elizabeth continued to complain about her husband. Matthew walked away, and Ellen tried to console her mother-in-law.

A nurse interrupted their talk and gave Elizabeth her medication. In the next moment Elizabeth returned to the present.

"Mabel Robertson was here to see me the other day. It's not the same as when Anna and I could visit. I miss Anna Robertson. We were such good friends. Why do all my friends die, and I keep on living?"

"Mother Anderson, you have a purpose for being here. Think of your children who love you and all those grandchildren and great-grandchildren. You help keep this family together."

"But I feel so worthless."

"No, dear, you're not worthless. We love you and we want you to stay with us."

Elizabeth looked out the window. "I miss my home. When I was home, I could look out the window or walk outside and see those beautiful hills. I could lift my eyes to the hills. That's where my help came from. From the God who made heaven and earth."

Chapter 12

"Mother Anderson, you remind us what's important."

Ellen and Elizabeth continued to visit. Their talking together reminded Ellen of days gone by when she and her mother-in-law had long talks. While they talked, Ellen felt a growing uneasiness about Matthew.

Finally, Matthew returned. He looked pale.

"John, where have you been?" demanded Elizabeth. "Why do you take off just when I need you?"

Matthew meekly objected.

In the next minutes, Elizabeth Anderson returned to a world she had experienced fifty years ago. Sometimes she spoke as if her children were small.

Matthew placed his hand over his heart. Ellen knew he was experiencing pain.

She tried to comfort her husband. "Matthew, we should get you to the doctor."

"No!" he stated emphatically. "I'll be all right."

Ellen knew better than to object. She said a silent prayer for both Matthew and her mother-in-law.

Matthew's mind replayed his mother's confusion. Ma had kept insisting he was his father, and then she seemed angry at her husband for leaving her there. Elizabeth Anderson was not herself. She was not the mother he knew.

Matthew finished cleaning the milking machines. Soon Lowell would be taking over, and he wouldn't have this responsibility. In some ways this was more work than in the days when he milked the cows by hand. These modern changes weren't always good.

The pain in his arms and chest usually went away, but this evening the pain persisted. Perhaps he should have taken Ellen's suggestion that he visit the doctor. He hated the smell of a doctor's office, and admitting a health problem was something Matthew found hard to do.

At times, he felt he wasn't getting air. The work seemed to take forever. Finally, he finished. He began to walk toward the house. The dizziness returned, and suddenly everything was swirling around. He stopped. He tried to focus on the house, but it seemed to be moving.

"Lord, help me! What's happening to me?" He stumbled and then sat down on the ground.

"Matthew, what's wrong?" It was Ellen. "I'm here." She grasped his hand and then let go. "I need to get help."

Matthew's mind told him he needed help, and Ellen didn't drive. He should have followed her advice and gone to the doctor.

He thought he felt Ellen's panic as he heard a car come up the driveway.

"Aunt Ellen, is something wrong with Uncle Matthew?" The voice was Larry's.

"Come! We need to get help. I'm afraid he might be having a heart attack."

Matthew placed his hand on his chest. It seemed that his chest would explode. He tried to speak but only garbled words would come out.

He felt himself being helped, almost carried, to the car by Larry and Ellen. He found himself in the backseat.

"I need to go back to the house. I'm getting aspirin and water. Aspirins are supposed to help." Ellen ran to the house, returning quickly.

"Get in the car, Ellen. I'll get him to the hospital as fast as I can."

The next minutes were a blur. There were moments he shouted in pain, and then temporary relief came. "Lord," he whispered, "there's nothing I can do. I leave myself in Your hands."

Ellen sat in the front seat, aware that Larry was breaking all speed limits as he drove to the River Falls Hospital. In the back seat, Matthew had moments when he was silent and still as death; at other times he thrashed about, shouting out his pain. These moments were all too reminiscent of that winter day in 1938, the day of Matthew's brush with death.

"I can't lose Matthew. I don't know what I'd do without him."

"We're not going to lose him," reassured Larry.

Larry maneuvered the car expertly from the township and county roads to the state highway. How thankful Ellen was that Larry had stopped at just the right moment. She knew that God caused people to be present at the right time.

Chapter 12

Larry stopped at the emergency entrance, quickly jumped out and rang the bell. An attendant arrived. Within minutes Matthew was on the gurney, being pushed to the examination room.

An officious nurse stood by the door. "Mrs. Anderson, why don't you and your son stay in the waiting room?"

Ellen experienced a combination of anger and frustration. "Doesn't the doctor have some questions?"

The nurse responded in her brusque manner, "Your son explained all the doctor needs to know."

"He's not my son. He's my nephew." Ellen held back tears and suddenly felt weak. The room seemed to be spinning around. She started to fall, but Larry took her arm and led her into the waiting room.

"Ellen, are you all right?"

"I'm afraid I'm overwhelmed. I thought for a minute I was going to faint. I think I'm all right now. But could you find a phone and call Margaret?"

"I'll do that.

Larry gently saw that she was seated and then left to park his car and call Margaret.

Ellen's thoughts returned to that time almost twenty-five years ago. She began to relive the awful fear that had filled her whole being. First, from her kitchen window she had seen the two men—one helping the other. Her first thought had been that her father-in-law must be ill. But it was Matthew. Father Anderson and she had finally managed to get Matthew to lie down. The agonizing hours that followed left an indelible mark on her memory. When Matthew stopped breathing, she felt certain his life was over. If Dr. Baker had not acted so quickly, Matthew would have been gone.

During that time, the children had been in the other room, listening intently. Johnie had run off in anger. "God can't take my father. That's not fair."

Ellen had waited alone in the hospital for hours that night. The worst thing was not knowing whether Matthew would live or die. Tonight, she was thankful that Larry was with her and soon Margaret would come.

Even with Larry present, she felt very much alone. She was plagued by fears that Matthew would not survive. Finally, the doctor appeared. For a moment she feared the worst.

"Mrs. Anderson, you may see your husband now. He's resting. He's had a heart attack."

"How serious?"

"It's a mild heart attack. Of course, any heart attack is serious business. Would you like the hospital to notify Dr. Baker? He's retired, but he still sees some of his former patients."

"That would be wonderful." Already Ellen felt the assurance that comes with having an old friend by her side.

"It's Room 203, the second room to the right. I'll check later."

When Ellen saw Matthew, her reaction was totally uncharacteristic. Usually, she was a woman who was very much in control. She saw how pale her husband looked, and she began to cry uncontrollably.

"Aunt Ellen, the doctor is optimistic. Matthew will recover. I know he will."

Ellen said nothing. Larry guided her to the chair by Matthew's side. She took his hand in hers. She felt reassured.

She dried her tears and began to speak. "All that's happened has been more than he can bear. Laura's death. Mother Anderson's confusion. Michael leaving us. Farm work and getting Lowell started with farming. This has been too much."

Larry placed his hand on her shoulder. "I'll see that the chores get done. Lowell was supposed to come tonight."

"I don't know what we'd do without you."

"I'm simply giving back some of what you gave to me. I don't know where I'd be today if it hadn't been for Uncle Matthew."

"There's something I realize about Matthew the longer we are together. He's always felt he didn't quite measure up. He didn't finish the eighth grade because his father needed him at home on the farm. All the other kids went through high school or beyond."

Larry interrupted her. "You know Uncle Matthew has more sense than most college graduates. He is second to none—except when it comes to his own health."

"Matthew has a deeper wisdom. His wisdom comes from the Lord. I think I started out as the leader in our marriage. When he came to faith, he became that strong leader that I love and admire."

"Uncle Matthew serves as my example."

"Would you pray, Larry?"

Ellen grasped her husband's hand as Larry prayed. She prayed silently the words that Larry spoke. As the prayer ended, Ellen felt peace settle over her.

Chapter 12

She listened to Matthew's steady breathing, feeling an assurance that all would be well. Sleep overcame her so that she did not hear Larry leave and Margaret arrive.

The restful sleep was preparing Ellen for what lay ahead.

Chapter 13

Matthew wasn't sure whether he was awake, or sleeping, or dreaming. He heard voices that seemed to drone on.

"Do you think we should call Johnie?"

Matthew realized the voice was Margaret's. He opened his eyes and tried to figure out where he was. The last hours seemed a bit hazy and unreal. He remembered finishing the chores and walking toward the house. That's when the pain and dizziness overcame him. What followed seemed like a bad nightmare.

"Let's wait and see," said Ellen. "We're not sure of his condition."

Suddenly, Matthew realized it must be morning. The cows had to be milked. Chores had to be done.

Matthew straightened up. Then he realized feeding tubes were connected to him. "The cows need to be milked. There's chores."

Ellen came to his side. "Thank God, you're awake. How do you feel?"

Margaret moved to the other side of the bed. "Dad, you gave us such a scare. You've been overworking."

"Right now, I feel fine—except for these stupid tubes. I hate them."

Margaret moved toward the door. "I'll get the nurse. Dr. Baker should be coming this morning."

"The cows. The chores." Matthew thought of the cattle, heavy with milk. He was too old to keep on milking cows and still be doing all the other farm work. The cows must be sold.

"Matthew, dear, don't worry." Ellen reached for his hand. "Larry has everything taken care of. Lowell is all set to take over. By now, they've finished the morning chores."

"I need to get home. Lowell and Larry don't know all that needs to be done. I can't stay here."

Ellen's voice became stern. "Matthew. You've had a heart attack—very likely a light one. But you're going to have to take it easy."

The minutes that followed involved what was as close to a family fight as ever happened with Matthew. There was Matthew's determination to get home and go to work clashing with his wife and daughter's determination to see that he should not exert himself.

The nurse interrupted their discussion. "Mr. Anderson, do you feel hungry enough for some breakfast?"

Matthew did not hesitate. "I'm starved."

"I need to check your vital signs first." She proceeded to take his blood pressure and his pulse.

Margaret and Ellen watched closely.

"Your blood pressure is good—maybe a little higher than the ideal. It's good."

"When can I get out of here?"

The nurse smiled. "Mr. Anderson, the doctor needs to see you. What happened could be very serious. You need to be patient."

"I need to get home," Matthew insisted. "I have work to do."

Ellen repeated the nurse's admonition.

"We'll have breakfast for you shortly." The nurse left.

Ellen was glad for an excuse to get out of the room. She needed to talk, and it was wonderful to have a daughter like Margaret.

"I don't know what to do with your father. I've known he's had some heart problems, yet he lifts heavy hay bales and insists on working hard. I'm afraid that even with Lowell on the farm, he'll do more than he should."

Chapter 13

"Mom, Joe and I'll do all we can to make sure he doesn't over-do. Even though Dad doesn't listen to us, he seems to take Joe seriously."

"You know, in many ways Joe is more like a son than a son-in-law."

"I can't see Dad living in town just yet. Maybe in another ten years he'll be ready. But Dad needs his space. He loves the country."

"That's true. He's better off being happy and free rather than cooped up in town. If it's his time to die, then so be it."

"Things will work out."

Tears came to Ellen's eyes. "But I need to take care of him the best I can. I can't let him take stupid chances."

"We're your family. We kids will be around. James will come home more weekends. We even managed to contact Carol, and she's planning to visit. We'll be talking to Johnie—probably when I get home."

"And Michael?"

Margaret hesitated. "We couldn't find him. I'm afraid we don't know where he is."

"That, I believe, is harder on your father than anything else. He placed so much faith in Michael. And Michael, with all his potential, has gone the way of the prodigal. It's not just that he doesn't want to farm. He did so well for awhile, but then went back to his old ways.."

"I know, Mother. But like the prodigal, he will return."

"I should have faith," said Ellen. "But I'm afraid I don't."

For Matthew, the hours that followed seemed endless. When he moved around, he discovered he was much weaker than he had thought. He began to realize he would not be able to do the chores.

During the afternoon hours, Margaret and Ellen went shopping. That left him alone, and he needed to nap.

Finally, in the late afternoon hours, Dr. Baker appeared.

"So, Matthew Anderson," Dr. Baker spoke slowly. "You decided to visit us again."

Matthew sat up. "And I'd like to get out of here."

"You're not ready to go anywhere yet. I'll examine you, but you're still weak."

Dr. Baker, now moving a little more slowly than in past years, began to poke and probe and ask questions. Matthew found himself becoming impatient.

"I've looked at your tests, Matthew, and I've examined you. It appears you've had a light-to-moderate heart attack. We hope that no serious damage has been done."

"I'm relieved."

Dr. Baker continued, his voice taking on the tone of one giving a lecture. "This is your second time of coming close to death's door. The other time you were at death's door, almost beyond. This is a serious warning."

Matthew grunted.

"I'd like to have Ellen present when I say what I have to say."

Matthew knew she would soon be back. He didn't have time to reply, for in walked Margaret and Ellen. They greeted Dr. Baker.

"I was just saying that I wanted you to be here when I talked to Matthew. And it's good that you're here as well, Margaret."

Matthew noticed those knowing looks of both his wife and daughter.

"Now, Matthew, my friend, you need to listen carefully. And, Ellen and Margaret, you can help by keeping him in line."

Margaret laughed. "That might not be easy."

"But you can do it. Matthew, you can ignore what I say and not take care of yourself and work yourself to death. Or, you can follow some guidelines and have a full and productive and meaningful life."

"I'm not ready to sit back in a rocking chair," protested Matthew.

"I'm not prescribing that. I am giving you some stronger heart medication. We need to keep that blood pressure a little bit lower. Ellen, you need to watch to see that he takes these every day."

"You can count on that."

"Now, for the present, you can do no lifting. Absolutely no lifting. But you should exercise by walking. Walking may be the best exercise you can do."

Matthew held back a groan.

"Even in the months ahead, you cannot lift those heavy bales or do some of the heavy work in the barn." He turned to Margaret and Ellen. "You'll have to make sure he obeys these restrictions Later on, he may be able to do moderate lifting."

Margaret interjected a comment. "Our whole family will take this on as a project. We can exert a lot of influence."

Chapter 13

Matthew began to realize he didn't have a chance to ignore doctor's orders.

Dr. Baker looked at Matthew squarely. "There's something else. Matthew, you've had a lot of stress and worry. You need to avoid all kinds of stress. It is stress that may have brought on this heart attack. I know you've lost your daughter-in-law, and your mother hasn't been doing well. My friend, there's nothing you can do about either of these situations. You can't take on all these problems."

"I haven't been a very good Christian. I've been worrying a lot."

"Matthew," said the doctor, "you're one of the finest Christians I know. You care about people, and you try to help. But there comes a time when there is nothing you can do. Right now, others will have to work out their own problems."

"Dad, you have five children. You were strong for us for many years. Now, let us be strong for you."

Dr. Baker held out his hand. "Can we shake on this? You will agree to follow doctor's orders—and your family's orders."

Matthew reluctantly shook Dr. Baker's hand. "I guess I have no choice."

Ellen felt a sense of relief when Matthew returned home. Lowell, with help from his father, took over the work with cattle as well as the other farm work. James came home alone for the weekend. His visit helped to ease Matthew's concerns.

Early the following week, Johnie made an overnight visit home. That visit seemed to convince Matthew even more that he must follow the doctor's restrictions. Ellen found herself relaxing.

A few days later, Ellen could see how difficult it was for Matthew to sit back and watch the men work as they brought in the trailer house where Lowell and Megan would stay. Their presence gave Ellen a sense of security. If something should happen, this young couple would be nearby.

After dinner at noon, Ellen had developed a habit. She watched her friends the Hughes on *As the World Turns*. Matthew retired to the bedroom and took his nap. He would lie down and read the newspaper and then doze off. Today, she could tell he was sound asleep.

As she turned off the television, she heard gentle footsteps in the kitchen.

"Mother, I'm home."

Ellen recognized her second daughter's voice. "My dear, Carol, I'm so glad you're home. Your father will be thrilled that you came."

Before Ellen could get up from the davenport, Carol was beside her. "How's Dad?"

"He's taking his afternoon nap. That's part of doctor's orders."

"I've been missing you ever so much. I wanted to talk with you before I see Dad."

In those minutes that followed, mother and daughter talked of the concerns about Matthew and the rest of the family. Ellen knew that Carol wanted to say something more, but she was having a hard time.

"Mother, I don't know how to say this." Then, she stopped.

Ellen was reminded of the times Carol had come as a child. Carol always found it difficult to admit she was wrong.

Carol looked down and away. "I'm beginning to realize how headstrong I've been. I've done some foolish things along the way."

Ellen remained silent, knowing it was best just to listen.

"I've rushed into marriage. I was a stupid teenager when I married Jeff Grant. I didn't understand all that he was going through after coming home from the war. He shouldn't have died the way he did. And I left Nick McKenzie when I shouldn't have. He was a good man. And now Hank is showing a side of himself that I didn't know existed."

"I'm sorry." Ellen dreaded what she would hear next.

"No, I'm not leaving him. I made a promise to love and honor him. I'm keeping that promise. If he decides to leave me, that is another matter."

"I'm proud of you, Carol. You've learned some valuable lessons."

Ellen saw tears in her daughter's eyes.

"I realized something that I'd never realized before. I've always felt I needed to prove myself. I knew I wasn't as smart as Margaret. And James was smarter than all of us. In many ways I was like Johnie, but he managed to work out his problems. I never felt I quite measured up."

Matthew spoke in his quiet manner. "I understand what you're going through." Ellen had not realized Matthew was standing there.

"Oh, Dad," she stood up. "I've been so worried about you. I had to see you." She ran to her father, who enfolded her in his arms.

The scene that followed needed no words for communication. The prodigal daughter had come home.

Chapter 13

Matthew reached out to Carol. "I never felt I measured up. My sisters and brother had all gone on to high school or beyond. I didn't even finish eighth grade. In school, I never felt I was quite as good as the rest."

Carol began to sob. "I did some awful things because I felt that way. I was nasty to both of you. And I was really horrid to Margaret. I did many things to prove I was somebody."

Ellen spoke with the assurance of a teacher. "Carol, you're a bright girl. You have wonderful talents that are different from those of the others. And, my dear Matthew, you have wisdom far beyond mine. We must accept our talents and individuality. We use our talents the best we know how."

"Mom. Dad. I've never understood or appreciated you until right now. I love you more than I can ever say."

The moments that followed were moments that were best enjoyed in silence.

Later that evening, Matthew and Carol walked down the lane to the east pasture. Matthew held his daughter's hand. There was a new bond of understanding.

Matthew pointed to the hills. "I will lift my eyes to the hills. That's where my help comes from. My help comes from the Lord, who made heaven and earth."

"Dad, I have much to learn."

"I have much to learn, too."

Chapter 14

October 1962

Seasons of life are much like the seasons of the year. Spring quietly changes to summer. Summer becomes old and dry and turns into autumn. The autumn leaves reach the height of their brilliance, and almost without warning they disappear. This was such a day for Matthew. Many of those leaves had fallen, but a few remained.

During Matthew's first days at home after his heart attack, he became restless. He did much walking and thinking. He wondered about this phase of life. It was all right to grow old, but he didn't like the restrictions. "Lord," he prayed, "why can't I be useful to those around me? I hate having to be so careful. I hate being on the sidelines."

As he regained strength, Matthew found there were some tasks he could do. Today was the day to dig potatoes. He couldn't carry the heavy sacks, but he could make many trips to the basement with a smaller pail of potatoes.

Matthew and Ellen worked together as they always had. Matthew, using the fork to get the potatoes out of the ground, enjoyed seeing the fruits of their labor. Ellen, still quite nimble, shook the dirt off the potatoes and placed them in pails.

"We're getting more potatoes and other crops than we can ever use," announced Ellen. "I imagine Lowell and Megan could use some. They have to work hard to make ends meet."

"And James and Johnie could use some as usual."

"We still have quite a few to dig, but we don't have to finish today."

Matthew paused and stood looking down the driveway. "I think we have our answer to that. I see Victoria coming down the driveway."

"Even after all these years, your sister drives far too fast."

Matthew smiled. "As much as she sticks to all the commandments and rules, she breaks the law when she speeds."

Victoria brought her car to a sudden stop and stepped out. "Hello Matthew. Hello Ellen. I thought I'd drive out. I have some news, and we need to do some planning."

Matthew wondered what news his sister could have.

Victoria didn't wait for any small talk, but hurried on in her usual brisk manner of speaking. "A week ago, I decided to call Martha. Mother isn't getting any stronger, so I thought this might be the last time Martha could enjoy being around Mother. Martha will be flying into Minneapolis tomorrow. I'm going down to pick her up."

"Do you think your mother will appreciate Martha's effort? Will her mind be clear?"

"Mother's been good this last week. Her mind seems clearer now."

Matthew agreed. "The last two or three times I've gone, Ma and I have visited a long time. This might be her last chance."

"I didn't mean to interrupt your work," said Victoria. "I should have waited until later."

In usual rural hospitality, Ellen made the invitation. "We'll go in for coffee. And maybe you can stick around for supper."

"I can't turn down coffee. And we need to do some planning for Mother's birthday party. She'll be ninety-four next week."

"But," said Ellen, "we celebrated her birthday this summer. Most family members were here. We can't expect them to come back."

"Oh, no, this is for the close family—we children. And for any of the grandchildren who are around."

Matthew sensed that if there was one thing that bothered Ellen about his sister, it was that Victoria could be downright pushy.

Matthew and Ellen put into pails the remaining potatoes they had dug. Victoria picked up a pail and joined her brother and sister-in-law as they returned to the house.

"Uncle Matthew," called Lowell from outside the barn. "Don't over-do. I can take care of the heavy work. I'll carry in those potatoes"

"Thanks for the offer," responded Ellen.

Chapter 14

"We're okay for now," said Matthew.

As they entered the back porch, Victoria began with her questions. "How are things working out with Lowell? I can't help remembering when Larry tried to take over the home farm. He didn't do well at all. In fact, the farm would have been completely ruined if he had stayed."

Matthew rarely spoke against this sister. "Victoria, you know very well that Larry made a complete turnaround. He made serious mistakes and even spent time in prison. But he's been a different man."

"What about Lowell?"

"He's learning. I don't think I could ask for a better person to take over the dairy and other work."

"But, apparently, he wasn't to be trusted with a young woman."

Matthew thought of things he would like to say to Victoria, but he held back those words. "The kids were young and impulsive. And they are married."

"Oh, Matthew, I guess I'm not as kind and understanding as you are. I'm still that strict old high school principal."

Ellen took out the thermos and poured the coffee. "I baked some chocolate chip cookies this morning." She put out the plate of cookies.

Victoria reached for a cookie. "I could never resist your cookies. If I were around here, I'd put on too much weight."

Their conversation turned to plans for Elizabeth Anderson's ninety-fourth birthday. Matthew thought back, remembering his mother as that strong woman rather than as the weakened and feeble woman he now visited. Growing old was not easy.

As the three were finishing their coffee and planning, Victoria changed the subject. "You know, Matthew, I'm afraid I was a bit judgmental about Larry and Lowell. I follow rules scrupulously, and I can be hard on people who don't. I'm sorry."

Matthew, surprised at Victoria's apology, remembered something else. "I'll never forget how you helped Carol get on her feet after she messed up her life. You saw that she got a good tutor, and you made sure she earned that high school diploma."

"I felt that was part of my job as principal. And even more so, part of my role as an aunt and a concerned person."

"We'll never forget," said Ellen, "all that you did for Carol and for all our kids. You have been that special person who always went the extra mile."

"Thank you." Victoria put down her cup. "Did you have a good visit with Carol when she was home?"

Ellen looked to Matthew as she began to answer. "Carol's making changes. We had some long talks. She realizes she's made mistakes, and she is trying to do what is right at this point in her life."

Matthew could see his sister checked her words as she spoke. "I hope that everything will turn out all right with the kids. Divorce is always hard on children."

Ellen continued to explain. "I think she realizes that leaving Dr. McKenzie was wrong. Now, she is determined not to make the same mistake again."

Victoria appeared to be pondering a problem. "I think I've come to realize something. Perhaps Carol and I are more alike than we want to admit. And when people are alike, they sometimes clash."

Matthew found this thought hard to believe. "My dear sister, if there are any two people who are different, it has to be you and Carol."

"Let me explain," said Victoria. "We are both headstrong and stubborn. That's a good quality in many ways. When I saw Carol as a teenager, I saw myself. I went through a period of rebellion, and even when I did my turnaround, I found myself stubborn in another way. I think I wanted to stand for something that was good and right. And Carol was and is strong and capable in so many ways."

The three continued to visit, and Ellen began to prepare supper.

Matthew decided he needed a break. "I think I'll go out and check the garden and see if I can't find a squash for you." As he stood by the door ready to leave, he added, "You know, we keep on learning about others and ourselves. Even when we're older."

Victoria laughed and added, "That's what we call life-long learning—part of the lingo in some education circles."

Margaret Anderson Nelson had little time for herself. With a husband and six children, her time was filled with every imaginable kind of duty. For a moment she looked at her list of tasks: "One: Check the children's sign-up for 4-H (she was both 4-H mother and club leader); Two: Order Christmas programs for Sunday School (she was Sunday School superintendent); Three: Check on Dad to see that he's taking care of himself; Four: Pick up groceries for Grandma's ninety-fourth birthday for cake and other things; Five: Attend PTA committee meeting tomorrow."

Chapter 14

"I need time for myself." She paged through the well-worn pages of her Bible. Her fingers moved to the familiar passage in Ecclesiastes: "For everything there is a season."

Sometimes life changed too fast. Dad's heart attack shocked her into the realization that he was older and wouldn't always be around. The loss of sister-in-law Laura was difficult. She and Laura were about the same age. And the children were growing up so fast. Matt was in high school, and the other five were moving through the grades in the country school over the hills, the same school she had attended years ago.

"What's really important in all this busy life?" she said aloud. "What will the children remember? It won't be my good housekeeping. It won't be all these things I do."

Margaret thought of her own mother and then of her grandmother. Ellen Anderson had been her role model from the earliest years. She had always wanted to be a farmer's wife and a teacher. But what did she remember most? It was those talks and times together in the kitchen or garden. And there were those memorable family events and gatherings.

And Grandma. Elizabeth Anderson was totally different from her mother, more prone to times of sadness. Always aware of the brevity of life, Elizabeth Anderson didn't expect to remain on earth that many more years. And now, in another week she would be ninety-four.

Margaret hadn't written in her journal for some time. She had followed the suggestion of James that she write about the happenings in her life and put down some of the thoughts and lessons that came to mind. She began to write:

"Life is filled with change. I can hardly keep up." She wrote about each of the children. Then she thought of Joe and how she had come to love him. When she was only eleven, she had looked up to him. Her crush had turned to love when she wrote to him and feared for his life. But Joe had survived the South Pacific and come home, eager to resume his life as a farmer.

"What is it that we remember? What do we remember most?" She stopped and her mind traveled through the years to many people and several familiar places.

"It is home we remember. It is Mother and Father and all those nearest and dearest to us, those we often take for granted. It is that love that makes life worthwhile and meaningful. It is God's love that flows through the family."

She sat at the kitchen table, forgetting about time, remembering all those she loved the most. Then something seemed to draw her into the living room, and she began to look at family pictures. She saw the growing stages of each of the children. For a moment she felt as if she were seeing each of the children as young men and women. Life was moving altogether too fast. It was as if she were on a Merry-Go-Round, wanting to get off.

"Margaret," a gentle voice called to her.

"Mother, I didn't hear you come in."

"We knocked. We're going into town to shop. We thought you might want to come along."

Margaret relaxed, experiencing a sense of well-being. Many things were changing, but Mom and Dad remained the same. There was this beautiful rhythm of life that continued.

The trip to town became a time when Margaret could talk with Mom and Dad—just like old times. Everything seemed to change, yet everything remained the same.

When she said goodbye to them, she added, "I think we're ready for Grandma's birthday. I wonder what it feels like to be ninety-four."

The day of Elizabeth Anderson's birthday celebration arrived with the sun shining bright on the fallen leaves. Ellen and Victoria and Margaret were busy in the community room of the nursing home, preparing for the party. Other family members had not arrived. Matthew sat in his mother's room, wanting to express the deep feelings he had for her.

Elizabeth Anderson put aside her Bible. Matthew was amazed that she could see so well even at her advanced age—except when she had those times of confusion.

"I'm ninety-four today," she announced. "I think it's time God took me Home. I'm ready to go any time."

Matthew hesitated, not knowing quite what to say. "Ma, we love you. We want to keep you around as long as we can."

Elizabeth reached out to Matthew and took his hand. "Son, I know I've had days when everything was a blur—when I didn't recognize you or others. I thought your father had come back, and I confused the two of you."

Chapter 14

"That's okay, Ma."

"But I knew I wasn't right. I had such awful feelings that I didn't quite understand. Then, everything was blurred and hazy. It was as if I was walking in cotton or string, and I was all tangled up. It was an awful feeling."

"But you're okay now, Ma."

"I'm ready to go Home."

"Ma, do you remember the time we went to River Falls for the family picture? Martha had come home, and we were all together."

Elizabeth tightened her grip on Matthew's hand. "Oh, how I miss Martha. I wish she were here. There's something special about a mother and her oldest daughter."

"I think we have a surprise. Martha's coming."

"Oh, Matthew, I'm so thankful. Why did she have to move to California?"

"That's where her children are."

Matthew wondered, too, why California had become such an attractive place. You couldn't beat Minnesota for beautiful scenery.

"I wonder why I remember that time so well," Matthew mused. "I was only twelve, but that day of the family picture stands out in my mind."

A sad look moved across his mother's face like a cloud obscuring the sun. "I remember why it was so urgent that we take that picture. There were two reasons. First, your father and I were celebrating our twenty-fifth wedding anniversary. But we had just had Lucille to the doctor for a thorough examination. The doctor told us that it was not likely she would live past her twenties."

"Did you tell us, Ma? I don't remember knowing that."

"We simply didn't talk about it. The older children seemed to know. I think you realized something was wrong."

"You know, Ma, Martha was always like a second mother. But when Martha left home, I turned to Lucille. She was always around. I remember how tired she was."

"We knew almost right away that Lucille was not healthy and strong like the rest of you. Mary was strong and healthy. But after her birth, I felt so depressed. I have no words to describe how low down I felt."

Matthew began to recall more about that day. Perception of life is different for a twelve-year-old boy. Matthew remembered how fascinated he was with the photographer's equipment and the pictures on display.

As Matthew had examined the equipment, the photographer had pointed to a portrait of a couple celebrating fifty years of marriage. The kindly man spoke even now in Matthew's memory: "I looked at that couple. I knew they would soon be separated by death. He died just a few months later."

The moments of silence meant a different kind of communication between mother and son. Words were not necessary.

Matthew spoke gently after those moments. "I've been thinking more about Lucille lately. She would have enjoyed our family gatherings. I could always tell how much she loved everyone."

Ma wiped a tear from her eye. "Last night, I dreamed I talked with Lucille. The dream was very real."

"If she were alive, she wouldn't be young anymore."

A familiar voice interrupted. It was Martha. "What's this about not being young anymore? I'm here to get you ready for your party. I have a corsage for you, Mother, and I'll fix your hair."

"O, my darling, come, give me a hug."

The rest of the afternoon moved along like so many other family gatherings. Ma, however, became very tired and said little. The stars of the show seemed to be the family members, each involved in their own drama.

Victoria and Margaret took charge of serving sandwiches and cake. Martha and Ellen accepted secondary roles and simply enjoyed visiting with family and friends. All six of Margaret and Joe's children came for their great-grandmother's birthday. James made a quick trip for the afternoon event, but his wife and children weren't with him.

A spectacular floral arrangement arrived with a note from Carol. Matthew breathed a prayer of thanksgiving that his wayward daughter seemed to be returning to the family, and to the faith and values she had experienced as a child.

Johnie and his three children arrived. The cousins found their own little corner to converse and play. Johnie tried to visit with his grandmother, but she seemed too tired to talk. She dozed off for part of the time.

Johnie motioned for Matthew to follow him outside. Matthew knew Johnie wanted to talk—and probably needed to.

As they walked outside, Matthew smelled the chrysanthemums, those last flowers of autumn. There was a special fragrance that Matthew associated with his mother. She raised those flowers; in fact, she had one plant that she kept inside for half the winter.

"Those mums remind me of Grandma."

Chapter 14

Johnie walked over to the bench, and Matthew followed. The blue of October skies and the cackling of black birds brought a liveliness to what could have been a somber mood.

"Are things going okay?" asked Matthew. "We haven't heard from you for a while."

Johnie sat down and looked away. "Oh, Dad, it's been terribly hard. I miss Laura more than I can ever say. I've buried myself in my ministry and in taking care of the kids."

Matthew thought of his own life. "I can't even imagine how it would be without your mother."

"I guess God doesn't give a person more than he can handle." Johnie stopped and then went on. "I thought this was all behind me, but I keep on remembering the horrors of the battlefield. Some of those scenes come back to haunt me. The dead and the dying. And then I think of Laura."

Matthew wanted to reach out and take Johnie in his arms the way he did when the boys were small. "There are no easy answers."

"It's comforting to know you and Mother are here. I think of you and the days back on the farm. I loved the hills and the fields. I always thought I'd be a farmer—just like you, Dad."

"We'll be here for you as long as we live."

"I have much to be thankful for." Johnie changed the subject, almost abruptly. "And there's Grandma. We've had her for so many years. I hate to lose her."

"I've had my mother for sixty-two years. Even so, I'll miss her. And today we managed to have a nice conversation, but then she seemed to fade away."

"It's hard to lose those we love." Obviously, Johnie was thinking of his own loss. "The children seem to adjust well, but I'm not so sure about me."

"You do what you have to do." Matthew thought of the challenges he had faced. "When I found P.J. owned the farm, I didn't know how I could go on. But then there was a new opportunity. I could buy the Nelson place and it became my farm. My farm is really my own, and it is better than the home farm."

"God doesn't guarantee easy times, but He sees us through the rough times."

"When I look at Ma, I begin to think more about Heaven. Our time on earth is short."

"Dad, I think you're a better preacher than I am. You live the Christian life. Yes, death does not have a real sting. Eternity and Heaven lie before us as believers."

"Amen, son."

Matthew felt a hand on his shoulder. It was his son-in-law.

"It's time for lunch," said Joe. "Margaret wants you to come in. And Johnie, they'd like you to lead with a few words and a prayer."

Johnie nodded his head. "I'll see what I can come up with." He reached for his small Bible, which he kept in his pocket.

The hour that followed was similar to many other gatherings. Matthew paid little attention to many of the words spoken. He looked at the frail lady who was his old mother. How precious are the saints in the eyes of the Lord! he thought.

Noisy fellowship followed the words and prayer. Four generations of Andersons milled about and visited and laughed and even cried. This was a celebration of life. Though Elizabeth looked tired, she responded to each of the people who came to her.

Margaret came over to him. "You know, Dad, it must be both hard and wonderful to be ninety-four. Think of all the wonderful memories. And look at all the people surrounding Grandma."

Matthew thought a moment. "Growing old isn't easy."

That evening, as darkness began to steal the light of day, Matthew stood on the front porch, looking to the hills. He thought aloud, "Those hills don't change, but everything else changes. I'm moving toward another season of life. And, Lord, You are here for me."

A cold breeze scattered the leaves across the lawn. Change was in the air. Everywhere.

CHAPTER 15

The words of President Kennedy kept repeating themselves in Matthew's mind. He had never heard the President make such a blunt speech. The President angrily and forcefully said that the Soviet Union had started to build missile and bomber bases in Cuba. Kennedy said that those sites could accommodate intermediate-range missiles that could strike "most of the major cities in the Western hemisphere."

Such war, probably nuclear war, was too terrible to imagine. Millions of lives could be destroyed. A peaceful way of life would end.

Kennedy's words continued to haunt Matthew. The President called the construction of these bases a "clandestine, reckless and provocative threat to world peace." These words were followed by his announcement that he would impose a naval and air "quarantine" on Cuba. He demanded that all offensive weapons be withdrawn from the island. Then, he threatened to retaliate against the Soviet Union if missiles were launched from Cuba against any country in the Americas.

Matthew thought of the familiar scripture: "There shall be wars and rumors of wars. And nation shall rise against nation. And kingdom shall rise against kingdom."

He had often felt those words applied to sometime in the distant future. But could this mean immediate war and catastrophe?

Ellen returned from the kitchen. "You're worried, aren't you, Matthew?"

Matthew looked away from the darkened television set. "We could be at war within days. It doesn't look good."

"I hate the thought of our grandsons going off to war."

"I keep remembering those dark times when James and Johnie were in the Army. I've been thinking of the time when Johnie was missing in action. I couldn't stand the thought of losing him."

"We must have faith," Ellen reminded him. "Think of the way God worked."

"Yes, there was Johnie's long road to recovery. When I look back at that rambunctious kid who wanted nothing more than to be outdoors, I'm surprised at the way he's turned out."

Matthew thought of the world that the younger generation faced in 1962. It was a different world—not so safe as it used to be. The Cold War could break into a hot war at any moment. Then, would anyone be safe?

"If war should happen," began Matthew, "I wonder if this isn't about as safe a place as any. No matter what would happen, we wouldn't starve. We'd have enough meat and potatoes and milk and other food."

Ellen smiled. "My dear, we've been through rough times before."

Matthew gave a deep sigh. Much about this day had been troubling.

The phone rang. Matthew missed the old-fashioned country telephone that rang three long. There was something impersonal about these new phones.

Ellen answered after the fourth ring. Matthew could tell by the conversation and by his wife's tone of voice that it was James. The conversation was short.

"Guess what," she announced. "There are teachers' meetings, and James can get time off on Friday. James and Ruth and the kids are coming for the weekend."

Matthew's mood changed immediately. "I miss having the kids around. I'm glad they're coming home."

In minutes the telephone rang once more. He could hear Ellen's enthusiastic words. "It will be great to have you home along with James."

"Johnie and the kids are coming home," she announced. "Both our boys will be home."

Chapter 15

The threat of war faded for Matthew. Somehow the safety and security of family pushed that danger away. And it seemed that people came back home in times of difficulty and danger. Home was a safe place.

He thought of Margaret and Joe nearby. That was such a comfort. And Carol, though far away, seemed once more to seek out the family.

But what about Michael? When would he come home?

Friday afternoon became a day of family activities. James and Ruth and Johnie and their children arrived early in the afternoon. The children scattered almost immediately and always found something exciting to do. James and Ruth and Johnie helped with the digging of the potatoes and other tasks, in that way carrying on a tradition from earlier years.

Matthew and Ellen fell into bed that night, exhausted from all of the family activity. The possibility of war seemed to fade far into the background.

Saturday morning, Matthew discovered that he was not alone in bed with Ellen. Four-year-old Leah had found her place and snuggled between the two. As he rubbed the sleep out of his eyes, Melissa, the youngest daughter of James, appeared. And then Johnie's eight-year-old, Janelle. Soon three girls were snuggling as close as they could to their grandparents.

"Tell us about our daddies when they were young," requested Janelle. The others chorused in agreement.

Ellen poked her husband. "Matthew, you can do that. I'll get up and start breakfast."

Matthew was beginning to get used to staying in bed. He didn't have to get up at the crack of dawn to do chores. He rather enjoyed his new freedom, yet there was always plenty to do around the farm.

Matthew began to search his memory. He thought of things he probably shouldn't tell his granddaughters. Then, he remembered the time Margaret, Carol, and Irene were lost. He relived and told how Johnie and he had found Carol in a hole or cave left by an uprooted tree. And then he told how he and Ellen had found the other girls in an abandoned house. He went on to tell of other adventures the boys had during the snowstorms.

These were precious memories that he treasured.

He began to smell the delicious aroma of bacon frying. It was at that moment that Janelle questioned her grandfather.

"Grandpa, will we go to war with Russia? And maybe all be killed?"

Matthew wasn't sure what to think or say. "Well, child—"

"I'm afraid." Janelle snuggled up even closer to Matthew.

"We're safe right here. And even if something does happen, we have plenty of food on the farm. We'll be all right."

Janelle and the others seemed reassured by Matthew's answer.

"Time to get up!" called Ellen. "No pajamas at the breakfast table. Hurry up and dress!"

And that is the way the day began.

October can have sunny blue skies, almost like an early fall day, or the day can be cold and rainy, almost like winter. This October day was one of those ideal days. That morning during breakfast, Margaret called, announcing that she would like to host a picnic at the home place. Matthew didn't have to think twice about an answer to that invitation.

Ellen moved into quick action, preparing potato salad and frosting the chocolate cake. Matthew's mouth watered as he thought of the food and fellowship at this family gathering.

Confusion and activity marked the hours that followed. The picnic was scheduled early—right before noon, so that Johnie could return to Maple Valley for his pastoral duties.

Much of what followed was traditional. The adults sat at the picnic tables while the children found picnic blankets and sat on the ground. Matthew sat back and simply reveled in the thought of most of his family being together.

The children finished eating first, and the younger children suddenly descended on Joe and their other parents. "Can we go play in the haymow? We like to jump. It's a good place to play."

After some discussion with Johnie, the three fathers consented to the haymow or hayloft as the place where they would play.

Matthew couldn't help wondering if the grandchildren who were city kids realized some of the dangers of those games. But he and

Chapter 15

Ellen had learned the wisdom of letting their own children raise their grandchildren.

The children went their way—most to the haymow, but others disappeared elsewhere. The sun shone brightly, and the remainder of the family enjoyed visiting. Matthew thought of Ma, who no longer was able to make such trips. And Victoria was not here. Then, Mary and Ed were far away in California. People separated and went their own ways. That's what happened to families.

Change was inevitable, Matthew knew, though not all change was good.

The sounds of the children's shouts and talk sifted through the air. The quieter voices of the adults reminded Matthew that there was continuity in life. New faces. Old ways.

He thought he heard Margaret's oldest, Matt, yell something. It sounded like: "Don't jump! That's too high for you!"

These words and other exclamations were followed by the sounds of hay bales tumbling down. The conversations around came to a sudden end.

"Something happened out there!" exclaimed Margaret. "Joe, please check on the kids."

Joe needed no invitation to action. He ran toward the barn, followed by James and Johnie. Matthew hesitated and then heard a scream, followed by wailing.

All kinds of dreadful images went through Matthew's mind. He remembered hearing about a boy who had fallen from a high balcony. That boy broke his neck and later died. Enough tragedy had already taken place.

Joe hurried and climbed the ladder to the hayloft. Matthew and others waited below.

"It's Janelle!" Matthew heard a voice say.

Matthew could see the anguish in Johnie's face. The crying continued.

"I'm holding Janelle." Joe's feet appeared at the top of the opening. "Let me hand her to someone. I think she wants her father."

Johnie stepped up on a bale of hay. A crying girl was soon in his arms.

"It hurts so terrible!" cried Janelle. "I shouldn't have jumped from that high balcony."

"There's nothing we can do about that now," soothed Johnie. "Tell me where it hurts."

"I feel terrible all over. But my arm hurts worse."

Joe came down the ladder and announced, "I'm sure her arm is broken. We need to get her to the doctor—or have the doctor come here."

Margaret hurried into the house. She would take care of calling the doctor. Adults and children hovered around Johnie as he carried his little girl out of the barn across the lawn and into the house. Janelle's sobbing quieted as she clung to her father.

Margaret motioned for Johnie to carry Janelle into their bedroom. "The doctor will be in his office in another hour. We need to make our little girl comfortable. Then, he'll drive out here."

Johnie tried to comfort Janelle. "Everything's going to be all right."

"My arm hurts terrible. I miss Mama. Why did God have to take her to Heaven?"

Margaret placed an ice pack on her arm. "This will help."

"It still hurts."

Matthew saw tears in his son's eyes.

Johnie spoke slowly. "I miss her, too. I wish she were right here with us. But some things we can't understand. God will take care of us."

Ellen entered the bedroom quietly, carrying a cup. "I brought you some hot cocoa. I know that always makes people feel better."

Janelle began to whimper once more.

"Don't you want my hot cocoa?"

"Oh, Grandma, it still hurts."

Ellen sat down beside Janelle, and held the cup as Janelle sipped.

Johnie smiled. "Mom, you have little girls and boys all figured out. No one can comfort a child better than you."

Ellen laughed. "I guess I had enough experience."

Matthew felt a sense of pride in what Ellen could do. He had found the best wife any man could want.

There was something about Janelle that reminded Ellen of both Johnie and Carol. It was almost as if she were once more a young mother.

Dr. Baker confirmed the obvious. Janelle had broken her arm in two places. He set the splints as the poor girl cried out in pain. He gave her medication that quickly made her groggy. Within a short while Janelle was in a deep sleep.

Ellen wanted to take her son in her arms, but he was a man trying hard to be strong and brave. "Johnie, why don't you let Janelle stay with us for a few days? I'll take care of her. Then, we can bring her back to Maple Valley."

Johnie hesitated. "I hate to take advantage of you."

"That's no problem at all. Your father and I would love to have a little girl around. I miss being a mother to my children."

By this time Jack and Leah had entered the bedroom.

"Can't Leah and I stay with Grandpa and Grandma, too?"

"Jack, you have school on Monday. And, Leah, remember you're going to Grandma Martin's."

"But we'll miss Nell," objected Leah.

"You can't leave me all alone, can you?" Johnie took his little daughter in his arms. "I'd miss you."

That seemed to settle the matter for Jack and Leah.

By now it was time for afternoon lunch. Margaret and Ruth brought sandwiches out to the picnic table and made more coffee and lemonade.

Johnie and Jack and Leah quickly ate some lunch and then drove away. Ellen felt an emptiness that she knew Johnie experienced. Johnie would return to the emptiness that was part of being without his wife.

Janelle seemed happy enough to stay with her grandparents. After that James and Ruth and their children, as well as Matthew and Ellen and Janelle returned home.

This was one of those autumn picnics that would be long remembered. The warmth of the earlier part of the day disappeared late that afternoon as cold clouds covered the sun. The season was changing from the warmth of summer to the cold of winter.

Sunday evening, Matthew switched off the television set. He felt an overwhelming sense of relief.

He turned to Ellen. "Do you realize what Kennedy's words mean?"

"Yes, I think so."

"We have avoided all-out war with Russia."

"And Kennedy's done the right thing."

"I know I didn't vote for him, and I've been skeptical. But Kennedy and Khrushchev have met, and war with Russia has been avoided. We can thank God for this."

As Matthew and Ellen sat quietly, Janelle came and sat between them. "I can't sleep."

Ellen got up from the davenport. "How about some hot cocoa? That will help you sleep."

Matthew thought of the many times he and Ellen and the children had sat at the kitchen table, drinking hot cocoa. It felt good to have this granddaughter with them.

The Cuban missile crisis was over. The children were safe in their homes—except for Michael. Janelle was safe in the care of her grandparents.

"God's in His heaven," Matthew said aloud. "All's right with the world. Almost."

CHAPTER 16

November 1962

Matthew relished his role as grandfather. He read and told stories to Janelle during the next days. Ellen got out old school textbooks and worked with Janelle's reading and math. The days would be long remembered.

Matthew felt a relief that the Cuban Missile Crisis had ended. The United States remained at peace—at least for now—though the Cold War talks continued.

That Friday night in November, the pleasant days ended abruptly. Saturday was to be a planned trip to Maple Valley. Matthew and Ellen would take their granddaughter back home. They would enjoy the rest of that day there, along with Sunday so they could hear Johnie preach. But that plan was not to take place.

Ellen returned from the kitchen. "Matthew, I have some bad news. You need to go to the hospital. Your mother broke her hip."

Matthew could say little. "Oh, no."

"It looks as if they will do surgery right away in the morning—even though it's Saturday."

"I wonder," thought Matthew aloud, "if she's strong enough to make it through the surgery."

"We'll pray. She's had a good and long life."

"Yes." Matthew went into the bedroom to get the car keys. "I'll pick up Victoria on the way."

"I'd like to go, but I need to stay with Janelle."

Sometimes life seemed to go in slow motion. Matthew experienced a kind of fear and uncertainty as he drove. The minutes were like hours. After he picked up Victoria, her nervousness didn't help matters.

"I can't imagine life without Mother." Victoria spoke the words slowly as Matthew drove toward River Falls. "She's been in my life all seventy-two years."

"Most children don't have their parents that many years."

Victoria didn't seem to have her usual self-control. "Life won't be the same without Mother. Caring for her in the nursing home seems like a way of life."

Matthew agreed.

The silence that followed told Matthew his sister was shedding tears. The strong reserve of this high school teacher and principal was breaking down. Perhaps Victoria needed to shed that stern exterior and show how much she cared.

Matthew stopped the car. "Well, sister, we're here."

As they walked toward the entrance, Victoria grasped her brother's hand. "Matthew, I knew this time would come someday. But I'm scared—really scared."

Matthew wanted to reassure his sister. "I guess I've never been able to imagine life without Ma. But she is still with us. She hasn't died."

When they entered Elizabeth Anderson's room, a nurse met them. "She's been sedated, but she's awake and wants to talk. I'm glad you're here."

"Is that you, Matthew?" Ma's voice sounded strong. "Victoria?"

"We're here, Mother." Victoria cleared her throat. "We'll be with you. We won't leave you."

"I'm so tired. Everything is hazy." Elizabeth Anderson's voice faded.

Matthew and Victoria found chairs and sat on each side of the hospital bed. The antiseptic smell triggered memories. Matthew thought of the time he had come close to death. It seemed like yesterday, but it was almost twenty-five years ago. He had returned to life, with a new purpose for living.

They waited silently.

Elizabeth Anderson's voice broke the silence. "I'm going Home. I'm going Home. It won't be long now."

Chapter 16

"Oh, Mother," protested Victoria. "These hip surgeries are becoming almost routine."

"I'm seeing a light. It's so bright and beautiful. It's so dark and dreary in this room."

Matthew remembered his brush with death. He had seen the farm with all its beauty, the hills, the fields, the lakes. He had seen each family member. He had felt overwhelmed by love for them. He had felt, then, a voice calling him back to life—a voice saying his life had a purpose.

"Mother," said Victoria as she clasped her mother's hand.

"Let me go, Victoria. Matthew. Don't hold on to me."

"I'm seeing all the sin and evil around me in this world. The darkness is so heavy. I see a light. Christ is standing there. He's beckoning me."

Matthew knew words were hardly necessary.

All at once, a peace settled over Elizabeth Anderson. Victoria felt her pulse. Matthew waited, thinking the end had come.

"She's still with us."

Throughout the night, Matthew slept fitfully. When he awakened, he listened for his mother's breathing. She breathed deeply and steadily. Periodically, the nurse came to check. Matthew awakened abruptly as the nurse entered to prepare Elizabeth Anderson for surgery.

Matthew and Victoria left the room. They returned to say reassuring words as their mother was wheeled into surgery.

A nurse turned to them and said, "You might as well go and have something to eat. You've been up all night. Your mother's in good hands."

"I'm hungry," said Victoria. "Let's go for breakfast."

Matthew smiled. "I'm starved. Let's head for the Falls Café. I haven't been there for a long time."

When brother and sister ordered their breakfasts, Matthew felt a burden was being lifted from his shoulders. He had deep thoughts that he wanted to express. Instead, Victoria began to talk.

"I've let go," began Victoria. "The outcome is in God's Hands. There's nothing we can do anyway. I feel at peace."

"I do, too."

"We've entered a different chapter of our lives—at least I have. I'm old. I'm seventy-two. My working years are over."

Matthew responded. "Yes, but I always find plenty to do. The yard. The garden. Help with milking. Or plowing the fields. The kids. The grandchildren."

"My life seems to center around the nursing home. After Mother's gone, I don't know how I'll feel about the place. Right now, I visit with people. I do some volunteer work."

"You do such a good job of tutoring students. That's important. And your adult Bible class is going strong."

"I'll always be a teacher, I guess. I love what I'm doing."

"You know, Victoria, we've seen lots of change. But look at all the changes Pa and Ma went through—especially Pa. He came from a different country. Learned a new language and way of life. I don't know that I could have survived all those changes."

"Dad and Mother were strong pioneers. I don't feel we have that same strength. At seventy-two, I'm too old to change."

"You've been making changes. I'm making changes all the time—learning new things."

Victoria reached across the table and took her brother's hand. "Matthew, you feel you don't measure up because you don't have formal education. You're amazing. You put me to shame."

"Thanks, Sis."

The waitress came and offered seconds on coffee. The two accepted refills and enjoyed both the coffee and the quiet moments.

Victoria began once more: "Our lives are much easier in many ways. Yet, I've had so many choices. My travels. It was great to travel to Europe and Sweden and to England. And I often think of this Cuban Missile Crisis and how we could have gone to war at any moment. We could still go to war."

Matthew quietly reminded her, "Victoria, do you realize we've been on the edge of war most of this century? World War I, the Great War. World War II. The Korean War. Some other skirmishes. And now what is called the Cold War with Russia."

Victoria smiled. "And I'm the history teacher. We've made it this far."

They sat, enjoying their coffee.

Matthew brought out his pocket watch. "I think we should get back. The surgery should be over by now."

They returned to the hospital and to Elizabeth Anderson's room. The doctor reported that surgery had gone well. Their mother was sleeping when they entered. They sat in their chairs, waiting.

A half-hour later, Elizabeth began to waken.

Chapter 16

"Hello, Ma," said Matthew. "You made it through just fine."

"We're so relieved," added Victoria.

"I'm still here," she said groggily. "I thought maybe I'd wake up in Heaven. I don't know why God wants me back here."

"We want you." Victoria took her mother's hand. "Can I get you anything?"

"Not a thing. I feel so groggy."

The nurse came in and announced, "We'll get you something to eat. And very soon the doctor will see you."

"I'm not hungry."

"The doctor feels we need to get you up quite soon. You need to move about."

Matthew heard his mother grunt. The nurse left.

In the next minutes Matthew wasn't sure what was happening. His mother mumbled some words he couldn't quite understand. Victoria asked what she said. Then, it seemed she fell into a deep sleep.

Matthew and Victoria sat for some time, not saying anything. Matthew couldn't say when the change came, but the atmosphere of the room became suddenly cold and empty. Deep within he knew what had happened.

Victoria reached over and clasped her mother's hand. "Her hand is cold." Then she took her mother's pulse.

Matthew looked down at his mother.

"She's gone," said Victoria. "We've lost our mother."

A deluge of emotions and remembrances bombarded Matthew's mind. The old farm home where he was born. Ma was always there. The new house. The little house Ma and Pa lived in. Ma was always there to welcome her children and grandchildren.

Then the words of the old hymn came to him:

> Though he giveth or he taketh,
> God his children ne'er forsaketh;
> His the loving purpose solely
> To preserve them pure and holy.

He began to sing the words softly. Tears clouded Victoria's eyes.

Victoria cleared her voice and spoke. "The Lord giveth, and the Lord taketh. Blessed be the name of the Lord."

Matthew held Victoria in his arms. They both wept.

"She is in a better place," said Victoria.

CHAPTER 17

Matthew felt a sense of unreality during the next days. He remained in the background as Ellen and Victoria called family members and made funeral arrangements. In reality, Ellen did most of the work.

Victoria, the woman who was usually in charge and in control, became a completely different person. She frequently broke down in tears. She forgot to take care of routine matters. She suddenly became one of those helpless women who needed someone to take care of her. Matthew couldn't help wondering what would happen to his older sister.

"It will be good," Matthew thought. "The family will all be together, just as we were last summer. A funeral is a time for people to come home."

The funeral was delayed until Friday so that family members could have time to come home. But the complete family homecoming was not to be.

During those next days Matthew felt a need to be outside. With only a small amount of snow, he found it was a good time to cut branches and burn some of the brush. The fresh air helped clear his mind and gave him an opportunity to think. The family had grown in numbers and had moved throughout the country. He found it difficult to keep track of everyone.

Wednesday evening, he and Ellen reviewed the family situation. Ellen, always the well-organized planner, had a list before her.

"I wish Martha could come. Is it possible she could come the last minute?" asked Matthew.

"Martha wanted so badly to come. I found out from Corrine that she got out of the hospital the other day. She isn't supposed to travel."

"I'll miss her. Will any of the kids come?"

"Corrine wanted to, but there isn't time to drive. And flying is too expensive."

"What about Mary and Ed? They'll definitely come, won't they?"

"I'm sorry, Matthew. Mary checked airline tickets. They're too expensive. And they can't seem to make the right connections. They feel they can't afford the trip. They want to come to Minnesota next summer."

"Then, it looks as if it will be our family. And, of course, Larry and Joan and their children." He thought a moment. "Have you gotten through to Carol?"

"I finally got through. Someone's staying with the kids. She and Hank went on a trip to Italy. They can't be reached."

Matthew sighed. "Our family is so spread out. We're losing family togetherness, I'm afraid. I'd like to have my sisters around. I miss them."

"That's part of life, dear. Children grow up and move away. Growth means that they spread out, and sometimes move far away."

"We're fortunate to have Margaret and Joe nearby. And James and Johnie aren't so far away that we can't visit them. Are you going to try to get Michael again?"

Ellen went over to the phone. Matthew still missed the old-fashioned wall phone. The black phone attached to the wall didn't have the same character.

Matthew heard only part of what Ellen said. "Are you sure he didn't leave any telephone number or address?" she questioned. "Thank you. If you find out anything, let me know."

Ellen put down the telephone receiver. "Something very strange is going on."

Matthew waited for Ellen to go on.

"Michael left suddenly. His landlady thought he was going to Illinois to work for an implement manufacturer."

"Did she know why?"

"I think the lady didn't want to hurt my feelings. She suggested that Michael was in some kind of trouble. That's why he left so suddenly."

Chapter 17

Matthew thought back to the events of the past. "He's been involved in drinking. That by itself is a problem. I'm pretty sure he was into gambling as well."

Ellen turned to go back to the kitchen. "I think we're going to have a hard time sleeping tonight. Perhaps some hot milk would hit the spot."

Matthew agreed. "Hot milk always seems to relax us. And problems don't seem so big."

"We've trained Michael in the way he ought to go. I have to believe what the Bible says. When he is old, he will not depart from those ways."

"He started out so well."

"Yes, he's like Johnie. He will return."

With those assurances, Matthew and Ellen relaxed and drank their hot milk.

Matthew had always been an early riser, except for sleeping late a few weeks back. Now that he was retired, he still wakened around five and got up soon after. There was always work to do, and today was Ma's funeral. However, when the telephone rang, he knew something out of the ordinary had happened. He checked the alarm clock, which read 5:30.

Ellen quickly hurried into the kitchen to answer. Matthew could tell little from the early conversation. Then, he knew it was Carol.

The conversation was one-sided. Ellen's expression told him that this phone call was a good sign. As the conversation appeared to come to an end, Matthew heard Ellen's reassurances. "We're all fine. No special news. James and Johnie and their families are here. We're a full house." A question interrupted Ellen's report. "No, Michael hasn't come. We haven't been able to contact him."

After that the connection seemed to go bad. There were the usual closing remarks: "We love you, Carol." A tear appeared in Ellen's eye. "Goodbye, my dear."

"Where did she call from?" asked Matthew. "What's the news?"

"She called from Rome. They're seeing all those statues and beautiful artwork. And guess what? They'll be home for Christmas."

Matthew could scarcely believe what he heard. "I still hope and pray we'll get our old Carol back. I think she realizes her mistakes."

Matthew and Ellen dressed quietly. When they entered the kitchen again, they found Johnie at the table, working on his sermon.

Without a greeting, Johnie asked a probing question: "How does a grandson preach a sermon and put into words the life of his grandmother? I don't see how I can do justice to Grandma."

Matthew saw the perplexed look on his son's face. "Remember, son, your grandmother asked that you deliver the sermon. It was her request."

"And," reminded Ellen, "you are preaching to the living. You invite people to come in faith to the Lord. And you comfort people."

"I'm afraid I forgot my manners. I didn't even say good morning." Johnie got up and gave his mother a hug. Then, he shook his father's hand firmly and moved to a hug. "I'm thankful to be here. And I'm glad I have the two of you."

"We had an early phone call," said Ellen.

"Did Michael call? Or is he coming?"

Ellen explained about Carol's call.

"I pray for Carol," said Johnie. "I think of her as that scrappy little sister. I'm afraid she's lost her way. I want her back."

"She'll come home," said Matthew. "Someday."

Johnie gathered up his Bible and notes. "I hope you won't think me unsociable, but I need time to prepare. I want to give Grandma a good send-off."

"Go. By all means, go." Then Ellen added, "We'll take care of the children."

"I'm off to the pasture and lake. That's where I think best."

Johnie walked west to the lake and in spirit became the young boy who'd played in those very spots. He remembered swimming in this lake with his sisters and brothers and cousins and friends.

A thin layer of ice covered the lake. He remembered the skating parties that were part of the young people's entertainment.

Something within prompted Johnie to leave the lake and begin walking to the east. This wooded area provided more protection from the early November wind. He arrived at the ponds and sloughs where he used to enjoy duck hunting.

All at once he became that fifteen-year-old boy who couldn't wait to get out and enjoy the outdoors and shoot ducks. It was a warmer November day. Dad had come out and joined him. It was at that time he came to realize who he was. He knew he needed a Savior. He remembered his prayer. "Lord, I know I've done some rotten things in my life. I know that I can't make it on my own. I need you. I commit my life to you."

He thought of the detours of his life. There were times he had wandered away from the faith. But today he felt secure in that faith.

As he stood looking toward the hills, a sharp wind blew. The snow swirled around him. His memory transported him to the Armistice Day blizzard. Mom and Dad had gone to the hospital because Uncle P.J. was seriously ill. He and his brothers and sisters were home alone, and Grandma was there. That was one of those times he felt especially close to Grandma. And today, he would preach the funeral sermon for her.

Johnie spoke aloud. "I can't do this trip down memory lane. I have to polish this sermon." He looked up to see the sun trying to break through the clouds. "Lord, help me bring together my thoughts. Help me think on You and show me what to say."

His father always looked to those hills as he walked and prayed. Johnie did the same. "I will lift my eyes unto the hills from whence cometh my help. My help cometh from the Lord who made heaven and earth."

Suddenly, the sun broke through, and the snow glistened like diamonds.

"How Laura would have enjoyed a walk on this winter morning! Oh, my dear wife, how I miss you. But you are in a far, far better place."

Johnie looked around at the brilliant white of the snow around him and then beyond to the hills. "This is home." He stared to the hills and something took him far beyond. "Yes, this is home, but Heaven is my real home."

At that moment, he knew exactly what he would say.

Johnie took his place at the pulpit and looked out at the congregation. Mom and Dad and Aunt Victoria sat in the front row with James and Ruth at the end of the row. He missed the presence of Martha and Mary and Ed. A whole segment of the family could not come home—even for this most important of funerals. Though time seemed to stand still, life had to move on.

For a moment he stood silently, looking over the congregation. He couldn't help thinking of Carol in Italy. And where was Michael? Why couldn't he be reached? What was happening to his little brother?

Johnie bowed his head. "Let us pray. Lord, we come to You in this time of sadness. Yet, it is not really in sadness because Elizabeth Anderson has gone Home. She has gone Home to be with You. Be with us the living as we remember our mother, grandmother, great-grandmother, friend, neighbor, relative, and much more. Guide us in our thinking. May we remember Elizabeth Anderson, but may we remember You, Lord Jesus, and think on that which is of eternal importance. We commit this time to You. In Jesus' name. Amen."

Once more he looked at the congregation and paused. "Last Sunday evening a call came. Grandma had died. Her death came as no surprise, but I felt the loss keenly. I'll be home, Mother, I said. I'm coming home.

"Home. What a precious word that is. How many memories the word evokes!

"Home. I think first of Mom and Dad and our home. Of course, I think of my home and my wonderful wife and our children."

For a moment he found tears coming to his eyes as he thought of Laura and her last days. He wondered if he would ever get over missing her.

"But Grandma, Elizabeth Anderson, has always been there. She lived with us during some of those critical times. Otherwise, she always welcomed us in her little house. Or later, there was always that smile as we greeted her in the nursing home.

"Grandma wanted me to preach her funeral sermon. That task is a hard one for me. I know that she was modest and didn't want attention called to herself. 'Call attention to Jesus,' she would say.

"Let us return home to that farm that we called the 'home farm.' It is 1937. I am a lad of twelve. John and Elizabeth Anderson are celebrating their golden wedding anniversary. Pastor Strand is speaking, and his key verse is this one: 'Jesus Christ, the same, yesterday, today, and forever.'

"The verse puzzled me at the time. Eternity is hard for us adults to fathom. It's even more difficult for a twelve-year-old to understand. But as I look at Grandma's ninety-four years, I have gained some insights.

"In all my years of visiting Grandma, she has always talked of 'Going Home.' After Grandpa died, she spoke of meeting him in Heaven. I used to think that was just something old people talked about. But along the way something happened to change me. Perhaps that first big change came when I was a teenager.

"It all happened one of those days before that famous Armistice Day storm. I was a fifteen-year-old kid. But something was happening within me. It was one of those days when we felt something in our bones—we knew a storm was coming. I was very much aware of those storm clouds of war. I couldn't understand how people would want to destroy the peace of a beautiful countryside. Why? Why? I kept asking myself.

"Then, I looked at people around me. I saw how kids treated one another. I saw bullies at work, intimidating others. I was ready to fight against such bullies. But at the time I realized I, too, was a sinner. I looked around and realized something: there was one answer. I knelt there in the woods. Jesus Christ is the answer. He is the only way out of this mess. At that moment in time I committed my life to Him."

Johnie found himself choked with emotion. He paused and gazed above the congregation. If he looked at his family, he knew he would lose control.

He began to search for the right words. "It's hard to find the right words. It seems that which is closest to our hearts is the most difficult to talk about. Speaking about our personal relationship with the Lord is not easy. Telling of our love for those closest is also difficult. It is at times like this that we declare that love.

"Though a funeral and memorial service honor the dead, the service is for the living. It is here we find comfort. It is here we remember what is important in life. It is at this time we tell our loved ones how much we care.

"Let me get back to my story. As that storm ended, I realized how much the Lord is involved in every aspect of life. That afternoon, I wanted to be out in the woods doing what I felt like doing. Yes, we were out in the woods, but it was for the purpose of hauling wood. A few days later, we realized we would have been in serious trouble if we had not brought home the wood. Others who had not taken care of such matters suffered great hardship. Yes, God prompted Dad to see that the work was done.

"In those years that followed, I experienced the ups and downs of a typical teenager. I'm afraid I went astray. The war came. I enlisted. Dad didn't want me to go. I was stubborn and went.

"The Lord guided and sustained me through those terrible times. When I was in the trenches in Germany, Christ became near and dear to me. But then the awfulness of war and the brutality of bloodshed got to me. It goes by different names. Shell Shock, some call it. All I can say is that those times were dreadful. I spent time in an army hospital. I don't remember much. I don't think I knew whether I was dead or alive.

"Once more, I returned home. This time the Lord granted me new life. I came to this very church. I looked at the stained glass windows. I saw Christ holding the lamb. In my mind I was that lamb, the prodigal who had come home from a far country.

"I experienced the words, 'Come unto me all ye who labor and are heavy laden and I will give you rest.' That meant I had truly come home."

Johnie paused and looked to his audience. "But there's more that I now realize. Yes, I came home to Mom and Dad and James and Margaret and Carol and young Michael. But I recognized what home really was. I came on bended knee to my Savior and Lord.

"And now I realize something else. On this earth, as Scripture says, 'We do not have an eternal abiding place.' This world is temporary—just a beginning. It is an introduction to eternity. We are students. We must prepare for this eternity.

"And how do we prepare? We must come to Him, acknowledging and confessing our sin. We have been separated. Only through Christ can we find this forgiveness. I invite you at this time to come home—to come before the Lord our Maker. Commit your life to Him. This is the way. And we may wander away many times. But He invites us back.

"And now how do we live? We must seek first His kingdom and His righteousness. We acknowledge that He has added so many blessings. We come to Him with thanksgiving.

"Elizabeth Anderson, my grandmother, was one of those blessings. We have other blessings—both material and spiritual—too many to count.

"As we seek His Kingdom, we are reminded of the greatest commandment: 'Thou shalt love the Lord thy God with all thy strength, with all thy mind—and thy neighbor as thyself.'

"What does this mean now in view of eternity? How does this translate and apply to our daily lives?"

Already Johnie had made his sermon longer than he had intended, but his audience seemed to be listening. He wanted to finish in a clear and direct way.

"First, let us live, realizing Christ is in this very room—this church sanctuary. He walks beside us. He has experienced the problems and temptations of being human. He understands our sadness as we stand beside the grave.

Chapter 17

"And what about loving our neighbor as ourselves? That's a big order. I learned this lesson the hard way. When my beloved Laura died, I realized how much time I wasted—the many times I didn't have time for her or for my children."

Johnie began to choke up as tears filled his eyes. He paused.

His family and other members of the congregation were silent and spellbound.

"I'm sorry," he apologized. "Perhaps my tears remind all of us how important our loved ones are. We must take time to be with them—to show them how much we love them. This love we have is God's love flowing through us. We must share that love generously.

"Again, I say: 'Jesus Christ is the same yesterday, today, and forever.' And I also remind us: `The Lord is from everlasting to everlasting, and underneath are the everlasting arms.'

"We have all come home to our Oak Ridge Church. We have come home to say goodbye to a woman we all love. May Elizabeth Anderson's life and example help prepare us as we look forward to going home."

Johnie spoke a short prayer. Pastor Young announced the familiar hymn, the family favorite. Johnie joined the rest of his family in singing.

> Children of the heavenly Father,
> Safely in His bosom gather.
> Nestling bird nor star in heaven,
> Such a refuge, ne'er was given.

Johnie loved those words. The family exited the church and walked to the cemetery. He remembered this same walk he had taken a few months ago. A cold November wind made the journey harsher. Leah and Jack and Janelle crowded close to him.

"Are we going to see Mommy?" asked Janelle. "We took her here last summer."

"No, my dear," Johnie replied as he stooped down and hugged her. "We'll meet Mommy in Heaven. She's not really here. Grandma isn't really here either."

As the graveside service ended, Matthew came over to him. "Johnie, my son, you did a wonderful job. I'm proud of you."

Aunt Victoria, who could be stiff and formal, was suddenly in his arms. "My darling nephew, I'm proud of you. You're a living example of what God can do in a person's life."

In the next moments, aunt and nephew were shedding tears that represented so much of the love the family members felt for one another.

Others came to speak to Johnie. Perhaps the words of James meant the most: "Brother, you said what we all needed to hear. You have truly become a pastor—and a good one. I'm proud to be your brother."

In a rare moment, the brothers hugged each other. "I love you, brother."

"And now," said Johnie, "I'm hungry. It's time for lunch."

What followed was one of those grand funeral lunches. The Anderson family and the church family feasted together. The words of the Table Prayer seemed to take on added meaning:

> Be present at our table, Lord.
> Be here and everywhere adored.
> These mercies bless and grant that we
> May feast in Paradise with Thee. Amen.

Later that night, Matthew sat at the kitchen table with Ellen and James and Ruth and Johnie. Through the years the family had a tradition of talking things over as they drank coffee. Or, if it was late at night, they would drink hot milk. Tonight was a night for hot milk.

"I don't know how Margaret does it," said Ellen. "With her six children she's taken your three, James, and your three, Johnie. That's quite a gang."

"They're loving it—and having a ball," said Ruth.

Matthew looked lovingly at Ellen. "My dear, Margaret's like her mother. You trained her well. She can handle just about anything."

Ellen blushed. "You're embarrassing me."

Johnie reached over, taking his mother's hand. Then he gave her a kiss. "Mother, I love you. And, Dad, too. I am truly blest."

At this moment Matthew wished time would stand still. He was together with some of the people he loved most. Would they ever be together again in this loving and intimate way? Fast-paced modern life had a way of separating people.

For the next moments, the Andersons were silent. Somehow the most tender moments can be ruined by speech.

Chapter 17

It was James who broke the silence. "I still have a dream. I'd like to write a family story and somehow capture the love and goodness and tenderness that we feel now. I don't know if that's possible. But I'd like to try."

Matthew couldn't help seeing the expression on his wife's face—that look of determination—a look he had seen many times.

"James, my son, that is something you must do. If you don't and you come to the end of your life, you will regret it. You must follow your dream."

Ruth smiled and took her husband's hand.

Johnie gestured with both hands. "If God could take this wild and restless kid and turn him around to become a preacher of the Gospel, He can take my scholarly brother and make him into an important writer."

Words of encouragement followed from each one present. They drank the last of their hot milk.

Johnie yawned. "I'm tired."

The others agreed and quietly said goodnight.

Later, Matthew spoke lovingly to Ellen. "My cup runneth over."

CHAPTER 18

At times Matthew wished for the good old days. Thanksgiving was here, but the family would not be together. James and Ruth and their children had decided to remain in Riverton. There were too many family and job obligations. Johnie's job as a pastor kept him in Maple Valley. Carol had returned from Italy and didn't feel her family could make the trip. And where was Michael? Why hadn't they heard?

Then, he thought of his own brothers and sisters and how they used to be together at Thanksgiving and Christmas. These gatherings would no longer take place with Martha and her family and Mary and Ed. They were all in California. And most of the nieces and nephews were far away.

This year, as in recent years, Victoria would join the family. This sister had remained the one and only sibling close by. He needed this sister and thanked God for Larry. This nephew had become like a younger brother. And Larry's son Lowell was the reason he could continue enjoying living on the farm.

This year, Margaret was hosting the Thanksgiving celebration. Margaret, with help from Joan, had insisted that she take care of the food and all the planning. However, Ellen always brought her special pumpkin pies.

For Matthew, the best part of Thanksgiving was the time after the meal. The men would go to the living room and relax. He could hear the women in the kitchen, talking as they washed dishes. Margaret and Joe's six children and two of Larry's children had gone to the little house where the kids could play their games and make all the noise they wanted to. The older children would probably be playing Monopoly, and the younger ones would play a different game.

Joe invited Matthew to take the easy chair, the most comfortable chair in the room. Everyone seemed to baby him since his heart attack. Joe and Larry sat across from him on the davenport.

The men sat quietly, listening to some of the words of the women. It was Larry who broke the silence. "You know, Uncle Matthew, when I was a kid, Thanksgiving and Christmas at your place were the most memorable times in my life."

Matthew thought a moment. "I remember those times as special. Even then you were almost like a little brother."

Larry seemed to have something he needed to say. "Uncle Matthew. Joe," he addressed them. "With Mother far away and my sister I don't know where, I feel alone—except for my wife and my children. But it's you two who have become my family."

Matthew began to reflect on the changes of the past years—the people who were absent from his life. He missed the way he and Ellen would get together with Mary and Ed—and he loved those talks he'd had with Martha. It wasn't possible to replace people, but they were far away.

It was Joe's turn to say something. "I don't know what would have happened to me if I hadn't had the Anderson family. Grandpa and Grandma Nelson were in many ways my parents, and Mom and Dad were too busy in the city. I was that tag-along that they didn't really want."

Matthew saw Joe's faraway look.

"When I came as hired man that winter, I became part of the family. Matthew, you became Dad to me. And I call you Dad most of the time. And Ellen is Mom. And if it hadn't been for Margaret, I don't think I could have survived those awful years in the South Pacific. Her letters and the thought of her kept me going."

Both Matthew and Larry listened intently.

"And now, I feel the Lord has blest me in so many ways. Margaret—I couldn't ask for a more wonderful wife and mother. I think I always wanted lots of brothers and sisters. Maybe that's why I was happy that we had so many children."

Matthew felt a keen desire to speak those feelings he so rarely communicated. "Joe, you've been not only a son but also a friend, a buddy. We both love the land in the same way." He paused and turned to Larry.

Chapter 18

"And, Larry, you have been my nephew, but you're more like a younger brother. I always felt I needed a brother."

"You became the family I needed." Larry began to recall what Matthew had almost forgotten. "I remember the kind of man I had become years ago. I was involved with criminals. I was going down the road of power and money. I was heading straight for hell. But when I was in jail, you and Grandma and Aunt Ellen visited me. You prayed for me. And then I found the Lord—or He found me."

Joe, usually not a man for words, spoke a fitting closing. "God has helped each of us in different ways. He's used this family to show His love."

Matthew sensed the truth of those words. God had been good.

Holidays always reminded Ellen of the changing scenes of life. In the traditional manner, the women cleaned off the table and began to wash dishes. Ellen stepped back and let her daughter be in charge. Margaret always did a superb job. Even Victoria was learning to step back and let the younger generation take over.

Joan nudged Margaret aside and began washing the dishes. "Margaret, I think it's best if you put away dishes. You know where they go."

Margaret turned to her aunt. "Aunt Victoria, why don't you sit down and rest? You're the matriarch now. You've earned some time off."

"I'm not ready to be put on the shelf—not quite yet."

"We didn't mean to do that," Margaret pulled out a chair. "You are our most special aunt. You've celebrated all our family events even though other family members are far away. You've always been so generous."

Victoria obediently sat down. "I cherish you more than I can ever say."

As they worked, the women talked. Ellen wiped dishes while Margaret put things away. Ellen became far more aware of the many changes that had taken place or were in motion.

"Carol," Margaret began. "Carol hasn't been around much for years. But I miss her especially now. As girls we were so different. I wish we could have the sisterly talks we had years ago."

"You're in company," said Victoria. "I miss both Martha and Mary. And Lucille has been gone for years. When Martha and Mary come back, they're always in such a hurry so that they can visit with everyone. We hardly have a chance to really talk."

"You need to go to California," suggested Joan. "You'd have more time then."

"I went once, but we did all that running around. I didn't really get to visit with anyone that much. The nieces and nephews are all busy with their jobs. I don't know whatever happened to women who stayed at home. I think children need their mothers—at home."

Ellen couldn't help being surprised at this comment. "That's an unusual comment, coming from a career woman like you."

"I guess I chose such a path. But I was still a believer in a strong home. The best homes had the strong stabilizing influence and strength of a mother at home. Some women didn't appreciate me when I said that."

Joan drained the water in the sink and began to run fresh water. "I stayed home for many years. But now I enjoy working in the kitchen at school."

Suddenly, Ellen felt dizziness come over her. She felt sharp pain in her stomach. She must have eaten too much, or else something didn't agree with her. She stepped back and lay down her towel.

"Mother, I think you should sit down," said Margaret. "You've earned a vacation."

Ellen sat down. The dizziness went away, but the pain remained.

"Are you feeling all right?" asked Margaret.

"It's nothing. I'll be okay." She felt better, but there was something unreal and indistinct about everything that was going on.

Margaret took a stack of plates and put them away in the cupboard. "I find it hard to believe, Joan, that you'll soon be a grandmother. You're too young for that."

"I'm ready to be Grandma any time. I miss my own parents. They died before their time. I guess that's how the Andersons became my family."

The women continued to talk about children and the younger generation. Ellen felt a distance from everything around her.

With dishwashing out of the way, Joan and Margaret joined Victoria and Ellen at the table. Many problems could be settled at the kitchen table. Ellen found herself returning to the present reality.

Margaret turned the conversation in a different direction. "Thanksgiving doesn't seem the same without Grandma. This is the first year she's not been with us."

Chapter 18

"Ninety-four years is a long and full life," said Victoria. "Most of us—maybe all of us—won't be around that long."

Ellen thought of the last years and the many visits to the nursing home. "The last years were hard for her. She missed so many of her friends."

"Even at seventy-two, I've lost several of my friends," Victoria observed. "The worst thing about growing old is losing your friends."

"Nothing remains the same." Ellen placed her hand on her stomach. The pain, though diminished, was still there.

"I've learned to expect change," said Victoria. "It happens whether we're ready or not. I don't know if there's anything to do to get ready."

Ellen sensed something was wrong within her. She was certain it wasn't her heart. The pain disappeared and then returned.

"Mother, you look pale. Is something wrong?"

Ellen hated to complain. "Oh, it's probably nothing. I think I ate too much."

Any further conversation ended with the next interruption. Matt, Margaret's oldest, entered the kitchen first, followed by his brothers and sisters and the two cousins. Standing outside were several young people from the neighborhood.

"Can we take Beauty and Max and go for rides? Beauty is gentle and the little kids can ride her."

Margaret didn't hesitate. "You'll have to ask your father." She looked at Lisa and Lorraine. "No, you'll have to ask your fathers."

The delegation moved into the living room. The requests were mixed with excitement. Noise and confusion replaced the conversation of the few minutes before.

Joe and Larry apparently felt this activity would be all right. Ellen heard the usual caution and warnings.

"Matt," called Margaret as he and the others made their exit. "Be careful. Especially with the younger children."

"Yes, Mother." Others echoed the same replies.

Ellen had learned not to worry. "Kids will be kids. We have to trust them. What happens will happen."

"Accidents are bound to happen," added Margaret. "There's nothing we can do to stop them."

The rest of the afternoon involved the usual confusion and commotion as the family had leftovers and pie and coffee. This Thanksgiving was a good one. Ellen would remember the family comradeship and closeness in the days that followed.

Soon after Matthew began driving home, he knew something was wrong. "Ellen, you don't look well. What's wrong?"

"Matthew, I'm afraid something's wrong with me. I think we need to see if Dr. Baker is home. I'm sick. It's more than acid indigestion."

Matthew slowed down and found a place to turn around.

He felt a sense of relief when he saw lights on in the doctor's house. He helped Ellen out of the car and up the steps. He knocked on the door.

Dr. Baker, recently retired from his practice, answered the door. He greeted them and took one look at Ellen. "Come in, Ellen, you need help."

Matthew waited as the doctor took Ellen into a room, which had once been an examining room. Mrs. Baker tried to speak words of reassurance and comfort.

Matthew listened to the voices. The wait seemed to take forever.

"Matthew," Baker spoke almost abruptly, "you need to get your wife to the hospital immediately. I don't know exactly what's wrong. There's some kind of obstruction. I'll phone the hospital. This could be serious."

Ellen, usually the strong one, the one who was never sick, looked weak and tired. "You should let Margaret know."

"We'll take care of that," said Mrs. Baker.

Dr. Baker helped Matthew get Ellen into the car. "She'll be okay. Just go directly to the hospital. They'll be ready for you. It'll be faster than calling the ambulance."

"Thanks Doc."

"I'll be there as soon as I've made the arrangements."

Matthew knew he had to remain calm. Lord, give me the strength to do what I have to do. Be with Ellen. Help!

Matthew drove the car at speeds beyond any speed he had driven before.

Chapter 19

Thanksgiving night was the longest night of Matthew's life.

He stayed close to Ellen. Her words did not make sense. Dr. Baker explained to another doctor her situation. The doctors took her to another examining room. Matthew paced the floor of the halls and waiting room.

Dr. Baker finally came to him. "Matthew, this is serious. There's a blockage. We don't exactly know the reason. They've called the surgeon, Dr. Turner. He's one of the best. Ellen will be in good hands. They'll do surgery around ten o'clock because it's an emergency."

"You mean, Doc, we could lose her?"

"It's not likely. But Dr. Turner can do wonders. More than likely, she'll be fine."

"I don't know what I'd do without her. I always thought I'd die first. She's always been the strong one."

"Matthew, you're stronger than you think. You have the genes of your mother and father. Look at them. Look at Elizabeth Anderson."

"Thanks, Dr. Baker, for being here. I know you didn't have to come."

"You're like family. I wanted to be here. Isn't Margaret coming?"

"I told her it wasn't necessary to come."

Dr. Baker walked over to the desk and picked up the phone. "I'm calling her. You need your family with you."

A few minutes later, the nurses rolled Ellen into the operating room. Matthew clasped her hand. "My darling, the Lord is with you."

Dr. Baker left, and a half-hour later Margaret hurried toward him.

"Dad, I could have come sooner. You should have told me how serious this was."

"I just found out. That's why Dr. Baker called."

Margaret nestled into his arms. "Dad, I'll be with you."

Matthew thought of the other times he had been in this same hospital. And he remembered being in the old hospital when he had his own brush with death. It was Ellen who had stayed beside him through that whole ordeal. Now, he would be with her. "In sickness and in health." The words of the marriage ceremony came to mind.

"Dad, have you eaten? It's been many hours since our big Thanksgiving dinner."

"I'm not hungry. I couldn't eat."

Father and daughter waited for what seemed like an eternity. It was well past midnight when Dr. Turner appeared.

"Mr. Anderson," he spoke gently. "Your wife came through surgery just fine. The blockage was caused by the gallbladder. We took the gallbladder. There were some giant stones. It's been rough for her, but she came through all right. It appears she has an infection, so that may take a few extra days of recovery."

"Why weren't there signs of gallbladder problems before?" questioned Margaret. "Usually, people know ahead of time."

"I would say that your mother has been working very hard. She probably ignored the signs."

"That's Mother for you," said Margaret. "She's been busy and she's had a lot on her mind."

"I suppose she was worried about me, and didn't let on to anyone."

Dr. Turner again reassured them. "She needs some recovery time, but she'll be okay."

Matthew and Margaret returned to Ellen's room.

The nurse entered. "You might as well go home and get some rest. She won't know you're here for quite some time."

"I'm staying," said Matthew.

"Dad, I'll be with you."

Father and daughter remained in the room, sleeping fitfully that night on chairs.

Chapter 19

The next days were hazy and unclear for Ellen. She was aware of Matthew's presence. She heard the doctor say that she would be having surgery at ten o'clock. Otherwise, she experienced the sharpest pain she had ever felt. The births of the children had been mild by comparison.

Ellen knew she needed to walk, but she did not feel like doing anything. The nurse was with her, and Matthew followed close behind.

Sometime during the third day, she became aware of what had really happened. "The blockage was taken care of with gallbladder surgery," said the doctor. "But you have an infection. You also have a touch of pneumonia. You're one sick lady, but you're on the mend."

Ellen couldn't quite take in all that was being said. The days that followed seemed to go on forever. She wished Matthew wouldn't hover so close by. Finally, she convinced him that he should go home and get some rest.

Pain does something to a person. Ellen, usually so involved with and concerned about others, could focus on nothing but her weakness and pain. She wanted people to leave her alone.

The doctor helped her in this respect. Visitors were to stay for only five minutes. The grandchildren came, but she didn't have the energy to enjoy their visit. Afterwards, she felt guilty.

Wednesday morning she awakened feeling much better. When the doctor came for his morning rounds, she made an announcement.

"I feel much better today. I'm ready to go home."

"Not quite, Mrs. Anderson," said the doctor. "You've been seriously ill with infection and pneumonia. Yes, you can go home soon. But you're going to have to take it easy."

"But Christmas is coming."

"That doesn't matter. You're going to tire easily, and that means you must rest. Or you'll be right back in the hospital."

Matthew stepped in at that moment.

"Yes, dear, you are going to be taking it easy. Megan is coming over to do the cooking for all of us at our house. We've got it all planned."

"But Megan's expecting a baby in a few months. She shouldn't be doing lots of extra work."

The doctor turned to leave. "I don't care how you do it, but you must take it easy. I believe Megan is a young, healthy woman, so the extra work won't hurt her."

Ellen laughed. "I guess I'm outnumbered."

The doctor left. Matthew stooped down to kiss her.

"Oh, Matthew, how I've missed you and everyone else. I can't wait to go home."

"Home isn't really home," said Matthew, "without you."

Matthew didn't know when he'd felt so alone. Ellen was home, but nothing seemed to be the same. When the doctor said Ellen would need much rest, he knew what he was saying. Ellen was resting or sleeping for many hours during the day. Ellen, usually so very busy preparing for Christmas, was able to do very little.

Matthew walked past the barn. "Is there anything I can do?" he asked Lowell.

Lowell didn't hesitate. "Uncle Matthew, you're supposed to slow down and not work so hard."

He had almost forgotten his own health concerns. But he knew he was ready to work again. He was tired of feeling so useless.

Matthew began to walk down the driveway. He looked toward the hills, but the Scripture didn't come alive. God seemed very distant. What had happened to his strong and vibrant faith? At the moment, life seemed dark and hopeless.

This past year had been filled with reminders of sadness and change. When the big family reunion took place this summer, Matthew somehow knew these family members would never again be together at the same time. That early celebration of Ma's ninety-fourth birthday had reminded him that she would not be around for long. Then the relapse of Laura's cancer and her death came soon after. And why did Michael have to leave in anger? And only a month ago, the Cuban Missile Crisis brought fear to everyone.

Ma's death was not a surprise. But it didn't seem fair that his young grandchildren should lose their mother. And now, Ellen, who was always so strong, lay in bed barely able to take care of herself.

Chapter 19

Matthew himself felt at his lowest point, physically, mentally, and spiritually. "I don't have the strength to go on," he said aloud.

The sound of a car horn interrupted his thoughts.

"Matthew, what's up? It's been a while."

Matthew looked up to see Glenn stepping out of the car.

He mumbled, "Hello." He wondered why he hadn't heard from Glenn when he had his heart attack or when Ma died.

"The wife and I just came back from a trip to California. I heard about your heart attack and about Mrs. Anderson and then about Ellen. You've had a terribly tough time."

"It's been rough." Matthew had missed the talks he used to have with this friend.

"How about we go into town and have a cup of coffee. Would that be all right with Ellen?"

Matthew thought a moment. "She's resting—needs lots of rest. She won't even miss me. Yes, let's go."

He got into the car. In minutes he was telling Glenn of all that had happened.

As they sat down in a booth in the City Café, Matthew couldn't help asking, "I suppose you'll be moving to California like so many people have? Mary and Ed. Martha and her family and many others."

Glenn laughed. "No thank you. California is a great place to visit, but I don't want to live there. Oak Ridge is the place for me. The wife talks about moving to Lake View. That's not for me. I'm a country boy, and I want to live and die in the country."

Matthew looked away. "I used to feel that way. In a way I still do. But with Michael gone, I'm not sure it's wise to stay."

"You have Lowell taking over, don't you?"

"Yes, he's doing amazingly well. But he'll be here for a year, and then he's going on to school."

"I can't see you living in town."

"The doctor's such a fuss budget. I know I could do much more work."

"It's time for us to slow down."

Matthew thought of some of the other farmers. "Several farmers have moved to town. Old Louis seems happy to go up town for coffee every day."

Glenn looked intently at his friend. "Matthew, there are times I think I'd like to try something else—maybe even pump gas at a filling station. We farmers work terribly hard."

"I used to think of going far beyond these hills around us. But I've come to realize that I have everything I could want here on this earth right here."

"The grass is always greener on the other side."

The two men kept on talking until they realized the noon crowd was coming in.

"Our wives will wonder," said Matthew. "We'd better go."

A short while later, when Matthew entered the kitchen, Ellen greeted him. "I was beginning to wonder what happened to you, but Lowell saw that you left with Glenn."

"I'm sorry. I should have told you, but you were resting."

"I need rest, but I need to exercise. I'll warm up the stew that Megan brought over. She's been such a great help."

"I've been thinking," began Matthew. "This is fine now that Lowell and Megan are here. But wouldn't we be better off in town rather than living alone out here in the country?"

Ellen didn't hesitate. "You know, dear, I've been thinking the same thing. If something should happen to one of us, we shouldn't be alone out here in the country. I didn't know if I should suggest it to you."

"I think we're ready. As ready as we'll ever be."

"Home," Ellen said slowly, "is not a house. Home is where your loved ones are. And if we're together, that's home."

"And now that you're back here, this is home."

Matthew rather liked the folk ballad, "Blowin' in the Wind." Yes, something was blowing in the wind. Change was in the air.

CHAPTER 20

December 1962

Christmas was fast approaching, but things were different this year. Ellen would not be arranging and planning the big family Christmas events. She was stronger, but not able to do all that she usually did.

Matthew missed the delicious aroma of cookies baking in the kitchen. Ellen had started to make meals but had refrained from doing the extra work in preparation for Christmas. This year he had a hard time getting into the Christmas spirit. Everything was changing.

On this morning in December, Matthew had helped in the barn as Lowell did milking and other chores. He hated sitting on the sidelines not doing any real work. He might be moving toward his sixty-third birthday, but he didn't feel that old. He still had plenty of life in him, despite that so-called heart attack.

As he entered the kitchen, Matthew knew Ellen was up and at work. The smell of sizzling bacon made Matthew's mouth water. Ellen had the pancakes ready.

"I'm feeling better. I figured you needed some extra energy now that you're helping out in the barn."

"Smells good."

Matthew quickly cleaned up and sat down at the kitchen table. Together, they prayed their short table prayer.

Ellen dished several pancakes onto his plate. "I haven't been myself for some time. I feel strong enough to do some more work now. It's almost Christmas, and I've hardly done a thing."

"Remember what the doctor said."

"I'll be fine."

Matthew and Ellen proceeded to eat their breakfast the way they had for almost forty years. Changes seemed harder to make even though such change might be necessary.

Matthew finished his coffee and began to get up. "I'm going to get out the snow blower. We need to make room for James's car. And maybe Johnie will come after Christmas."

"I don't know if that machine with its jerking is good for you, dear. Shouldn't you let Lowell do that work?"

"I've already had the machine out once."

Ellen smiled. "I guess it's no use to object."

As Matthew left, he kissed her on the cheek. "Afterward, I'll take a walk."

The snow blower started easily. Matthew experienced a certain pride and satisfaction as he looked at the area he had cleared. It would be good to have James and Johnie and their families around in a few days. And Carol would be home, but she was staying at Ma's little house on the home farm. When everyone left after Christmas, Ellen and he would be alone.

What about Michael? He kept asking himself that question. James and Johnie had confronted Michael about his habits and way of life. This youngest son had left in anger and had not been heard from since. Oh, how he missed this prodigal. Why would a young man with such promise reject his family this way?

Somehow, he thought Christmas would bring Michael home. But that would be too good to be true.

Matthew put away the snow blower. A voice interrupted his reverie.

"Uncle Matthew." The voice was Lowell's. "Don't over-do. Remember what the doctor said."

Matthew felt a mixture of annoyance and appreciation. "My boy, I'm tired of being useless. I feel much better."

"I was just concerned."

Chapter 20

"I appreciate your concern. I couldn't keep this farm in operation if you weren't here. I hope you realize how much that means to me."

"You're helping me and Megan out of a tight spot. The timing is perfect."

"I guess the good Lord is watching over us."

"I guess so." Lowell began to walk toward his trailer house and then turned to Matthew. "I'm heading into town to get a load of ground feed. Perhaps you'd like to come along for the ride."

Matthew hesitated. "I'd like the company some other time. But I'm not exactly feeling as if I'd be good company."

"Maybe you need company then."

"Thank you. Ellen and I are getting ready for our Christmas company. She's starting to do some work, so I need to help her."

"Megan and I will have you over sometime. So long."

Lowell hurried away.

Matthew had a sudden desire to be alone. He walked past the barn and toward the lake, where so many family picnics had been held. The depth of the snow was just right. He had to exert some effort, but the walk was not difficult.

He trudged out onto the ice. He thought of the children and their friends skating and having fun at this very place. He thought of how he and Ellen had enjoyed their youthful laughter and games. But they now were all adults with their own families. That feeling of emptiness kept crowding into his awareness.

He couldn't put Michael out of his mind. "Why, Lord, haven't you answered my prayer about Michael? I've placed him in Your hands. I've committed him to You. Why don't we hear from him?"

Matthew surveyed the world around him. The frosted trees across the lake glistened in the sunlight. Usually, he would find this beauty uplifting. But now he felt depressed. He had thought he would never again experience despair or sadness like this, but the despair would not let go.

"Where is my faith?" he said aloud. "Lord, where are You now? You seem so far away. Why does my life seem so empty?"

Matthew's mind moved backward and forward. His childhood at the home place. P.J. and the way he took the farm that should have been his. His own brush with death. His forgiveness of P.J. P.J.'s death. Then his mind moved to the children growing up on this new farm, the farm that was truly his. The darkness of the war. The fear that Johnie was killed. Then, when Johnie returned but not fully alive.

More recent times filled his mind. The family reunion last summer. Ma. Victoria, Martha, Mary. Grandchildren. Nieces. Nephews. The complete family together for that short time. Then, Laura's death. And Ma's death.

His own siblings used to be close, but now both Mary and Martha and a major part of their families were in California. In the old days, they would drive over to see Mary and Ed. And Martha would frequently come and visit. Now, they were all far away.

"I miss my loved ones. Life is not the same."

Matthew began walking, unaware of time. He felt almost nothing except emptiness. What was happening during this part of life? He kept on walking along the edge of the lake. He looked to the east and the swampy area where they had looked for the missing girls those many years ago.

A voice interrupted that winter quietness. Someone was calling his name.

Matthew reached down for his pocket watch. His watch told him it was after 1:30. Ellen must be worried about him.

"Uncle Matthew!" Lowell's voice echoed down the winter trail.

"I'm here!" Matthew called back.

Out of breath, Lowell ran toward him. "Where have you been? Aunt Ellen's worried sick about you!"

"I'm sorry," Matthew apologized. "I'm afraid I lost track of time. I wanted to walk and be alone."

Lowell repeated himself. "We've all been worried about you. Aunt Ellen always wants to know where you are."

Matthew repeated his apologies.

"I can see why you like walking out here. I don't think we could find a more beautiful spot any time of the year."

"We've had many family gatherings here. I think you must remember some of them. We're near the picnic spot."

"Yes, I remember. As kids we had fun. But I haven't been back here for a long time. We need to hurry. Ellen's worried."

The two men walked faster.

"Lowell," Matthew addressed his nephew. "It's tough getting old."

"But you're not old," objected Lowell. "Look at Grandma Elizabeth."

"I feel old today."

Matthew had a hard time keeping up with Lowell.

Chapter 20

When he walked past the barn, Ellen hurried toward them. "Matthew, where have you been? It's almost two o'clock—long past dinner."

Matthew apologized. "I lost track of time."

"Come, it's time to eat. I'll heat up the meat and potatoes."

Ellen breathed a sigh of relief as she warmed up the meat and potatoes. Matthew bowed his head and ate silently.

"Matthew, I know something's wrong."

"I've been thinking about lots of things."

"Matthew, dear, you and I know that the Lord will see us through whatever changes we need to make."

"It's not easy."

Ellen knew what her husband was thinking. "I miss him, too. Somehow, I wish Michael would come home for Christmas."

"That would be the best gift ever."

A knock at the kitchen door interrupted their conversation. The door opened and Lowell stepped in.

"I picked up the mail. It looks as if you have a letter."

He set the mail on the table.

Ellen thanked him and added, "How about some coffee?"

"No thanks. You have your letter, and I have work to do."

Ellen held up the letter. "We may have good news. It's a letter from Michael."

A smile spread over Matthew's face. "Read it!"

Ellen ripped open the letter and began to read. "Dear Mom and Dad. I should have written sooner, but I haven't known what to say. I don't have the skill with words that James and Margaret have.

"You will notice by the return address that I'm in a small town and mail will get to me from General Delivery. I'm the Prodigal Son, no question about it. I will return someday, but I'm not ready."

Matthew sighed. "I was hoping he'd come home soon."

Ellen continued reading. "I have a reason for traveling around. When I'm at home in Oak Ridge and Lake View, I'm not really me. I'm a part of you. I'm Matthew Anderson's boy. Whatever it takes, I have to discover myself. Who am I, really?

"I left Minnesota soon after Johnie scolded me. I can't stand the thought of the tension I would cause, simply by being around.

"I have no trouble getting work. I've had several jobs since I left Minnesota. I have discovered I'm a pretty good salesman."

Matthew interrupted. "Michael's like Johnie, but I always thought he'd stay on the farm. He has so much talent. He can do almost anything well."

"He has to make his own decisions."

Ellen resumed reading. "There's not much more to say. I just wanted to say I'm okay. And I want to wish you Merry Christmas. I'll pick up my mail at General Delivery for the next week or two.

"I want to say that I love you both and think of you every day. I'll be back someday when I get my life in order. Until then, I love you. Michael."

Ellen remained silent. There was nothing to say. She could see disappointment written all over Matthew.

"I was hoping he would be coming home."

"I need to write so the letter goes off tomorrow. He should get it right after Christmas."

"We have to tell him about Ma. And about your gallbladder operation and the infection."

"And," Ellen added, "about your heart attack."

Matthew stood up. "I think I'll go outside."

"Don't disappear again."

"No, I think Lowell is cleaning the calf pens. I'll help." Then he added, "I think we need to consider a move. We're eligible for Social Security. We can move to town."

Ellen felt a sense of relief that Matthew was changing his mind. "We'll move when we're ready. When we sell the farm."

Matthew walked slowly toward the barn and the new building that contained some calf pens. It always helped to keep busy.

He looked toward the hills. From them he usually experienced new strength. Today, that energy and strength did not come to him.

"Lord, I love this farm. I love the country. But I think it may be the time to leave."

Chapter 20

He walked into the new building.

Lowell greeted him. "I'm almost finished cleaning. You don't need to get yourself dirty. Maybe you could hoist that straw bale over. It's not heavy."

Matthew picked up the bale and lifted it over the railing. Lowell spread the straw around. Matthew reached down to pet one of the calves.

"Raising cattle has changed. When you have so many, it's not personal. The kids used to name all the cows. Now the cows seem to be a number."

"We have to make enough money to live," said Lowell. "We can barely make ends meet."

Matthew sighed once more. "That's the way it is today."

CHAPTER 21

"Mom! Dad! I'm home."

A familiar voice wakened Matthew from his afternoon nap. He realized the voice belonged to Carol. She had planned to arrive home later in the day for this much-anticipated Christmas visit.

For some reason, Matthew had a difficult time rousing himself. He had many concerns on his mind, and he hadn't slept well the night before. Apparently the same had been true for Ellen, who was taking her nap on the davenport in the living room. Both Matthew and Ellen had been told by their doctors that extra rest was absolutely necessary.

"Anyone home?" called Carol.

Once he was awake, Matthew jumped out of bed. He didn't hear Ellen moving yet. "Carol, I'll be right out."

He entered the kitchen. "You're home." He opened his arms to his daughter. Carol gave him the warmest hug she'd given him in years.

"Oh, Dad, I'm so happy to be home. Where's Mother?"

"She's resting."

Close behind Carol came Nick and Nicole, two of the grandchildren he barely knew. And by the door stood grandson Jeffrey and Carol's new husband, Hank Stevens. This son-in-law and grandchildren seemed like strangers.

Matthew shook hands with Hank, and the younger children gave dutiful hugs. Jeffrey shook his hand.

"Is Mother okay? Is there anything wrong?"

"It's good to have you here. Your mother is still napping, I think. Our doctors have ordered us to take naps, and I guess we both slept more soundly than we thought. We're feeling better."

Ellen appeared in the doorway. "I'm sorry I didn't hear you come. I must have been sleeping soundly. I'm glad you're here."

Carol rushed forward. "Mother, you're so thin. I didn't realize what a rough time you've had. I should have come."

Carol hugged her mother.

"No, dear, that was not necessary. I'd have been terrible company. When I'm not feeling well, I just want to be alone."

Carol turned to her children and Hank.

Ellen stooped down to hug and welcome her grandchildren. "Hello children. Nicholas. Nichole." She looked up at her grandson. "And, Jeffrey, you're so tall."

"Hello, Mrs. Anderson." Hank stepped forward and shook Ellen's hand. "I'm glad we can spend Christmas with you."

"I am, too. We've seen so little of you and the kids. We hardly know them anymore."

Carol quickly responded. "We're going to remedy that. We want all our children to know their grandparents." She turned to sixteen-year-old Jeffrey. "Say hello to your grandmother."

Awkwardly, Jeff went over to Ellen, stooped down and gave her a hug.

Ellen stepped back and looked up at her grandson. "I can't believe I have a grandson this tall. You're not a little boy anymore."

"I'm over six feet. That's not little."

By this time, Ellen had collected her thoughts. "Have you eaten? It's still a few hours before Christmas Eve supper."

"We're fine. We had some lunch along the way. We wanted to stop here first before we stopped at Margaret's."

"Why don't you all sit down at the kitchen table? I can at least make some coffee and hot cocoa."

In minutes Ellen had the coffee, hot cocoa, and cookies on the table. To Matthew it seemed he was getting to know strangers. But in reality this woman was his little girl, the one who had given him all kinds of trouble. He felt his love for her, and now he wanted to get to know the daughter who had been away so long.

Chapter 21

These grandchildren weren't like the others. They had grown up in a different world. However, between Carol and Ellen, the conversation kept moving along.

Matthew tried to start up a conversation with Nicole. Most of his granddaughters liked to sit in his lap and cuddle against him. Nicole seemed almost suspicious. He supposed that attitude came from living in the city, where people couldn't be trusted.

After an hour of visiting, Carol announced that it was time to go over to Margaret's and get settled in the little house. The little house would be small compared to the mansion where they lived in Chicago.

As they drove down the driveway, Ellen looked to Matthew. "I'm glad they're here, but those kids aren't like the others. They seem so distant."

Matthew thought and added, "Sometimes they don't even seem like our grandchildren."

A few minutes later, James and Ruth and their children arrived. That meant the normal confusion of a family together at Christmas.

Margaret had everything under control for the Christmas Eve meal. Aunt Victoria had come early and helped. Deborah and Judith set the tables. Joe and the boys were finishing chores in the barn. Mom and Dad, along with James and Ruth, were coming up the steps.

"Merry Christmas!" she called out. "Take your wraps into the bedroom. Christmas Eve dinner is right on schedule. The lutefisk should be just right. The Swedish meatballs and everything else is ready."

The greetings and confusion were followed by the predictable customs of Christmas Eve.

"Mother," Margaret instructed, "you are to take it easy. You sit down at the kitchen table. We have everything ready. We've expanded the old oak table, and we added some card tables, so we have room for everyone to sit down in the living room."

Her mother smiled. "Well, my dear, you have everything planned and organized."

Above the conversation Margaret called out: "Men and children. Out of the kitchen—into the dining room. In fact, you can find seats at the table or sit down in the living room." She turned to her younger daughter,

"Marlene, why don't you run down to the little house and tell Carol and her gang that we're almost ready to eat. They should come up now."

At this point Joe and the boys entered.

"Down to the laundry room to wash up," commanded Margaret. "I've got your good clothes down there. You can change there and come up for supper."

"My dear niece," said Victoria, "you are amazing. You have all the qualities and organization of the best of teachers."

Margaret blushed. "Thank you, Aunt Victoria."

The little girls returned. "Aunt Carol was still changing clothes," said Marlene.

Within minutes Joe and the boys came from the basement. They had done a complete changeover into their good clothes. Everything was ready.

In some ways Margaret enjoyed all the delightful confusion. She continued to work and give orders at the same time. "Everyone sit down at the dining room table or card tables. Joe, you help everyone get seated. Save places with the adults for Carol and Hank. We're almost ready."

Margaret checked again and noticed that Carol and her family had not arrived. She thought to herself and said under her breath, "I can get a meal ready for twenty people, and Carol has to be late."

Margaret, Aunt Victoria, and Ruth began getting the various platters and bowls filled with the food.

Margaret called out to her brother: "James, would you come in here a minute?"

"I thought men were banned from the kitchen," James joked.

"I think you better go down to the little house. Set a fire under Carol. She needs to come up right now. In a few minutes we'll be eating."

James obeyed his sister and returned in minutes without Carol and her gang.

As if by clockwork, the tables were filled with food. Margaret invited everyone to be seated. "We'll start. We don't want the food getting cold. I've asked Aunt Victoria to pray."

Aunt Victoria stood up, tall and erect, though strands of gray could be found in her dark hair. A gentle far-away look in her eyes replaced the stern look of earlier times. Everyone from the youngest to the oldest bowed heads.

"Heavenly Father," she prayed solemnly in her clear and distinct manner. "We come before You, thankful for the blessings of another year. Though we are missing several and two of our loved ones went to be with You this past year, we are thankful to be together as a family. Thank You for family. Thank You for sending Your Son as a baby in a manger. Grant that all in this family may come to know You and believe in You. Thank You for this special Christmas meal and for Margaret and all who had a part in preparing it. Bless this food and our fellowship. In Jesus' name. Amen."

The prayerful quietness ended. Family members passed platters and bowls of food. Conversation escalated during the next minutes. Margaret kept wondering why Carol and her family were slow in coming. Soon everyone had a first serving of food.

Finally, there was activity on the back porch and the kitchen door opened.

"We're here," called Carol. "Merry Christmas!"

Carol, followed by her husband and children, entered the living room. She looked surprised and turned to Margaret.

"I didn't realize you were in such a hurry. I'm sorry we're late."

"Well," said Margaret, "we have a tradition of always eating on time. And we didn't want the food to get cold."

"Things haven't changed," mumbled Carol.

"Take your wraps into the bedroom. And hurry up so your food won't get cold."

Carol and Hank found their places. Jeff looked bored with the whole situation, and the younger children found their places with the other children.

While people ate, the conversation quieted down. That made young Nicole's words stand out. "I can't eat this stuff. Lutefisk tastes terrible."

"Nicole," said Carol. "You don't say things like that when you're invited out. Eat the rest of your food."

"I thought it was supposed to be so good."

Margaret tried to make the best of the situation. "Not everyone likes lutefisk. It's something you grow up with and learn to like."

Aside from the disruption of the latecomers, the Christmas supper went fine. Margaret observed that Hank remained rather quiet, as did Jeffrey. Carol tried especially hard to be part of the various conversations.

By the time family members had filled themselves with the lutefisk, meatballs, creamed peas, and home-grown potatoes, they weren't very hungry. Even so, they ate their dessert of Swedish rice pudding, and they found it hard to turn down the Christmas cookies.

Margaret continued to call out directions. "Put any bones in these bowls and clean off your plate into the same bowl. Pass your plates this way. Ruth and Carol and I will take care of cleaning up and dishwashing."

"I'll help, too," interrupted Aunt Victoria.

"I'm certainly capable of helping," added her mother.

"Okay, Aunt Victoria, but Mother, you still need to take it easy. Mother, there is a job for you. I'm afraid we neglected it the last few years. I would like you to read the Christmas story the way you did when we were growing up. I have a King James Bible on the dresser in our bedroom. Would you do that?"

Her mother smiled. "Yes, but some of the kids could do the job beautifully."

Her aunt broke in quickly. "No, Ellen, no one does it better than you. I still remember that Christmas when you were expecting Michael. I cannot imagine a more beautiful picture."

"Well," answered Ellen, "I should look over the King James Version. I've been reading these modern translations."

And so a Christmas Eve tradition was revived. It was a large group that filled the living room in the year of our Lord, 1962. While the Cold War continued and other world problems were escalating, Ellen quietly read the Christmas story:

"In those days, there went out a decree from Caesar Augustus——

During the next hour, Margaret observed a quiet family togetherness. Hank tried to be sociable. Carol took time to talk with her nieces and nephews. This was one of those Christmas Eves that she would long remember.

Christmas Day was another day of delightful confusion. Once more, the family gathered at Margaret and Joe's place. This group included the Christmas Eve group along with Larry and Joan and their girls as well as Lowell and Megan. Johnie and his three children had arrived in time for dinner. Ellen loved having the family together. She wished, though, that she could take care of more of the work.

Dinner was over, and the younger generation scattered. Some would ski on the hills nearby, while others skated down at the lake. The men retired to the living room, and the women began the task of cleaning up and doing dishes.

All at once, Ellen felt dizziness come over her. She didn't want anyone to notice, but Margaret did.

"Mother, what's wrong?"

Ellen hated to admit it. "I guess I'm a little dizzy. There's been so much happening. I guess I can't take it as well as I used to."

"Mother, you need to lie down."

Ruth and the other women echoed the same sentiments.

"We should call the doctor," said Ruth.

"No, I'll be okay. The dizziness is gone. That just happens when I've been hurrying around. And I think this room is a little warm."

Margaret came over and took her arm. "I'm taking you to one of the bedrooms upstairs."

Ellen obeyed and followed her daughter. "Oh, why am I so weak?"

Once she lay down, sleep overtook her. For the next hour she experienced a deep sleep.

"Ellen. Ellen." Her husband gently called her. "I think you better get up. Carol and Hank have to go back to Chicago."

Ellen sat up, wiping the sleep from her eyes. "I don't understand."

"Hank had a call. Some business problem he has to take care of."

"But they just came yesterday. They were supposed to stay several days."

Matthew helped her out of bed. "I know. It doesn't seem right that they have to leave so soon."

"Oh, I wish I'd get my strength back."

Carol greeted her. "Mother, I wish we didn't have to leave. But Jeff is staying with Mrs. Grant, and he'll be over to see you."

"I'm sorry you have to leave. I was hoping we'd have more chance to visit."

Hank's loud voice called out. "Carol, hurry. We've got to get going."

Carol gave her a hug. "We'll be back. This summer."

"Oh, I miss you. But I'm coming outside to see you off. I'm not that weak and sickly. I'm getting better."

James and Johnie were soon both beside her.

"You've still got us," said Johnie. "And you always knew I was a handful. I still am, and I'll be here three more days—along with the kids."

"Yes," added James, "and Ruth and I and our kids will be here as well. You'll have your hands full."

Ellen, with her sons beside her, went outside to say goodbye to Carol and Hank and her younger children. Margaret placed another jacket around her mother.

They stood there on that cold December day. Ellen remembered other times when she had said goodbye to loved ones. But this was the way life was.

Nicholas and Nicole each gave her hugs—this time those hugs were warmer and friendlier. Hank embraced her, but he always seemed cold and distant. Carol gave her another hug, a very quick one, and then got into the car.

She felt Matthew beside her.

"It's hard to see her go," said Matthew.

"I wish she could have stayed longer."

"Come, Mom and Dad," said Margaret. "It's cold out here. We need to take care to keep you in good health."

Ellen wasn't sure she liked the idea of her children taking care of her. She was used to taking care of them.

While Carol's departure dampened some spirits, the Christmas celebration continued. Most of the adults went down to the lake to watch the skaters and other activities. Ellen stayed inside with Margaret and Victoria. After all, Margaret and Victoria had to prepare for afternoon lunch. Ellen wanted to help, but they seemed intent that she should take it easy.

During the next days Matthew found his strength and energy coming back. With six grandchildren staying at their house and with the six others often visiting, there was lively activity. James and Ruth were good at organizing the household. And Johnie provided that extra energy for the skating and skiing and tobogganing parties.

"I'm proud of my family," he told Ellen many times.

Saturday, Johnie and his children left for Maple Valley. After all, Sunday was a pastor's work day. Sunday afternoon, James and Ruth and their children packed their suitcases and returned to Riverton.

That left Matthew and Ellen in a house that seemed terribly empty.

Chapter 21

The last day of the year arrived. Matthew returned from the mailbox with the daily paper and some advertising circulars. As he sat down for morning coffee, a letter fell out.

"It's from Michael!" exclaimed Ellen.

Matthew trembled from within. Even though the last letter had come only a short time ago, it seemed such a long time since there had been contact with Michael. He feared the direction Michael was taking.

"Read it!"

Ellen cut open the letter and began to read. "Dear Mom and Dad. I must apologize for being away. I hope you will understand why at some point.

"I'm so sorry that I missed Grandma's funeral. I am glad that I had the chance to see her last summer during the family reunion celebration. She has been such an important part of our lives.

"Dad, I would have come home if I had known about your heart attack. I'm glad you're doing okay. Mother, I had no idea that you were in the hospital."

Matthew couldn't help interrupting. "Why didn't he let us know where he was? There's no way we could reach him."

"Dad, I wish I could give you an answer about the farm. Right now, I need to find myself. I can't see myself working on the home farm the rest of my life. There's a big world out there. I want to go beyond all that and do something more.

"I'm glad Lowell's doing such a good job in running the farm. Dad, I wish you wouldn't hurry and sell the farm. The family needs a place to come back to.

"Give me a few more months to think through some things. I'm returning to Minnesota in a few days. I think I can have my old job back. And then one of these weeks I'll surprise you and come home. But please don't tell James and Johnie. I don't want another one of their lectures.

"I love you both more than I can say. I know I've been a rotten son. Someday, I hope I can make you proud of me. All my love, Michael."

Matthew looked out through the kitchen window. He loved those hills and lakes and fields. There was no more beautiful place in the world. He wanted to live and die in this home.

"I miss that boy. I wish he would come home."

"I don't think we can depend on that."

"When Lowell leaves, we have to sell the cows and rent out most of the land."

"Matthew, that's the only way."

"And if something happens to me, I don't want you here alone in the country."

"Or the other way. You shouldn't be here alone."

"We have only one choice. Sell the farm."

Matthew thought a minute. "I can't give up hope. Michael could come home."

CHAPTER 22

January 1963

Matthew's life settled into a quiet winter routine. He and Ellen prayed together about Michael and Carol and all of the other concerns.

Ellen said it well: "Lord, we have done our part. We have tried to raise up our children in the way they ought to go. We will pray for them. But, Lord, we place Michael in Your hands. Watch over him. Please bring him back to You and to us. But we commit him to You. We entrust him to Your loving care. In Jesus' name. Amen."

Matthew felt a peace that he did not fully understand.

He regularly helped Lowell with the chores, but he also took time to have coffee with Glenn Robertson. Such friendships were important, and a person never knew when such a friendship would end in death or another kind of departure.

Most of the time Matthew felt he could speak his innermost concerns to Glenn Robertson. On this morning in mid-January, they sat in a booth in the far end of the Lake View Café. Coffee had a way of loosening the tongue.

"You know, Glenn," Matthew began, "I don't know what I'd do with myself if I lived in town. My whole life has been hard work. I like to read more than ever before, but you can do only so much reading."

"I'd feel the same way. I'll stay on the farm until I drop."

"I've been thinking about that. If something happened to me, I wouldn't want Ellen alone out in the country. And if something happened to her, I wouldn't want to be alone."

"But you'd be alone in town. It wouldn't be any different."

Matthew thought a moment. "But in town there would be people around. A fellow could go up town for coffee."

"But there's a lot of other time in the day."

"I don't know what I'd do without Ellen."

"I guess we men are pretty helpless with some things. We work hard and have this physical strength, but when it comes to matters of the heart, we don't do well."

Matthew's mind filled with images of the hills and the beautiful countryside. "I love the land. I love my farm. I feel when I'm plowing the fields or mending fences, I'm closer to God."

"I hadn't thought of it that way. Sometimes the outdoors are harsh—almost vicious. I think of the cold winters I'd like to get away from."

"Those cold winters make the work go faster."

"I'd like to go to Arizona or California for the winter. I think I could enjoy walking around or just sitting down by the ocean."

This was one time Matthew could not understand his friend. "I think part of me would die if I had to leave the farm."

"Well, Matthew, then don't leave. Stay!"

"But Ellen feels it would be all right to be in town. Maybe I'd be better off in town."

Glenn slammed his fist on the table. "That is plainly stupid. You can stay on the farm. Rent out the land. Raise some beef cattle. Raise some chickens and a garden. And one of these days Michael will get some sense into his head and move home."

Matthew, surprised at the force of his friend's words, said nothing.

Glenn went on, "If you love your farm so much, why leave the place? You said part of you would die if you had to leave the place. You're not ready to die yet. The doctor says you're better off now than before the heart attack. Look at how long both your ma and pa lived. Don't do anything stupid."

Matthew smiled. "You may have a point."

Glenn repeated some of what he had previously said and then added, "Where's your faith, anyway? You always said God gives strength for what you should do."

Chapter 22

The waitress came and filled their cups with coffee.

"You've given me something to think about."

"Well, you better think hard."

Matthew took a sip of coffee and then set down the cup. "You know, Glenn, you're right. We can stay on the farm. Rent out some of the land. I'll have some beef cattle and a few chickens. Then, I'll still have time to enjoy life. And I find that gardening is something I love to do."

"Now, you're talking."

Once more, Matthew felt there was hope.

Margaret stood by the window, alone in the kitchen. Joe was out doing chores as usual. She should do more work outside, but cooking and taking care of six children demanded much of her time. And, now, another possibility or opportunity had been placed before her.

"Please, Mrs. Anderson," the county superintendent of rural schools had said, "we need you to go back and teach this winter. We're in short supply of good, qualified rural school teachers."

The words replayed in her mind. The money would definitely come in handy. Keeping the six children in school clothes was not an easy task. If she took this job, the children would have to take on much more responsibility at home. But would that be fair?

And then she thought of Mom and Dad. They were in the middle of decision-making about their future. She wanted to have time for them. On top of this, Michael continued to be a major concern for the whole family.

"Why does life have to be so complicated?" She spoke the question aloud as she put away the last of the breakfast dishes.

A gentle knock on the door interrupted her thinking.

The back door opened. "Hello sis. Surprise!"

It was Johnie. He stood before her, smiling, but his eyes showed sadness and concern.

"Hello brother. What brings you home this morning?"

Immediately, Margaret knew something was wrong.

"I've been to see Michael. I saw him for just a short while. I'm afraid it doesn't look good."

"Oh, dear," said Margaret. "What's he up to now?"

"It's a long story."

"Why don't you sit down? I'll put on some fresh coffee."

Margaret brought out the new electric coffeemaker and filled in the coffee grounds. "I don't know if this newfangled coffeepot makes better coffee. I still like the old way, but I'm giving it a chance."

"The coffeemaker is a little easier. I have it on all the time in my church office. We drink lots of coffee."

Margaret hesitated but asked the questions. "Is Michael all right? Has anything happened?"

"Not yet, anyway."

She sat down, facing her brother. "Tell me everything. Don't spare me because I'm your little sister."

"I came here because I wanted to talk with you first. I don't know how much I should tell Mom and Dad. I don't think telling them the whole story would do any good."

"Stop stalling. I want to know the truth."

Johnie smiled at his sister's annoyance. "Let's have coffee. First ve have coffee."

Margaret laughed at her brother's imitation of the heavy Scandinavian accent. She brought out cups and then reached for the cookie jar and put some cookies on a plate. She poured their cups of coffee.

"Now, fire away."

"It's a long story. I'm not sure I know where to start."

"Tell me everything."

"To start with, he worked in the Twin Cities. I managed to have contact with the woman who was his landlady. She said he came in as a clean-cut farm boy—hard working and all that. Then, something changed. He started staying out late at night. Gradually, she could see that he was involved in drinking. She would not tolerate anything like that. She warned him at first. He paid little attention to that. Then, she asked him to leave."

"Well, we all know he started down that road while he was at home. But he had resolved to change."

"That resolve did not last." Johnie sipped his coffee and enjoyed a cookie. "His landlady rented rooms to two other young men who worked at the same place. They said he quit a few days later."

"What happened then? I thought Mom and Dad had a letter when he was in Illinois."

"Before he went to Illinois, he had several other jobs. He'd start out doing just fine, but then he'd show up late."

Chapter 22

"How did you find this out?" asked Margaret.

"These other young men took an interest in him and seemed to find out about him from time to time. Then, he disappeared. I spent a bit of time doing detective work."

"You do have a way with people."

"That's when he went to Illinois. I then contacted one of my pastor friends—we were together in the seminary. My friend Lee did some checking. Michael followed the same pattern in Illinois. He'd show up at first, doing a great job. Then, he would be late or absent. As far as Lee could find out, he became involved in gambling."

"But," interrupted Margaret, "he was supposed to return to the Twin Cities. And I thought he would come home at least for a visit."

"Maybe those were his plans, but he had his check mailed to one of the towns on the Iron Range. So that's where he went."

"Did you follow him?"

"That may have been a mistake. I followed him and caught him as he came from work. He wasn't too happy. He had plans."

"What happened then?"

"I confronted him. I may have come across as the old-time fire and brimstone preacher. He kept on saying he needed to be his own man and live his own life. He threatened to disappear again if I didn't leave him alone. I tried to appeal to his concern for Mom and Dad, but he would hear none of that."

"Why? I don't understand why."

"As far as I can tell, he feels he's a disgrace to the family. The community looks down on him, and he doesn't want to face that criticism."

Margaret thought of students from her classrooms. "I think of my students who felt they didn't measure up. They either fought hard to measure up, or they gave up. Some felt the answer was to get away from the home and community."

"What's happened with Michael is that he's determined to stay away. He feels he can't come home. And if we pursue him, he'll run further away. He threatened to disappear completely if I hounded him."

"What are you going to tell Mom and Dad?"

"I have to tell the truth, but not the whole truth."

"Isn't that a white lie?"

Johnie blushed. "Margaret, will it help for them to know all about the drinking and the gambling? And even the possibility of drugs?"

"Does he have a job right now?"

"One thing about Michael, he's a brilliant mechanic. Yes, he has a high-paying job with a company that contracts with the mining company. If he can only stay with his job."

"I wish there were a solution."

Johnie stood up. "I think I'd better go over to Mom and Dad's. I have to tell them something."

"Why don't I call them and invite them over for dinner. Then, you can tell them what they need to know."

"That would work. A meal always eases any problem."

The minute Matthew greeted Johnie, he knew there was a problem. And that problem or concern had to be Michael. He was almost afraid to ask, but he waited for Johnie to say what he had to say.

As usual, Margaret prepared a delicious meal. Matthew had come to enjoy her special meatloaf along with scalloped potatoes and green beans and onions. It seemed Margaret did everything to perfection.

Matthew had that terrible feeling in his stomach every time he sensed a problem.

"Dad," said Margaret, "why aren't you eating? I've made your favorites."

Ellen didn't hesitate. "I think we know you have something to tell us—and it's probably about Michael. Your father is uneasy, that's why."

Margaret looked to Johnie. "You might as well tell."

Johnie put down his fork. "It's always best to tell the truth—the whole truth."

"Don't try to shield us," said Ellen. "We know the situation is not good with Michael."

"I'll make a long story short. I've tried to keep track of my little brother. I've confronted him, and I've had friends check on him. He's still trying to find himself—so to speak. He's searching for something. It seems he's running away, trying to find his own identity."

"Tell it to us straight, son." Matthew trembled as he spoke the words.

"Right now, he's on the Iron Range. He has a good job with a company that contracts with the mining company. So far, he's left several jobs in the Twin Cities and some other jobs in Illinois. He's a good worker and brilliant mechanic. He does well for a while, then he shows up late, then he's absent. Then, he often leaves and moves elsewhere."

Ellen pleaded, "Have you told him how much we want him to come home? To visit us."

"Is he still drinking?" asked Matthew. "Is he into drugs?"

Johnie avoided his gaze. "Well, I don't know."

Ellen gave the knowing look that only a mother can give. "You think so. In fact, you're certain he is."

A smile spread across Johnie's face. "Mother, I guess we kids never could fool you. When we'd been up to something, you knew right away."

"That's part of being a mother and a teacher."

Johnie's face grew serious once more. "I'm afraid there's nothing we can do. Michael will do his own thing and go his own way."

"We can pray," Ellen reminded.

"I should know that."

Their talk was interrupted by the ringing of the telephone. Margaret quickly got up and answered.

Matthew heard one side of the conversation.

"I'm sorry, I can't take on the job right now. I simply have too much to do right here. I have a husband and six children to care for."

The voice at the other end kept on talking.

Margaret's voice gained a firmer edge. "I am sorry, Mr. Grant. I must absolutely say no. I cannot accept the contract."

After a few more words she said goodbye.

Joe spoke up. "Margaret, you're sure that's your decision? The kids and I don't want to be selfish. If you would like, we'll manage."

"You're more important than any teaching job—or the money it brings in."

Matthew saw the tenderness in the eyes of both Margaret and Joe. These two had truly enriched his life.

Margaret announced, "It's time for dessert. It's plain old strawberry-rhubarb sauce. Nothing special."

Matthew enjoyed some rich farm cream on his sauce. Conversation returned to the ordinary.

Time passed quickly.

"You men, go in the living room. Take a rest. Johnie, you're tired from driving. And, Dad and Joe, you've been working outside. You need a break."

Soon the men relaxed in the living room. Life was good. It would be even better if Michael came home.

That evening, Matthew felt a need to go outside. Milking was done; the barn was dark. Lights shone from the windows of the big house and from Lowell and Megan's trailer home. The moon reflected on the snow, producing a silver coloring.

Matthew looked beyond toward the hills. "How can I ever leave? I love these hills and everything here. This is home; I wish it would be home until I die."

He bowed his head and looked into the night. "Lord, bless and guide Michael. Bring him in Your own way."

He said to Ellen when he entered the living room, "It's a beautiful night out. We can't wait for Michael. We have to go on and make plans."

Chapter 23

March, 1963

March had come in like a lion. The snowstorm kept Lowell from returning home and picking up Megan and their young son. Lowell's absence meant that Matthew was left with the milking of almost forty cows that morning.

Now that evening had arrived, Matthew found himself exhausted. Fortunately, Lowell returned before evening chores. This was more work than Matthew had done when he was a young man. He would turn sixty-three in less than two months, and it was time to slow down.

The action of television's *Raw Hide* had failed to keep him awake. Usually he enjoyed the lively action of the Western and the clear evidence that good won over evil. But now a troubled sleep had settled over him.

Ellen's voice interrupted his sleep. "Matthew, dear, I think you better wake up. Margaret and Joe are coming over."

Matthew wakened slowly.

"Did you hear what I said?"

"Yes, but why are they coming over on a snowy night like this? Lowell and Megan and the baby barely made it back this afternoon."

"Margaret sounded secretive—as if they have something up their sleeves. I think they've been plotting and planning. I don't know what it's all about. I suspect it could be about our anniversary. After all, we've been married forty years."

Matthew got up to switch the channel. "We might as well watch Mitch Miller. I like his music."

The familiar sounds of the Mitch Miller program filled the room.

"Matthew, something's bothering you. Ever since Glenn Robertson stopped over, you've been quiet. What did he have to say? You might as well tell me."

"It's nothing definite."

"Obviously, it's worrying you."

"We'll talk about it later. After the kids have left."

"I won't bother you about it. When you're ready, you can talk.".

From the back porch came the sounds of people stamping their feet to get rid of the snow. Margaret and Joe opened the kitchen door.

"Hello, Mom. Dad, we're here."

Ellen and Matthew went to the kitchen to greet them.

Joe greeted Matthew and Ellen. "I wanted to finish *Rawhide* before we came. The bad guys always get what's coming to them."

Matthew chuckled. "I started watching, but I dozed off."

"Your dad's had a hard day. He didn't doze, he was fast asleep."

Margaret and Joe sat down at the kitchen table across from Ellen and Matthew just as they had done so many times before. This time seemed different to Matthew.

"Why didn't the kids come?" asked Matthew.

"They were busy," said Margaret. "They were into all kinds of work and projects—and even some school work."

Ellen looked squarely at her daughter and son-in-law. "I think something's up. Otherwise you wouldn't have come over on this wintry night."

Matthew couldn't help thinking something was wrong.

"We have a surprise." Margaret smiled. "Let me put on the coffee. We can celebrate."

"Oh, no," objected Ellen. "I'll take care of things in my kitchen. You tell us and satisfy our curiosity."

Ellen proceeded to fill the new electric coffeepot with water. Then she measured the grounds carefully.

It was Joe who spoke up. "Margaret and I got together with James and Ruth and Johnie, and we talked to Carol. We figure it's time the two of you had a real vacation."

Chapter 23

Margaret held up an envelope. "We thought it was time the two of you traveled to California. We have the plane tickets. We'll take you to James's in Riverton, and he'll take you to the Twin Cities airport. You fly out March 19, and you'll be back in ten days."

Matthew began to object. "I don't know if I want to fly. Being up in the air scares me."

"Don't be silly," objected Margaret. "Flying is much safer than driving a car."

"But there's work to be done here. We can't just leave the house and take off."

"That will all be taken care of." Margaret took out the tickets. "Lowell and Megan can move in here. Lowell is already taking care of the chores and other work. He can handle that all by himself when you're away."

"But what if Lowell needs some advice or help?" questioned Matthew.

"I'm a few miles away," said Joe. "It's time that Lowell takes care of things on his own. He shouldn't be depending on you all the time."

Margaret didn't wait for comment from her parents. "Don't you want to visit your sisters? Mary and Martha have both been hoping that you'd come for a visit. You can't disappoint them."

Deep within Matthew knew the decision had been made. Though he had some fears about flying, this might be his opportunity to go far beyond these Minnesota hills. He would see a part of the world he had dreamed about seeing.

Once more, Ellen objected. "What about Michael? What if he comes back and we're not here?"

Margaret's reply was uncharacteristically sharp. "If he comes when you're gone, it's time that he misses you—and realizes he's been a first rate jerk!"

Joe added, "We're here. It's time for Michael to take responsibility."

Ellen served the coffee as they continued discussing travel plans. Matthew began to look forward to an experience he had never had before. In those moments, he forgot the choice that was bothering him.

Perhaps this was a new opportunity, carrying hope with it. This new chapter in his life might not be so bad after all.

Sometimes Ellen was completely frustrated by her husband. Something was bothering him, but he wouldn't say what it was.

She slipped into bed beside him. "Tell me, or I won't sleep all night."

Matthew remained silent a moment. "Glenn stopped by today."

"I didn't even notice."

"He didn't stay long. He said Tim was interested in buying the farm. He thought we should talk serious business."

Ellen sat up. "Matthew, what's that boy up to? He bought the Olson farm two years ago. Is he trying to buy up all the farms so he can have one of those corporation farms?"

"I don't know. Glenn said he's ready to offer a good price."

"Do you think we should take it? After all, we're not hearing from Michael, and he isn't ready to settle down here."

"I'm bothered by it all."

Ellen turned off the lamp. "The more I think about it, I think we should sell and move into town. That could be better for both of us."

"I don't know that I'm ready right now. Maybe in a few years. We can rent out the place. I can cut down the amount of work I do."

"We'll think about it and pray. And besides, we have this wonderful trip to California. We can look forward to that. We'll see Mary and Martha and their families."

Matthew mumbled approval.

"You know, Ellen , that trip may be the right time to think about the future. We can decide when we come back."

Ellen agreed with Matthew. It was always good to sleep on something before making a decision.

Monday afternoon, Glenn and his son Tim drove up the driveway. Matthew knew immediately they were coming to talk business.

Matthew had been working in the tractor shed and getting the snow blower ready for the next snow fall. He liked working around the farm. Somehow living in town didn't appeal to him.

Matthew greeted Glenn and Tim.

"We'd like to talk business," announced Glenn. His tone was different from the usual friendly casual tone.

Chapter 23

Tim greeted Matthew. Tim seemed restless and uneasy.

"Come in. We'll have coffee," invited Matthew. "Ellen's just made some chocolate chip cookies. Tim, I think you'll like those."

"Ellen makes the best."

The men chatted about weather and work as they proceeded to the house. When other talk didn't come easy, weather served as an acceptable topic.

Ellen had the coffee ready, so they sat down immediately. She poured coffee for each of the men and put out a plate of chocolate chip cookies along with some sliced date bread. After the preliminaries Glenn got down to business.

"We've come to make an offer. Rather, Tim is ready to make an offer."

"You mean," said Ellen, "you want to buy our farm. The whole farm."

"Yes," said Glenn, "all 320 acres. Tim wants to expand his farming operation. He has the new heavy equipment. That means he can handle more field work."

Matthew cleared his throat. "I'm not sure I'm ready to sell."

"But you talked about moving to town," said Glenn.

"But," continued Matthew, "you suggested that I could live on the farm and rent out the land."

"Tim is ready to make an offer."

Matthew gulped. Things were moving too fast.

"I'm ready to offer you $55,000 for this whole farm—320 acres."

The offer seemed too good to be true. "The offer sounds good."

Matthew didn't know that he liked the idea of doing business with the son of his best friend. Sometimes friendship and business didn't go well together.

Before the silence became awkward, Ellen spoke up. "Matthew and I always talk things over. And we'll pray about it."

"I don't think you'll get a better offer. Tim is ready to give you $20,000 down. The rest he'll pay during the next fifteen years."

Glenn and Tim looked to Matthew for an answer. Matthew wasn't sure what he should say. He was thankful when Ellen spoke.

"We like to talk over these big decisions with the kids. However, we would want everything handled through the bank. I'm not sure it's a good idea to spread those payments over fifteen years. We might not be around for fifteen years."

"We're friends," said Glenn. "If you can't trust us, who can you trust?"

"The unexpected can happen," said Ellen. "There can be serious setbacks. But we'll talk this over between ourselves and then the kids." She got up, brought the coffeepot over, and offered more coffee. "By the way, Matthew and I will be flying to California the week after next. That will be a good time for us to think this over."

"Don't think too long," warned Tim. "I'm looking at other property. By that time it may be too late. I may have found another farm."

"We'll have to take that chance," said Matthew.

The remaining part of the visit seemed somewhat strained. Matthew felt relieved when Glenn and Tim left.

To Matthew, the thought of selling the farm was like expecting a death announcement. He spent his days thinking about selling or not selling. At the same time he hoped that by some miracle Michael would call and decide to come home.

Several days later, a call did come. Matthew and Ellen were getting ready for bed. They had decided not to wait for the ten o'clock news on television.

The ringing of the telephone startled Matthew. People didn't call this late unless something was wrong.

Ellen hurried in to the kitchen to answer. Immediately, Matthew knew it was Michael. They had prayed for something like this. Had Michael finally come around? Was it possible that he would return home, where he belonged?

"It's Michael," she said to Matthew.

Matthew stood close to the phone in order to hear what Michael said.

"I've been thinking about you," said Michael. "I just wanted to talk. I'm sorry it's been such a long time."

"Where are you Michael?" asked Ellen. "When are you coming home?"

Matthew strained to hear every word.

Chapter 23

"I'm working for this company that has a contract with the mining company. I'm busy. I'm making better money than I could anywhere else. It's great to finally have some money."

Ellen spoke what Matthew was thinking. "Remember: money isn't everything. There are more important things in life."

There was a moment of silence. "Mother, don't start preaching to me the way Johnie does. I'll make my own decisions."

"I'm sorry, son, but we're concerned about you. We haven't seen you for such a long time. We miss you."

Matthew heard a catch in Michael's voice. "I miss you, too. But I need to sort things out. I need some time."

Matthew took the receiver from Ellen. "Son, I miss you so very much. Please come home for a weekend. We want to see you."

An awkward silence followed.

Ellen then spoke: "Your father and I will be going to California." She proceeded to tell him some of the details and then added, "We have an offer on the farm. We're thinking about selling."

A short pause followed; then came explosive words. "Don't sell. Please don't sell."

Ellen calmly explained. "We're just thinking about it. Does it really make any difference to you? You're not around."

To Matthew, Ellen's words sounded harsh.

Matthew again took the receiver, trying to soften those words. "Oh, son, we miss you. There's nothing we'd like better than having you home, running the farm. But we need to make some changes."

"Dad, I'm sorry. I know I can never measure up to the others—especially Johnie. I wish I could, but I can't."

Always the quick thinker, Ellen responded. "But Michael, we don't expect you to be another Johnie. You are you. You are unique."

"Yes, Mother, you say that, but you really compare me to Johnie—and to James and Margaret. I can't measure up to them. Never."

"Just come visit us," said Matthew.

"We love you no matter what," said Ellen. "We miss you."

Some noise at the other end interrupted the conversation.

"Mom, Dad, I've got to go. I love you. I'll call again. I'll come home for a visit." He stopped and added, "I love you. Don't sell the farm. Not yet."

Neither Matthew nor Ellen had a chance to respond.

"Goodbye."

Matthew and Ellen talked late into the night.

"What do we do? Keep the farm?" asked Ellen.

"I'm not sure we can or should wait."

"Do we sell?"

"And," asked Matthew, "will Michael come back to the farm because Glenn's offer forces him to?"

"That wouldn't be right."

"I think there's a little hope, at least," said Matthew.

CHAPTER 24

Ellen had her own fears about flying. She and Matthew had never been on a plane. They had been to the airport several times because James took them there. They always enjoyed the hubbub of people coming and going, and there was a fascination with the planes as they ascended into the skies.

She knew Matthew had dreamed of traveling—of going beyond those hills of home. How would he take to this entirely new means of travel? She wasn't sure how she would react. She hoped that neither of them would become airsick.

Matthew sat by the window. He wanted to see the landscape below. Ellen sat in the middle seat, and a businessman sat in the aisle seat. He was intent on reading his magazine, and his ear plugs told them he was not going to talk.

The doors of the plane closed. The pilot announced take off. The grinding of the engines caused Ellen to experience a new kind of excitement. Matthew sat silent, looking outside at the runway. He had that calm look she always appreciated.

The flight attendant went through her directions. Ellen reached over to check Matthew's seat belt. In minutes they were in the air. Matthew's eyes focused on the landscape below. She could tell he thoroughly enjoyed what he saw.

Matthew pointed out the window. "This is like riding a bus, only you see more scenery."

"You're not feeling any airsickness, are you?"

"No, I never felt better. If I'd known how simple it was to fly, I think I'd have wanted to take a trip a long time ago."

Ellen saw how Matthew kept looking out the window until they were above the clouds. Then, she saw him relax and begin to doze off. This trip would be a good break for both of them.

Several hours later when the plane began to descend, Matthew awakened abruptly. Ellen felt a sharp ringing in her ears.

"We'll soon be in the L.A. airport," she said. "Let's enjoy the family out here and not think about any decisions we have to make."

"We'll leave everything in God's hands. We don't have to make any decision right away anyway. God's plan and timing will be perfect."

Matthew felt himself pushed along as he and Ellen left the plane and entered the terminal. The energy and vitality of the crowd might be exciting, but in that moment he wished he were back among the hills of Oak Ridge. This life was fine for a vacation, but he much preferred his simple life on the farm.

"Corrine wrote that we should go to the baggage claim," said Ellen. "Someone will meet us there."

Matthew balanced his carry-on bag and took Ellen's from her. They walked briskly, following the crowd. The crowd seemed to know exactly where to go.

Strangers were all around them. Matthew would occasionally see a face that he thought looked familiar, but instead it would turn out to be someone who looked like someone he knew back home. He had never experienced such a mass of humanity.

After several elevators and halls and stairs, Matthew and Ellen found their way to the baggage claim area. Their baggage claim turnstiles showed no movement.

"Uncle Matthew! Aunt Ellen! We're here."

Matthew turned to see his favorite niece. Corrine hurried toward him, and he wrapped his arms around her. Warren followed close behind.

Chapter 24

Matthew could not find words to express what he felt. In a sea of strangers were two relatives who were also his friends. A wave of comfort swept over him.

The two couples were soon busy talking and asking and answering questions. In a few minutes the turnstiles moved and bags began to arrive. Matthew and Warren moved up close to the turnstile. This world was a new one for Matthew. Why would people want to live and exist in such crowded conditions? There was too much humanity in close quarters.

Matthew waited impatiently. Most of their fellow passengers collected their bags, but still their bags had not come. Finally, Matthew saw the familiar blue and black suitcases arrive. He supposed their bags went on the plane first; that meant they came off last. One of Matthew's virtues was not only being on time, but being early. Such was the penalty of an early arrival.

As Warren navigated the Los Angeles freeways, Matthew thought of the rolling hills and fields and lakes of home. Though there was something fascinating about this fast-paced city life, he found himself feeling homesick.

The family had already planned Ellen and Matthew's ten-day California vacation. They would stay the weekend with Warren and Corrine. The first gatherings would include Warren and Corrine's children as well as Corrine's sisters and some of their families. Sunday evening, Mary and Ed would come and get them, and they would spend time with them. Then, they would come back and spend time with Martha. Finally, Warren would take them to the airport.

The whole weekend became a time of activity—to Matthew it seemed frantic. Warren and Corrine were the two relatives he knew and loved. But somehow the other sisters and all these great-grandnieces and nephews, the members of the next generation, had the Anderson look. Otherwise, they seemed like strangers.

Something was happening all the time. They were always eating. Whether it was a picnic or lunch or another meal, this was the time the family members gathered. Matthew found it hard to keep track of all the relatives and how they fit together.

During the times in between, Matthew and Warren managed to talk. Matthew wondered how people could be happy in the midst of all the frantic freeway driving and all the hurrying around.

"Are you happy here in California?" asked Matthew. "Don't you miss Minnesota and the kind of life we have?"

Warren didn't hesitate. "We had some hard times in Minnesota, but there were more good times. Yes, I miss the life that I knew so well."

"You drive the freeways like a pro. I don't think I'd want to drive here."

"It takes getting used to."

"Do you really want to stay here the rest of your life? Wouldn't you want to come home?"

Warren scratched his head. "Well, Matthew, it's this way. I'd like nothing better than to go back to Minnesota. But the job's here. And now the kids are all settled around us. And Corrine has her sisters and their families here. It's home to them. I don't know that this place will ever seem like home to me."

"You'll come back to visit, won't you?"

"Yes, but that costs a lot. We hope to come back two years from this summer if we can afford it."

Matthew looked closely at his niece's husband. The man had grown older. Matthew himself was now almost sixty-three. Warren was only ten years younger. Warren's forehead had worry lines, and his hair had turned from brown to gray.

"You realize, Warren, we're not so young. If we put off these trips, we may not see each other again in this life."

"I'm finding it hard to realize I'm as old as I am. My father died when he was two years older than me. I'm not ready for that."

"Life has no guarantees," said Matthew.

This conversation was like many other talks they had had. Matthew came away missing the friend he used to enjoy on a regular basis.

Sunday afternoon, a larger family gathering took place. Mary and Ed drove up from San Diego. There must have been more than thirty people—it was fun, but noise and confusion reigned. However, this was family.

As Matthew and Ellen rode to San Diego with Ed and Mary, everything seemed like old times—at least at first. One big difference was evident: the children were not in the picture. Two of the children, Irene and Jake, now lived in Minnesota, and Beth had her own life.

And their lives were completely different. No longer were the main topics of conversation the various farm problems and the children growing up. Now, Ed was retired, and he was struggling with back problems. And Matthew and Ellen had been through their health problems and now had decisions to make.

As Matthew and Ed talked, the problems surfaced.

Chapter 24

Ed announced, "Mary and I are talking about coming back to Minnesota."

"It would be great to have you back. What about Beth here in California?"

As Ed spoke, Matthew couldn't help noticing how much weaker and older this once robust man looked.

"Beth's busy with her teaching. We hardly ever see her. And she can afford to come home to Minnesota. If we move to Minnesota, we should see Irene and her family. And Jake might even come around."

Matthew repeated himself. "It will be nice to have you home again. We used to be together every week."

"Those were good times."

"Our lives weren't so rushed then," said Matthew. "It seems to me that all you do is rush around here. Fast driving on these freeways. Everything else moves fast."

"You're right. And it takes its toll on us. I don't think she wants me to say anything, but Mary has been diagnosed with cancer, breast cancer. She'll be having surgery after you leave."

For a moment Matthew was stunned. He couldn't quite believe anything could happen to his younger sister. The odds were that he as a man would die before his little sister.

"I don't know what to say. It doesn't seem fair. Mary went through so much with her TB, and now this."

"Sometimes, God makes me very angry!" Ed began raising his voice. "Why does He permit these terrible things to happen to a good person like Mary? I don't understand."

Matthew saw Ed's clenched fist. He wanted to say something, but realized it wouldn't help. "I'm sorry. I don't understand either."

"I wonder," continued Ed, "if God really cares anyway. I wonder if He actually exists."

"Oh, Ed," pleaded Matthew. "He does exist. And He loves us and cares so very much."

"Rubbish!" shouted Ed.

"We're in a fallen world. That's why these things happen. He sees us through whatever trial we face."

Ed grunted.

Matthew wanted to say much more. "I was on the edge of death years ago. You know that. As I was on the edge of eternity, I experienced God's presence. He was there. He would have taken me over if it had been my time."

"You've always been good, Matthew. I'm not you."

"Jesus stands at the door. He invites all of us. He says for us to come unto Him. We labor and are heavy laden. He gives us rest."

"I'll think about it, Matthew."

That ended that conversation. Other talks followed, but Ed avoided anything too personal.

On the evening before they were to leave, Mary suggested to Matthew that they walk down a few blocks to a park. Matthew had longed for a time when they could have such a brother-sister talk.

Matthew could see that Mary was deeply upset. They stopped as they approached the park. "I know about it. Ed told me."

"I didn't want to spoil your vacation. I've known for some time that something was wrong."

"We'll be praying for you."

"Oh, Matthew." Mary's tears began to flow. "I wish we could somehow go back to the way things were. Life was so much simpler. The family was all together."

Matthew took his sister in his arms. "We can't go back. It probably wouldn't be wise. We forget some of those hard times."

"I remember when we were all kids with Mom and Dad. Then, Martha got married and lived nearby. And Victoria and P.J. went to off to school and work. Life was good then."

"Yes, it was," said Matthew. "I believe those were gentler times."

"I recovered from TB. But will I recover from this cancer?"

Matthew wished he knew. "Our lives are in God's hands."

"I believe that. I know that. But Ed is always so angry. Sometimes he seems to blame me. I think he blames God."

"It's not easy for him. And he's not well."

"Do you know what's wrong?"

"It's his back. But I think he's afraid to go to the doctor."

Brother and sister walked on through the park, finally sitting down on a bench near a flower garden.

"Some things don't change," said Matthew. "The flowers. The trees. All of nature."

Chapter 24

"You love the land, don't you? I love the land, too. I wish we were home in Minnesota. I liked California at first because I escaped the Minnesota winters."

"Ellen and I will be happy to have you back home where you belong."

Mary began to reminisce. "Remember some of those crazy things we did as children? Think of the time when I climbed high up on the windmill and was too afraid to come down. You finally talked me into not looking down. And I managed to get to the bottom."

They talked of other adventures and soon were laughing at the antics of childhood.

Mary reached over and took her brother's hand. "We need to do this more often. I needed a talk with you."

"It was about time we did this."

Matthew would long remember these moments with his sister. He kept wondering why life had to become so complicated. But then he realized how normal this was: more people meant life became more complex. And the family had grown and would continue to grow.

The time with Mary and Ed passed quickly. As they said goodbye at Martha's apartment, Matthew felt profound sadness. Would these special people return home? Or would they somehow be lost in this distant state?

Martha had lived many different places. Her personality permeated this small and cozy apartment. As Matthew observed his new surroundings, he saw that there were family pictures crowded everywhere—on the walls or placed in other spots. He recognized an old chest of drawers, the one piece that she had brought from the home place.

"I'm giving you my bedroom. I'll sleep on the davenport. That's what I always do when company comes."

"No," Ellen objected, "you have a pullout bed. Matthew and I can sleep here."

"I'm the hostess," said Martha, "and I won't hear of it."

That settled the matter.

That night, Ellen went to bed early. Matthew and Martha talked late into the night. There were things he could talk about to Martha that he couldn't seem to express to anyone else. In his earliest years she had been like a second mother.

"Matthew, something's bothering you, isn't it?" Martha always seemed to sense her brother's concerns.

"I'm worried about Mary and her cancer. And then Michael hasn't come home for a long time. He's trying to find himself, but I'm not sure he will."

"I know all that," said Martha. "I think there's something more."

Matthew began reluctantly. "I didn't know how much the farm meant to me until I thought about selling it. It's almost as if a part of me is dying. I can't see myself living in town with nothing much to do."

"But, Matthew, do you have to sell? You can live in the house comfortably."

"I think about Ellen. If something happened to me, she'd be out there alone. And if something happened to her, I couldn't stand being out there alone."

"Isn't there some chance that Michael could come home? He always loved the farm."

"It doesn't seem possible now. And Tim Robertson just made a fantastic offer. We have to decide quickly."

"Now, Margaret and Joe have the place that is really the home farm. You could go and live in the little house that Mother lived in."

"Ellen and I don't want to be a burden to our children as we get older. That's not fair to anyone."

Martha began to change the subject: "You know, I sometimes get really homesick for Minnesota and the home area. I wish my family didn't live out here. There are times when I'd like nothing better than to roam the hills of the home place. Or even just walk in the pastures of your farm."

"Why don't you plan for a long visit?"

"I'm afraid money's tight for me. And my girls aren't exactly doing that well financially either. The cost of living here is terribly high."

"Maybe we can figure something out."

"I'm not sure we can, Matthew," began Martha. "I'll be seventy-five in a few weeks. I don't expect to live to be as old as mother. I find it difficult to travel."

"You need to come home. We want you to."

"I'll think about it." Martha glanced away from Matthew. "I know I don't have a strong heart. The doctor confirmed that. I begin to think more about Heaven and home. It's really not so bad to think about dying."

Chapter 24

"Don't say that," said Matthew. "We want you here on earth."

"Sometimes, I'm so tired. There are many things I'd like to do, but I can't. I think of all the friends and family I've lost. My husband. Mother. Dad. My young son years ago—they'd call it a crib death. Two grandchildren. My sister. My brother."

"Your life hasn't been an easy one. You've had more hard times than the rest of us."

"I'm sorry, Matthew, I didn't mean to dampen your spirits. But it's the way I feel. It's what I'm thinking about."

Matthew stood up. "I think it's time we get some rest. I feel guilty about taking your bed for tonight."

"It's wonderful that we've had this time together."

Matthew stooped down and kissed his sister on the cheek. He would long remember their talk.

Family members walked through Matthew's dreams throughout that night.

Two days later, Matthew and Ellen flew back home.

"I've made a decision," said Matthew. "At least it's what I feel is the right way—but only if you feel this is okay."

"Darling, I think I know your decision. And I'm all right with that."

"I think we sell the cows when Lowell's year is over. We can live on the farm and rent out the fields. I'll have plenty to do as it is. And we can arrange to collect Social Security real soon. And then if Michael comes home, we'll still have the farm."

"If or when it's time to move, we'll know the time is right."

As the plane descended, Matthew looked below and saw the plowed fields and brown areas where the snow had disappeared. Spring had arrived.

Matthew turned to Ellen. "I can't wait to get home. I want to do some field work at least one more year."

Matthew felt peace within, but he knew that peace might be challenged.

CHAPTER 25

May 1963

"I think we got it today," announced Matthew as he put the mail on the kitchen table. "Our first Social Security check. That means we're retired." He handed Ellen the letter.

Ellen slit open the envelope. "You're right. Our first retirement check."

This was one of those days that marked a turning point in life. The hard work of the old days on the farm was forever in the past. Matthew and Ellen now faced a future that was far different from anything they had known.

"I'll go into town and deposit the check. Maybe Glenn and I can go for coffee."

"You can go ahead. When you're in town, I'll go over to be with Megan. She wants me to show her how to make my rhubarb pie and rhubarb preserves."

"I'll change clothes for town," said Matthew.

"Dinner's almost ready. About five minutes."

As they sat at the table and ate dinner, Matthew thought out loud. "You know, if we sell those cows we'll have money to do something special. We can stop watching the pennies the way we have all our lives."

"I don't know if I can think any other way. I've always been thrifty. I think I've known how to make the dollar go a long way. I don't think I can change."

"We're not going to change. We can give more to church and missions."

"We're entering a new chapter of our lives. We can sit back and enjoy some of what we've worked hard for. But there's one thing I keep wishing for."

"I know," Ellen paused, "if only Michael would return from that far country of indecision and rebellion."

Matthew delayed his trip into town. Weariness had come over him, so he decided to take his usual afternoon nap. This nap lasted longer than the typical fifteen minutes. Change or decisions about change often bring weariness.

That nap brought Matthew into a dream world, reminding him of the distant past. He was once more a child. His brother P.J. was once more teasing and tormenting. Again, he saw P.J. standing above him and repeating those devastating words: "The farm is mine. I have complete control."

P.J. had been dead more than twenty years. Even so, his deeds lived after him. This brother had changed the course of Matthew's life. The pressures of change had brought Matthew to the edge of eternity, but he had come back. And for twenty-five years he had lived and farmed a bigger and better farm. But now he was on the edge of another decision.

"Matthew," Ellen called. "I thought you were planning on that trip to town. You've napped longer than you intended, I think."

Matthew yawned and sat up, rubbing his eyes. "I had one of those dreams. About P.J."

Ellen picked up her recipe book. "Every time something bothers you, you have nightmares about P.J."

"When I'm tired and weak or when my faith falters, I have the dream. I should know better. The Lord will take care of us."

Ellen smiled. "I'm going over to be with Megan."

Matthew left for town.

Matthew deposited their first Social Security check. He wasn't sure he felt that much security with money. However, it did feel good to be

Chapter 25

getting that monthly check. He and Ellen could live on the farm quite comfortably.

As he left the bank, he heard the familiar voice of Glenn calling. "Matthew, it's time for a cup of coffee and a sweet roll. My treat."

"Sounds good."

Within minutes the two friends were sitting in a booth at the City Café.

Matthew knew Glenn had something else on his mind. As he finished the sweet roll and took a sip of coffee, he decided to be direct. "What's on your mind, Glenn? I have a feeling you want to ask me something."

Glenn cleared his throat. "Yes, but it's more for Tim."

"If he still wants to buy the place, I'm not ready. In fact, Ellen and I are thinking about staying."

"Are you sure? Mabel and I are talking seriously about moving into town."

"If I do decide to move, it would be good to have you here. I'll think about it."

"Tim might be interested in just buying the 120 acres to the west of your farmstead. I think he might make you an offer on that land."

Matthew looked puzzled. "But if he's buying land, why doesn't he buy to the east? That has richer soil and places where there aren't so many hills. That would be a better deal."

"You'll have to ask him."

At that moment Tim walked in. He quickly came over to the booth and sat down beside his father.

"Hello Dad. Hello Matthew. I guess I'll have some coffee, too."

The waitress came over and refilled their cups and poured a cup for Tim. Tim ordered a sweet roll.

"I was just telling Matthew that you might be interested in buying some of his land—the 120 acres to the west."

Matthew repeated what he had said to Glenn about the better land to the east.

Tim replied, "I guess I have a fondness for the land on that side. We've had picnics with you on that land."

Matthew didn't have to think very long. "That's probably the land we'd like to keep. We've even talked about building a cabin down there by the lake."

Tim didn't hesitate. "That would take a lot of money and work. I'm prepared to make a good offer."

"You couldn't go wrong," added Glenn.

The conversation continued, and Matthew felt two guys had ganged up on one—just the way children did back in grade school days.

"If you want to make your offer, I'll talk it over with Ellen and with Margaret and Joe. We talk over everything."

Tim's facial muscles tightened. "The offer's good now. I'm not sure how long I'll keep the offer on the table. I'll be looking elsewhere."

Matthew felt his stomach muscles tighten. That always happened when he felt any kind of pressure.

"I'm offering $30,000. That's half of what I offered for the whole farm. You can't go wrong on that. The offer is generous."

"That's a good offer," added Glenn. "That's more than I would offer, but that's the way my son operates."

Matthew couldn't help wondering. "I'll talk to Ellen." He got up. "Right now, I think it's time to go home."

Tim repeated his offer and added an extra $5,000.

Matthew moved away from Glenn and Tim. Then he turned. "Thank you for the coffee and sweet roll. I'll see you in church."

A few nights later, Matthew and Ellen drove to visit Margaret and Joe and the kids. The kids stayed around to dutifully greet their grandparents and then went off their individual or group ways. A neighbor picked up Matt, now finishing his freshman year, for the freshman-sophomore party at Lake View High School. The others were active in different ways.

As the four sat at the kitchen table, Matthew was ready to tell about Tim's offer to buy land when Margaret brought up some new information.

"I don't know if you've heard the latest," Margaret said, "but apparently Aunt Rita sold their lake place to some Illinois people. She must have done it a few years ago. I always thought Larry would get something from his mother."

Ellen's look told Matthew what she was thinking. "I never liked that place. I won't forget when P.J. had us go into that hidden room. That's where his ill-gotten records and gains were kept. There's something evil about that place."

Chapter 25

Joe, usually slow to speak, surprised Matthew with his words. "It's still an evil place, I'm afraid. The new people moved there. They seem to have lots of parties, and there's a lot of traffic coming and going."

"We're not having a repeat of the Chicago underworld moving in, are we?" asked Ellen. "I thought we were all done with that."

Margaret replied, "I don't think so. The people may not be like people around here, but they're the rich city people having a noisy time. Things will quiet down in a few months."

"I found out something else," added Joe. "Several new houses are being built near P.J.'s place. I've heard that some of these city people are going to live there during the summer."

"And," interrupted Margaret, "I learned that the value of lake property on our lake is going sky-high. We had a realtor approach us about buying our pasture by the lake."

"He offered what seemed a good price, but I know he'd make a bundle of money when he sells lots."

Ellen gave Matthew a knowing glance. "I think you'll find this interesting. Matthew and I have had offers for our farm. At first, Tim Robertson wanted to buy the whole farm. Then, he offered a good price for the 120 acres west of the farmstead, the land near our lake. I'm afraid there are some other motives behind this."

Margaret raised her voice. "You mean Glenn Robertson knew about this? And Tim? I used to think he was a nice guy. I went out with him, and he even asked me to marry him."

Matthew avoided his daughter's gaze. "I feel sad. I can't believe my best friend would be in on anything like this. I'm disappointed."

"At least now we know," said Ellen. "We know why Tim Robertson was so insistent that he should buy those 120 acres."

Matthew stood up. "I'm not ready to sell now. And I won't be ready to sell for quite some time. We have a comfortable home. I'll rent out the land."

"I'm interested in renting, too," said Joe. "Matt might be interested in farming in a few years. And Michael could come back as well."

Matthew looked at Ellen. He knew what she was thinking. "Our minds are made up. We keep the farm. We live there. When we sell, the land will stay in the family."

Joe got up from the table. "Dad, I think the kids would like to show us their 4-H calves and other projects. It's too nice to stay inside."

The remainder of the evening Matthew and Ellen interacted with the grandchildren. "How blest we are," Matthew said to himself.

The next afternoon Matthew had visitors: Glenn and Tim Robertson. They talked of a number of things, but Tim was obviously intent on business.

"This is my final offer," said Tim emphatically. "I've upped the offer twice. You'll be sorry if you don't take the opportunity."

Matthew felt anger and disappointment within. He tried to weigh his words.

"I'm not selling. I understand lake property is becoming quite valuable. But I'm keeping the land in the family."

Glenn looked away, embarrassed. "Maybe that's best."

"Let's go, Dad," said Tim. "We have work to do."

"We'll have coffee next week," added Glenn.

Matthew did not insist that his friend come in for coffee. Their friendship had been strong for years, but now he felt keen disappointment that Glenn would help Tim try to take advantage of his situation.

Matthew felt a need to be alone. He walked down the driveway and across to a lane that led to the east pasture. He went to the highest hill on his property and turned to look in all directions. One moment he was bowed down like an old man. In the next moment, he stood tall as youthfulness and vigor returned.

"I will lift my eyes unto the hills from whence cometh my help. My help cometh from the Lord, who made heaven and earth."

He felt God's presence anew. "Lord, lead me all the way."

Chapter 26

August 1963

Ellen put aside the afghan she had been working on. The sound of a car coming up the driveway announced company.

She smiled as she heard the car come to a sudden stop. "Things haven't changed. That has to be Victoria. As law-abiding as she is, she always drives a little too fast."

Ellen proceeded to the back porch to welcome her sister-in-law.

Victoria briskly got out of her new Buick. Strangers who saw her energetic walk would hardly believe this lady had reached seventy-three. "I've been doing a lot of thinking. I have some ideas I'd like to talk over with you."

Ellen knew that when Victoria had ideas, that meant some kind of action.

In a few minutes Ellen and Victoria were seated at the kitchen table, and Ellen had plugged in her new electric coffeepot.

"Ellen, you look tired."

"It's been a busy summer. I enjoyed having the kids around, but I'm all tired out."

In a tone that sounded sharp, Victoria replied: "Those kids take advantage of you. You do too much work for them when they stay here."

Ellen, annoyed at Victoria's judgment, found herself becoming tense. "No, when the kids come, they do most of the work. And I do things for my children because I love them, and I want to. Give me a few days of quiet and rest, and I'll be back to full strength."

"I do worry about my family."

"We're not as young as we used to be. What do you hear from our California people?"

Victoria cleared her throat. "That's what I came over about. I have good news about Mary. She's doing quite well. But Martha isn't. I'm afraid it's her heart."

"We realized that when we visited her this spring."

"I have an idea. I'm planning to go out to California, and I want to bring Martha back home with me. She's alone in her apartment, and her children aren't around that much. I'd like to have her here, and I'll take care of her. I'll see that she goes to the doctor. We have good doctors here."

"Do you think she'll accept your offer? Will she want to be that far away from her children?"

"Oh, I think she'd come back. She wrote to me how homesick she's been for her home here in Minnesota. And her children think it's a good idea."

"It would be good to have Martha back home. She's been like a second mother to Matthew."

Ellen poured the coffee and reached for a plate of cookies.

Victoria added cream to her coffee and then looked squarely at Ellen. "Something's bothering you. What is it? Is it Michael?"

Ellen checked to see if Matthew was coming. "Yes and no. We haven't heard from him in quite some time, but he said he will come home for a visit. I think he's working hard to make money—probably so he'll buy a fancy car."

"I don't understand that boy."

"I'm concerned about Michael, but I think I'm worried more about Carol and her family. I talked to Mrs. Young. She has some contact with Mrs. Grant, though Mrs. Grant is too high society to spend time in church. It's Jeffrey. Mrs. Grant plays the part of an indulgent grandmother. Some of her indulgence helped destroy her own son's life, and now she's doing the same with her grandson. Jeffrey's been getting into trouble."

"What does Matthew think?"

"This is something I just heard. I haven't told Matthew. He's worried enough about Michael and Carol as it is."

Chapter 26

"I thought Matthew was handling this quite well. He says it's all in the Lord's hands. He seems quite relaxed."

"He's gotten much better at dealing with stress, but this is still stressful. We've decided to stay on the farm, but he wonders about the future. And I think it hurt him that Glenn Robertson would encourage Tim to take advantage of our situation."

Victoria reached across the table and grasped Ellen's hand. "My dear sister-in-law, Matthew is the kindest man in the world. He's so tender-hearted, that's why he gets hurt. Glenn was a real jerk for trying to buy that land."

"It was Tim, but he felt hurt about Glenn's part."

"Let's get back to Jeffrey. It's his grandmother who needs a good talking to. And I'm not afraid to do it."

"Be careful. Carol said she was coming this summer. And Jeffrey is her responsibility. She said she was going to surprise us."

"There's still another week or two." After a quiet moment, Victoria set down the coffee cup with force. "I have two jobs. I shall arrange to get airline tickets to California. I am positive Martha will come back with me. And, second, I shall immediately talk with Mrs. Grant. She has to come to her senses."

"Be careful what you say."

Victoria rose from her chair with great determination and dignity. "I will weigh and consider every word."

Ellen smiled. She wondered what Victoria meant by weighing and considering.

"Thank you, Ellen. I'll let you know what happens." Victoria left in the same brisk manner in which she arrived.

Ellen mused aloud, "There could be some interesting developments in the near future."

The next afternoon, Matthew finished sweeping out the machine shed. He looked with satisfaction at the new combine, which had been put away. A large car with Illinois license plates caught his attention. Immediately, he knew Carol had arrived.

His pace increased as he approached the house. He had long hoped that Carol would actually come for her promised summer visit.

As Matthew entered the kitchen, Carol ran toward him and threw her arms around him. "I've never been so happy to see you."

"We're glad you came." Matthew looked around after they finished their hug. "Where are the kids?"

"Hank and the kids are coming in a few days. I came sooner because we have a problem to take care of. Jeffrey's been in trouble. He wrecked another car."

"Was he hurt?" asked Matthew.

"Fortunately not. Grandma Grant gives him everything and then wonders why he gets into trouble."

"He belongs with his mother," said Ellen. "He needs to go back with you."

"Aunt Victoria told Mrs. Grant in no uncertain terms that he should be with me. In fact, I gather that she really put the old woman in her place. Something that only Victoria could do."

"Did it help?" asked Matthew.

"I'm not sure. I think Victoria's talk made her even more determined to take care of the problem. Otherwise, I think Mrs. Grant might be relieved to have Jeffrey leave. He's getting to be a real handful."

"Teenagers can be that way," said Ellen.

Carol smiled. "I'm afraid I was a handful. I realize now how terrible I was."

"We love you, dear." Ellen led the way into the living room. "Let's sit down and visit. I'll start supper in a few minutes."

Carol began to unburden herself. "I've made so many mistakes through the years. And now my children are suffering the consequences. I've been a bad mother."

Matthew was speechless, surprised at his daughter's words. As Carol tearfully spoke, Ellen tried to comfort her with words of hope. "The children are young. You've changed. They can change."

Carol continued to talk of her children and the ways she hadn't been the right kind of mother. "Mother, I can never be the kind of mother you've been to us. I never realized what wonderful parents I had until now."

"My dear Carol, you can't be me, and I can't be you. God created each of us different. We have to develop our own personalities. My mother was a unique mother; I'm completely different. You need to practice being a mother in your way. And the times and situations are different today."

"I can't do it. I feel as if I'm breaking down and can't go on."

Chapter 26

Ellen's voice sharpened. "Carol, that's not you talking. You've been a strong-willed child from the beginning. Now, give that strength over to the Lord, and use it as a mother. You can do it. I know you're not one to give up."

"Do you really believe that?"

"Yes," Ellen said without hesitation. "I don't know if I dare say this: you and I may be more alike that we realize. I have a very strong will, and it wasn't until I gave the Lord the reins that I became what I am."

Carol began to cry once more, but these tears were different. "I'm sorry, Mother. I'm sorry, Dad, for all the grief I've caused you. Please forgive me."

"Oh, we do, but we've made our mistakes as well."

"And..." Carol faltered, "Lord, forgive me for being the wayward child. Show me how I can change. Show me what I can do."

That evening, Matthew and Ellen and Carol talked of past and present and future. Matthew sensed a closeness that had not existed for years. Under his breath he whispered, "Thank You, Lord."

Late the next morning, Carol and Ellen drove into town. It was no use putting off that meeting with Mrs. Grant.

Ellen dreaded a confrontation with Mrs. Grant. She had never liked the woman. Though the woman had a high position in the Lake View community, she always seemed jealous and critical of the Andersons. Then, later, she had tried to take custody of Jeffrey away from Carol. That showed her to be a formidable enemy.

As they walked up the sidewalk to the Grant mansion, Ellen reminded Carol, "You do the talking. I'm here for moral support."

"I know the Bible says to love your enemy. I am not able to love this enemy. She has been my enemy for years."

Ellen remembered the many encounters. First, Mrs. Grant disapproved of Carol's friendship and marriage to her son. Then, she tried to have Carol declared an unfit mother. And she tried in a host of other ways to make trouble.

Carol pressed the doorbell.

Ellen heard someone moving around inside. There was still no answer.

Carol pressed the doorbell a second time.

The door opened, and Mrs. Grant appeared. "Good morning." Her greeting was cold and formal.

"I came to talk with you and my son." She looked around and saw no evidence of her son's presence. "By the way, where is Jeff?"

"Come in," Mrs. Grant invited. "Jeff had breakfast—he messed up the kitchen—and then he took off on his motorcycle. I don't know where he is."

"I thought you would have grounded him after that last accident. He's had more accidents than most people have in a lifetime."

Mrs. Grant's facial muscles tightened. "You have not done a good job of bringing up that boy. I can't undo your mistakes."

Ellen wanted to speak out in anger, but she remained silent.

Carol looked amazingly calm. "He has not behaved well, but the two wrecked cars happened while he was with you."

Mrs. Grant ignored those words. "Jeffrey Grant would have a position in this community. He is an heir. He needs a good education. I'd like to see him finish his senior year here. He'll settle down when school starts."

"I see no evidence that he will settle down."

"Jeffrey belongs with me. I promised him some advantages—advantages that a person in his position has a right to. "

Ellen and Carol stood patiently as Mrs. Grant continued to talk about all that Jeffrey would gain by staying with her.

When Mrs. Grant's storm of words subsided, Carol spoke. "What about the two wrecked cars? Are you going to give him another?"

"No, he will not be driving for six months at least. Anyhow, the first accident wasn't his fault. I've talked with Jeffrey, and he understands what he has to do."

Carol smiled. "He really has you fooled. Your grandson is as smooth a talker as you'll find anywhere. He can con anyone."

"He'll make a wonderful bank president. I have the power to put him in that position. I am the main stockholder. As it is, I decide who comes and who goes."

Carol held back her words. "What he wants to do with his life is up to Jeffrey."

Mrs. Grant's manner changed suddenly. "I'm sorry; I should invite you in for a cup of tea. I was about to have a cup myself."

Ellen didn't trust Mrs. Grant's new tactics. She waited for Carol to speak.

Chapter 26

"I suppose we could, so long as you understand that Jeffrey is to be with his family on Saturday and in church on Sunday morning. And he will go back to Chicago with us."

"Yes, but what if Jeff won't go with you? What if he decides to stay here?"

Carol smiled a confident smile. "He won't decide to stay with you. Now, let me help you get the tea."

The next hour passed rather pleasantly. The three women talked about a growing and changing community. Discussion about a troubled teenager faded into the background. Ellen felt motherly pride in the way Carol handled herself.

As Ellen and Carol were leaving, Mrs. Grant made an announcement. "I will see that Jeffrey is with you on Saturday morning."

Life is filled with both the expected and the unexpected. That was true of the days that followed. The next day Matthew and Carol walked over the woods and hills and talked of many things. It seemed as if those many years between had faded away. And yet he saw Carol as a mature and beautiful woman.

Carol broke off a piece of goldenrod. "Sometimes, I wish I could go back. I remember the way it was when I went to our little rural school. Life was so simple. I think the goldenrod reminds me of that time."

"We've had a good life here. Your life seems so busy and complicated compared to ours here at Oak Ridge."

"Our lives have gotten out of hand." Carol brushed her long light brown hair aside. "Something happened that's changing everything."

For a moment Matthew feared what Carol was about to say. "Is something wrong?"

"Well, yes and no. Hank's been working awfully hard. The doctor took a look at his blood pressure and checked his heart. The doctor warned him to slow down and take care of himself, or he might not be around much longer."

"But Hank isn't even forty."

"He'll be forty next year." Carol stopped talking as they approached a pond. "I see something. It's one of the blue flowers—a gentian I believe. I love these, but they never last when you pick them."

Carol stooped down to look closely at the flower.

Matthew knelt and touched the flower. "They're meant to be enjoyed in their natural habitat. I think that's the way it is with people. They are best off in their natural home—their natural habitat."

"Oh, Dad, I've been missing so much. And when you see Hank, you'll realize that he's trying to change. We've had some serious talks. Hank is taking medication. It's been hard, but he's delegated many of his responsibilities to others. And, already, life is better."

"How about the kids? How are they taking this?"

"They're seeing more of us. We're doing things together. They like it. That is, all except Jeffrey. He's in that rebellious stage—you and Mom know that."

"That can be a hard age." Matthew remembered all too well what Carol was like at seventeen.

"I guess I wasn't that great. I caused you lots of grief. And Jeffrey may be a lot like me." Then she smiled. "Apples don't fall far from the tree."

Matthew laughed.

"Hank and I have changed. Now we go to church every Sunday. Nicholas and Nicole are in Sunday School, and they like it. We've even gotten Jeffrey to go to the youth group meeting once in a while."

"The Lord is in the business of changing lives."

Carol drew back. "Yes, but we'll take it one step at a time."

Matthew wanted to say more. At the same time he wished these moments would last. There was enough of autumn in the air to remind him of the changing seasons.

Father and daughter stood silently by the pond. Some beef cattle grazed nearby. They could hear a few grasshoppers in the vegetation.

Matthew missed the days when the children were all with him—when they all lived in the safety of home. But this was life. Children became adults; they had their own lives to live. They moved away, sometimes far away. They established their own homes. Oh, how he wished Carol were nearby so that he could see her changed life and appreciate those grandchildren.

Matthew reached out and picked a cattail. "The seasons are changing. Autumn is all around us. And the seasons of life are changing as well."

"Dad, I didn't realize you were a poet."

"I'm not. But life has its seasons. Your mother and I are moving into another season. Autumn is beautiful."

Carol snuggled up to her father. "Dad, I love you."

Chapter 26

The weekend became a hubbub of activity. Johnie and his children drove home to Oak Ridge on Saturday. James and Ruth and their three also came for the day, as did Margaret and Joe and their six children. Victoria joined the family, as did Larry and Joan and their girls, along with Lowell and Megan and their little boy. It was a day of confusion and delightful family togetherness.

Mrs. Grant kept her promise and brought Jeffrey to his mother. Though he was sullen at first, he gradually joined in with the games and other family activities.

One family tradition was a softball game. Matthew and Ellen and Victoria sat back and watched the younger generations play.

"My how life changes, but it remains the same," observed Victoria. "I remember a generation ago when Mom and Dad sat back and watched us as we played with your children and Mary and Ed's. It was a different world then."

"Those were good times, but life goes on," said Ellen.

Matthew picked at a blade of grass. "Sometimes, I think I'd like to go back."

Ellen quickly responded. "My dear, we forget the hard times we went through. The storms. All the uncertainties. Those we forget."

Matthew remembered the struggles only too well.

"By the way," asked Ellen, "how was your visit with Mrs. Grant? Carol and I visited her. She was rather unfriendly at first, but then her tone changed."

Victoria straightened herself. "Well, I said plenty. I reminded her of Jeffrey's dad and his wildness and drinking back when Carol married him. I was rather direct. I spared no words."

That was typical Victoria, thought Matthew.

"I think she had it coming," said Ellen. "I think that talk helped. Jeff is out there playing with the rest of his cousins, and I think he's enjoying it."

"Somehow," Matthew mused, "I wish Michael were here. Then the family would be complete."

And so the day and the Sunday that followed passed all too quickly.

CHAPTER 27

September 1963

Matthew always hated saying goodbye. Carol and Ellen were having their personal talk together. Nicholas and Nicole had to make their last visit to play with the kittens. Even seventeen-year-old Jeffrey wanted to play with the dog they called Sport.

Matthew helped his son-in-law Hank Stevens put luggage into the two cars. Hank didn't seem anxious to leave.

"Matthew," Hank began, "I can't tell you how much I've appreciated this weekend. Now I understand the kind of woman and family I married. I thank you."

"We're glad that we had this chance to get to know you. It's the first time we've really had time with you."

"I'm afraid that's been my fault. I have to be honest: at first I wasn't sure I wanted to meet you. Then, I was always too involved with the business. Long work hours. I never quit. But I've learned some lessons."

"Carol told us."

"The realization that I could have died or could die at any moment gave me something to think about. I began to take a different look at life and what's most important."

Hank paused. Matthew waited for him to go on.

"My dad died when he was forty-nine years old. Mom lived only a few years after that. At the time I was too busy to spend time with them. I had my work. I was serious about getting ahead. Now, I realize what my dad was saying. He was trying to tell me that he'd missed something in his life."

Hank looked down, avoiding Matthew's gaze.

Matthew motioned for his son-in-law to sit down on the lawn. "Let's be comfortable. It's good to talk about these things."

The two men sat in the shade of the old oak tree.

"The last time I saw my father in the hospital, he kept saying there's got to be more to life than just this work. There's got to be more."

"Is that when he died?"

"He died about a week later. He was a strong man. I thought he'd be home in a few days. In fact, the doctors said he could go home in a day or two. I've felt guilty ever since about not going to see him again."

"I'm sure your dad understood."

"But there's something more. Dad and Mom were brought up in the church, but they drifted away. They sent me to Sunday School and confirmation. They thought I should have some religion, but they were never involved. I didn't rebel until later. Then, I wanted nothing to do with the church. I didn't feel God was important."

Once more, Matthew waited for Hank to go on.

"I realize now I've been missing something. I don't find the reality of God in a lot of churches, but I felt some of it in your Oak Ridge Church."

Matthew prayed for wisdom in knowing what to say. "God is a personal God. He reveals himself through Jesus Christ. That comes down to a personal relationship."

"That's what I've been looking for. That's what I need."

Matthew saw the intensity in Hank's eyes. He meant business.

"It is so simple; yet so deep—so profound. For me it began when I truly acknowledged I was a sinner and couldn't make it on my own. When I was at death's doorstep, I asked Him to come into my life and to show me the way. My life was never the same after that."

"Could that happen to me? You have what I need. Ellen has it, and so many other Andersons seem to have that special something."

Matthew never wanted to be pushy. "Why don't you ask Him?"

"I've never been much of a praying man—except when I thought I was going to die. Then I sent up some desperate prayers."

"You can ask Him."

Chapter 27

Hank paused a moment and then bowed his head. Matthew didn't know what he was praying, but he sensed the depth of the prayer. Only the final words were audible. "Lord, guide me."

Matthew stood, placing his hands on Hank's shoulders. "Lord, You've heard Hank's prayer for help. Guide and direct him. Grant him a safe journey home. Be with him and Carol and each of the children. I ask this in Your precious name. Amen."

Hank stood up. "I feel different."

For the first time Ellen saw her daughter as a mature woman. "Carol, I'm glad we had this time together. I understand much better what you've been facing."

"I've made some mistakes, but I think we're getting on the right track." She looked out the window to see her father and husband deep in conversation. "I'm surprised Hank hasn't been hounding us to leave. And the kids must be busy, or they would have been itching to leave, too."

"Let me put together a package of cinnamon rolls. You can lunch on the way back."

At that moment a car came up the driveway at an unusually high speed. Instantly, Ellen knew who it was.

"Someone sure is driving here fast." Carol looked out the window. "It's Aunt Victoria. She never changes. She still drives too fast."

Ellen placed the cinnamon rolls in a small box, and she and Carol went outside.

Victoria got out of her car and called out: "I wanted to come over and say goodbye. I didn't get to do that when we were together."

By this time Jeffrey and Nicholas and Nicole appeared.

"Hello, Aunt Victoria," greeted Carol. "We're almost ready to leave. We should have been on the road an hour ago."

"No rush," interrupted Hank, "Matthew and I have been having a good talk. So what if we get back late in the evening?"

Hank and the children greeted Victoria. Ellen noticed that Jeffrey respectfully said hello to his grand aunt.

Victoria motioned to Carol and Ellen and drew them aside. "Carol, I wanted to say a few words to you. I'm sorry if I was harsh with you and your mother-in-law."

Ellen noted the surprise in her daughter's face.

"Aunt Victoria, you did the right thing. Yes, I've made some mistakes. And Mrs. Grant needs to be put in her place."

"I may have butted in where I shouldn't have. I want you to know how much I love you, and I want what's best for you."

Carol placed her hand gently on her aunt's shoulder. "My dear Aunt Victoria, I should have paid more attention to you long ago. You tried to get me on the right track, but I was stubborn."

Ellen couldn't help noticing how Victoria's reserve was breaking down.

Victoria's words came out quietly and slowly. "I was a teacher and a principal for so many years that I have some habits that are hard to break. I'm afraid I come across as a bit brusque and bossy. It's been my way."

Victoria, tall with graying dark hair, looked suddenly older. The woman who had stood tall and straight for so many years now did not stand so straight.

Ellen was about to say something, but Carol spoke first. "Aunt Victoria, we knew you loved us. You were always around to help and encourage us."

Ellen witnessed something she had not seen before. Victoria was shedding tears. The stern school teacher reserve had broken down. Carol moved slowly into her aunt's arms. A thirty-five-year-old woman and a seventy-plus-year-old woman experienced a connection that rarely happened.

Through her tears Victoria spoke, "My dear Carol, you have truly come home. You are home in spirit, no matter where you live."

Carol backed away slowly and walked toward her car. "Yes, I've come home. And it hasn't been until now that I realized how much my family means to me—how much home has meant."

"Don't get all mushy now, Mother," interrupted Jeffrey. "We're supposed to be in school tomorrow."

Carol wiped her eyes and turned to her son. "Someday you'll understand these things. I'm not usually this way."

The next minutes were filled with laughter and tears as each individual said goodbye to the others. This was the first time in all these years that Carol and her family had taken time to say goodbye. They usually rushed away with only a few departing words.

Ellen watched as the two cars went down the driveway. Whenever the children left home, she felt their absence. At the same time she experienced a joy that Carol had returned home in spirit.

Chapter 27

"Come," Ellen turned to Matthew and Victoria. "Let's go in. We'll have an early dinner."

"And afterwards," added Matthew, "let's go for a ride. There's a hint of autumn, and the scenery is beautiful."

Matthew loved the evenings of early September. He gazed at those hills as he had so many times before. He thought of what lay beyond. He had been to California. He and Ellen would be going to Chicago. But was there anything more beyond those hills that he could not find here? The only lack he felt was the absence of his children.

Matthew, Ellen, and Victoria had gone for a long ride through the hills of the Oak Ridge area. He never tired of looking at those familiar places. When they returned, he had gone out to the barn to help Lowell with the milking and other chores. Somehow that occupation brought him back to the realities of life.

As he looked at the large healthy dahlias near the house, he observed that the most beautiful blooms came before the frost. "Does that happen in the lives of human beings?" he mused. "Can we produce some of the most beautiful flowers during our final years?"

Matthew had been thinking more about this last phase of life. After all, he was sixty-three. His father had died at seventy-seven. Ma had been ninety-four. There were no guarantees, but there was a good chance that he had several more good years ahead. What should he do with that time?

After their drive and supper, Victoria had stayed and visited. It seemed she had a need to talk and be with family. She and Ellen were now busy talking about those matters women talk about.

The shadows of evening deepened. Matthew heard the crickets and cicadas. These creatures were always at their loudest this time of year. It was almost as if they made the loudest appeals as their lives were about to close.

The lights in the house beckoned him. He hastened to the back porch as a cool breeze reminded him of the changing season.

The women greeted him.

"You must have been enjoying this early autumn weather," said Victoria. "This is my favorite time of the year."

Matthew smiled. "That's because school starts."

"Yes," Victoria replied, "and in some ways I miss the challenge of another school year. I miss the other teachers, and I miss contact with the students. Yet, there is so much hard work, and I was getting older, so I knew it was time to retire."

Matthew began to sit down. "Aren't we all getting older?"

"Come, Matthew," said Ellen. "Let's go to the living room. Victoria has something she wants to talk with us about."

Matthew had thought something was up.

Matthew settled into his easy chair while Ellen and Victoria sat on the davenport. He waited for Victoria to speak.

"I've been doing a lot of thinking." Victoria seemed to be looking at him, but far beyond. "I'm not young anymore. I'm ten years older than you. I want my life to count for something."

"Victoria, you've had a tremendous influence on thousands of kids. Your accomplishments are something you can be proud of."

"I'm not thinking about the past. I'm thinking about the present and the future. I want to do something for the next generations."

Once more, Matthew waited for his sister to go on.

"I've been thinking about your grandchildren. They face a completely different world. I'd like to help them have a better start. Now, I've lived frugally all my life. Except for some traveling these past years, I have never spent much. Actually, I've accumulated a substantial nest egg."

Victoria's substantial nest egg was not a surprise to Matthew. Though she had always been generous with gifts for the children, he knew she watched carefully where her money went.

"Many of your grandchildren will go on to college or get some other type of education. I want to help them in that way. But if Matt decides to farm, I want to help him get a start in the farming business. What I am saying is that I want to help establish those children so that they have a good life."

"That's wonderful that you would do this," said Matthew.

"I've established a trust fund. I have made some specific recommendations about the distribution. If something happens to me, I want you to carry out those wishes."

Matthew didn't hesitate. "Ellen and I are grateful for all that you're doing."

"There's something else I want to do. I remember our childhood and the way things were. I'm starting to write down those memories. There are things that the children will find interesting after I'm gone. And I think of all our other family members—that is, our cousins and other distant relatives. I want to tell how they're related so the next generations will know they have these connections back here."

"That's an ambitious project," said Ellen. "I've started to write some notes about my life and my family. At least James is interested."

"There's so much I'd like to ask Pa if he were here," said Matthew. "He never talked much about the old country. I wish I knew more about his life before he came to America."

"I found out a few things," said Victoria. "I'm writing them down, but it was almost as if Dad and other pioneers put that part of their lives far behind them. They wanted to forget the separation and hardships."

"They had a hard life in the old country." Then, Matthew added, "We've got it pretty good here. We live like kings."

Victoria began to reminisce. "I think about Lucille. I remember the last time we talked."

Matthew couldn't help remembering his reactions to Lucille's death. For a long time he had doubted the goodness of God. How could God permit a good person like Lucille to suffer and then die? God didn't seem fair.

Victoria's dark blue eyes displayed a faraway look. "She knew her time was short, but she wanted desperately to live. I think a young man by the name of Bill had been interested in her, and she wanted the love she had to go to him and to their children. But that was not meant to be. I shall always remember the peace that she had about her. During that last talk, she said she had finally come to forgive all those who had wronged her. And she had asked forgiveness from all she had wronged."

Matthew discovered he had thoughts and feelings that had long since been relegated to a past life. Lucille became very much alive in his mind. "Lucille was one of the kindest people I've ever known."

"I never knew Lucille when she was alive," said Ellen, "but her influence has lived on long after her death."

Another thought came to Matthew. "It's so important to live at peace with all men. Scripture tells us that. I think of Michael. I keep praying that he'll come back to us."

"That's been hard for you, hasn't it?" Victoria's words showed more and more of the softness and kindness that had not been evident before.

"Somehow, I wish those accidents and problems had never taken place. But one can't undo what's past. I think we may have expected too much of Michael. We always felt he would follow in Johnie's footsteps."

"You can't blame yourself, brother."

"I know I have to make something else right." Matthew fidgeted. "I have to talk with Glenn. We've been friends too long to let anything come between us."

"He tried to take advantage of you." Victoria's sharp tone told Matthew his sister defended him. "If you had sold that land, you would have lost thousands of dollars."

"Glenn was trying to help his son."

Their talk of people and situations continued late into the night. Ellen convinced Victoria to stay the night and go home in the morning.

Thoughts of the day followed Matthew until he slept. Sometime that night or early morning, Matthew resolved to take action.

Chapter 28

Though Matthew had decided to act, he discovered there were delays. He had wanted to visit Glenn, but discovered Glenn and Mabel had gone on a short trip. He had decided to visit Michael in person, but found out that his son had moved on to a better job.

"There is reason for delay," thought Matthew aloud. "I wasn't ready to talk to either Glenn or Michael. I might have said something unwise. I need to speak cautiously and carefully."

It was on one of those sunny September days with a hint of cool crispness in the air that Matthew decided to drive into town. He needed to have the oil changed in his car, and that might mean a visit with Larry, his favorite nephew.

Larry's service station had grown from a one-man operation to a bigger station with several men working. The two men working for Larry could take care of everything.

"Uncle Matthew, do you have time to come into my office? I'd like to talk with you about something."

"Sure, I'd like that." Matthew couldn't help wondering if there was something special happening.

Larry closed the door. "How about some coffee?"

Matthew wondered if all this coffee was good for a person. "I'll take half a cup."

Larry poured the coffee into a "Larry's Garage" cup. "How is Lowell working out at your farm? He seems to like what he's doing."

"He's doing a great job. I'm just wondering how long he'll want to stay."

"That's part of what I wanted to talk about. He's beginning to feel it's time for him to go back to school and finish his degree. What he's doing now is good experience, but he'd like to be in one of those farm management programs or related research. He's looking to the future."

"Farming isn't what it used to be. You have to go into something in a big way, or you can't make a good living. But it's been a good way of life for me." Matthew almost hated to ask the next question. "How long is he planning or willing to stay?"

"He's willing to stay through next spring or summer, but after that he wants to move on."

"I can understand how he feels."

"But, Uncle Matthew, there's something else on my mind. This is a matter for prayerful concern. It might come as a surprise to you."

"This doesn't sound good."

"Oh, you don't have to get upset or concerned. It's something that means a big change for me."

A phone call interrupted at this point. Larry arranged for a tow truck to be sent out for a stranded motorist. Matthew could see why Larry's business had grown. This nephew had become a dependable and reputable businessman.

"You've made me curious."

"During these past months, I've been struggling with some questions. My business here is highly successful, but I've been having the feeling that the Lord has something else for me to do."

"Your work here at this service station is a real ministry. You've kept some of these young men from going in the wrong direction. You've made a place for them to hang out. They've come to know the Lord, and you've helped train some good mechanics."

"That work will go on." Larry looked down at a sheaf of papers and held up an application. "I have an application for work at the state prison."

"Why would you want to work there?"

"Uncle Matthew, I spent time in jail and in prison. I learned some serious lessons. You and Grandma helped me. And a prison worker and a volunteer showed me the way to go. There are hundreds of young men who need a turn-around experience."

Chapter 28

Matthew began to realize what his nephew was saying.

"I've become aware of some of the opportunities in prison work. I might be a prison guard, but I can be much more than that."

"That would mean moving. What about Joan and the girls?"

"Lisa is a senior. If we move sooner, she'll stay here for her senior year. Lorraine is fifteen, and she doesn't seem to mind the idea of moving. In fact, she's excited about it."

"I do understand," said Matthew. "I'll miss you, and I'll miss Lowell when he moves on."

"If I get the job, we'll only be a hundred miles away. I'll be close to James. James will be at the college, and I'll be at the prison. Interesting, isn't it?"

Matthew smiled, but felt a sadness about the changes. "I'm finding once more that life is filled with change. I'm not sure I like all these changes. I'd like to keep people close to home."

"We'll always come home. People have a way of coming home, don't they?"

Matthew realized a profound truth. "Yes, home is like a magnet. We return to those we love most."

He couldn't help wondering if that magnet would draw all his children and friends back to the fold.

As Matthew left the garage, a familiar voice called, "Matthew, it's time for lunch. How about coffee and a roll at the bakery?"

The voice belonged to Glenn. He was back from his trip, and now Matthew had his chance to talk with his friend.

Matthew had long wondered what he would say to Glenn. How could a fellow approach his best friend about the wrong he had done? Did Glenn even feel he had done anything wrong? Anyhow, he had to clear the air, or at least tell Glenn why he felt as he did.

After the walk to the bakery and the usual talk about weather and cattle and crops, Glenn changed the subject. He put down his jellied roll. The man whose face and demeanor usually displayed confidence now showed hesitation and timidity.

"We've been friends a long time." Glenn paused a moment. "I'm afraid I've taken you for granted. And I've taken a lot of other things for granted."

"I've done the same. But I'm realizing that life sometimes changes fast. Ma died a year ago, and Martha isn't doing so well."

"Families and friends drift apart," added Glenn. "It happens, and we don't even realize it's happening."

Matthew nodded in agreement. He wanted desperately to speak his own concern, but Glenn seemed determined to go on.

"Matthew, I have something that's bothered me, and I know it's bothered you. It's what Tim did. I didn't realize all that he had in mind. He thought he could buy your land and make some quick money."

Matthew avoided the gaze of his friend. "I felt hurt. I couldn't believe you would take advantage of a friend that way."

"I'm sorry, Matthew. I didn't completely realize what my son was up to. These kids get ideas. If I'm honest, right now I don't trust my son. Something's happened to him. He's become a different kind of person."

"I guess that's the way the world is today."

"It was wrong for me, a friend, to do what I did. I knew your land would be a good investment for Tim, but I didn't realize what he had in mind."

"There's something Pa used to say. 'Beware of selling land to friend or family member.' That can mean trouble. And I can't help thinking of P.J. and the way he stole the farm. He was desperate to claim that ownership."

"Matthew, I can't tell you how sorry I am. I did wrong, but Tim is making an idol of money and property. Even though he's pushing toward forty, I need to get after him. He'll hurt himself and others."

"I begin to understand." Matthew looked across the room at the other customers. "We try to help our children. And sometimes we can't help them. We just have to let them make their own decisions—and their own mistakes."

"I don't know that I can sit idly by and let Tim take advantage of others. He'll soon get a bad reputation. And that could be my fault."

"Yes," said Matthew, "we do have an obligation to speak up when our children do wrong. But there's no way we can control their choices."

"I will never again let something like a land deal or anything else hurt our friendship. I promise."

Chapter 28

Matthew extended his hand. "Agreed. Doing what is right comes first."

The two men sat in silence for a few moments.

Glenn broke the silence. "I've been uneasy about many things. This cold war with Russia isn't over. The Berlin Wall. The so-called hot line between Washington and the Kremlin. It doesn't make sense. A telephone line won't stop a war!"

"Lots of things don't make sense."

"I don't understand what's happening in the South. I can't help admiring Martin Luther King. If we truly lived as Christians, his dream would come true. We'd look at one another and not judge on the basis of skin color or nationality."

"Not everyone is lucky enough to be Swedish." Matthew's face broke into a big smile. "It might not be good if we were all Swedish."

Glenn let out a hearty laugh. "I hadn't thought of it that way. We seem to be quite a mixture of people here in Lake View and in the area. Norwegian. Swedish. German. English. And quite a few other nationalities. Even several blacks over in River Falls."

"It comes down to relationship, doesn't it? We have our differences, but we get along."

"Some of those families over toward Prairie Center aren't so great. They drink a lot and get into fights. Their Saturday night dances are rather wild."

"They've always been that way. All we can do is live and speak and act in a way that we feel is right."

"Matthew, you should have been a preacher."

Matthew chuckled. "Hardly. I didn't even finish eighth grade."

"You have such a strong faith. I feel weak compared to you."

"It's not my faith that's important. It's Christ. I keep getting to know Him better."

"I know, but there are times when He seems far away."

"That happens to all of us. I know then that I'm the one who moved. Not Him."

Matthew returned home that afternoon, feeling his friendship with Glenn was secure.

"Rest in the Lord. Wait patiently for Him." Those words kept repeating themselves in Matthew's mind.

That evening, Matthew related the events of the day to Ellen—his talk with Larry as well as his talk with Glenn. "I guess I haven't been very patient. And I can see God took care of everything in His own time. Now, I keep hoping that something will happen with Michael."

"There's nothing to do except pray and wait."

"I have the feeling that something is going to happen soon."

"You mean about Michael."

"Yes, but I may feel that way because I desperately want for it to happen. But so much is happening. I feel there's something more. Something even bigger."

"God has a way of preparing us for what we have to go through."

"I don't know if I'm ready."

Matthew's uneasiness increased. That night was filled with nightmares. P.J. once more made his appearance. He tormented Matthew just the way he had done when Matthew was a child. His sisters appeared in that nightmare, and they were calling for help.

That morning the nightmares faded. Matthew forgot the details, but he remained uneasy.

Several days later his uneasiness was confirmed. Two separate events or messages reminded Matthew how quickly life could change.

At mid-morning when Matthew and Ellen were having their coffee break, a car came up the driveway at high speed. There was no need to guess who was arriving. Victoria walked briskly to the back porch and let herself in.

"Matthew, Ellen, I have some serious news."

Matthew greeted his sister. Ellen motioned for her to sit down.

"It's Martha. She had a heart attack last week. She can't go back home. She needs someone to take care of her, or she may need to go to a nursing home."

Typically, Victoria didn't wait for questions or response.

"I'm going to California," she announced. "Martha wants to come back here, and it seems her girls feel that I can take care of her—and the nursing home is better here. She wants me to come and get her as soon as possible. And I'll drive out because there is stuff she wants brought back."

"But, Victoria," said Matthew, "do you plan to drive to California all by yourself? I don't think that's a good idea."

"Matthew, I'd like for you to come with me. I need help to get Martha back home."

Matthew stumbled over his words, not sure what he should say or think. "That's happening awfully fast."

Ellen didn't seem to hesitate. "Matthew, if you feel it's okay to go, I can stay here by myself. I'll be just fine. Lowell and Megan are close by."

Victoria looked to her brother for his answer.

Matthew always liked to think something through carefully. "This is sudden. There are things here I should do. I was going to do some more plowing."

Ellen reminded him, "Lowell has everything under control, and he can do the plowing."

Victoria added, "Matthew, you enjoyed California. You can use a vacation."

"Go ahead," said Ellen. "And Victoria needs you to be there with her."

Matthew knew the decision had been made. "I guess I can go."

Victoria stood up. "We'll leave tomorrow. Bright and early."

Matthew gulped. This was faster than he had anticipated.

The second event of the day came just before noon. As was his custom, Matthew went to the mailbox. The mail brought a letter from Johnie. This letter would be Johnie's reply to Ellen's weekly letter.

As they finished the meal, Ellen cut open the letter. It was always the custom that Matthew would sit back and enjoy the communication as Ellen read it aloud.

Ellen's surprised look told Matthew that this was not an ordinary letter.

"I think we're in for a bit of news." Ellen began to read: "I finally managed to catch up with Michael and visit with him. I thought of calling you, but then thought it best to write down the essence of our visit. We must continue to pray.

"Michael seems to harbor a kind of resentment against me. He thought you always compared the two of us, and he felt that he never measured up and could never measure up. I told him how wrong he was. He was a much better student than I—I was a rascal when I was in high school. I never saw the sense of school until the Lord nudged me about becoming a minister.

"I believe some mending of fences took place. We talked for hours. Though he has this high-paying job in construction, his first love is farming. That's what he wants to do. But he feels he must do this on his own. He wants to prove himself."

Matthew couldn't help interrupting. "He doesn't have to prove himself. He can come back here. I'd give him the farm."

Ellen put down the letter. "Matthew, dear, that's exactly what he doesn't want. Remember how great you felt when you bought this farm on your own? That's what our son wants."

Tears came to Matthew's eyes. "I miss that boy. I'd give anything to see him. I wish so many things had never happened."

"We can never go back." Ellen went on reading, "There is another interesting development. Michael has a girlfriend. She comes from a farm in eastern Minnesota. I met her briefly and she seems very nice. I think Michael is serious about her. She is an elementary school teacher and the same age as Michael.

"Michael has turned around with respect to the drinking and wild parties. But now he is equally determined to prove himself in a different way. I think I understand what he's going through, but he doesn't understand forgiveness and grace. But now I must close, so that the letter gets in the mail."

Matthew had a sudden desire to go outside. "Ellen, I need to think about this. You need to write to Michael and tell him how we feel."

"Yes, Johnie sent his address. I know that you need to walk and think. I'll write the letter and encourage him to come home for a visit."

Matthew lost track of time as he walked through the woods toward the lake where so many family gatherings had been held. There were moments when he felt he heard the laughter of the children and the conversation of the adults. He recalled how Ma and Pa had enjoyed being together with the family in this very spot.

Matthew looked at the still blue September water. He stooped down to look closely at the dark blue gentian. This flower brought together the best of September. The yellows and reds of the trees seemed to shout praises to the Creator. God's presence brought a peace to Matthew that passed all human understanding.

"I can face all the changes that I need to face," he said aloud. "The Lord will guide me through it all."

He turned from the beauty of the lake and the gentian and looked to the trees and the hills.

Matthew wanted to shout the words: "I lift my eyes to the hills. My help comes from the Lord, who made heaven and earth."

CHAPTER 29

October-November, 1963

Life's been moving too fast," announced Matthew to Ellen on a mid-October day. "I feel as if I've been on a merry-go-round that's out of control."

"Go. Take a walk. You need to relax."

And that is what Matthew did. He needed to think about and place the many happenings of the past month in perspective. Things had happened so fast, he felt he was once more a student who couldn't quite keep up with his fellow students. He walked west toward the lake. That was always a place to think. He began to review the happenings of the past month.

The trip to California had been a whirlwind trip. Victoria did most of the driving in her Lincoln, a rather fancy car in Matthew's estimation. A state trooper pulled her over once for exceeding the speed limit. She managed to charm the young man out of giving her a ticket. Victoria had a way of moving fast in whatever she did. Anyhow, Matthew wasn't used to city driving, and he hated that kind of driving.

The words of the doctor kept ringing in Matthew's ears: "Your sister has recovered remarkably well. However, her heart is not good. She could live for years. But if there is stress or too much excitement, she could die quickly. Your quieter life in Minnesota may lengthen her life."

What the doctor said and didn't say gave both hope and warning. Martha, who had been like a second mother, was the sister he wanted around the rest of his days. Seventy-five didn't seem old when he thought of his mother's ninety-four years.

The three days in California were filled with hectic activity. Martha's three girls and their children and grandchildren visited at Corrine and Warren's, the home where everyone gathered. Matthew had a hard time keeping track of all those nieces and nephews. The family had grown and couldn't help drifting apart.

Matthew had somehow thought these family members and the generations that followed would always be close. That closeness seemed impossible with this part of the family three thousand miles away. But that's what happened with families. They drifted apart with their new families and concerns.

The trip back was largely uneventful. They stayed in motels three nights. This time Matthew did more driving. Victoria seemed tired out, and she was busy seeing that Martha was taken care of and comfortable.

Martha survived the trip amazingly well. In Lake View under the care of Victoria, she regained much of her strength. Matthew wanted to hope for the best, but underneath he felt a gnawing uncertainty.

"Lord, I commit Martha to You. Keep her from hurt and pain. If You call her Home, she will be far, far better off, but I will miss her."

Peace drifted over him. As he walked along the shore, he began to dream. There were many spots here that would be perfect for a cabin. They could move a trailer home down here, and the family could come here and spend time each summer. That would simplify life in so many ways. The family could continue to gather for picnics in this special place.

"I hate to think of selling the farm, but I'm afraid it's the way we have to go eventually. I don't have the strength and energy to take care of all these things. We can keep this lake property for the family."

Matthew remembered an episode almost two years ago. One of those Minnesota blizzards had blocked them in. Fortunately, they had electricity, but Matthew had become ill. The chores had to be done. Matthew, with Ellen's help, had managed to do all that was necessary. In no way would it have been possible to get to the doctor.

It was Ellen who had said firmly, "We shouldn't be way out in the country at this point in our lives. We need to move to town. There's no question about that."

Chapter 29

Winter would soon come. This year, Lowell and Megan would be nearby. But after that, they would be alone. Matthew dreaded their move, but he knew it needed to come.

The sun that had shone brightly disappeared under a cloud. A cold breeze blew, reminding Matthew of approaching winter. The trees, except for the red oaks, were bare of leaves. Suddenly, life seemed empty and cold.

Turning away from the lake, he began walking home. Would he ever feel at home away from the country? The question plagued him as he looked around at all of the familiar places.

October would soon be over. Matthew thought of the winter that loomed before him. The prospect of the winter chores bothered him. Everything would have been fine, but Lowell made a sudden decision to attend university classes two days a week. That left Matthew with all the chores during those days.

"I don't think this arrangement with Lowell is working out." Ellen put away the last of the supper dishes. "When Lowell is away, you're working harder than ever."

"I hate the thought of the winter chores."

"It's alright that you help out," continued Ellen, "but Lowell needed a place to live and some income. He agreed to take over all the farming, but he's backed out of part of that."

"I hate to back out. It's been tough for him. He needs to take those classes at the university."

"Matthew, it's not fair to you in any way."

"I thought we could hang on to the cattle and the farming in case Michael came back. But that doesn't seem likely now."

"We need to move forward. You're not going to stay here and work yourself to death. You're not young anymore."

Matthew knew Ellen was right. "It's useless to keep on with all this work. We can live here a few years more and then sell and move to town."

"Finally, you see the light."

Beyond This Home

This final Saturday of October was gray. Ellen missed the activity of family. All of the family members seemed busy, going their own ways. She decided to bake a batch of chocolate chip cookies. Perhaps someone would drop in.

A gentle knock interrupted her baking and reverie.

Before she could open the door, a man opened it and entered.

"Mother, I'm home."

Ellen threw off her apron and rushed to him. "Michael, you're home! Your father will be thrilled. I'm thrilled you're home."

Michael enfolded her in his arms. He looked older. Some of the boyish qualities were gone. His shoulders had broadened, perhaps the result of the construction work he had been doing.

"I've finally come." He paused and looked around. "Mother, where's Dad? You're usually having coffee by this time."

"Your dad's still out doing chores."

"I thought Lowell was renting the land and taking care of the cattle."

"Yes, that's the way it started out. It worked well at first. But Lowell is more concerned about getting back to college—and that's good. So, your dad has been doing more work. He takes over the milking and chores two days a week—and sometimes more."

"That's not right. I'll get out there and help."

"Your dad should be back any minute." Ellen motioned for her son to sit down. "I want to talk with you. I'm worried about your father."

Michael could not avoid his mother's steady gaze. "I should have come home sooner."

"I'm glad you're here now. Your father's been tired. And we've been concerned about Martha. Some other things have happened to cause Matthew a good deal of stress."

"I'm afraid I've been taking so many things for granted. I'm sorry."

"Your father and I have been talking. We're going to make some changes. We can't go on this way. All this farm work is becoming too much for Matthew. We're thinking about selling again."

Michael looked away. "Somehow, I thought this farm and home would always be here. I can't picture this place without you and Dad."

Chapter 29

"Remember, we're not so young. We're not going to be around forever."

"I'm afraid I've been thoughtless."

Ellen looked at her son and smiled. "Son, let's not dwell on this. We're so happy to see you. What's been happening with you? Tell us about yourself."

"It's a long story. I don't know where to begin."

Ellen heard Matthew on the back porch. "Wait. You can tell your story to both your father and me."

Michael walked toward the door and opened it. "Dad, I'm home."

Ellen's eyes filled with tears as she saw the joy on Matthew's face.

"Michael." Matthew tried to say more, but other words would not come. "Michael, my son, Michael," he repeated.

The two men embraced. Ellen saw tears in the eyes of both.

"I've come home," said Michael. "I've come home."

"Have you come home to stay?" Matthew asked the question that Ellen had wanted to ask.

"I'm sorry. I'm home for now. I have to get back to my job. I'm sorry."

"We're so glad you're here," said Ellen. "Sit down. Tell us about yourself. You've been so many places."

"I've had all these jobs. In the Cities. In Illinois. Then, in northern Minnesota." He began to tell about the jobs and places.

Finally Ellen asked the question she had wanted to ask: "Have you been happy? Have these jobs brought you true satisfaction?"

Michael looked down. "In a way, they did make me happy. I've been making good money. I've seen more money than I'd ever seen in my life. I want to use the money in a special way. I'm making some changes."

Michael stopped. Obviously something of greater importance had taken place.

Ellen wanted to do something about the awkward moment. "Can I get you something? You must be hungry."

"I don't need anything. But I always enjoy your dinner."

Ellen remembered the hamburger in the refrigerator. "I can make your favorite meal, and it won't take long. I have the makings for Swedish meatballs. And you can tell about everything as I peel potatoes."

Michael relaxed. "Some things are hard to talk about."

"We love you," said Ellen. "We'll understand." She began peeling potatoes.

"I've made lots of mistakes. Before I left home, I did some rotten things. I'm sorry for all of that. And I tried to blame other people."

"We've forgiven you," said Matthew. "And we aren't perfect parents. We've made our mistakes."

"Johnie talked to me several times. At first I wouldn't listen. In fact, I blamed him and you because I thought you felt I had to live up to him, and I couldn't."

Ellen placed the potatoes in a pan of water. "Michael, you were actually a far better student than Johnie. You looked so much like Johnie, it was like having another Johnie."

"This is hard to talk about," Michael repeated. "I've realized something about myself. I realized how rotten I was—that I was a wayward son—a dirty sinner. I've come back to the Lord."

"We're so happy!" Matthew exclaimed.

"I committed—or re-committed—my life to Him. I'm not sure what He wants me to do. I have some serious thinking and praying to do."

"We'll pray for you," said Ellen. "We've been praying for you all along."

"There's something more. I've met a wonderful girl. She's a fifth grade teacher. She has a beautiful Swedish name. Elise. I love her, and I'm going to marry her."

"When do we get to meet her?" asked Ellen. "I can't wait."

"Soon. One of these next weekends."

"What's she like?" asked Matthew.

Michael took out his billfold and brought out a picture. "Here. Isn't she pretty?"

Matthew and Ellen eagerly examined the picture.

"She has all of the Scandinavian features." Ellen added, "She looks as if she's an Anderson already."

"You'll love her. She's petite. She has deep blue eyes. She has brown hair, and her face is the most beautiful I've ever seen. I'm so lucky that she loves me and wants to marry me."

The three talked as Ellen prepared the noon dinner. Michael gave exclamations about how he had missed his mother's cooking. And Matthew and Ellen brought him up to date on his many nieces and nephews.

Michael stayed that night. They went to church as a family. For Sunday dinner, they gathered at Margaret and Joe's and enjoyed one more family reunion and celebration. Then, it was time to say goodbye.

Chapter 29

Sunday evening, as Ellen turned out the light, Matthew reflected: "The Prodigal has returned. Our lost son is home once more."

Ellen moved close to Matthew. "The Lord has answered our prayers."

"Is it possible that Michael will come home to the farm?"

Mid-November was that time of year that caused Matthew to become depressed. On this day the clouds were heavy above. Snow had fallen earlier in the month but did not yet cover the ground. Everything around seemed brown and drab.

On such a day, Matthew wondered if change wouldn't be good. Though he hated the thought of leaving the farm, living in town might be the answer.

Ellen greeted him at the door. "Margaret called. She asked us to come over for noon dinner."

Matthew eagerly agreed. "We need a break. These chores get harder all the time. If Lowell wants to keep renting and working, he can't take off this way and leave me with all this work."

"I think we need to make some changes."

"Sometimes, I think it's time to make the big move into town."

Ellen gave him one of those knowing looks. "Even Glenn is thinking about that move."

Matthew quickly changed out of his work clothes, and they drove the six miles to the home place. He had a feeling that Margaret had something to tell them. What could that be? He didn't anticipate any more family news.

When they arrived at the home place, everything went on in a routine way. They visited about the weather and the kids and those many farm concerns. Yet, Matthew knew Margaret had something on her mind. She would tell them about it in her own good time.

As the four settled back to finish Margaret's apple pie and savor a cup of coffee, Margaret spoke.

"I have some good news—and some bad news," she announced.

"I sensed you had something to tell us," said Ellen.

Joe broke in. "I finally heard from my brother. After all these years, he wants to be a family."

"That part is the good news," added Margaret. "Gerald somehow felt the family should be together. Joe's mother isn't doing well. And now, after these many years, it seems she wants a relationship with Joe and our family."

Matthew remembered only too well how Joe's parents had rejected and ignored him. And the brothers had pretty much ignored Joe as well. But Joe, in his goodness, would always forgive the other person.

"What are you saying?" asked Ellen.

"Well, it's about Thanksgiving. Joe and I talked it over. We felt we had to accept their invitation. That means we drive to Cloquet for the day. I'm sorry, but we can't have our Thanksgiving together."

"We understand," said Ellen.

Matthew wasn't sure he did understand. Why should this family who had so completely rejected their younger son and brother finally have this claim on him and his family?

"You'll still be together with Aunt Victoria and Aunt Martha, won't you?"

Matthew remembered his last conversation with Victoria. "Victoria decided to make a Thanksgiving feast for those who would otherwise be alone. I think she's planning to have it in the church."

"I'm sorry," apologized Margaret. "We just felt we had no choice."

"Your father and I will have a nice quiet day alone. We'll be fine."

"What about Michael?" asked Joe. "I thought he was bringing his new girlfriend home. That could be a special time for you and them."

"We hear from him regularly now," said Ellen. "But Michael and Elise are going to spend time with her folks. We'll be fine."

"What about Johnie?" asked Margaret.

"He has Thanksgiving services," replied Ellen, "and a church Thanksgiving dinner, I think."

The two couples talked during the next hour, but their spirits were dampened at the prospect of missing the usual family Thanksgiving. Somehow a quiet holiday did not appeal to Matthew.

Later that evening, as Matthew and Ellen were getting ready for bed, Matthew made an observation. "Everything's changing. All the kids are going their own ways. Victoria and Martha are helping with a community Thanksgiving for people who are alone. And other families have moved away. We seem to be left alone."

Ellen smiled. "That's not so bad. We have each other."

Matthew looked across the room at his wife. "I love you, Ellen. I don't know how I'd live without you."

Chapter 29

"And I love you. And we are fortunate to have a good family. They don't have to be around us all the time. Besides, I don't know if I'd have the energy to have the whole gang around for Thanksgiving."

Matthew reflected for a moment. "That's the way God meant it to be. I think He meant for us to have time for ourselves—to make sense of our lives in a new way. He is with us always."

"Even to the end of the world."

Matthew yawned. "I think the good Lord is telling us to slow down."

Ellen got into bed. "I think of the prayer I taught the children. 'Jesus, Tender Shepherd, hear me. Bless thy little lamb tonight. Through the darkness be Thou near me. Keep me safe 'til morning light.'"

Matthew switched off the light and got into bed beside his wife. He felt an overwhelming sense of God's goodness. Changes would come in many different forms. But "Jesus Christ is the same yesterday, today, and forever."

As he drifted off to sleep, he thought, "Life is good. God is good."

CHAPTER 30

Friday, November 22, 1963 had started like any other day. Matthew had helped Lowell with some of the chores and now was in the bedroom lying down for a short nap. Ellen had finished the noon dinner dishes and turned on the television.

Ellen missed her old radio friends like Ma Perkins and the Youngs. Recently, she had started watching *As the World Turns*. The Hughes were interesting people, but they had such complicated lives. She took out her knitting and soon found herself immersed in the trials and tribulations of the Hughes.

Suddenly an announcer interrupted the story, and there on the screen was Walter Cronkite. "President Kennedy has been shot. We do not have the details. We're coming to you live from Dallas, Texas."

Ellen gasped. "Matthew," she called out. "Come quickly! The President's been shot."

Matthew appeared quickly. "What did you say?"

"The President's been shot," repeated Ellen.

Ellen and Matthew sat glued to the television set. They were too shocked to speak.

A half hour later, the news shifted to Malcolm Kilduff, who gave the official word. "President John F. Kennedy died at approximately 1 p.m. Central Standard Time today here in Dallas. He died of a gunshot wound in the brain."

Ellen watched as she saw tears in Walter Cronkite's eyes. He repeated the shocking news. "The President is dead."

"What's this world coming to?" Matthew placed his hand on his heart and looked away. "Such things shouldn't happen. I didn't think they could happen in America."

Ellen got up and switched off the television. "It's a reminder of the kind of world we live in."

The telephone rang its two long rings.

Ellen guessed who it was. Margaret would be the one to call.

"Mom, I can't believe it. How can such a thing happen? Things like this shouldn't happen."

Ellen listened for the next minutes as Margaret expressed her shock and sadness. "I'm sorry, too, but these tragedies have happened before. And I am afraid they can happen again."

"I guess I know that."

Matthew switched on the television once more. Lyndon Johnson was being sworn in as President of the United States.

Ellen was about to say goodbye when Margaret surprised her with her last comments. "Oh, I've been thinking, and Joe and I have been talking. We don't want to drive more than a hundred miles to Joe's brother, who hasn't had time for us for years. We might not make that trip at this time. We might stay right here, and make the trip some other time."

Ellen smiled. "Oh, if you do, then your dad and I won't have to be alone."

"I'm sorry we didn't think of that before."

"We'll be fine either way. But we'd love to be together."

This phone call and what followed reflected what was happening in millions of homes across the country. Husbands called wives. Children called their parents. Friends who hadn't touched base in years called each other. The tragedy brought the nation together. Suddenly the country was one. Republican. Democrat. Catholic. Protestant. Jewish. Everyone came together.

"I wonder if there will be other phone calls," said Matthew. "I wish all the kids were home under our roof."

Chapter 30

That afternoon, as James returned to his office from his twelve o'clock class, he noticed a buzz in the halls. He caught snatches of conversation. Whatever had happened sounded serious.

"Dr. Anderson," called one of his students. "Did you hear? Kennedy's been shot. It just happened."

James groped for words. "How serious is it?"

"We don't know. I guess I need to get to my next class."

The secretary for the English department greeted him. "You've heard, haven't you?"

Two other professors entered the office. Soon they were all listening intently to the radio and the up-to-the-minute reports. Time seemed to stand still during that hour.

A half-hour later, the announcement came. "President Kennedy died at approximately 1 p.m. Central Standard Time." James' reaction was one of disbelief. The other professors reacted in the same way.

James walked slowly to his two o'clock advanced creative writing class. He had planned on having them analyze a short piece of fiction and then read the beginnings of their short stories. He wasn't quite sure what he should do. If the students felt as he did, their thoughts would be elsewhere.

These ten students were the "cream of the crop," so to speak. They were silent at first. Then, it seemed they wanted to talk and to ask questions. Why? Why would anyone want to shoot a popular President such as this? Then, their discussion focused on death and the whole business of facing death.

James couldn't help thinking of the poem by A. E. Housman about the athlete dying young. He quoted some of the lines:

The time you won your town the race.
We chaired you through the marketplace;
Man and boy stood cheering by,
And home we brought you shoulder-high.

"I believe Kennedy will be remembered just as this athlete is remembered in the poem. The athlete dies at the height of his career. He has broken records. He will never find himself forgotten. He will never wear out his honor. Kennedy will be remembered better because he died young."

James began to notice several students were writing in their journals. "Profound thoughts may come to us at times such as this. Let's write these thoughts in our journals."

Some students wrote quickly and easily. Others seemed to stare out the windows; one student put his head down on his desk. Quietness filled the room for the remaining minutes of the hour.

Like so many others in the country, James wanted desperately to be in touch with Ruth and the children. He usually worked late in his office and arrived home just in time for supper. Now he wanted to get out of the office and hurry over to the school where Ruth taught. He could be there just as she dismissed her sixth grade students.

As his students wrote, James wrote. His thoughts centered on family. How much he loved Ruth and Richard and Coleen and Melissa. He wanted to take them all in his arms and tell them how much he loved them.

"Life is fragile and can change quickly," James wrote. "How much we take for granted that our leaders will continue to govern in the same way. Then, our President is shot. Life comes to a standstill. We suddenly realize the transitory nature of life. All at once the future seems to be in jeopardy. Life will never be the same."

He set down his pen. Feeling restless, James stood up and walked over to the window. The students, he observed, also seemed restless and unsure of how they should act. He looked across to the main campus building. Below, on the sidewalks, a number of students were walking.

James made a spur-of-the-moment decision. "I believe we'll end class early today. Bring your journals with you on Monday, and share some of what you've written. Have a good weekend."

The students, talking among themselves, left. Some wished him a good weekend. He had never observed such a subdued atmosphere on a Friday afternoon when students prepared for weekend activities or a trip home.

"Everyone seems to be leaving early," announced the secretary. "Dr. McDonald and Mr. Martin have already left."

"Why don't you go home?" suggested James. "All I want to do is see my family and find out what's happening."

"Thank you, Dr. Anderson."

Matthew collected a few papers and books, putting them into his briefcase.

That evening, James and Ruth and the children were glued to the television set, anxiously watching the story of the assassination of a

President. They were silent much of the time, but felt a closeness in the sadness they experienced.

James felt a strong need to call home to Mom and Dad. Twice the circuits were busy, and several more times their line was busy. Finally, he heard his mother's voice at the other end of the line. He felt a sense of relief and well-being as he was assured that some things in life remained the same.

Disbelief seemed to permeate all of the conversations, including this one with his mother. He felt a need to be together with as many family members as possible. Perhaps this was the time to cancel the work and activities they had planned. He knew it was the right time to go home.

Home could be a terribly strong magnet.

Johnie had scheduled Friday afternoon, November 22, to do pastoral visits. He finished his sandwich and a glass of milk and said aloud to himself, "I probably shouldn't have eaten. I'll have coffee and goodies, so I'll be stuffed with fattening food by this evening."

He looked at his watch. It was 12:30. He knew Mrs. Lindgren watched her story. It seemed a tradition for the women and sometimes their husbands to settle back and watch *"As the World Turns"*. All he knew was that the Hughes family had plenty of problems, the staple of television soap operas.

It was at quiet times like this that he missed Laura. The two of them would have lingered over a cup of coffee and talked about whatever was on their minds. "At times like this," he said aloud, "I feel so very much alone."

Johnie decided not to listen to the radio as he began his ten-mile ride out into the country. Mrs. Lindgren lived alone on the family farm. Johnie figured she was around fifty, and her children had grown up and moved away. Even after the death of her husband three years ago, she had decided to remain on the farm. She rented out the land but kept a flock of chickens, raised a few beef cattle, and maintained a big garden. She had invited him for lunch, but Johnie had declined the invitation. Instead, she said she would give him dessert.

He decided to drive through some back roads so that he'd arrive at the right time. Mrs. Lindgren's story would then be over. He wouldn't want to interrupt that.

These back roads reminded him of Laura. It was in such a setting as this during a stormy winter night that he met her and rescued her in the midst of her car trouble. "Lord, I still keep wondering why you took Laura away from me and our children."

He returned from his detour to the Lindgren road. He got out of the car and walked up the steps to the kitchen door of this grand old farm house—a rather big house for one lady living alone.

He knocked on the door. No one answered. He could hear the television, but it sounded more like a newscast than a soap opera.

"Mrs. Lindgren," he called out. "I hope I'm not early. I didn't want to interrupt your story."

The woman appeared. "Oh, I'm sorry. No, you're not early. In fact, you're late. But haven't you heard? The President's been shot. It's terrible. Walter Cronkite cut in on my story, and I've been glued to the television ever since."

"Why? This is hard to believe."

"Come in," she invited. "But, please, call me Ruby. I'm not quite old enough to be your mother."

Johnie followed her into the spacious living room, a room that gave witness to a successful farmer who amply furnished the room with the best furniture and finest pictures. He caught the words of Cronkite, saying that President Kennedy had died.

Both Johnie and his hostess remained silent as they watched history unfold.

Ruby went to the kitchen, returning with coffee and a plate with a generous piece of strawberry-rhubarb pie topped with a generous portion of whipped cream. Johnie's mouth watered.

For awhile the two said little as they watched the scenes on television.

"President Kennedy was so young," said Ruby. "Too young to die."

"I didn't vote for Kennedy, but I've come to like and admire him. It's hard to imagine our country without him."

During the next hour something happened. Ruby Lindgren and Pastor John Anderson spoke of life and change and loneliness. Pastor and parishioner talked as two hurting human beings, reaching out to someone nearby. Johnie spoke freely of the burden he felt as a widower and single father. As Johnie got up to leave, he made an observation.

Chapter 30

"Ruby, today I didn't do my job as a pastor. I think you took on the role of minister to me. I needed that, and I thank you."

Ruby didn't hesitate. "I needed to be needed. You're just a few years older than my son. If I were twenty years younger, I'd go after you. Sometime you'll make another woman a wonderful husband."

"I'm not ready for that. But I don't want to be alone for the rest of my life."

The telephone rang. "I bet that's my son. I knew he'd call."

Johnie reached out to shake hands, but then Ruby embraced him.

"Thank you for understanding," he said. "I want to pick up the kids at school. I need them, and they need me. And we'll find some way to go home to Mom and Dad."

"Joe," Margaret called out as she hurried toward the barn. "Something's happened. It's terrible."

Joe, who had just returned from errands in town, stepped out of the pickup. "What's wrong?"

"The President's been shot. He died just an hour ago."

All at once, Margaret felt she wanted to be near all those she loved. She had called her mother immediately after hearing the news. And now she breathed a sigh of relief that Joe had come home from town.

Joe looked stunned. "He's dead, you said."

Margaret proceeded to fill in some of the details.

"How could such a thing happen in America? It doesn't seem right."

At that moment Margaret saw tears in her husband's eyes. He was a sensitive and caring man, but he had difficulty showing any kind of deep feeling.

She moved close to him. He enfolded her in his arms. She felt safe and secure.

Words were not necessary for the two to communicate their love and need for one another. Margaret would long remember this moment. The President was dead. The country would never be the same. A kindness and innocence had been destroyed at the same time.

Margaret thought to herself, "I'd really like to be near Mom and Dad."

Joe spoke the words Margaret was thinking: "Let's stay right here for Thanksgiving."

"Darling, thank you."

Carol quickly paid the waitress. She had to get away from the people at this ladies' luncheon. These social gatherings seemed increasingly frivolous and empty. There had to be more purpose to life than these.

The news of the President's death had come as the ladies finished their luncheon. They, too, had seemed stunned but tried to continue with small talk.

Carol decided to do something she rarely did. She had come in from the suburbs by way of the train. She called a cab and gave directions to her husband's office building.

During the hour since she had heard the news, her mind moved about like one of those fast-paced movies. One common element that remained indelible was a scene with her parents at their farm home. She wanted to gather Hank and the children and go home.

When she entered Hank's office, he greeted her but did not seem surprised that she was there. "I figured you might do something like this."

"President Kennedy is dead," she said. "I can't believe it. I feel I've been attacked, and we're not safe."

Hank smiled and gave her time to continue talking.

"You know, I haven't been homesick for Oak Ridge in a long time. But now I am. I keep thinking of those days back on the farm. I've never appreciated Mom and Dad as I should." She continued to ramble on about home and childhood.

Hank finally interrupted her. "I think you'd like to go home to Minnesota. How about if we go back for Thanksgiving? How's that?"

Carol forgot herself for the moment. She moved around Hank's desk and threw herself into his arms.

"That's what I wanted to do, but I was afraid to ask. I thought business would keep you here. Thank you."

She kissed her husband on the cheek. Then his arms circled around her, and he kissed her fully on the mouth.

Chapter 30

Carol had not felt this way in a long time. She felt giddy and happy, despite the national tragedy. She had a phone call to make. She was going home.

Exasperated, Michael put down the receiver. "Will these people never get off the phone!" he muttered.

It was past ten, and he wanted to call home.

They had been sitting in Elise's apartment, watching the television coverage. She seemed to understand what he was thinking.

"You want to go home for Thanksgiving, don't you?"

"Yes, very much. But I promised I would have Thanksgiving with your parents."

"You've met my parents, but I haven't met yours."

Michael felt that special tenderness whenever Elise showed this sensitivity to him and what he was thinking. "Would you be willing?" he asked.

"Yes, I've been wanting to meet the Andersons."

Michael kissed Elise on the cheeks and hurried back over to the phone. "I'll try one more time."

This time the phone rang. His father answered the phone.

"Dad, it's me, Michael."

He heard the joy in his father's voice. "Son, I'm so glad you called."

"Dad, I'm coming home. Is Thanksgiving okay?"

He heard a catch in his father's voice.

"That will make Thanksgiving perfect."

CHAPTER 31

Matthew had never experienced a time like the days that followed the assassination of President Kennedy. It wasn't just a family mourning the death of a loved one; it was a nation stopping to reflect and mourn. He felt this deep sadness for the country and for Jackie, now alone with two young children. But life was moving on. Within hours, Lyndon Baines Johnson was sworn in as thirty-fourth President of the United States.

This morning the church sanctuary was unusually full. Even those people who were frequently absent on Sunday morning had decided to come. The younger children seemed to sense something was different. The organist had chosen to play music of a more quiet nature because of the recent tragedy.

The service moved along with several hymns and Scripture readings. Pastor Young introduced the next hymn.

"Our hymn of the month is more appropriate than I ever realized when I considered it as a new hymn for us to learn. Notice how the words remind us of our choice—or choices. Each man and nation has choices. Choices for good or evil. We have seen someone who chose evil. Now what choices are we going to make?"

The organist played the introduction, and then Matthew and the congregation joined in singing the words written by James Russell Lowell:

Once to every man and nation
Comes a moment to decide,
In the strife and truth and falsehood,
For the good or evil side;
Some great cause, God's new Messiah,
Off'ring each the bloom or blight,
And the choice goes by forever
'Twixt the darkness and that light.

Matthew tried both to sing and think the words. There was mention of truth being noble. Truth had its martyrs with the cross in the background. New occasions would teach new duties. But truth was always on the scaffold.

The final words spoke reassurance to Matthew:

Yet that scaffold sways the future,
And behind the dim unknown,
Standeth God within the shadow,
Keeping watch above his own.

Pastor Young began his sermon. "This is what we sometimes call Judgment Sunday. It's not the kind of sermon that I like to preach, but I must. It is part of Scripture, and it is my duty to preach all of the truth.

"Today in our Scripture, we see God as a judge. This is a serious reminder to us about our relationships with people. About our relationship with the Lord Himself. About our actions and decisions and their consequences."

As the pastor spoke about sin and sin's consequences and judgment, Matthew felt a deep and profound sadness. The assassination was a blight on a nation that had stood for what was good and right. The tragedy was jarring his conscience, as well as the conscience of a nation.

Would something good come out of this? He wondered. Could the tragedy cause people to think about the more important things in life? Could it bring people home to the truth of Scripture and of God? Would eternal values be a greater consideration?

Pastor Young's words penetrated Matthew's awareness. "Are you and I drifting away from Christ and from the truth of Scripture? Are we forgetting that we should be seeking first the Kingdom of God and His righteousness? Are we instead seeking first our own comfort and pleasure as we rush along from day to day?

Chapter 31

"Is this national tragedy a call? Is the Lord calling out to us to return to Him? I hesitate—or maybe I don't—to use a word we don't often use: Repent. Next week as we move into the Advent season, we'll hear John the Baptist saying those words. It is time to look at the whole of our lives. Repent means to turn around. Don't we need to turn around—turn away—from some of our attitudes and actions? We must come to Christ, repenting of those wrongs, and seeking Him as we seek to make our lives and our world a better place."

Matthew thought of his role as a father. His sons and his daughters still came to him. Sometimes they sought advice, but many times they just wanted to talk. His role was now to pray and encourage them. And there were all those wonderful grandchildren. He loved them, and they loved him. They were growing up so fast, and they were involved in school and so many activities. Even so, he could point them in the way they ought to go.

As the service came to a close, Pastor Young spoke a different kind of prayer—a powerful one, Matthew thought. "And now let us move forward after this time of national tragedy. Let us resolve to live and to seek first the Kingdom of God. Let us seek God's strength and Spirit to love our family and neighbors and to become better Christians and better Americans. Let us become servants, asking what we can do for others and our country, not what our country or they can do for us.

"And now may the Lord and Judge and King bless you and keep you. May He guide you into better understanding of His Kingdom and will. May His face light your way as you seek to live a better life. And may He give you the peace that passes all understanding as you go on your way. And this is only possible as we pray in the name of the Father, the Son, and the Holy Spirit. Amen."

There was a hushed silence.

After the silence, the congregation quietly sang, "God be with you till we meet again, By His counsels guide, uphold you, With His sheep securely fold you. God be with you till we meet again."

Matthew experienced a new peace in the midst of sadness.

Ellen listened to the sermon, but at the same time the image of Jackie Kennedy remained imprinted on her mind. Jackie holding her dying husband in her arms. Jackie standing in the background as Lyndon Johnson was sworn in as President. Jackie and those two young children.

Ellen had never been politically involved. She had not voted for Kennedy. She voted in the tradition of her husband and the family of her youth. But she had come to love and admire this young couple and their two children. She thought of poor Jackie's loss of her baby a few months before.

And now, Jackie would be left alone to raise two children. She couldn't imagine bringing up her children without Matthew by her side.

She agreed with Pastor Young. There was something wrong when a youthful President was killed in this public place. And Lee Harvey Oswald, what could have prompted him to commit this atrocious crime?

At this moment it almost seemed as if the whole American way of life was under attack. Would this country ever be the same? Trust had been destroyed. Was this violence a sign of the times?

Ellen usually talked with several people after the service, but today she didn't. There was a short choir practice for the Thursday Thanksgiving service, anyway. Some of the usual visiting took place, but the choir members were more subdued.

Margaret was now the choir director. She handed out the music, and the pianist began playing the introduction. They began to sing the arrangement of several hymns of Thanksgiving. No one seemed in the mood for serious work.

Margaret was about to go over some troublesome parts when Glenn Robertson hurried to the front of the sanctuary where the choir was seated.

"They got him! They shot the guy. I just heard it on the radio. Someone shot Lee Harvey Oswald."

"That's not the way to do things," thought Ellen.

Margaret acknowledged the news. "I think it's best we come early Thanksgiving morning and run over these parts. Our minds are on other things now."

Ellen had always looked to the future with optimism. Somehow the events of this morning and the past days cast a dark cloud over tomorrow.

Chapter 31

Matthew always looked forward to Sunday dinner, and today was no exception. Today was special because they were invited to Margaret and Joe's.

Matthew and Ellen visited with Glenn and Mabel Robertson and others following the short choir practice. There was something about this terrible assassination that brought people together. It was almost as if they needed to huddle together for safety from the dangerous and evil forces out there.

"Dinner's almost ready," announced Margaret when they entered the kitchen. "You can put your wraps on our bed and sit down at the table."

"Can I help?"

"Thank you, Mother. My girls need to learn their way around in the kitchen. You can just sit down."

Eleven-year-old Deborah mashed potatoes while ten-year-old Judith filled glasses with water in the dining room.

Matthew went on into the dining room, and his namesake, fifteen-year-old Matt, took the coats into the bedroom. He noticed Joe in an easy chair in the living room. He was sound asleep.

Matthew stood beside his son-in-law, looking down at him. Joe had brought so much comfort and happiness to Margaret and the rest of the family. As Joe dozed, Matthew looked at his thinning brown hair, now beginning to turn gray. He hadn't noticed that before. Matthew himself was growing older—sixty-four in April, and Joe would be forty-three. His children and their spouses were mature adults now. All except Michael.

"Dad," called Matt. "We have company, and you're sleeping."

Joe jerked forward. "I'm sorry. I guess I was more tired than I realized."

Margaret and the girls entered with the platters and bowls of food. "You can all sit up in your usual places." She turned to her husband. "Joe, you've been working too hard. You shouldn't have bought those extra milk cows."

Each person took his or her place. Little Marlene cuddled up to her grandfather; she always managed to sit next to him. There was one empty spot.

"Where's David?" asked Margaret.

The other children looked to Matt. "David kinda had a little fight."

"But he came home from church with us," said Margaret. "He sat in the backseat when we drove home."

Everyone looked to Matt for the explanation. Matthew couldn't believe David would fight. He always seemed to be such a polite, well-behaved boy.

"Well," Matt began, "he and Gaylord Robertson had a fight. Gaylord tends to be a bit mouthy, and David put him in his place. He has a black eye, and it just started to show."

"Where is he?" demanded Margaret.

"I think he's out in the barn."

"Everything's hot. We'll pray and then eat."

The family prayed together their table prayer.

Joe got up. "I think I need to get him. That Robertson boy has been acting up, and it wasn't all David's fault. I'm sure of that."

Some things never change, thought Matthew. It seemed only yesterday that Johnie had fights with his cousin Jake. Even at David's age, Johnie couldn't stand unfairness of any kind. At that point in his life, his fist was his answer to the problem.

The rest of the meal was uneventful. David returned quietly. "I'm sorry I'm late."

During the meal nothing further was said about the black eye.

After the meal, Margaret let the children go their own ways. Mother and daughter washed and dried dishes. Joe and Matthew went to the living room. David stayed behind. No doubt he wanted to talk.

Joe looked at his son. "You know that's not the way we settle problems."

With tears in his eyes, David replied. "But Gaylord was making fun of Matt and some of the other kids. I couldn't stand it. He was a stupid jerk."

"Maybe he was, but a fist fight never solves the problem."

"He got what he deserved."

Matthew smiled at his grandson. "David, you have the right values. I'm proud of you that you wanted to defend those who didn't fight or couldn't fight. But as your father says, try to work it out differently another time."

"It's hard to stand back."

Matthew hesitated. "You know, David, you are so much like your Uncle Johnie. He became angry at any kind of injustice. He was in a few fights, but he learned better ways."

"Your grandfather has a point."

David grunted. "Uncle Johnie's a great guy, but I'm not going to become a minister."

Chapter 31

Joe smiled. "That's what Uncle Johnie said."

"I'd like to stay on the farm or run some of those big new machines. That's what I want."

"And I'd like to have you right here," said Joe, "but it has to be what you want—what you really want to do."

David nodded, saying nothing.

"Why don't you go out with the other kids? It sounds as if they're having fun."

David left. Matthew couldn't help thinking and saying, "It's amazing how some things have changed drastically. And yet in some ways life is just like it was years ago."

At the same time Matthew said the words, he wanted to appreciate his family at that moment. There would be changes; there might never be another chance like this.

Matthew saw that Joe had closed his eyes. Joe was working terribly hard—such was the life of a farmer.

Matthew closed his eyes and enjoyed the sounds of children playing games and of Margaret and Ellen in the kitchen. Life was good.

A half-hour later, Margaret turned on the television set. The sounds of the funeral procession were haunting, along with the serious commentary of television announcers.

The funeral cortege traced in reversal the path that John Kennedy had traveled in his festive inaugural parade down Pennsylvania Avenue from the White House to the Capitol. The somber beat of drums had an almost hypnotic effect.

Poor Jackie Kennedy. She followed with Caroline and little John. What a loss to the family and to the nation!

The children returned, at first talkative and noisy. Then, as the cortege continued, they joined the adults in the silence of mourning the President.

Monday, November 25, 1963 was like no other day Matthew had ever experienced. That morning, he helped Lowell with the chores. Then, he and Ellen did something that was highly uncharacteristic: they sat glued to the television set.

The events of history moved before them. Matthew felt he was present there in Washington D.C. and Arlington as he saw thousands of people pass before the casket of President Kennedy in the Capitol Rotunda. What a somber scene! Never before had he seen a whole nation come to a standstill to mourn.

"Is the Lord telling us something?" Matthew said to himself. "Have we as a country somehow lost our way? Is there something more behind this dreadful tragedy? Is there some kind of plot or conspiracy?"

Life moved on. The funeral cortege moved to the cathedral. The mass was held. The Cardinal gave the funeral sermon. The sprinkling of holy water and the whole service seemed so foreign to Matthew with his different background and life. It all seemed so unreal that this youthful President could be dead.

Then came the procession to Arlington and the burial. He viewed Jackie kneeling beside the casket.

All at once the funeral was over.

Ellen switched off the television set. "Let's have some coffee."

"You know," replied Matthew, "I'm hungry. I didn't eat much at noon."

Ellen agreed.

It was the middle of the afternoon. The rays of sun shone through the kitchen windows. And it was time for life to move forward. The world had changed during those hours. The Anderson family was changing as well.

Chapter 32

The house was a beehive of preparation that Tuesday evening. Matthew and Ellen's house was the larger one; therefore that would be the scene of the Anderson family gathering on Thanksgiving. If weather permitted the morning travel, every member of the Matthew Anderson family would be together, at least for a short while. Added to that number would be Larry and Joan and their family, including the next generation with Lowell and Megan. And Victoria and Martha would come by later in the afternoon. What an event Thanksgiving would be!

"Dad, why don't you clean out the garage?" said Margaret. "You can make room for another car in case we have cold weather and snow."

Matthew knew the women wanted to get him out of the way. Margaret and the two girls, Deborah and Judith, had come over to help clean house and get everything ready for the influx of company on Wednesday evening and Thursday. Ellen needed to slow down. Margaret and the girls had a way of getting things done quickly.

Matthew wasted no time in getting out to the garage. He enjoyed this triple-sized garage, but it had become a storage place for much else. Not only did it include his car and the pickup, but also the lawn mowers and some junk. Matthew began to move the mowers and other stored paraphernalia.

As he tried to arrange a lawn mower in the far corner, a voice interrupted his thoughts.

"Uncle Matthew, let me help you. There's something I wanted to talk with you about."

It was Lowell. Matthew gulped, almost fearing what Lowell had to say. "Yes, I guess that would be good. Some of these machines are awkward to move."

Lowell helped his uncle rearrange the machines and boxes and discarded objects that came from various places—even some of the memorabilia that belonged to the children. Now there would be room for still another car.

"You said you had something to talk to me about?" questioned Matthew.

"I guess I've been putting it off." Lowell looked away, avoiding his uncle's gaze. "Last Thursday, I received a letter. I have a great opportunity."

"I can guess."

"The School of Agriculture has a job for me. I'll work as I go to school, and I'll have a salary. Everything will be paid for."

Matthew didn't need to think long. "You can't pass up an offer like that."

"The only problem..." He paused. "The work begins January first."

"I understand." Matthew looked at Lowell, seeing in him something of both Larry and P.J. There was something about genes and family tendencies that he knew was there, though it was hard to understand.

"I know it puts you in a difficult situation."

Matthew hesitated. "I've been putting it off, but it's time for me to get out of the cattle business. Too much work for an old man."

Larry apologized once more.

Matthew knew he had to act soon.

The minute Ellen heard Matthew's steps on the back porch, she knew he was troubled. That's the way it was with couples who had been married for forty years.

"Dad, what took you so long?" questioned Margaret. "We called for you. We've had the coffee on."

"I guess I didn't hear."

Chapter 32

"Is something wrong?" asked Ellen. She knew something was wrong even as she asked.

Margaret and the two girls sensed what Ellen knew.

"I guess I might as well tell you. Lowell was over. He's quitting. He needs to leave by January first. He's got a good deal going for him. He can work and go to agriculture school at the same time. I can't hold him back."

"Dad, you shouldn't be doing all that work by yourself. That's too much. And some of that lifting isn't good for you."

Ellen saw the strain in her husband's face. "Matthew, I think it's time."

"Yes, my dear, it's time to sell the cattle. We can stay on the farm. I'll rent out the land and maybe keep a few beef cattle. It's time to move on."

"Oh, Grandpa," pleaded Deborah, "we'll miss all those cows. It won't be the same."

Margaret hastily replied, "Deborah, your grandfather shouldn't be doing all that heavy work. When you get older, you're not supposed to work as hard."

"But he looks the same."

"Maybe we should move to town," said Matthew. "A number of farmers are doing that. It would be good to get away from all the hard work out in the country."

"You can't move to town," said Judith. "That would be terrible."

Matthew smiled at Judith as she snuggled up to him. "That may happen someday, but we'll probably stay on the farm for now."

All at once, Ellen felt very old. A nice little house in town might be the answer. Keeping up this big house was getting to be too much.

"When the family is together, let's not say anything about selling the cattle or possibly moving," said Matthew as he sat down at the kitchen table for his morning coffee.

"They're going to have to know, but we can wait." Ellen stopped a minute. "Matthew, perhaps you could go into town. I think we need some more butter and a few other odds and ends for Thanksgiving. I'd go with you, but I have so much to do."

"Sure thing. I think this might be a good time to pick up Glenn and have another cup of coffee at the café."

In minutes Matthew swung by Glenn's farm, and the two men were talking together as they had done for many years.

The City Café was their favorite place. They were soon eating sweet rolls and drinking more coffee.

"Matthew, I think something's wrong," began Glenn after a few moments of quiet. "I can tell something's bothering you."

Matthew proceeded to explain that Lowell would soon be leaving for school. "I think it's time for me to move on."

"You know, I understand how you feel. Now that Tim is taking over completely, Mabel and I think about moving to town. Perhaps we could go south for the winter. I heard Texas is a good place to go."

"I don't think I like the idea of Texas for me. But I'm getting tired of all this work on the farm. Even so, I love the land and what it means. I always think: If you're good to the land, the land will be good to you."

"I feel the same way. But I also feel ready to go."

The two men continued their talk. One minute, they were ready to move; the next minute, they wanted to live in the country for the rest of their lives.

Glenn broke the line of confusing talk. "This is ridiculous. We're acting like two kids who don't quite know what to do."

Matthew laughed. "We're two old men who aren't quite so sure about our future."

"You know, Matthew, I think I have a temporary solution. Tim's boys are old enough to help in the barn. He doesn't need me. What if I come over and work with you. We'd have a great time working together. And then you could wait for the best price for your cattle. Or maybe Michael might decide he wants to come home."

"I wouldn't want to take advantage of you."

"Matthew, I feel I need to make up for what happened earlier. I shouldn't have been taken in by Tim when he wanted to buy your place. I still feel awful about that."

All at once Matthew felt better. Changes lay ahead. But there were ways of working out any kind of problem. God would show a way. And people would be there to help.

Chapter 32

Matthew and Ellen awakened early Thanksgiving morning. There was work to be done.

Ellen put the turkey in the oven, a twenty-pound turkey, which should be enough for the family. This year they would eat after one o'clock—not at the usual twelve noon time. That would allow everyone adequate travel time.

Matthew brought the card tables down from the attic. He hadn't been to the attic in a long time. That attic contained memories of forty years of marriage—old books, trunks, and old dresses and suits that were long out of style. Ellen had said that they really needed to clean out the place. This is something they needed to do if they moved to town.

The aroma of coffee and oatmeal cooking on the stove drew Matthew to the kitchen.

Ellen poured a cup of coffee. "It's amazing the way this tragedy of an assassinated President draws people together. A week ago, we thought we'd be alone for Thanksgiving, and now the family will be complete, God willing."

"I can't quite believe all that's happened. I keep thinking Kennedy should be alive and on the news."

"I hope everyone makes it here by one—or close to it."

"James and Ruth and the kids must have come to Margaret's last night."

"Margaret didn't call. I assume they were busy. And I'm sure they came."

"And everyone else comes this morning."

"Johnie had his Thanksgiving service last night, so he said he'd be here about noon. The congregation made changes so he could be home with his family. Carol and Hank and the kids were staying along the way and should be here by one. Then, Michael and Elise will come by one, and Elise's parents may be coming as well."

"We'll be a full house tonight."

The two finished breakfast and together set the tables for the Thanksgiving feast. Matthew felt thankful that he didn't have to be in the barn doing chores. He could be a part of the preparation for this family event.

They worked and peeled potatoes until Ellen announced, "It's time to get ready for church. The service is at 10:30 today."

Thanksgiving Day, 1963, held much promise.

"I'm disappointed," said Matthew to himself. "We have much to be thankful for, and look at how few people are at the service this morning." He looked around. Glenn and Mabel weren't in their usual spot. Tim and his family came periodically on Sunday mornings. So many other members were not present. At least Margaret and Joe and all six of their children were present.

Margaret leaned over and whispered to her father. "James and Ruth came late last night. That's why they're not here. They were starting to get up when we left."

Matthew didn't want to be critical, but he felt they could have made some extra effort. Sometimes people forgot the values they grew up with.

The service was like so many other Thanksgiving services. Was it possible that tradition sometimes detracted from the true meaning of Thanksgiving? All at once the words of Pastor Young's sermon caught his attention.

"There is a sin of ingratitude. It may take the form of taking our blessings for granted. A few weeks ago, we took for granted our President Kennedy. We thought he would be our President for another year and a few months, and then likely for another four years. Yet on that fateful Friday, his life came to an end.

"Let us now enjoy the blessings we have. And the family and friends we cherish. We know not when change may come. We know not when we face tragedy and the unknown."

Those words stuck in Matthew's mind.

The service ended with an old favorite hymn, "God Be with You till We Meet Again." This was the favorite closing of so many family reunions, and it served as a reminder that some present here might never see one another again on this earth.

Matthew, followed by Ellen, turned to leave. And, to his surprise, there in the back of the sanctuary stood Carol with Hank and all three of their children.

In a moment, Carol was in his arms. "Dad, we're here. We wanted to come to church on this day of days."

Matthew felt himself choking back deep emotion. The prodigal daughter had truly come home.

Chapter 32

"Thank You, Lord," he whispered under his breath.

The wall clock chimed one. Ellen settled back as Margaret took charge. The potatoes were ready to be mashed, and Ruth was ready to do that task. Margaret prepared to carve the turkey. And Joan and Carol dished up vegetables. All that Ellen had to do was find more bowls or utensils. It felt good to have others helping.

Everyone had arrived except Michael. He was supposed to be here with his fiancée, Elise, and her parents.

"I think we need to go ahead and eat," said Margaret. "Everything is ready—just right. We can't wait."

The other women agreed.

Ellen called to those in the living room and dining room. "Matthew, boys, why don't you get everyone seated? The food is hot, and it's coming."

Commotion followed, as always during a family gathering, but quickly the food was dished up and people were seated.

The family became quiet, ready for the prayer. Ellen nodded to Johnie.

"Dear Lord, we come to You with grateful hearts. We thank You for our country and pray for Your guidance and blessing during this difficult time. We are thankful that all of us could be together and fellowship. And we pray for Michael and Elise that they may reach us safely. How thankful we are for family! We miss those who are not with us."

Ellen saw that sad look in Johnie's eyes. These times were not easy for a single father and widower.

"We thank You, Lord, for bountiful blessings. We ask Your blessing and guidance on each member of this family. We pray that each has come or will come to know You in a personal way. Bless this food and those who have prepared it. Bless each of us as we fellowship together and enjoy each other. May what we do and say be done to Your glory and Your honor. In Jesus' name. Amen."

There were choruses of amens, and soon the members of the Anderson family were devouring the food and visiting at the same time.

Margaret insisted that Ellen remain seated. She and Carol took charge of seeing that all the bowls were filled. What a change had taken place in Carol; she had truly returned in spirit to the Anderson family.

At this point a door opened, and Michael called out. "I'm home! We're all here. I'm sorry we're late."

Ellen and Matthew each rose quickly.

"Welcome," said Ellen. "Put your coats down. We have places for you. Come in and sit down."

Michael continued to explain. "We came across an accident—not terribly serious, but we had to help. That's why we're late."

"We understand."

"This is Elise," announced Michael. "She's my girlfriend. And her parents, George and Sarah, and they are Andersons as well."

"We'll do the rest of the introductions later," said Ellen. "Let's just enjoy our meal and our being together."

Ellen breathed a silent prayer of thanksgiving, and she knew Matthew was doing the same. At long last, the family was complete. Michael had returned. They were all home.

The interruption seemed only to spur on the conversation as well as the eating. When the food was passed, people took seconds and thirds.

As people began to slow down and stop eating, Michael stood up. Ellen hadn't realized that he was taller and huskier than Johnie. But he had grown older. His blond hair was beginning to darken, as usually happens when people mature.

Ellen couldn't help remembering all of the hopes they had pinned on Michael. That hadn't been fair. Even so, she secretly hoped that Michael might return home and take over this farm. That would take care of all of their concerns.

"I want to properly introduce Elise at this time. This is Elise Anderson. She is a fifth grade teacher in her local school. She's the most wonderful girl I've ever met. And she has consented to be my wife."

"Congratulations!" were called out. "We're happy for you."

"When's the big day?" called out Margaret.

Ellen noticed how petite this girl was. She couldn't be more than five foot two, with bright blue eyes that complemented Michael's and a sweetness and gentleness, yet the strength needed to take charge of a classroom of students.

"After school's out—at the earliest," replied Elise. "Now, I've heard about all of you. I want to meet and get to know each one of you. And my parents also want to get to know you. You see, I'm their one and only child."

Sarah Anderson stood up, an older and slightly taller and heavier version of Elise. "Elise's father and I are older parents. For years we thought we could never have children. And then out of the blue when I thought my child-bearing years were over, Elise was born. She has been our pride and joy. And since we are older, we wanted to see our daughter safely taken care of and married. We are so delighted that Michael will be joining our family. And that will bring our two families together."

The Andersons applauded and called out words of congratulations and welcome.

Each person introduced himself or herself. Some introductions were followed by jokes and humorous comments. This Thanksgiving became a true celebration of home—of being home.

Victoria and Martha stopped by late in the afternoon. For so many years they had been integral parts of the family celebration. Now, it seemed they were moving to the background. And besides that, Mary and Ed and their children were no longer around.

Time seemed to fly that afternoon. Ellen wanted to enjoy every moment, but time kept moving forward.

Evening approached. Margaret and Joe and their six children left. After all, they were farmers, and it was time to do chores. Lowell left to do chores, and Larry went with him to help. Joan and the girls went over to the trailer house to be with Megan and the baby. George and Sarah Anderson left so that they could visit George's brother in eastern North Dakota. Then, another exodus followed. When James and Ruth left for the "little house," the other children chose to spend the night with their cousins.

That left a smaller group. The women congregated in the kitchen while the men sat in the living room, talking and watching the news.

Ellen suddenly felt very tired. After all, she was almost sixty-five. She couldn't believe how these years had flown by. She saw Martha yawn. Martha showed the signs of her age more and more. She had begun to look weak and frail.

Ellen began to remember. "Remember, Martha, Victoria, how the two of you used to come out the night before and help me get ready for the big events—both for Thanksgiving and Christmas. That was a special time."

"We were in the old home place, then," said Victoria. "The new house is much like the old one, but it's not the same. I guess we've come to enjoy your bigger place. This seems like home. You and Matthew have made it that way."

Victoria's words evoked memories in Ellen and the others. Soon, they were taking their trip down memory lane. The journey through past years only reminded her of the many changes that had taken place. And now, with the growing family of grandchildren, change seemed to accellerate.

Carol's next words surprised Ellen. "I'm afraid I was so busy being a rebellious teenager that I didn't appreciate the wonderful family I had. I wish I could go back. I'd do so many things differently."

Victoria didn't hesitate to respond. "You know, Carol, each one of us has to make his own mark. I was like you in many ways, only I struck out to the university and became a teacher."

Carol smiled. "Aunt Victoria, I can't believe we're saying we're alike in so many ways. But that's the truth."

"Carol, dear," replied her aunt, "I saw all the ability you had. I saw myself at your age. I think that's why we clashed at that point in our lives."

"I've finally grown up."

"And I have, too," said Victoria.

Ellen couldn't believe what was happening. It seemed to her that it was God-ordained that people should come together in this way.

Elise spoke up for the first time in a while. "I love the history of this family. Being an only child, I missed out on so much. I'm glad I'm marrying into a big family."

In her forceful way, Victoria responded, "We're glad to have you in the family. But we might be somewhat overwhelming at times."

"I don't think so."

Ellen began to prepare the supper. Victoria and Carol came to her side to help. Martha remained quiet.

Typically, food seemed to inspire people to talk. The smaller group visited as they sat at the dining room table. Martha and Victoria left for their home. Then, quietness gradually settled in as one or two at a time went up to bed.

Chapter 32

As they lay in bed in their downstairs bedroom, Matthew and Ellen couldn't help overhearing the talk their sons were having. Apparently, the boys had trouble sleeping and had decided to come to the kitchen for a glass of milk.

Johnie's voice carried well, even though he spoke quietly.

"Michael, I'm sorry for all the misunderstandings. I know I came down hard on you. I should have been more understanding."

Michael didn't hesitate. "No, I deserved everything you said—and more. I was being a complete jerk."

"You have to believe me when I say that I had no idea you felt the family expected you to be like me. I wouldn't want that. I've made enough mistakes of my own."

"Oh, brother, I wouldn't mind being exactly like you. Only I don't think I'm cut out to be a minister. Someday, I think I'd like to live on a farm."

There were some moments of silence. "God has created each of us for a different purpose. You go ahead and pursue what God has called you to be and do."

"I'm more convinced than ever that God put Elise in my life. In some ways, I'd like to marry her tomorrow. But I'm not sure what He wants me to do in the job department. I love the farm, but it's hard work. There doesn't seem to be much future in farming."

"That's for you to decide. I'll love you and pray for you whatever you decide to do."

"It's your prayers and Mom's and Dad's that brought me back. Otherwise, I don't know where I'd have gone."

"Life's been really hard for me." There was a crack in Johnie's voice. "I don't know what I'd have done without the Lord—and my family. Thanks for coming home. We're truly a family again."

Matthew couldn't hold back a cough.

"I bet we're keeping Mom and Dad awake. Let's get up to bed. It'll be like old times—except James isn't with us."

"Yes, brother."

The boys got up and turned off the kitchen light.

"I love you, brother," said Michael. "It's not easy to say that, but I do."

"I love you, too. And right now, I need a brother more than ever."

In the hallway, Matthew saw the two brothers embracing. Then, they tiptoed upstairs.

"This is too wonderful for words," said Ellen. "This is a Thanksgiving miracle."

"Where is your faith, my dear? We've been praying about this for months. Even years."

Ellen moved closer to him. Matthew encircled her with his arms.

"You know," said Matthew, "Elise's father says that Michael is a farmer at heart. He said someday he'll be back on the farm. This farm."

"Can we wait?" questioned Ellen.

"How about another miracle?"

A peace and serenity settled over Matthew and Ellen and the rest of the household. The peace surpassed all their human understanding.

Chapter 33

December 1963–January 1964

Matthew always anticipated Christmas, but this year the holiday could hardly surpass the wonderful events of Thanksgiving weekend. It was amazing how the whole family came together for the first time in years. And it was not just coming together; all the members of the family were at home in spirit. He would always remember those times.

The uncertain future still loomed before Matthew. Glenn was willing to help with chores for awhile, but even so this might be the right time to sell the cattle and make other plans.

The day of Christmas Eve always involved extra preparation in the kitchen. And Ellen was in charge. As he did most days, Matthew helped Lowell with the milking.

Ellen spoke as Matthew entered the kitchen. "You shouldn't be doing all this extra work. Lifting isn't good for you."

"I avoid the heavy lifting. I'm doing okay. But, Ellen, you're supposed to be slowing down also."

"I'm just baking some sprits. And I'm getting the rice pudding ready. The kids have come to like this Swedish tradition."

"Most of the kids don't seem to like the lutefisk. You'll have to make plenty of the Swedish meatballs."

"Some of these Swedish traditions seem to be dying, but we're Americans—not Swedish Americans anymore."

Matthew looked wistfully out the kitchen window. "We've always lived through change. Look at what Pa went through when he left Sweden and came here. He had to learn a whole new language and much more."

"We sometimes forget what our parents went through in this new land. They had to make many changes."

Matthew noticed a car drive up. It had to be Victoria. She still hadn't slowed down—even at almost seventy-four years.

"Oh, Matthew, I forgot to tell you. Victoria and Martha are coming—just like in the old days. I thought it would be a good change for them to stay over."

"What if some of the rest of the kids decide to come?"

"Carol and Hank aren't coming. They have plans for their family. Michael will be with Elise's family. Johnie has a funeral either on Friday or Saturday, and he needs to be around. And James and Ruth often stay in the little house by Margaret and Joe's. Otherwise, we'd be all by ourselves."

"But Margaret and Joe are coming, aren't they?"

"We take that for granted."

Matthew saw that Martha was having difficulty walking. He hurried outside without even grabbing a jacket. Brother and sisters greeted each other.

"Martha, let me help you. I'll take your packages."

Martha gasped for breath. "I'm old, I guess. I can't get around the way I used to."

Matthew took Martha's packages. "Victoria, we were supposed to keep this gift exchange simple."

"There's more in the car. And I brought some cooking oil. Ellen and I are making doughnuts and phutimun."

"I haven't had homemade doughnuts or phutimun in a long time."

"It's Christmas—time to do special things."

Matthew returned to Victoria's car twice for more packages.

"You're too generous," said Ellen to Victoria. "You've always gone the second or third mile."

"Well," said Victoria, "the main gifts are for Margaret's children. It's tough to take care of six children. And I'd rather be generous while I'm living. Now is the time when they can use some extra help."

Chapter 33

"You have no idea how much that means to Matthew and me—and, of course, to the kids."

In minutes Ellen and Victoria were busy in the kitchen. That gave Matthew the opportunity to visit with Martha.

Matthew proceeded to share with Martha that which concerned him the most, especially the possibility of leaving the farm. Martha seemed to understand him better than almost anyone else—except Ellen, perhaps.

"My dear brother, I think I know how you feel. It's hard to give up the things and the places we love. But there comes a time. Perhaps you should stay right here on the farm, but be ready to make a move if necessary."

"The future is always scary. I like the life we have right here—except that there's too much work for one man."

"Matthew, you're not so young anymore."

Matthew sat back, comforted by the kindness of Martha.

"I've been through many changes. We had hard times in Wisconsin when Carl died. I've done so much moving around ever since his death. I guess Lake View and this Oak Ridge area still seem like home. I'm thankful you were here to keep the family together—to give them a place to come back to."

"I hadn't thought of myself in that way."

Martha continued, "I think we need a person and a place to come back to. There are so many changes in the world. Wars and rumors of war. A President shot to death in a most horrible way. And that's when we feel the need to come home."

Matthew thought back to Thanksgiving. "That Thanksgiving gathering was the most wonderful family gathering we've had—at least all five of our children and their families."

"Home." Martha said the words with a kind of reverence. "I think of a different kind of home. I haven't said much about it, but my heart isn't good. I have a strong feeling that my time is short."

"Don't say that," protested Matthew. "Look at Ma. She lived to be ninety-four."

"I don't think that will happen to me. I think my time is coming soon."

Matthew and Martha talked and spent moments in silence. There was a kind of security that Matthew felt as he listened to the chatter of Ellen and Victoria. Changes might come and go, but some things remained the same.

God was good. Life was good. The Lord would see them through anything that might come their way.

Matthew missed the way farming used to be. In the earlier days he had a dozen cattle or so, and knew each one by name. Now, there were more than fifty, and everything seemed impersonal. Even so, he thought of that old Scandinavian tradition. He went around after the carefully allotted feed had been given and added more. This was Christmas Eve and the animals should have that extra share.

His thoughts suddenly moved back to childhood days. Pa was instructing him to give that extra share of feed to the cattle. He could hear Pa's words: "On Christmas Eve at midnight, the cattle are given the power of speech. They come alive in a new way as they worship the Christ child. That is why we give them this extra portion of food."

Lowell interrupted his reverie. "Would you check those cows at the end of the line? Something's not quite right."

"Sure thing, Lowell."

Matthew made sure the machine was attached right. Once more, he thought of the old days when he would be milking the cows by hand. Sometimes he felt arthritis in his hands, no doubt from work done years ago.

As they finished the work, Matthew wished Lowell a Merry Christmas.

"And Merry Christmas to you," said Lowell. "Uncle Matthew, I want you to know how much having this place to live and this work has meant to me. I don't know what I would have done if you hadn't helped. I thank you."

"I'm glad I could. And you helped me through a difficult time."

"I'll miss you and Aunt Ellen. Now, I understand why Dad cares so much for you."

"We go back a long way. Your dad was almost like a little brother rather than a nephew."

Lowell extended his hand for a handshake. And in a moment the handshake turned into an embrace.

Chapter 33

Within the next hour, Lowell and Megan left to be with her parents. Margaret and Joe and the six children arrived. In minutes the house was filled with the joyful sounds of a Christmas gathering.

As the family sat at the table ready to devour the Christmas meal, Martha quietly announced, "I'd like to ask the blessing tonight."

"Dear heavenly Father." Martha's voice faltered, lines of pain evident in her beautiful face. "You have brought us through a difficult year—a year with many changes. We thank You for a country that is free. We seek Your guidance, and may our leaders look to You for strength and direction. Now, I thank You for this family gathered here. Bless and guide them and the rest of my family so far away. We thank You for this bountiful meal. Bless this food and our fellowship. May we honor and glorify You this night and throughout our lives. In Jesus' name. Amen."

Matthew felt an aching sadness deep within. Somehow, he knew what Martha said was true. But he thought to himself, "Man knows not his time."

The rest of the evening proceeded in the same way so many other Christmas Eves had. They ate their fill of the traditional lutefisk and Swedish meatballs and other delicacies. Some of the children refused the lutefisk.

After the dishes were done and put away, Margaret turned off the main lights in the living room so that only the Christmas tree lighted the room. Quietly, they sang "Silent Night." Then, Ellen read the familiar Christmas story. Six-year-old Marlene snuggled close to her grandmother. This Christmas would indeed have been an empty one had it not been for the six children.

The festivities concluded with the family going to the Oak Ridge Church and the Christmas Eve candle lighting service. Once more that night the Christ child was born in the hearts of believers. He came quietly into their lives that night.

Other Christmas gatherings took place during the week. James and Ruth came and spent a day, thus necessitating another family gathering.

Christmas 1963 came and went. Life was moving on—almost too swiftly.

New Year's Day, 1964. Ellen yawned as she left the kitchen after doing some more cleaning. She was tired, for it had been a long day. And she was worried that Matthew would overdo with Lowell no longer around. Glenn was supposed to come over and help, but she wondered about that arrangement. Glenn had not come over today, but had said he would help tomorrow.

Matthew sat in his easy chair nearly asleep. Michael, with his arm around Elise, sat watching television.

"Matthew," she said, "I think it's time for us to go to bed. Even if it is a bit early."

Michael sat up. "Please wait a few minutes. There's something Elise and I would like to talk with you about."

Ellen yawned. "I guess it is a little early."

Michael continued. "Elise has consented to be my wife. You know that. We're definitely planning to be married in June."

"We're happy for you," said Ellen. "Elise, already you seem like one of the family."

Elise turned and looked into Michael's eyes and then at Matthew and Ellen.

"I feel that way, too. And I love the family and the farm and everything about it."

Michael began tentatively. "We've done a lot of talking and thinking and praying. Elise and I would like to come here. I know, Dad and Mom, you planned that I would take over the farm a few years ago. But I goofed off rather badly. I'm wondering if you're still okay with that."

Ellen saw Matthew's face brighten.

"Are you ready to settle down?" he asked. "Farming isn't easy, but I guess you know that."

"I love the farm. Every day I go to work, I miss the farm and home."

"We've been saving money," said Elise. "We want to buy the farm. And for now, we'd like to rent the trailer house that Lowell and Megan lived in."

"And," Michael added, "I'd like to earn some more money. The mechanic's pay is good, and I'm saving every penny I can."

"You know the answer," said Matthew.

Though she and Matthew were tired, they both came alive in the next hours. Ellen could see Matthew's lines of worry disappear. Michael and Elise talked of their dreams for the future. And Ellen realized their prayers had been answered.

Chapter 33

Matthew found himself energized during the next weeks. He had a future to plan for. He would not be saying goodbye to the farm he loved.

Glenn did keep his promise to help during the weeks that followed. The two friends often had coffee and talked for hours. At the same time Matthew began to hope and dream about the future as he and Ellen talked about building their own house. Then Michael and Elise would move into their house.

As they finished their noon dinner, Ellen brought out several magazines. She put one house plan before him.

"I've been studying this plan. I think it would be an ideal house for you and me. We'd have our own place. Our own privacy. Yet, we'd be close to Michael and Elise."

"I think we can afford it. Let's build a nice place that we can enjoy."

"Look at this plan for the living room—or the family room as they call it today. I want this large enough so many of the kids and grandkids can gather there."

"We'll make everything convenient," said Matthew. "We're getting old. We might not get around as well as we do now. We have to think about that."

"You're right, Matthew, we'll do ranch style. The basement can become another family room if we have kids coming home."

Matthew thought a moment. "This is an answer to prayer. Growing old may not be so bad after all."

Ellen laughed. "It's part of life."

"I can't wait until spring. And when Michael comes home."

"We have lots of work to do."

A few minutes later, Matthew and Ellen walked outside. Matthew excitedly pointed to a spot. "That will be the right place for our new home."

Ellen looked around. "I love the view.

Living life meant change.

And Matthew eagerly anticipated this change. A new chapter in their lives.

Chapter 34

May 1964

Matthew always marveled at God's creation. He stood on the front porch and looked out at the grain fields with their rich deep green color. Like life itself, these fields held the promise of a bountiful harvest. Michael had moved home, and that was good.

He spoke aloud the words of the creation story. "And God said it was good. It was very good." Life had been good to him. "God is very good."

The familiar sounds of the John Deere tractor broke into his reverie. Michael must have finished planting the last of the corn. He and Michael had finished another season of planting—his sixty-fourth season of life.

Matthew had a way of thinking aloud. The thoughts seemed clearer when he spoke them. "This past year has been a rough one. My heart attack. Ellen's surgery. But that is past. And Michael is back with the family. Michael's return is an answer to prayer."

The tractor sounds stopped. Matthew enjoyed the silence of the country as he looked to those hills and drank in the beauty of spring. The Garden of Eden could hardly have been more beautiful. The lilacs in full bloom and the apple trees and their blossoms brought bright colors to the green that could be found everywhere.

"I can't imagine why I ever thought of going elsewhere." Matthew pictured California and a few other places where he had been. No other spot could compare to these hills of home. He looked down on the lawn. "I think I need to mow the lawn this afternoon."

He sat down on the porch swing and began paging through a *National Geographic* magazine.

"A penny for your thoughts." Michael sat down beside him.

"Finished?"

"The corn's in the ground. Now, we can use some rain any time."

"Farming is always a gamble." Matthew paused a moment. "But I can't imagine living any other kind of life."

"It took me a little while to realize the same thing. I know I could make more money elsewhere, but I don't think I could find the same peace of mind."

"I'm glad you're taking over the farm."

Michael added, "I'm glad you didn't go ahead and decide to sell."

The two men sat in silence for a few minutes.

"Dad, I've been thinking." Michael stopped and then went on. "Tomorrow night, maybe we could do the milking early, and then I could drive over and pick up Elise for the weekend."

"Michael, you leave early. You don't need to drive late at night. I'll take care of the milking."

"But, Dad, remember I'm supposed to be taking over. You're supposed to be retiring."

"I'm not ready to sit around and do nothing. I intend to help you as you take over the farm. You'll be the boss now, but I'll help."

"Thanks, Dad. You're the best."

The screen door opened. Ellen announced, "Come in and wash up. Dinner's almost ready."

Michael rose quickly. "I'm starved."

"Some things never change."

"What is that delicious smell?" questioned Michael. "There's something that smells especially good."

Ellen placed the potatoes and gravy and pork roast on the table. "Oh, I made your favorite pie. Rhubarb. The first of the season."

Chapter 34

"Oh, Mom, you're the greatest." Michael walked over and stooped down to kiss his mother on the cheek. "The only thing I'm afraid of about marriage is that Elise won't cook as well as you do."

"Come, now, Michael, she does everything else so well, I'm sure she'll cook every bit as well as I do."

"That's not why you're marrying her," added his father.

"I love her so much. I can't wait for us to get married. Then, we'll be together all the time."

Ellen looked at her husband and smiled. Michael reminded her of Matthew when they were young and in love.

The three sat down.

"Matthew, you pray."

"Heavenly Father," Matthew began. "Thank You for springtime and for planting being done. Thank You for the beauty all around. Thanks for Michael and for bringing him back to the family. Bless and guide him as he works and begins a marriage. Thank You for this food and bless it and our fellowship together. In the precious name of Jesus. Amen."

Ellen immediately passed the food to Michael. It was fun to cook for her son and see the way he gobbled down his food. She missed having children around to cook for.

As they finished their meal, Ellen dished up the rhubarb pie. "Matthew, are you going to be busy this afternoon?"

"I think I should mow the lawn."

"Dad, let me do that."

"Well, Victoria called first, and then I talked to Martha. Martha is feeling much better, and there's something she would really like to do."

"Sure, if it's something I can do, I'll do it."

"Martha would like you to take her out and see the fields and pastures and lake at the home place. Joe said he would do it, but Matthew, she really wants you to take her."

"That I can do."

"I'll call her when we finish our pie. I think you should take your nap and then go over and pick her up."

"Yes, I do get tired, and the nap helps. Taking a walk with Martha will be like old times."

Ellen tried to hide her concern for her sister-in-law. "Be sure you take all the time you need for this walk. When you walk and talk, you should never have to hurry."

Matthew stopped the car in the east pasture. "Well, Martha, here we are: the place where we walked and played years ago."

"I've wanted to come here for such a long time. It's been years since I came here."

Matthew couldn't help noticing that Martha looked older and frailer. "We'll get out and walk, but I don't want you to over-do."

Martha reached to open the door. "Victoria and others have been very helpful, but I'm tired of being pampered. I'm used to helping people."

Matthew hurried out to open the door. "Sister, it's about time people took care of you. You've spent your whole life taking care of people."

Martha leaned on Matthew as she got out of the car. "I guess I'm not as strong as I used to be. I fall more easily, and every once in a while I get dizzy."

"I'm glad you're with Victoria. It's good to have you home where you belong."

Matthew guided his sister down the hill through a wooded area to the lake.

"I remember how I would come with you and Mary to this very spot. Then, we would walk along the lake to the place where P.J. built his home."

"I remember. I was terribly shy and afraid as a boy."

"You were small for your age when you started school. I was afraid for you when you walked through the hills. Lucille was sickly, so she was absent much of the time. Otherwise, she could have been there for you."

"I loved exploring some of the places. I would skip stones on the water and walk among the trees. I imagined all kinds of things. In that respect, I was like James."

"I can see you in each of your sons—each in a different way."

Matthew thought a minute. "The farming blood certainly is in Johnie and Michael. I suppose the imaginative part is evident in James."

Martha took hold of Matthew's arm. "Let's find a place and sit down. I can sit down if you help me up."

Matthew agreed. He guided her over to a soft grassy spot.

Martha had a faraway look in her eyes. "Think of all the changes we've seen. I recall that New Year's Eve of 1899. Mother was expecting you in the spring. She was having a difficult time."

Chapter 34

"I never realized until much later how difficult a time Ma had at the time I was born, and afterward when Mary was born."

"Mother wasn't herself those years. I think she felt her family was complete, and then you and Mary came along just a little over a year apart."

Brother and sister sat in silence for several minutes. A breeze rustled the young leaves of the birch trees. The oak leaves were barely out.

"Matthew, I think I talked about this once before, but I remember all the excitement of 1900. That New Year's Eve, Victoria and P.J. and I went down to the school house. I would have been eleven. An older boy, with help from the rest of us, rang the bell 1900 times. That is something I will remember to my dying day. It was such an exciting time."

"The school's still there, but the bell has been taken. The school building is deteriorating. Someone bought the land and building and wants to keep it the same. But the building is sadly in need of repair."

"Nothing stays the same." Martha continued, "There were such hopes that centered around the new century. Some people thought education and religion and science would help us to become better and better. We would become better and better, and then we would be ready for the Lord's return."

Matthew sighed. "That hasn't happened. World War I. The Depression. World War II. The Korean Conflict. This terrible cold war and the threat of nuclear war. It seems to me the world has become worse and worse."

"I fear for my children and grandchildren." Then she added, "And great-grandchildren and the generations that follow."

"I look at farming. I don't feel at all comfortable with the new machines and the new ways and methods."

"The new generation must move on and take over."

Matthew sensed that something more was happening during this conversation. Could they be saying goodbye to a way of life? Was this Martha's last journey to the home farm? Was this a goodbye to a place and a way of life?

"I'm glad, Martha, that we went for this walk. We don't take time for one another. We're always in such a hurry to do something or to go another place."

"We don't take time to tell people how we feel, or how important they are. I wanted to say something to you. Aside from my three girls, you have meant so much to me. You and Victoria are the ones I come home to. And I am happy I have come home."

"You miss your children and grandchildren, don't you?"

"Yes, I do. But they're busy with their lives."

Once more, they sat in silence.

"Matthew, there's something else I wanted to say. I fear that we—that is, the rest of us in the family—always took you for granted. You were always there. Dad let you stay home from school to do farm work. That wasn't fair. He took advantage of you."

"He was a wonderful father."

"You're the one who has kept this family together—connected. You have given us a reason to come back."

"You are the one who always encouraged me. I felt I didn't measure up to the others, but you always believed in me."

"My dear brother, I think I realized more than anyone else who you really were. You always underestimated yourself."

Matthew thought a moment. "It was only after my brush with death that I realized I had a special purpose in life. That was the beginning of my serious study of Scripture."

"And you were a lot smarter than you thought."

Matthew smiled. "You're never too old to learn."

"As I look back on my life, I think I understand much more now. I understand the pressures that Mother and Dad faced. There have always been changes and challenges. The longer I live, the more I admire the way Mother and Dad handled their lives."

"Yes, I don't think I could have handled the changes half so well as Pa did. He left the old country and adjusted to a whole new world. New language. Completely different life."

"Do you remember when you and Mary wandered off into the cornfield, and you scared us half to death?"

"We were very young, but I do remember Pa's stern talk."

That memory gave way to others. The two sat on that spot and talked for several hours. A bonding took place that happens rarely, even for brother and sister.

As they walked back to the car, Martha turned and looked at the intense blue of the lake. "I think I just experienced a bit of Heaven—a foretaste of Heaven."

Those words Matthew would long remember.

Chapter 35

June 1964

"I'm afraid I have some bad news."

Matthew gulped and felt instant fear as Victoria's words came through loud and clear on the telephone. "What's wrong?"

"It's Martha." Victoria's voice cracked. "I went into her room a few minutes ago because I thought she should be up. She was lying there so peacefully, but she was gone. She died during the night."

"Oh, no."

"I have to hang up. The undertaker has just come."

"Ellen and I will be at your place as quickly as possible."

Matthew put down the receiver. The message seemed unreal. He had felt that somehow Martha would always be around, almost like a second mother. He had to pinch himself to realize that what he had heard was true.

Ellen entered the kitchen with a clothes basket in hand. "What's wrong? You look pale. What's happened?"

"It's Martha."

"My dear, what happened?"

"Martha died last night. The undertaker just came."

The door opened and Michael burst into the room. "Is the coffee ready? I need to get the mower ready. It's time to cut hay."

"Sit down, Michael, we've had bad news. It's Martha. She passed away."

"Oh, no. We were going to honor her at our wedding."

Matthew proceeded to explain. "All I know is that Martha didn't get up this morning. A little while ago, Victoria went in to check. And she had died."

"We need to get into town."

Matthew looked away. "I'm going to miss her. Oh, how I'll miss her."

"Dad. Mom. You're upset. I'm driving you to Aunt Victoria's."

For the first time Matthew felt a comfort in knowing Michael would be there to help. Something was happening. For years, the children had depended on Ellen and him in one way or another. Now, he felt himself wanting to depend on the children. He couldn't help remembering how Ma had depended on him.

Matthew and Ellen followed Michael to the car. Though death had claimed a loved one, life moved on. There were decisions that needed to be made.

Ellen knew she had to think clearly. Michael was too young to know really what needed to be done. Victoria, strong as she usually was, had broken down in tears the minute the three came to the door. The undertaker had already taken the body.

"We have to make calls," said Ellen.

"I've called Corrine. She'll let all of Martha's family know."

"Is Corrine coming?" asked Matthew.

"She had already planned to come to the wedding. And so, I believe, have Mary and Ed. I think they're all coming Wednesday, the day after tomorrow." She turned to Michael. "I'm so sorry this happened right before your wedding."

"That can't be helped."

During the hours ahead, they went to the funeral home to make arrangements. Both Victoria and Matthew were too emotional to be of real help. Ellen had a sense of what needed to be done. She felt a sense of relief when Margaret came to help with calling and making decisions.

Chapter 35

After much talk back and forth, the funeral was set for Friday, even though the wedding would still be held on Saturday.

Later in the afternoon, Matthew and Michael left. After all, other work and the milking had to be done. Ellen found much comfort in the realization that Michael was home and was taking charge.

Margaret drove Ellen and Victoria to the home place, where the women talked more of what needed to be done. Ellen turned to Margaret and Victoria. "You know, we need to be thinking about supper. We just grabbed those sandwiches for our noon meal. There's a hungry family to feed."

Margaret smiled. "I thought of that already. I took out some frozen meatballs, and I've got enough ham to feed an army. Mom, you take what you need."

"My dear, you think of everything. And Victoria, you shouldn't be alone tonight. You come and stay with Matthew and me and Michael."

Victoria wiped her tears. "I'll be okay. I've been alone most of life. It's just recently that Martha's been with me."

"Come," repeated Ellen, "at least have supper with us."

"You need a ride home, Mom. It's good you have a grandson who drives. I'll have Matt take you."

Ellen and Victoria worked together to put supper on the table. Matthew and Michael finished chores and came in.

"Isn't it strange," said Victoria, "how we return to the ordinary business of living and eating after we've lost a loved one? It might seem odd, but I feel quite hungry."

A different kind of routine resumed.

Thursday evening, the twilight shadows lengthened. Though Matthew loved having the whole family around, he felt overwhelmed by the numbers. Family gatherings were great, but he had only a few fleeting moments with his children and grandchildren.

James and Ruth and the children had come from Riverton and were staying at the little house by Margaret and Joe's. Johnie had left his three children to stay with their cousins at Margaret and Joe's. Carol and Hank had decided to stay at the local motel to simplify the housing situation. Elise, of course, stayed in the bedroom that would become Michael's and hers, but her parents stayed in town. Mary and Ed arrived that afternoon and joined the group, while Corrine and Warren had come the day before and stayed with Victoria. More people would arrive in the morning.

A number of people stopped at one time or other. Family members and friends filled the farmhouse. People seemed to be everywhere. Matthew felt the need for a few moments alone.

As always, he walked outside and looked to those hills nearby and in the distance. "I will look unto the hills from whence cometh my help. My help comes from the Lord who made heaven and earth."

He heard rustling in the grass and a voice. "Dad."

"Johnie, I'm glad you came out. Too many people at one time."

"I wanted to talk. Aunt Martha was really very special to you. I realize it's hard to lose a sister. I can't even imagine what it would be like to lose Margaret or Carol."

"Yes, Martha was special—almost like a second mother to me. When I was small, Ma needed to take care of Mary, so she left me to Martha. I think Martha understood me better than almost anyone else."

Johnie picked up a blade of grass and put it between his teeth. "It's going to be strange—preaching a funeral sermon one day and giving a meditation at a wedding the next day. I can't help thinking of Grandma's funeral—and not long after my own wife's funeral. I still miss Laura more than I can say."

"You've survived well."

"You know, Dad, I've thought about many things. I do know I don't want to be alone the rest of my life. And I don't know how I'd survive without my children."

"Our children are a blessing from the Lord." Matthew paused a moment and placed his hand on Johnie's shoulder. "You are a special blessing."

"Dad, you once said a man always needs a father. I think most men need someone older to look up to as a father. I realize how much I need you, Dad. I'm glad you're here. It's part of coming home."

Matthew smiled. "You know, even now I think of Pa and miss him."

Chapter 35

The two men stood in silence for a few moments. The last rays of light showed in the distance.

"I've been working on my sermon. I think I'm using one of the same scriptures for both the funeral and the wedding."

"I suspect I might even guess the Scripture."

Johnie spoke the words with strength and conviction. "Jesus Christ the same yesterday, today, and forever."

The words brought a host of memories to Matthew. "I think the first time I really thought of that verse was at Ma and Pa's Golden Wedding. Pastor Strand spoke those words. I was both puzzled and amazed."

"The words are powerful. Jesus Christ is eternally the same. He is our strength. He does not change."

In that moment, Matthew felt a new awareness of God's presence. From that awareness came a renewed strength to go on.

A pastor's perspective is different from the perspective of the man or woman sitting in the pew. Sometimes, Johnie felt that his perspective was almost omniscient. As Pastor Young conducted the service, announcing the hymns and soloists, Johnie looked out on the congregation.

Most of these people were family. Yet, the family had grown and moved on. He didn't know many of the people, especially the children.

He looked down at the front row. There sat Victoria, surrounded by Martha's children. Corrine and her husband Warren were next to her. He recognized the others were his cousins Jane and Rachel, but he didn't know them. But that's the way life is. Families grow and drift apart.

In the next row, he saw his mother and father. Matthew and Ellen had weathered many storms in their lives, but he could see they were growing older. In that same row sat Aunt Mary and Uncle Ed. It seemed so long since he had really visited with them. Mary and Ed and their children had been such a regular part of his life during his growing up years. Suddenly those growing up years seemed out of the distant past.

Martha's nieces and nephews sat in the rows that followed. James and Ruth, with their three children plus his own three children. The next row was packed with Margaret and Joe and their six children. Then came Carol and Hank, but the oldest son was noticeably absent. Michael was absent from this scene, since he was one of the pallbearers. Then came cousin Larry, with his wife Joan, along with Lowell and Megan and the girls.

Johnie hardly recognized his favorite cousin, Beth. He remembered how he and James had thought of her as if she were one of the boys. She lived in California and had been teaching for a number of years. He barely recognized Irene and her brother Jake. They both had families, but apparently they hadn't brought their spouses and children with them. He hoped Jake had changed from the days when he acted the part of a nasty bully. He still remembered the nasty things he had said about James. Even now, he wanted to protect people from that kind of bully.

Johnie thought of himself. He did indeed come from sturdy stock. But, more than ever, he wished Laura was present.

The family filled just about the whole half of the church sanctuary. A woman caught his eye. She looked like an Anderson. She must be some distant cousin or something. Yet, there was something strangely familiar about her. Who could this woman be?

All these people had come to a place that had been home. Home had such a powerful attraction. During time of crisis or problems or special occasions, people inevitably came home.

In the next moment, James moved to the front of the church. The organist began quietly playing the strains of that familiar old hymn. In his rich tenor voice, James began to sing.

> Softly and tenderly Jesus is calling,
> Calling for you and for me;
> See on the portals He's waiting and watching,
> Watching for you and for me.
> Come Home come Home,
> Ye who are weary, come Home;
> Earnestly, tenderly, Jesus is calling,
> Calling, O sinner, come Home!

Johnie found himself caught up with the words. This would be the core of his message today—his sermon and his tribute to his aunt. The words spoke of Martha, who had gone home. And those same words had a message to the living: "Why should we tarry when Jesus is pleading?"

Johnie thought of Laura. In that moment he felt a peace and happiness that she was at rest.

Chapter 35

> O for the wonderful love He has promised,
> Promised for you and for me;
> Tho' we have sinned, He has mercy and pardon,
> Pardon for you and for me.

As James finished singing the last "come home," Johnie rose and walked to the pulpit. Tears came to his eyes as he looked at his congregation, his family. He wiped the tears away and spoke.

"Aunt Martha has gone Home. We miss her, but she is in a far better place. Today we mourn, but not as people who have no hope. We are saddened by her passing, but we are here to celebrate her life."

For a moment Johnie wasn't sure how he should proceed. He had forgotten all those well-planned words.

He began slowly. "At times like this we are at a loss for words. How do we celebrate Martha Anderson Carlson's life? How do we look at these seventy-six years of living? What does all this mean?"

Johnie began to tell some of the family stories about Martha. The stories all seemed to focus on what she had done. Hers was indeed a life of service.

"Martha Carlson's faith had found a resting place. And that resting place was in Christ, the same yesterday, today, and forever. And now what does that mean to us? What message would Aunt Martha give to us? I believe the message would be both simple and profound."

Once more Johnie paused and looked out on the congregation. "Some of you have traveled many miles to come here. You have come home—perhaps to the place where you grew up or to this area where your family is connected. This is one home. This is an earthly home.

"The Lord invites us to prepare for a heavenly Home. This life here on this earth is but an introduction. It is an introduction to eternity. Let us live each day with these eternal values in mind.

"We heard earlier a hymn with an invitation. It was last Sunday or Monday the invitation from the Lord came to Martha Anderson Carlson. He called her Home. She was weary and ill. He called her to her eternal rest.

"He calls us here in a different way. Jesus has invited all those who are weary and burdened to come to Him and find rest. That is His invitation to you and me as we mourn our special aunt and sister and cousin and friend. He invites you and me to come to Him—to follow Him each day of our lives.

"There's a simple children's song that many of us sang in Sunday School." Johnie began to sing.

Into my heart, into my heart,
Come into my heart, Lord Jesus.
Come in today.
Come in to stay.
Come into my heart, Lord Jesus.

The congregation slowly joined him. As he repeated the verse, everyone joined in singing. There was not a dry eye in the congregation.

Johnie looked up. There was nothing more he could say. "Amen."

Matthew suddenly felt weak and tired. Martha was one of his closest connections to childhood, except for Ma and Pa. There would be no graveside service. Martha's body would be taken to Wisconsin to be buried beside her husband. Somehow, it didn't seem right that Martha wouldn't join the rest of the Andersons in Oak Ridge Cemetery. But then, Martha was not really here. Her soul had departed.

The funeral service ended, and the mourners left their seats. Matthew felt a sense of pride in Johnie's funeral sermon. Matthew and Ellen followed Mary and Ed to the church basement and sat at the same table for the traditional funeral lunch.

"How are you, Mary?" Matthew asked. "Tell me."

Mary looked into her brother's face. "I've had these bouts with cancer. Right now, the cancer is in remission. I can never tell. I take one day at a time."

"It's hard to grow old, isn't it?"

Mary put down her cup. "Yes. I so much want to live."

"Have you thought about coming back to Minnesota?"

"Beth's out in California," replied Mary. "She's single, and we hate to leave her alone out there."

"She could come back here."

Ed spoke. "I think she should. I'm afraid my health isn't so great. I have these back problems—they keep coming back. I think we'll be back. In fact, we're going to be looking into it."

Chapter 35

"If you move to Lake View, that would be like old times."

At this point their conversation was interrupted. Other people wanted to talk with them.

Matthew managed to talk with nieces Beth and Irene, nephew Jake, and other relatives. Some of the conversations took place quickly and were interrupted. But that's the way it is with such large family gatherings.

The crowd began to thin out. Matthew left the church basement to go outside. He hadn't seen Larry. He just had to see him. He missed the many visits they had.

"Larry," he called out. "I haven't had a chance to talk. How are things?"

"Uncle Matthew, I'm so glad to see you." Larry opened his arms, and the two men embraced.

"How is your work?"

"It's great. I know that God led me to work in a prison. From my experience, I understand some of what the men are going through. And right now, I'm working with the prison chaplain. I think it's really making a difference in the lives of the inmates."

"I'm proud of you, my boy."

Larry smiled. "Not too many people can say my boy. I like that. But I'm afraid I have to go right now."

"I wish we could visit more."

"Uncle Matthew, yes, we can. Tomorrow and the next day. But I have something else. And, tomorrow, I'll have a surprise for you—a big surprise."

"You've made me curious."

Larry hurried away.

Life is full of surprises, thought Matthew. I wonder what this one is.

CHAPTER 36

The wedding day for Michael and Elise began quietly. But it turned out to be a day with many surprises—especially for Matthew and Ellen.

Ellen strongly believed parents weren't supposed to have favorite children; each child was to be treated fairly in terms of his or her personality. Underneath, though, she realized James was her favorite. He seemed to have inherited so many of her values as well as part of her personality.

The morning of the wedding, James and Ellen sat in the kitchen, enjoying second and third cups of coffee. This was their time to talk. Ruth had gone over to the church to help decorate and get everything ready. All the children were over at Joe and Margaret's. And Johnie and Matthew were outside, having their talk.

"How is everything really going?" asked Ellen. "There are so many people around we haven't had a chance to talk."

"Life is moving altogether too fast. I'm busier than I ever thought I'd be."

"How about your writing? That's always been your dream."

James sighed. "I've written articles on teaching and literature, but I haven't had time to write what I really want to write. And the kids are growing and active. It's hard to keep up with them."

"Yes, they're what's most important now."

"I have a good life. I love my teaching and all the work at the college. My children are great; I wish I had more time for them. And I try to squeeze in as much work at the church as I can. I sing in the choir every week."

"I'm proud of you, son."

"I still have that dream. Maybe I can't write the great American novel, but I can write a novel. I've written some parts, and I have many stories to tell."

"James, I've lived long enough to know you won't be completely happy until you've pursued that dream. It's something you must do."

James looked outside to see Michael and Elise out by the garden, obviously deep in conversation. "I know it's something I must do. I see Michael out there, and I want to convey the family story and the family love in a great novel. I have to do that."

"Someday, you will."

"Mom, it's hard to picture life without you. You've been such a part of my life and the lives of my sisters and brothers—as well as the grandchildren and a host of nieces and nephews. Yes, I want to do that family story now, but I have too much else to do."

Ellen reached out for her son's hand. "My dear, someday you will, but do it in my lifetime and your father's. Don't delay too much."

"Mother, what about your dreams?"

Ellen thought a moment. "My dreams were always of teaching and being a mother. I have realized the results. Now, with Michael, my children are grown and seem to be on the right track. I'm proud of each of you and what you're accomplishing."

"You've done a great job. But now you can sit back and enjoy the fruits of your labor."

Ellen reached up and ran her fingers through her hair. "Right now, I better do something with my hair. But I do have something else I want to do. I want to write down the history and stories of my family—my parents and brothers and sisters. You don't know them so well. And I want to collect what I know of the Anderson history and stories. I've already started that."

"That is wonderful, Mom. I'd sure like to help you."

"You're busy. But I warn you: I can't write the way you can. But I'll get the stories down, and you can do something with those stories."

"We'll be a team."

Ellen stood up. "I need to get myself presentable for the wedding. After all, I am the mother of the groom."

"You look great. And I'm the best man. I need to make sure the groom gets ready."

Ellen once more looked outside to see Michael and Elise walking down the driveway. "I think those two lovebirds are so engrossed in each other that they've forgotten they need to get ready for their wedding."

"I'll go out and remind them."

And so Ellen said a silent prayer for Michael and her other children. Right now, everything seemed right with the world.

At the same time, Matthew walked in the yard and talked with Johnie. Like Ellen with James, Matthew somehow found that Johnie had inherited his love of the farm and the beauty of the outdoors. They had that special understanding of one another.

"I love this land," said Johnie. "I guess I'm a farmer at heart. I keep on using many farm illustrations in my sermons."

Matthew thought of his earlier dreams. "I always thought you would take over the farm. You not only loved the land, but you were good with machines."

"Dad, I think I would like to preach in a country church and live on a farm at the same time. That would be perfect."

"It might happen that you will someday."

Sadness clouded Johnie's face. "I don't think I'd like to live out in the country alone. I'm busy in the ministry, but I miss Laura so very much. I don't want to be alone the rest of my life."

"Son, there may be a young woman out there who will make you a wonderful wife."

"She could never replace Laura."

"She can't and shouldn't. Make that need a matter of prayer."

"Thanks, Dad, for understanding."

James interrupted them. "It's time to get ready for the wedding. It looks as if I have to remind the bride and groom."

The surprises began for Matthew as he was cleaning up so he could dress for the wedding.

Victoria called out as she entered the kitchen. "Matthew. Ellen. I have something I wanted to take care of."

"I'm surprised to see you," said Matthew as he came out of the bathroom. "We're getting ready for the big event."

"I knew you'd be getting ready, but there's something I wanted to give you." She held out a check. "I've decided to pay for 120 acres of your farm to be given to Michael. Getting started in farming is tough. I wanted to help."

"But, Victoria," Matthew objected, "that's far too much. You've been too generous."

"No, it's something I want to do. You and your children are special."

"Thank you."

Ellen quietly came forward and echoed a thank you.

"I want to give to people while I'm living. I don't want to leave an inheritance that people will fight over."

"You have many good years ahead of you," said Ellen. "Look at your mother. She lived past ninety-four."

"Yes, that's possible. I had some preliminary papers drawn up. I'd like you to give that land to Michael and Elise. I'd like to tell them."

"I think you should. They're both upstairs, getting ready." Ellen called for Michael and Elise.

In the minutes that followed, Matthew saw Michael receive the papers.

"Aunt Victoria." Michael seemed at a loss for words as he showed it to Elise. "I don't know how to thank you. This is too much."

"You are my nephew. You are special, and I wanted to show my love."

Elise moved toward Victoria to embrace her. "I'm so privileged to become a part of this family. Thank you."

First, Victoria opened her arms to Elise. Then Michael, with his overpowering six-foot-two frame, enclosed his aunt in his arms. "Thank you, Aunt Victoria."

Then, Victoria stepped back, her typical reserve taking over. "Now, kids, it's time to get ready for your wedding."

Matthew stood motionless as Victoria hurried out the door, and Michael and Elise went back upstairs. The gift was a surprise, but so were the actions and words of Victoria as well as those of Michael.

The day proceeded. However, more surprises came Matthew's way.

Chapter 36

Most wedding days at Oak Ridge had many similarities. In fact, the family interaction that went on at both weddings and funerals was somewhat similar. But this wedding day was in some ways very different. This wedding of his last son was a "coming home" celebration.

Matthew felt uncomfortable in the fancy suit he wore. Some men called it a "monkey suit." He wanted to do what was expected. Even Oak Ridge Church, with all its informality, became more formal during a wedding celebration.

At two o'clock sharp, sixteen-year-old grandson Young Matthew, known as Matt, ushered Ellen to her seat on the groom's side of the sanctuary. Matthew followed close behind. It was hard to believe that this grandson was now taller than both his father and grandfather.

The strains of "Jesu, Joy of Man's Desiring" began. Carol entered first in her pale green dress, carrying a bouquet of yellow roses. She had become a beautiful woman. Then, Margaret, really a young version of Ellen, entered. What a beautiful mother and wife and teacher. Then followed a friend of Elise's. He wasn't even sure of her name, but the maid of honor looked as if she could be Elise's sister.

At the front of the church the groom and the groomsmen gathered. Matthew couldn't get over how muscular and tall Michael was. His light hair and piercing blue eyes reminded Matthew of his own youth. James stood close to his brother but was obviously several inches shorter. Then, Joe took his place as groomsman. After that came a friend of Michael's whom Matthew didn't know.

James stepped forward. The organist played the introductory notes, and James sang the familiar words of the "Song of Ruth." Matthew waited for the words that he remembered so well. "Thy people shall be my people. And thy God my God."

The song soon ended, and Johnie began to intone the familiar words of the marriage ceremony. "In the name of the Father, and of the Son, and of the Holy Spirit. Amen. Dearly Beloved: Forasmuch as Marriage is a holy estate, ordained of God, and to be held in honor by all..."

Matthew found himself lost in thoughts about his children and other weddings and family happenings. Suddenly, he realized the couple was in the middle of the vows.

Michael spoke slowly and distinctly the vows he had written. "The Lord has summoned me to come home. I wandered in places I should not have wandered. I have asked God's forgiveness and my family's forgiveness. I now come to Elise. I have been seeking God's direction. I come to her with my flaws and imperfections and pledge to honor and stay by her all the days of my life."

Johnie began to direct the final vows. "I, Michael, take thee Elise to be my wedded wife…" The other words were altogether familiar.

After Michael finished, Elise's words came as an answer to Michael. "The Lord has called me to this place—to a wonderful family. He called me to be a teacher, and now a wife—and I hope and pray a mother. God has led me to a man who is becoming a strong man of faith. I now come in my weakness and imperfections and pledge to honor him all the days of my life."

Johnie directed Elise in the familiar vows.

I'm gaining a daughter, thought Matthew.

Ellen and Matthew joined the receiving line and shook hands with relatives and friends and strangers. Ellen's hands became sore. Following that custom, the women of the church served a generous wedding lunch.

Ellen wanted to visit with as many people as possible. She tried especially to see those family members and friends who came from a distance.

As the crowd left the gathering, Matthew's sister Mary came over. "I was hoping we'd have a chance to visit."

Ellen saw how pale Mary looked. "How are you, really?"

"I live one day at a time. I haven't been feeling my best today."

"Do you have to take more treatments?"

"I'm due for a checkup when we get back to California."

"We have good clinics and hospitals in Minnesota. Why don't you move to Lake View?"

"We think about it. It's possible we will in another year."

The day had been filled with interruptions. This time James and Johnie both hurried in and practically swept their mother off her feet. "We have a surprise. And you need to come and see the couple off."

"I was visiting with your Aunt Mary. You interrupted us."

Chapter 36

"Aunt Mary," said James, "you come, too."

Ellen never liked the customs of decorating the car of the newlyweds and attaching cans and other junk. But that is what had been done. She arrived on the scene as Michael was opening the door for Elise. She kissed each of them. Matthew did the same.

The couple drove off. Michael drove fast and then made a surprise turn. No other cars managed to follow.

As people began to go home, Ellen noticed that James, Johnie, Margaret and Carol stayed close to Matthew and her. What could this surprise be?

James spoke first. "It's time for our surprise—or rather surprises. Johnie, you go first."

"In another week when you are coming to see me, I'm taking a week's vacation. We're going on the North Shore Drive along Lake Superior into Canada. We know you love the area, and you haven't been there for years. That's my part of the surprises."

"That's too good to be true," said Ellen.

"We've always been too busy on the farm," said Matthew. "Or else we felt we couldn't afford the trip."

"And we'll get to be with your children," added Ellen.

Johnie seemed to glow with happiness. "The kids are excited. They wanted to be with Grandpa and Grandma."

Johnie stepped away, and James took the spotlight. "Next, Ruth and I want to show you a good time in Riverton. But we're going to take you on a number of short trips. We'll take some time to go to the Black Hills. After that, we'll go into Wisconsin and the Dells."

Carol then clasped Ellen's hand. "Hank and I are meeting you. Then, we're taking you with us. There's a lot to see in Chicago, but we know you like the outdoors, so we'll take you all kinds of places. We have dozens of parks, and the lake is always beautiful. We'll take you on boat trips."

Ellen couldn't quite believe all she was hearing. She had always dreamed of seeing more of the world—more of the beautiful United States.

"You kids are doing too much."

"And," Margaret said, "Joe and I will be around home to make sure everything goes smoothly for Michael and Elise. Michael's been away so long, he may need some help. Joe and I will be here for that. And we'll take care of the chores when Michael and Elise are on their honeymoon."

Ellen hugged Margaret and then each of the others. "You kids are doing too much." She paused and added, "Our cups are full to running over. Thank you."

"Thank you," said Matthew. "You are so good. God has blessed us."

Matthew had almost forgotten. There was one more surprise that Larry had. But during this whole wedding celebration, he hadn't managed to talk with Larry.

Almost all the cars had left. Only a few people remained at the church.

"Uncle Matthew," a woman's voice said, "I don't think you even recognize me. It's been years."

Larry stood close to the woman, his face beaming. "This is my surprise."

"Noreen, this has to be you. You have your father's good looks."

The handsome, well-dressed woman with dark eyes and dark hair kissed her uncle on the cheek. "It's good to be home."

"We've hardly seen you in the last thirty years."

Ellen moved forward. "Welcome, Noreen. You should have come to the wedding. If we'd had your address, we would have invited you."

Noreen looked away. "I'm afraid I didn't deserve an invitation or anything else. I've ignored the family for so very long."

"We've always wondered," said Matthew.

"I'm so glad I've finally found my sister. I realized, with Mother away, I needed my family—my sister—more than ever. Larry had to do some hard looking until he found me."

Larry looked down at his sister. "We've had our differences. But now, at this stage in life, I need a sister."

"And I need a brother."

What followed was a reunion where people tried to catch up on what had happened through the intervening years.

As the reunion came to an end, Larry announced, "Noreen is staying with Joan and me for a while this summer. When you visit James, we'll get together. We have to make up for lost time."

For a moment, Matthew looked at her dark features and good looks. P.J.'s shadow momentarily crossed the landscape of his mind.

Chapter 36

But now his niece and nephew were home, and the unpleasantness of the earlier time was part of the distant past.

A week later, with the honeymoon over, Michael and Elise looked down the driveway as Matthew and Ellen drove away.

"We're here alone," said Michael. "This home and farm is becoming ours."

"Already I feel at home."

Michael took his new bride's hand. "We're the new generation. We're the future of this land. I've seen some of the dreadfulness of life. I want to live and work for a better life."

"Yes, Michael dear, we are here for a purpose. May the Lord help us somehow to make this small area of the world a better place."

"I have to be me. I have so much I can learn from Dad and Mother. Even though I'm like him, I can't be another Johnie, that's for sure. But I can do something for my family, and I can work for the good of this community."

"I married you, and I love you for what you are."

"But my dear, I'm going to grow and change. That's what's happened with Johnie. He was pretty messed up when he came back from the war. And he changed."

"And the Lord changed you," added Elise.

"I want children—lots of children. They'll run and play just as I did—and as my brothers and sisters did."

"And I'll never be alone—the way I was alone as an only child."

"We'll grow old together. We'll have children around us—or we'll have our children coming back home."

Michael and Elise looked out and to the hills. They scarcely knew all that lay ahead. There would be joys, and there would be sorrows. Change would come—both the expected and the unexpected.

Michael repeated a verse his father had spoken many times. "I will lift my eyes unto the hills from whence comes my help. My help comes from the Lord, who made heaven and earth."

Epilogue

September 1964

Matthew looked around the kitchen in their new home as he and Ellen sat down for their morning coffee. He spoke his thoughts aloud. "Everything seems new and unfamiliar. I'm not sure what to think."

"You'll get used to it. Remember how quickly we got used to the Nelson house after we moved from your home place."

"We were younger then."

"This new little house will soon be home."

Matthew thought of the many pleasant days. "I guess that's right. I'm glad to be here. I admit I enjoyed seeing so much of the country with the kids and grandkids. It was quite an experience. I'd always dreamed of traveling, but somehow I thought such a trip would never happen."

"Trips," corrected Ellen. "We did the North Shore and Canada. And then west to the Bad Lands and more—plus Missouri and parts south, and Wisconsin. And Carol showed us the big city, and we actually went to Washington D.C."

"Let's look at our pictures tonight."

A knock on the door interrupted them. Michael stepped in.

"Mother, could you go over and check on Elise? She's sick. She's been throwing up. When she decides not to go and teach her fifth graders, she's in a bad way."

Michael and Ellen left, leaving Matthew to finish his coffee alone. The day stretched out before him. He thought about going out to plow the east forty. Instead, he opened their Bible and looked once more at the verses they had read earlier. He kept looking at the words: "Seek first the Kingdom of God, and all these things will be added unto you."

"We have a small kingdom here," he thought. "We have a beautiful home and farm. God's Kingdom is within us. But His Kingdom is not of this world."

Matthew couldn't help thinking about this chapter of his life—so different from all the earlier chapters. The children were grown and established in their lives. He had the role of grandfather, a wonderful role. He could help Michael and the other children when needed. He had more time to read and enjoy the life around him.

Ellen returned a few minutes later with Margaret.

Margaret stooped down and kissed him on the cheek. "Dad, I thought I'd stop and see how you like your new home."

"It takes some getting used to."

A knowing look passed between mother and daughter. But Matthew realized there was something special they knew.

"What's up? There's something more," he added.

"Michael just took Elise to see the doctor. I'm pretty sure we're going to be grandparents in about six months."

"Wow!" was all Matthew could say.

Margaret walked over to the cupboard and took a cup. "I guess we can celebrate with coffee."

Soon the conversation of the three was going in many directions.

An hour later, Margaret looked up at the clock. "I have to be going. It's time to get dinner ready for Joe."

"Life goes on," said Matthew. "We always have to move forward. And the whole world is changing."

Margaret stood up and moved toward the door. "That reminds of more change. Matt—and I can't believe he's sixteen—talks about college and going into the Peace Corps."

"I think we have a James in the next generation," observed Ellen. "For a while he seemed so much like Johnie, but now Matt is more like his Uncle James than James's own children."

Epilogue

"And Matt is talking about all kinds of things—perhaps teaching overseas."

Matthew sighed. "Life used to be so simple. It's not that way anymore."

Ellen picked up the cups and placed them in the sink. "I think Matthew and I like the idea of having our children and grandchildren close by. But life doesn't work that way."

"This is home," said Margaret. "In Oak Ridge we have our roots. It's the place we come back to. Remember how almost everyone in the larger family came back for Grandma's birthday? But, like Abraham, people have been called to go far beyond the home where they were born."

Matthew thought of the comparison with Abraham. "I always thought I'd go beyond those hills someday. It was not until this last summer that I ever went very far. I discovered something, though. I didn't need to travel a big distance. I had everything right here. And I realized I was called to stay right here. Others—my children and grandchildren and even my sisters and brother—were called to go beyond this place."

"Dad, you're quite a philosopher. And now I really must leave."

Matthew, with Ellen following, walked outside. Margaret got into her car and drove away. He looked to the hills. He looked at the house that had been theirs for so many years. He thought of the home place and the house he had grown up in. And he glanced at the new house they now lived in. This new, smaller house was now becoming home.

"Our lives are moving into uncharted territory. We have a new purpose in living. We've never gone through this before."

"My dear Matthew, all of life is uncharted. This chapter in our lives is different from any of the earlier chapters."

Matthew wanted to savor the moment of discovery. He felt God's presence as he looked around to the hills and the houses and then the garden. Several late fall dahlias, and gladiolas, and zinnias, and other flowers showed off their intense colors.

And he felt the unseen presence of family. It was as if Ma and Pa were present. His sisters and brother were there. And James and Johnie and Margaret and Carol and Michael were laughing and playing about.

The sun broke through the light autumn clouds and the garden and hills around became even more vivid in their beauty.

"Words can't describe what we're seeing," said Ellen.

"Or what we're feeling. God is present. And God is good."

Matthew and Ellen walked toward the garden. A car came up the driveway.

Suddenly, Michael's voice broke the silence. "I'm going to be a father! You're going to be grandparents once more."

Matthew and Ellen smiled.

"That didn't take long," observed Matthew.

Life always moved on whether a person was ready or not.

Contact Information

To order additional copies of this book, please visit
www.redemption-press.com.
Also available on Amazon.com and BarnesandNoble.com.
Or by calling toll free 1 (844) 273-3336.

Printed in the USA
CPSIA information can be obtained
at www.ICGtesting.com
LVHW042148161023
761298LV00032B/206

9 781632 322111